MURDER
IN SAINT-
GERMAIN

MURDER IN SAINT-GERMAIN

CARA BLACK

As always, for the ghosts

In memory of Alice et Alice,
both of whom departed too early

Published by
Soho Press, Inc.
853 Broadway
New York, NY 10003

Library of Congress Cataloging-in-Publication Data

Black, Cara.
Murder in Saint-Germain / Cara Black.
An Aimee Leduc investigation

ISBN 978-1-61695-770-4
eISBN 978-1-61695-771-1

1. Women private investigators—France—Paris—Fiction.
2. (Paris, France)—Fiction. 3. Leduc, Aimee (Fictitious character)—Fiction.
I. Title
PS3552.L297 M7988 2017 813'.54—dc23 LC 2016059289

Printed in the United States of America

10 9 8 7 6 5 4 3 2 1

"Hardly any man is clever enough to know the evil he does."

—FRANÇOIS DE LA ROCHEFOUCAULD

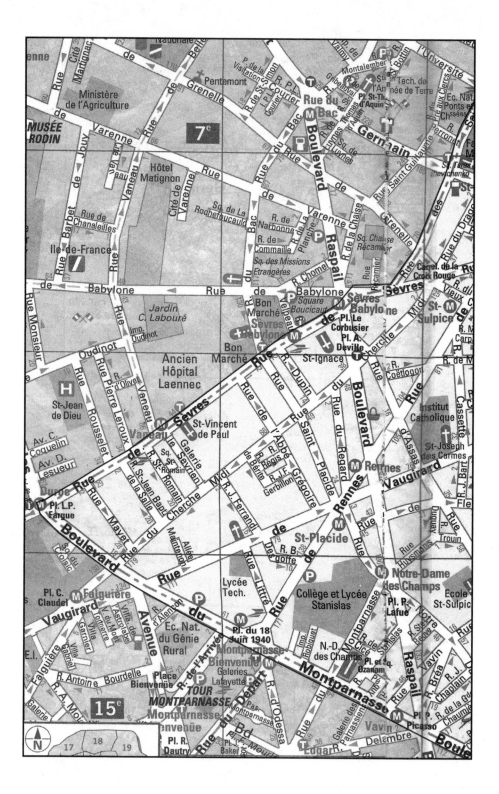

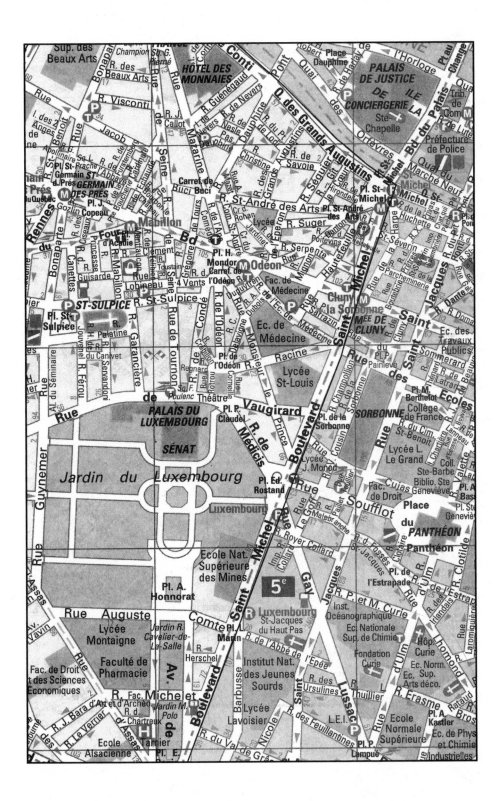

Paris, Jardin du Luxembourg · July 1999
Tuesday, Early Morning

THE BEEKEEPER ROLLED up his goatskin gloves, worried that the previous day's thunderstorm, which had closed the Jardin du Luxembourg, had disturbed his sweet bees. He needed to prepare them for pollinating the garden's apple trees, acacias, and chestnuts that week. Under the birdsong he could already make out the low buzz coming from the gazebo that sheltered their wooden hives. As he approached, he passed gardeners piling scattered plane-tree branches, their boots sucking in the mud.

What a mess. On top of the cleanup, he had a beekeeping class to teach here this afternoon. The buzzing mounted— had a hive been knocked over in the wind? As he adjusted his netted headgear, he felt a lump, something squishing under his boot.

Pale, mud-splattered fingers—a hand. Good God, he'd stepped on a human hand protruding from the hedge surrounding the apiary. Horrified, he stepped back, pushed the dripping branches of the bushes aside. He gasped to see a woman sprawled in a sundress. One hand clutched her swollen throat; buzzing bees, like black-gold jewels, covered most of her body.

Even before he shouted to the gardeners for help, he knew it was too late.

Paris · Tuesday Morning

AIMÉE LEDUC'S BARE legs wrapped around Benoît's spine as his tongue traced her ear. His warm skin and musk scent enveloped her. Delicious. Early morning sunlight pooled on her herringbone wood floor.

She didn't want him to stop. A sniffling cry came over the baby monitor. *Non.* The cry grew louder.

"Yours or mine?" Benoît sighed.

She'd know her daughter Chloé's cry anywhere; these were the cries of Benoît's niece, Gabrielle. "Yours."

One of the phones on the floor beeped. He looked at her again.

"Mine," said Aimée.

Benoît nuzzled her neck, disentangled himself, and found his shirt. She reached from where she lay on the duvet to the pile of clothes on the floor and found her cell phone.

A voice mail. Unknown number. She dialed in, heard the tone, and waited. "It's Dr. Vesoul." A clearing of the throat. "Our patient, Commissaire Morbier, went into emergency surgery. We're calling the family. He was asking for you."

Aimée's heart scudded. A knifelike pain wrenched her gut. Morbier. Her godfather . . . the man responsible for her father's murder.

The man she'd gotten shot two months earlier.

The man who had taken her to ballet lessons when she was a child. The man who'd lied to her for years.

Go hear him lie again? Never, she told herself. Kept telling herself that as she slipped into the work outfit hanging in her armoire—a black pencil skirt and white silk blouse—and as her shaking fingers struggled with the straps of her Roger Vivier sandals.

BRONZE SUNLIGHT STIPPLED the worn tiles on the kitchen floor. Miles Davis, Aimée's bichon frise, licked the spilled milk under Gabrielle's high chair. Holding her *bébé*, Chloé, on her hip, Aimée handed Benoît a freshly brewed espresso. He responded with a long kiss on her neck.

She would have liked that to go on forever. His scent lingered in her hair. "Tonight?" she asked.

"I've got meetings."

Benoît, a Sorbonne professor, tall and dark haired, lived across the courtyard at his sister and brother-in-law's. Stretching a long weekend, they'd asked him to babysit. His niece, Gabrielle, shared a caregiver, Babette, with Chloé. The babies were only a month apart in age.

"Playing hard to get?" she whispered. Stupid. Why couldn't she set boundaries, as the *ELLE* relationship article counseled? Keep him wanting more, not pull Gabrielle's uncle into her bed every night.

"Look for me around eleven," he breathed in her ear. His hand slipped into her blouse and traced the edge of her lace bra. "I'll bring the champagne; you provide the chaos. And wear that."

He waved goodbye to Gabrielle, seated in her high chair, and greeted the arriving Babette, who chattered about her upcoming Greek vacation. Aimée sat eight-month-old Chloé in the high chair next to Gabrielle's—like two peas in a pod; she never got over that. Chloé mashed a raspberry in her pudgy fingers, then smeared it on the stuffed bunny Morbier had given her at her christening.

For a moment, Morbier's face flashed in Aimée's head. She wanted to throw the bunny in the trash. But as she eased it from Chloé's sticky hand, the baby emitted a little cry. *"Désolée, ma puce."* Aimée tossed the favorite bunny into the hamper.

She could do this, couldn't she? Pull off being a working *maman.* She'd scored with a sweet caregiver for Chloé and a hunk who lived just across the courtyard.

She flipped open her red Moleskine to her to-do list, half listening to Babette's vacation chatter. A handwritten phone number glared up at her. Morbier's handwriting. Her insides trembled. Her godfather's presence was everywhere in her life. She pictured herself at his deathbed, imagined his accusations. Felt a beat of pain and drew a deep breath.

One thing at a time. Compartmentalize. Her goal these days was to put things into mental boxes, deal with the non-priorities later. Hopefully, by the time she got to the most unpleasant item, it would have gone away.

She picked up Chloé and inhaled her sweet baby smell.

"Give *maman* a *bisou,*" said Babette, folding diapers by the window and puckering her lips.

Chloé cooperated with a raspberry-scented slobber. Her daughter's grey-blue eyes were so like those of Melac, the girl's biological father, and reminded Aimée of him every day. Melac had a new wife, and he and Aimée had a custody truce—life was good, wasn't it?

For a moment, in her sunlit kitchen, with the Seine gurgling below the window, Babette's bustling faded away. All Aimée wanted to do on this muggy July day was sit back down and play with her rosy-cheeked Chloé. Forget about the day ahead . . . and Morbier.

Her phone rang in the hallway.

"See you tonight, *ma puce*." She blew a kiss.

At the coatrack she grabbed her trench coat, found her phone in her bag, and hit answer.

"*Allô*, Aimée? It's Jojo Dejouy. Got a moment?"

An old *commissaire* who'd been a colleague of her father's—and Morbier's. Not now of all times.

"*Oui*, can I call you later? I'm off to work . . ." She held the phone against her ear as she hurried down the marble stairs, grooved with age, to the ground floor.

"Morbier's asking for you, Aimée. I thought you should know."

First the doctor and now Jojo. She wanted to yell, *Leave me alone!*

"Not a good time, Jojo. *Désolée*." She shooed a stray black cat out of Chloé's stroller, parked next to Gabrielle's by the stairs. Brushed off the cat hairs.

There was silence on Jojo's end of the line. Aimée stepped over the courtyard's puddles. She held the phone between her shoulder and ear, dumping her bag in her motor scooter's basket.

"I know how you feel about Morbier," he said finally.

Like hell he did. She checked the spark plug. Kicked the tires. Good enough.

"There's not much time," said Jojo. "If you don't hear him out, I think you'll be saddled with more guilt than you feel already."

Guilt? "That's not the word I'd use, Jojo."

"It's for your sake that I called, not his," said Jojo. "It's you who's got to live with the consequences. Like I do.

Never leave things unsaid, Aimée. Come to terms with Morbier."

"*Alors . . .*" Her heel skidded on a fallen pear from the courtyard tree. Crushed on the cobbles, the fruit emitted a sweet scent.

"Wait, Aimée." Jojo's voice rose. "Your father meant a lot to me. I didn't show it when they kicked him off the force. That was wrong. To my last day, I'll regret that. But I know you're a bigger person than I am. You find the good in people. You're generous, like your father."

Aimée wiped her heeled sandal on a cobble. "Got to go, Jojo."

"You're afraid of his accusations?"

"I've as good as killed him."

"The CRS shot him, not you. Morbier's an old dog," said Jojo, "been around long enough to know the score."

She hung up. Grabbed the handlebars of her faded pink Vespa so hard her knuckles hurt. Couldn't she put the past aside for once and get on with today?

Yet she'd known Morbier all her life. She wondered what her father would have done.

A mist filled the quai, the plane-tree leaves rustled, and a siren whined as she gunned over Pont de la Tournelle to the Left Bank.

Find the good in people? Generous? She didn't feel generous.

But maybe she did want to hear whatever Morbier had to tell her. Could she face Morbier? Or would she end up kicking herself later? Would she regret it even more if she didn't hear him out?

At the traffic light beyond the quai, she turned left instead of right, heading toward la Maison de Santé du

Gardien de la Paix, the pale brick police hospital that bordered the Latin Quarter. Of those who went in, half made it to the country rehab clinic; the rest came out in a box.

The gathering clouds promised more rain after yesterday's storm. The humid heat was like a blanket lying over the streets. What she wouldn't give for a whiff of breeze. Her damp collar stuck to her neck, her fingers trembled, and she almost turned around.

Perspiration dried in the cleft of her neck. She'd come this far. Determined, she hurried up the hospital stairs. A few minutes, that would be all. She'd hear what Morbier wanted to tell her, then go.

Cool antiseptic-laced air met her in the old-fashioned wood-paneled lobby. Near the reception desk, she caught sight of Jeanne, Morbier's middle-aged girlfriend. Jeanne leaned against the wall, her hands covering her face. Too late?

The disinfectant odors couldn't block the smell of two old men on Aimée's left, each standing with the support of a walker. "Good job. Take another step. We're almost there," said a perspiring young nurse. Aimée recognized one of the men—Philippe, from her father's old *commissariat*. A haggard face now, one side of him drooping, drool hanging from his chin.

Sobs came from another corridor. Aimée shuddered and stepped back. Her fault, all her fault.

Jeanne saw her and beckoned.

That cold, wet night came back to her—Morbier reaching for what she thought was his gun, her signaling the SWAT team, the shots, the blood, all that blood, Morbier wheeled into emergency surgery.

Guilt, sadness, and anger washed over her.

Aimée couldn't push that scuffed door open. Couldn't face his dying. She shook her head at Jeanne, felt a tear course down her cheek, and turned around.

"Aimée, come back," yelled Jeanne.

A minute later, she'd jumped on her scooter and taken off.

Tuesday, Late Afternoon

AIMÉE CHEWED A paper clip as she stared at the computer screen in her temporary office at the École des Beaux-Arts on the Left Bank. She was in a former seventeenth-century cloister, overlooking the Cour du Mûrier with its Chinese mulberry tree. The steel of the minimalist Danish chair bit into her hip as she ran scans of the art school's database system.

There, with birds warbling from the courtyard, Aimée monitored eye-glazingly boring accounts, checked the interface and server IP logs. Slog work, but lucrative; she counted herself lucky for the contract with the prestigious crème de la crème art school. This was the bread-and-butter computer security work her detective agency survived on. She'd been referred by her best friend, Martine's sister, an editor at *ELLE*. It was the third time Sybille, *la directrice*, had hired Aimée.

Only rarely did a low conversation drift up from the garden; the classical statues seemed abandoned along their painted arcades. The school was deserted of students for the summer; the few staff on the premises were those jurying fall student submissions. Aimée stifled a yawn and reached for the fizzing glass of Perrier by the screen. Behind her lay a sun-drenched back terrasse, covered with ivy, hidden and intimate—not a bad job perk.

What a place to work, she thought. Almost the heart of Saint-Germain-des-Prés here by the Seine and surrounded by historical monuments.

Aimée checked her phone for messages. One from Babette, as usual—she was diligent about updating her. Chloé had eaten her yogurt, and the girls had gone down for a nap.

She imagined her Chloé in the crib, light from the window dancing on her blanket. Safe. That's how Aimée got through the day—check-ins with Babette, a little babble time with Chloé in the afternoon.

No more calls from Jojo. A wave of relief mixed with guilt passed over her. She rechecked the configuration options, the database scan—all in order—and finished up running the system's daily maintenance.

She grew aware of a shadow just before a man sat down next to her. The air stirred, and she caught a scent of something she couldn't put her finger on. Chemical, medicinal, oil based?

"Jules Dechard," he said, introducing himself. She recognized the well-known art history professor and critic. He was lean, russet haired, thin faced, tanned. He looked healthy for an academic. But then, what did she know? Benoît was an academic, too, and Aimée certainly found him fit enough.

Jules Dechard leaned forward. "Sybille says you're discreet."

"Discreet" meant many things. None of them good.

"Do you have a problem with your computer, Professor Dechard?" Probably he wanted her to scrub his hard drive—the usual request. She doubted he wanted to discuss the current art scene.

"Mademoiselle Leduc, I want to hire you."

Hire her? She toyed with the paper clip. "That could bring up a conflict of interest with my contract here,

Professor Dechard. I'm afraid that would prevent me from working for you."

"It's personal." He was staring at her Gigabyte Green nails.

What kind of problem could he have? A cheating wife? A son kicked out of a prep school? "My scope's limited to computer security."

"I know you can help me. I've read about you."

Who hadn't? Morbier's shooting, the ministry corruption, the widespread police fallout. *Paris Match* was having a field day.

"It's a simple job, Mademoiselle Leduc." He pushed a folded yellow Post-it into her palm. On it, in neat, slanting handwriting, was an email address, *aft@agt.fr*. "Computers mystify me. I'm old school. But I'm trying to collect any emails to and from this email address. Quite easy for you, I'd imagine. Maybe there's just some simple way you can check the whole . . . what's it called, the server? Collect all the emails from this sender? Even if they have been deleted—there's a way to do that, *non?*"

She could do that in her sleep.

She smiled. "I'll fax you a contract from the office."

Dechard laid his hand on her arm. Clammy. He slipped a wad of franc notes into her open secondhand Hermès bag. A large wad of franc notes.

"Keep it between us, please," he said. "I'm counting on your discretion. Cash and no accounting."

Strange. René would kill her—he hated working off the books. But for such a simple job, maybe she didn't need a contract. "All right, Professor. I will compile any emails that came in to you from this address and check in with you tomorrow."

"Not emails that came in to me," he said, lowering his voice. "In fact, please do not search for emails to me. I need to know who else at this school has been receiving emails from this address."

He was spying on his colleagues, and he thought he'd enlist her? As if she would jeopardize her contract. "*Désolée,* Professor, but I cannot help you. Email is private."

"I assure you it's not," Dechard said. "This is a Ministry of Culture–funded institution. Any correspondence undertaken under the school's name should be free and available to the public."

Aimée thought about that. She wasn't sure what he said was correct, but she was sure taking a private contract to hack staff members' emails for another staff member would cause her nothing but trouble.

"I'd like to help you, but . . ."

"You're worried you'd get in trouble. But I guarantee that won't happen. Sybille, the directrice, recommended I ask you to help with this. She's my sister-in-law. Besides, nothing I'm asking for would violate ethical considerations."

Aimée hesitated. "If Sybille suggested I do this, she should ask me herself."

"Check with her to verify if you must," Dechard said. "But please be discreet. Tell no one but Sybille."

The wad of money would probably cover childcare, the office rent, for months. Maybe even a few days away on *vacances.* If Sybille approved, how could Aimée say no? But something about this felt off to her. Why was Dechard so insistent on secrecy? What was he hoping to find evidence of? Usually these types of jobs involved an extramarital affair, or some other love-life indiscretion. Was Dechard married? He didn't wear a ring. Or was this something else entirely? A rivalry with another faculty member? She'd heard academia was cutthroat.

She'd talk it over with René—they'd return Dechard's money if they had to.

"I'll see what I can find," she said.

IN THE EARLY evening, Aimée stepped out onto the narrow street leading away from the Seine. The heat had barely cooled even as the shadows of the seventeenth-century building lengthened. No taxi in sight and a scorching three blocks to the Métro. Forget the bus with traffic at a standstill. Only a ten-minute walk if she hurried through the Left Bank. But before she could even cross the street, the sky opened. Late July was nothing but heat, showers, and tourists here in Saint-Germain.

She ducked back under the glass marquise awning. Above her, rain drummed in three-quarter time. She belted her trench coat and debated unfurling the umbrella to battle the sheeting warm rain. *Mais, non.* Caught, she'd wait it out.

Aimée's grandfather Claude used to complain the Saint-Germain he knew in the old days had disappeared. It had tipped beyond the reach of the working class, the students and artists who used to populate the quartier. She knew Oscar Wilde had died in a fleabag hotel near the school, penniless and alone, rumored uttering the line "Either this wallpaper goes, or I do." Today the fleabag was a boutique hotel, and the streets surrounding it were chock-full of antiquaries, art galleries, and prestigious publishing houses. Claude had been in love with an artist's model who had posed at the École des Beaux-Arts—before he'd met

Aimée's *grand-mère*, he'd assured her—and his nostalgia for that time had colored his thoughts, she suspected. Saint-Germain was a shadow of its storied past, her *grand-père* would tell her, a far cry from what it had been when Delacroix, Picasso, and Manet had lived here. Café les Deux Magots, where de Beauvoir and Sartre once wrote all day nursing a single coffee, had quadrupled its prices for tourists.

Still, in her time here back when she was a premed student, she'd loved Saint-Germain's bustling street life. The tiny art-house cinemas, the rue de Buci market, the bistros, the old cellar jazz clubs that closed at dawn. Change was inevitable, and Saint-Germain mixed old and new—like where the surviving fragments of a twelfth-century wall built by King Philippe Auguste had been repurposed into part of a parking garage.

As quickly as it had begun, the rain stopped. She started down rue Bonaparte and paused, startled to see a familiar face beckoning her from a *café tabac* doorway.

Suzanne Lesage—Melac's former undercover partner, head of an elite undercover counterterrorism squad. Suzanne, blonde and fit, had always looked sharp, and today's outfit proved no exception: flared gaucho pants, a crop top, metallic sandals, and gold hoop earrings. Usually dry and cool as a cucumber, Suzanne had rings under her eyes.

"*Quelle surprise,*" said Aimée. "So you just happen to be on rue Bonaparte?"

There was no such thing as a coincidence with top cops like Suzanne.

"I see you're back in shape after your *bébé,*" said Suzanne, kissing Aimée on both cheeks—the customary *bisous.*

"Chloé's eight months now. Got one more kilo to lose,"

said Aimée, ruing the previous day's *tarte aux abricots* at the pâtisserie. Despite the shadows under her eyes, Suzanne's face, makeup free apart from red lipstick, looked fresher than her own in the humidity. Aimée's mascara had clumped in the heat, her eyelashes sticking when she blinked.

"Your partner told me you'd be here, Aimée. Working at École des Beaux-Arts."

Her partner René?

"He said you'd be delighted to offer assistance in an investigation."

The traitor.

"*Un café?*" Suzanne gestured to her table inside.

Acid roiled in Aimée's stomach. She hoped she wasn't getting mixed up in another sting operation.

Suzanne ordered, then lasered in on Aimée. "Do you remember that favor I did for you, Aimée?"

Aimée nodded. Her heart pounded. What was Suzanne about to ask her to do?

"I'm calling it in, Aimée. You owe me."

Join the club, she almost said. Juggling work and child-care demanded all the favors she could call in and then some. Still, Suzanne had helped her out when she'd been desperate—Suzanne had used her professional connections and put her own career on the line to help Aimée track down a kidnapper when Zazie, the daughter of the propri-etor of the café below Aimée's office, had gone missing.

"Of course, Suzanne." Wary, Aimée wondered what she was agreeing to.

"This is strictly between us, *comprends?*" Suzanne checked her phone. "I trust you, but I can trust no one else right now." Then her face broke into a small grin. "Plus I know where you live. *Un moment.* I've got to take this call."

While Suzanne paced in the street on her cell phone, Aimée plopped two brown sugar cubes in her demitasse. She stirred, uneasy, wondering what this was about. In the mist, a bus pulled up down the street, disgorging dry passengers who were promptly replaced by damp ones. She inhaled the scent of Saint-Germain: a whiff of perfume from passersby, cigarette smoke, the smell of butter wafting from a boulangerie.

Suzanne sat back down. Thin lines creased the bridge of her nose. "*Alors*, it's crazy right now. I've been called in; a car's going to pick me up in five minutes. So I'll make this quick. I need your help."

Aimée nodded. "Why the cloak-and-dagger?"

"No one must know we've talked. It's off the book, Aimée."

"Unofficial?"

Suzanne looked around. "I'm not speaking to you as an officer now. I'm another mother, okay?" She leaned over the café table. Her thick, stylishly blunt-cut hair swung over her shoulders. "Last night I stopped at my local *café tabac* to get my Loto ticket, like I do every Monday." Her voice had dropped to a whisper. "I saw him, Aimée, in line at the counter." Her hand twitched on the demitasse handle. Aimée realized Suzanne was shaking.

"Saw who?"

"I saw a ghost."

Tuesday, Early Evening

"A GHOST?" ASKED Aimée. "Explain."

Suzanne was rational, practical, a highly trained operative. A woman Aimée respected. A woman who was right now casting furtive glances behind her.

"Last year my unit was part of an international team of military personnel and advisors. We were put together by The Hague and headed by a big-shot Dutch prosecutor, Isabelle Ideler. We were sent to Foča in Bosnia to work with the local Bosnian force," said Suzanne, her voice low. "Our mandate was to assist in arrests of fugitive warlords. We were operating under the jurisdiction of the International Criminal Tribunal for the former Yugoslavia, the ICTY."

"*Alors*, Suzanne, let me pull the reins in on this right now," said Aimée. "I do computer security, not international crime—"

"Hear me out," said Suzanne. "In a few minutes, a car's picking me up and taking me to Lyon to give a report to Interpol."

"Won't you find better help than I can give there, Suzanne?"

"*Non*, the report's unconnected." Suzanne gave a dismissive wave. "*Attends.* My team had sealed indictments empowering us to bring to justice war criminals who committed atrocities during systematic ethnic cleansing in the Bosnian War. We're talking war crimes. Massacres."

Aimée blinked. "The Bosnian War? Wasn't that over three years ago? I thought there was a peace accord."

A bitter laugh. "Bosnia's the wild west. A lot of war criminals are still in hiding. Some of them have been camped out in remote villages for years. And now, with the war in Kosovo, all the unrest and the massacres, the old warlords are making a fortune off of the conflict, smuggling arms, you name it." Suzanne shook her head, her eyes dark. "Aimée, you cannot imagine what it's like there. We were sent to Foča, a remote town surrounded by dense forest, accessible only by winding roads. It was the site of some of the worst ethnic cleansing during the Bosnian War. On Milošević's orders Serbian forces had destroyed mosques, burned villages, tortured men, and tossed their bodies into the river. These animals used little Muslim girls as sex slaves and forced their grandmothers to watch." Suzanne paused. Her nervous fingers balled up a sugar wrapper. "We were there when they were exhuming the bodies from one of the mass graves. That day's burned into my brain." Suzanne stopped again and took a breath. Her eyes closed. "The tiny bodies of young girls, raped, then shot. All piled together—and their parents who had watched them be murdered . . . Horrific."

Aimée sucked in her breath. "Terrible. Yet why tell me?"

Suzanne gripped Aimée's wrist, pulled her close. "Aimée, let me finish. We'd made no headway in tracking down one of our targets in Foča, a Serbian thug. Finally, we managed to wheedle a tip from a survivor. Those animals were so cocky, thinking they could hide near the scene of their crimes. Isabelle—that's the prosecutor—she insisted we had to do it by the book. The ICTY needed a proper arrest for the indictment to stick. So we bided our time, got the Bosnians to issue the warrant, set up the perfect textbook house raid. Somehow they smelled us. They opened fire, riddled our car with bullets, killed my bodyguard. Two of them holed up in a tunnel. A grenade went off—one of ours. No one in the tunnel could have survived the explosion. Our mission was aborted. The NATO ground crew collected the remains for DNA samples."

Suzanne opened her bag, pulled out an envelope, and slipped it across the table to Aimée. "Mirko Vladić. The one responsible for those little girls in the pit. I saw body parts being dragged out of the tunnel. His body parts."

Aimée sipped her espresso, willing the sweet jolt to dispel the bile in her throat. "So this man was killed in the explosion." She studied the photo on an ICTY document from the envelope. A grainy black-and-white head shot of a mustached man, early thirties, Slavic cheekbones, nothing that stood out, except for the eyes. The flat, dead gaze of a killer. The next photo showed a bombed-out cluster of charred stones and wood beams, a partial view of a cobbled street torn up by a bomb crater. It was strewn with kitchen utensils; in the middle, a birdcage lay on its side. "I still don't understand why you need me."

"Last night I saw Mirko Vladić in the café buying cigarettes. Around twenty after eight. Mirko Vladić, the butcher of Foča. The war criminal I surveilled. I'd know him anywhere."

"What are you saying?"

"He survived," said Suzanne. Her voice quavered. "The man I thought was dead. Who we were mandated to capture. Bring to trial."

Aimée controlled her disbelief with effort. Tried to be rational. "*Attends*, didn't you just tell me you saw his body taken away after the explosion?" None of this made sense. "Back up. Why were you even in Bosnia? You're based in Paris."

"I just returned from a year's posting in The Hague," Suzanne said. "Paul"—her husband—"is doing a term as a legal advisor in the Hague Tribunal—it was a career move for him. The brigade got me a position on secondment to ICTY's war crimes investigative unit. We put our girls in the local Dutch schools. I worked with that team until the case fell apart."

"Suzanne, you must have mistaken someone else for this man. It's just someone who looks similar."

Suzanne shook her head. "You know how surveillance works—I knew everything about him, how he walked, how he moved, every hair on his head."

Aimée respected Suzanne's skills too much to truly doubt her. But why would a supposedly dead Serbian war criminal be here in Paris? "Okay, let's say there is a chance this Mirko got away in the skirmish—it was chaotic, right?" said Aimée. "Shouldn't you report this to the ICTY? Isn't this their investigation?"

"I have no proof." Suzanne glanced at her phone, which was vibrating on the marble-topped table. "I'm going to talk to a contact at Interpol. But meanwhile, my own team doesn't believe me. My boss has put me on desk duty," she said, her tone grimly sarcastic.

"You told your boss you saw this man?"

"He called me crazy. Ordered me to back off. And now he's breathing down my neck about this report. Scrutinizing my every move to see if I've lost it. If I don't watch it, they're going to send me for posttrauma psych evaluation."

Aimée felt a rush of sympathy for Suzanne. There were

so few women who'd reached her position in the field, and
they always had to be twice as good as men. Especially in
the competitive crème de la crème squads.

"Aimée, I admit it's shaken me up. I'd had a long day when
I got to the *café tabac*. I was tired, dropped my purse, and
coins scattered everywhere on the floor. People bent down to
help pick them up, but one man didn't. That's why I noticed
him. By the time I had registered who he was, he'd gone."

Aimée wondered what more she could say, went back to
the most logical explanation. "You said yourself it had been
a long day. What if it's a case of mistaking this person for
Mirko, Suzanne?"

"I can't get it out of my mind," said Suzanne, her tone
intent. "After dinner I got online to check the ICTY investigations database. Mirko's listed as *presumed* dead. No DNA
proof to match. And the arrest order's void. I printed out his
picture. That's when I knew for sure." She reached over the
table and grasped Aimée's wrist hard. "It was him, Aimée."

Uneasy, Aimée looked around. "But Paul—what did
he say?"

"Like I could tell him. He'd just worry. He's working in
Nantes this week. There's nothing he could do to help. I
queried the ICTY to check for any reports or updated sight-
ings, et cetera. But sometimes they don't update everything,
so I emailed two of my old team members."

"*Et alors?*"

"Isabelle hasn't replied. The other couldn't tell me anything new. I'm not sure how or in what capacity they're still
involved in sealed indictment cases."

"Suzanne, okay, say Mirko survived. Somehow. How
could a wanted man travel across several countries?"

"Search me."

"You think he came after you personally? Why not in disguise?"

Suzanne shrugged. "Sloppy technique? Arrogance? He's a thug. He talks with guns. He's not a finesse criminal."

"And he just walks into your local café . . . Did he see you?"

"I don't know." Suzanne's hands rattled the demitasse, clacking the saucer. Dark tan foam spilled.

He'd gotten under her skin; Aimée could tell.

Suzanne tossed back her espresso. "Aimée, it's those girls. I can't get them out of my head." She raked back her hair with one hand. "No one's being prosecuted for the crimes that were done to them." She gripped Aimée's hand tight. "One of those girls was just about eight years old, the same age as my Hélène. They practically tore her in two. Dead but still holding her doll." Her lip quivered. "Sick doesn't describe it. He's an animal. You've got a daughter, Aimée. Wouldn't you want this animal caught?"

Chloé's rosebud mouth flashed through Aimée's mind. Her trusting grey-blue eyes.

"I can't open an investigation because the case is closed, and jurisdiction resides in another country," Suzanne said. "Interpol can, if they listen. But the justice system's too good for these men. I should have put a bullet in his skull. If the ghost is here, I need to finish the job we were sent to do."

Suzanne dropped a ten-franc note on the table as a black car pulled up in front of the café. She nodded to the driver, who'd stepped out. "I can't let this go until I know you'll help, Aimée. I called in favors for you last time. Big favors."

She owed Suzanne. "What can I do?" said Aimée, hesitant. "I'm not a trained operative."

"That's better. No one knows you. You don't have restrictions like we do."

Aimée's heel stuck to a gummy spot under the table. "What do you mean?"

"Do what you do best," said Suzanne. "Use your imagination. Snoop around. I need you to find proof that he's here."

In her spare time? She had an eight-month-old, a babysitter going on vacation, a business to run.

"I know I'm asking a lot," said Suzanne. "But no one knows you. There's no connection between us. I'm back in two days." Suzanne's gaze bored into Aimée. "Find out what you can, and I'll take it from there."

"I just don't have time for this right now," Aimée blurted. "Suzanne, I want to help you. Really I do. But there's nothing I can do for you in the next two days." She didn't add that René would kill her if he found out she was trying to hunt down a heinous war criminal. She shivered picturing Mirko Vladić's dead eyes.

Suzanne leaned back in her chair and folded her arms. "According to the police grapevine, you put Morbier in the hospital. I heard he's not going to make it." Suzanne's gaze locked with Aimée's. "I'm not judging you. Things happen. But you do know what that means."

She did know. She was a former *flic*'s kid, and the police were still "family," regardless of the fact that they'd drummed her father out of the force, and no member of a "family" turned on one of her "own." Ever. She'd broken the unspoken rule. After Morbier's shooting, the *flics* had labeled her toxic, persona non grata. She needed to hold on to Suzanne as a contact. That was how it worked. And Suzanne was reminding her.

Just a little legwork, Aimée told herself. Just some sniffing around for a friend.

"*Alors*, I'll give it my best shot," she said.

"*Merci.* Maybe I'm crazy, overworked, and seeing things."

"Time to change jobs?"

Suzanne pushed a small gift-wrapped box with a pink bow into Aimée's hands.

"A baby present? Suzanne, you shouldn't have," said Aimée, touched.

"I didn't. It's a disposable phone, the drug dealer special. I'm the only contact." Suzanne, all business, passed Aimée another envelope. "There's sensitive data in there. I'm not even supposed to access it."

Merde. A burner phone, sensitive data, a ghost with a blood vendetta, and a babysitter going on vacation. Just another day at the office.

At least she could count on Madame Cachou, her concierge, to fill in holes in her childcare situation.

Aimée grabbed her bag and followed Suzanne to the curb. The words came out before she could bite her tongue. "How's Melac?"

Suzanne looked both ways before she opened the door of the car waiting at the curb. Paranoid? Then she turned and smiled, as if they were just two old friends saying goodbye.

"Seems there's trouble in paradise," she said. "But you never heard that from me."

ON RUE DU Louvre, at the kiosk in front of her office building, Aimée bought a copy of *Le Parisien* and a chichi art magazine.

"Don't tell me—you're taking up painting?" Marcel, a one-armed Algerian war vet, grinned, handing her change.

"*Moi?* With all my free time, Marcel? It's research."

Aimée nodded to the building concierge mopping the

tiles in the foyer, tucked her mail under her arm. She climbed the winding staircase, feeling last night's marron glacé on her hips. She had such a sweet tooth these days. *Quelle horreur*—all those pool laps she needed to make up!

Even stepping carefully, she almost slipped on the damp wood of the landing, which reeked of the pine soap the concierge swore by. Too often lately Aimée was still here at the office when the concierge did her nighttime house-keeping.

Balancing her overloaded Hermès—a flea market trea-sure bought for a song—she caught her breath at Leduc Detective's frosted glass door. Punched in the security code, heard the click, and turned the knob.

Inside, she bumped the door closed with her hip, kicked off her Vivier sandals, and plopped everything on her desk. In the soft evening sun, the carved woodwork of the nine-teenth-century ceiling gave off a dull luster. The overhead fan whirred, rotating the hot air.

Saj, their permanent part-time hacker, looked up from his tatami mat, from which he was monitoring several computer screens.

"Where's René?" Aimée wanted to punch him for let-ting Suzanne corner her.

"Still running the seminar at the Hackaviste Academy."

She'd forgotten. *Merde.* Her *maman* brain was addled by sleep deprivation. Not to mention this heat.

Still, she wanted to run Suzanne's problem by René. Pick his brain on how to find a "ghost." Plus, she needed to talk to him about Jules Dechard.

Incense wafted from a burning cone by an altar to Shiva to the left of Saj's tatami. Aimée's nose itched. Her kohl-smudged eyes watered. "I'm allergic, Saj."

"You weren't yesterday." Saj's blond dreadlocks swung over his pale aqua Indian shirt as he stretched and unfolded his long legs. "But I've finished the cleansing."

He snuffed out the smoldering flakes. Opened the window onto rue du Louvre, letting in a breeze and the sounds of bicycle bells, a car horn. "Bad karma, Aimée. There's an imbalance. Unhealthy auras persisting." He raised his eyebrows, giving her a pointed look.

Since Morbier's shooting, Saj maintained, she'd ruined her karma, misaligned her chakras. She couldn't deal with that right now.

"I don't need your judgment, Saj," she said.

"Judgment's not my style, Aimée. Your nonalignment disturbs all beings connected to you. All of us."

"Please don't start, Saj. There is one thing you can help me with, though." She showed him the Post-it Jules Dechard had given her, explained the assignment.

It was only minutes before Saj called her over to his laptop screen. "You might want to look at this, Aimée."

"You scrubbed the school's server already? That's fast, even for you."

Saj was a whiz. Before Aimée and René had found him, he'd hacked into the ministry's files so many times that, instead of throwing him in prison, they'd recruited him to help them strengthen their security.

"The sender's IP address is physically located at the Galerie Tournon." Saj pulled his dreadlocks back, and she noticed a string of turquoise around his neck. "There are emails to and from two different faculty email addresses at École des Beaux-Arts."

She'd heard of Galerie Tournon, an upscale art gallery in the sixth.

"Here," Saj said. "Read the emails first."

There were two sets, all from the last week. The first was a chain of four emails:

From: aft@agt.fr
To: ms90@edba.fr
Subject: sale

tried calling you. making sale thursday.

From: ms90@edba.fr
To: aft@agt.fr
Subject: RE: sale

too late. do what I said.

From: aft@agt.fr
To: ms90@edba.fr
Subject: RE: RE: sale

he's your problem, got a buyer.

From: ms90@edba.fr
To: aft@agt.fr
Subject: RE: RE: RE: sale

I told you, forget it.

Odd. Vague, but still fishy.

"A drug deal?" Aimée wondered. "Would an École des Beaux-Arts faculty member be stupid enough to email about a drug deal?"

"You'd be surprised how stupid smart people can be about their email," Saj said. "But it could be nothing, too. Could be about a piece of art, or real estate, or anything. Look at the other chain, though."

From: aft@agt.fr
To: jd86@edba.fr
Subject: your secret's out

Professor Dechard,

You should have found an envelope on your desk from me. I assume you've looked at the contents. Now you know what I know. No one but us has to find out, but I need to be able to trust you.

From: jd86@edba.fr
To: aft@agt.fr
Subject: RE: your secret's out

What do you want from me?

From: aft@agt.fr
To: jd86@edba.fr
Subject: RE: RE: your secret's out

Left instructions on your voice mail.

From: jd86@edba,fr
To: aft@agt.fr
Subject: RE: RE: RE: your secret's out

I agree to your terms. Thursday drop-off?

From: aft@agt.fr
To: jd86@edba.fr
Subject: RE: RE: RE: RE: your secret's out

No more communication by email. Call my mobile.

Her gut clenched. "Jules Dechard is being blackmailed." She wondered if Dechard was in real danger. Why had he insisted on discretion?

"Who is he, exactly?" Saj asked.

"A very famous art critic. The chair of the art history department at École des Beaux-Arts." She picked up the art magazine she'd bought at the kiosk, flipped to the review page, and pointed to Jules Dechard's current column.

Saj sat back down on the tatami. "Maybe the sender's a gallery owner and blackmailing your professor for a good review, or maybe an angry artist threatening him after a bad one? Just off the top of my head."

Unease roiled in Aimée's stomach. "Now I wish I hadn't read the emails." Or taken the job in the first place, she thought.

"The art world is full of cutthroat competition. Reputation—that's everything." Saj flexed his arms over his head. "Dechard's got enemies, if this article's anything to go by."

The professor had seemed decent enough. Yet as Aimée's

father had always said, everyone's got something to hide—
just scratch and dig. But that wasn't her business; she'd
gotten the job she'd been paid for done.

She paced across the room and scanned René's desk to
see if there was anything that needed her attention. It was
littered with papers, but there was also a box holding a new
indoor-outdoor nanny cam. The thing was tiny—no bigger
than a box of paper clips. Had he gotten so paranoid he
wanted to spy on Babette in the park?

While Saj ran system analysis for their new accounts,
Aimée updated her last report for an ongoing client. Finally
she pulled out Suzanne's envelopes.

What could she do?

Even if this Mirko, a wanted war criminal, had survived—*unlikely*, based on what Suzanne had told her—his
appearing in a café Suzanne frequented seemed even less
likely. Too coincidental. If he somehow had made it to
Paris, why would he risk letting himself be seen? And so
randomly, in one café among hundreds?

Her father had always said with criminals there are no
coincidences, only mistakes.

If she didn't at least make an attempt to investigate, she'd
feel guilty. She'd do some simple digging and get home in
time for Chloé's bath.

She copied Mirko's photo, trimmed the border with her
manicure scissors.

Seeing her at work, Saj asked, "Does that have to do with
Dechard?"

Saj was an outside-the-box thinker, and she appreciated
his take on things. She decided to tell him about Suzanne's
request, despite her insistence Aimée keep it between them.
"Did you tell Suzanne Lesage where to find me today?"

"She sounded disturbed. A cosmos in turbulence."

"Next time leave me a message so I'm warned, okay? But here's the deal."

She explained her connection to Suzanne and what Suzanne had asked of her. "I think she mistook this man for someone who's dead."

"Never dismiss a visitation," said Saj. His brows furrowed. "The path souls take after death can be fraught."

He'd been reading the Upanishads again. Next he'd insist they start doing yoga before beginning their workday.

She had another few hours before Babette would need to leave Chloé. In the meantime, Aimée would nose around. She riffled through her disguises in the back armoire: the generic security suit, the fifties vintage velvet cocktail dress, the France Télécom overalls, the nurse outfit, and the Paco Rabanne chain-mail mini—her standby for impromptu party invitations. She chose a secretarial look: frameless glasses, brown wig, ballet flats, and khaki Céline safari jacket.

"How do I look?"

"Definitely clerical. A drone in an office."

"*Parfait.*" Always good to go incognito. Not that Aimée was worried. But since Morbier's shooting, she took precautions. Chloé needed her *maman.*

Her gut told her the trauma of what Suzanne had witnessed in Bosnia had taken its toll, made her see things. Nevertheless, this was personal, and Aimée owed her. She'd do everything she could.

See things. On a whim, she tucked the nanny cam into her bag as she walked out the door.

THE EVENING CROWDS filled the narrow sidewalks around Saint-Sulpice Métro station. Aimée spotted the *café tabac* she was looking for: a neon orange-red carrot glowed above the door. It was only steps away from the Métro entrance. Aimée's first thought was that the Métro would provide an easy getaway. But why and from whom?

The café was just around the corner from Suzanne's flat.

Stepping inside, Aimée was met by the whoosh of milk steaming and the slap of coins on the counter. The shop hummed with conversation. Locals visited their neighborhood *café tabac* for the cheapest espresso, a *tartine jambon*, Loto tickets, cigarettes, their *carte grise* (car or motorcycle registration) a look at *Le Parisien*—there was always one on the counter—or a chat with *maître*. The proprietor knew the pulse of the quarter, her father always said.

She debated ordering a glass of wine, but she needed to be alert and focus. *"Bonsoir, un epresso s'il vous plaît."*

The man she figured for the proprietor wiped down the steamer wand of the shiny coffee machine, whacked the coffee grounds into the trash, slotted in the aluminum filter, brimful of fresh ground beans. A moment later he set down a steaming demitasse on a saucer and passed her the round bowl of sugar cubes.

"Merci." She set the copied photo of Mirko on the counter. "Do you remember seeing this man last night?"

The man stared at the photo. Then at her. His muttonchop whiskers drooped down his cheek. "My staff served more than three hundred customers last night." He shrugged. "Not a clue. Nor am I a public service."

Helpful, the proprietor. "Does he look like a regular?"

"We get all types. Most from the *quartier*."

Further down the counter, Aimée recognized an older woman with her Chihuahua—an actress who had been in movies in the eighties.

"Don't remember you as local," the owner said.

Aimée saw suspicion in his narrowed eyes. This wasn't going well.

"Don't recognize him, as I said." His eye caught on a customer's empty wineglass as the man motioned that he wanted to pay.

No use beating a dead horse, as the old saying went. Aimée slid some coins across the counter. Downed her espresso.

One down, how many more to go before she went home with a clear conscience? What would be due diligence? She stood and headed to the crowded *tabac* section of the shop. As she waited in line, she eyed the cigarettes, noticing foreign brands. She suppressed that Pavlovian itch to smoke. Looming over the *tabac* line, a man in overalls stood on a ladder as he installed an overhead fan unit. An irritating whine came from his power drill.

The young woman stacking cigarettes finally turned to her.

"Have any Serbian cigarettes?" asked Aimée.

"What brand?"

"I forget, but from the former Yugoslavia."

"Hmm." The woman checked. "We normally carry Auras. But I'm all out."

Behind her Aimée heard shuffling in line. She whipped out the photo. "Did this man buy a pack last night? Maybe he bought you out?"

The woman glanced at the photo and lifted her shoulders in a shrug. "Beats me. I'm off on Mondays."

"Can you ask . . . ?"

A long line had formed behind Aimée, and shouts came from the back. A young *mec* stepped inside and signaled to the *tabac* girl.

"We're unloading a new shipment right now," she said.

"You want the Auras, come back later." She motioned Aimée to the side. "Next in line. Monsieur?"

Twenty minutes later she'd visited all the open businesses on the streets around the corner café: a dry cleaner and key maker, two boutiques about to close for the day, a coiffeur's shop, and the art gallery.

No one recognized the man in the photo. No one remembered him as a customer.

Before going home, Aimée would try once more.

She showed the *café tabac* girl the photo again. "Do you remember him ever buying those cigarettes?"

"I see hundreds of people every day. You want the Auras or not?"

She bought them. Left the *café tabac*.

The only thing she'd gotten out of this fruitless quest was a desire to smoke and a pack in her hand.

She passed the tall doors of a fire station, where a fireman with SAPEUR-POMPIER printed across the back of his blue shirt chatted with a highly made-up girl. Notorious, these fireman—and the groupies who clustered around them. Something about a man in a uniform, Martine always said.

Behind the *café tabac*, Aimée glimpsed the young man who had unloaded the new shipment. He was leaning on the wall in his creased black Levi's and a T-shirt, smoking.

"Got a light?" she asked him.

In answer he flipped open his lighter, cupped the flame. She leaned in. Took a drag. The Aura was harsh and woody.

That faithful jolt hit her lungs.

She stifled a cough.

"*Merci*. Thank God you got these in," she said, playing

with the packet. There was some kind of Cyrillic script on the box. "My friend must have bought you out last night."

"These? I prefer KOOL lights myself. Menthol."

Thought that made him special. She could tell.

"Did you see my friend?" She whipped out the photo.

He glanced and gave a quick shake of his head. "You don't look like a *flic*."

"Smart *mec*. I'm not." She hoped her nondescript outfit made her look like an office worker. "Didn't you work the *tabac* last night?" she said, taking a guess.

"What if I did?"

Now she was getting somewhere. Time to use her imagination, as Suzanne had suggested. Come up with a story, then go home.

"It's personal. He's more than my friend, if you know what I mean . . ."

"*Désolé*, but . . ."

"Look, he kicked me out. Changed the locks."

He shifted on his Converse sneakers. Uncomfortable. "Why ask me?"

She sensed something. Showed him the photo again. "Take another look. I don't even know where he's working now. All I want are my things. Please."

"A domestic quarrel? *Désolé*, but not my problem."

She groaned inside. This wasn't going well. And her ballet shoes were chafing her heels in the humidity.

"So you did see him? *Alors*, I'm stuck, need my clothes back so I have something to wear to work. Please."

She sniffled, tried to summon a tear. All she felt was the perspiration on her neck.

The guy looked at the photo. "Can't say . . . Customers come and go all the time."

She persisted. "Even the ones who smoke Auras?"

"There's one I remember, an old *mec* with a limp. Comes early every morning for a *café-clope*."

The Parisian breakfast of an espresso and cigarette.

"He's got an accent. Émigré."

She brightened. "Do you think the émigré knows Mirko?"

A shrug. "If anyone does, he would."

She scribbled the burner phone's number on a receipt.

"*Merci*, and in case Mirko comes back, here's my number."

He took it—not that he wanted to—ground out his cigarette with his toe, and disappeared into the *café tabac*. The sunset faded into a pale band above the *grisaille* rooftops.

Bon, she'd pass the émigré's info on to Suzanne. Let her chase the phantom. Aimée was done.

Yet it niggled at her.

She could relate to Suzanne's obsession. Thoughts of Morbier haunted her, waking her up in the middle of the night. She would lie awake on the floor by Chloé's crib, listening to her sleeping breaths, wishing she could fall asleep herself.

Alors, she'd explore every thread, as she'd promised Suzanne. Do a little more legwork.

Back in the café, she sat down at the bar, checked the time. Now she had to hurry. In her red Moleskine, she noted down whom she'd questioned and, on her to-do list, wrote, *old émigré—café-clope*. As she shoved the Moleskine back into her bag, her hand hit the nanny cam.

Behind the counter, a middle-aged woman bantered with the clientele. The suspicious proprietor Aimée had first questioned was nowhere to be seen. This woman seemed a talkative type, so Aimée decided to try again.

After she'd ordered another espresso, she pulled out the

photo and said, "My friend Suzanne said she thought she saw this guy here last night."

A steady brown drip filled the demitasse.

The woman wiped the counter down as she peered at the photo. "Ah, Suzanne. I remember she was here . . . but I serve so many people, I can't remember who came and went, and with the tourists . . . Maybe if it were November, when it's slower . . ." She trailed off and went to serve another customer.

Aimée took her espresso to the window. Blocking her hands from view with her bag, she put René's new nanny cam in one of the window boxes filled with ferns. She focused the lens on the counter, hit the RECORD button, saw the answering green light. She called Saj and told him what she'd done, whispering under the clamor of the café patrons.

"René's new nanny cam?" Saj said. "He'll blow steam out of his ears. You know it's highly illegal to mount surveillance in a place of business."

"Even with a nanny cam?"

A sigh over the phone. "Try arguing that to the *flics*."

She almost blurted out that she was doing it for a *flic*. Forget the nanny cam. The light in here was terrible anyway. She shoved it back in her bag.

"I'd recommend you look around for any surveillance cameras at nearby businesses. Like a bank."

Why hadn't she thought of that? Why hadn't Suzanne? Across the street was a branch of her own bank, Paribas, now closed.

"You sure this *mec*'s a ghost, Aimée?"

"I'm going to find out."

Tuesday, Late Afternoon

TODAY, IN THE middle of summer, the school yard was empty of any sounds but the thrush's chirping. A sweet fragrance drifted from the ripe tomatoes in the abandoned student garden as Pauline tossed a bottle in the nearly full recycling bin. There were no children's shouts or laughter; the school bell was silent.

But Pauline was not alone.

There were the ones who had stayed behind, who couldn't leave on their journeys. Forever doomed to inhabit this world. Pauline's world.

Fabienne, ten years old, a TB victim, skipped rope in her long white pinafore. Louis, the old caretaker who had suffered a heart attack in the loge, stopped pushing his broom long enough to wave. Pauline waved back.

"Not again," said Pauline's mother.

"Don't get jealous, *Maman*. If I couldn't see them, I couldn't see you."

Her mother, apron tied around her waist, tsked. She'd been the school's *gardienne* until 1989, when she stepped in the crosswalk and a bus squashed her flat as a *crêpe*. Right here in front of Jardin du Luxembourg. Pauline had taken over as *gardienne* then and had been here ever since.

Here with her mother and the other ghosts.

Pauline never spoke about it, but people in the quarter knew she had the sight. She called her visits manifestations.

Now and then a parent would beg her to read the

tarot. To help them communicate with a lost loved one. The butcher had sought her out, and the old general's daughter.

Sometimes the loved one spoke. Even when they didn't, Pauline felt them. In their room, on the street—wherever they had died.

Pauline refused payment or gifts—that would be wrong; she'd never asked for this sight. She asked only to stay here at the school. With them. To keep them company.

Now the new headmistress, a no-nonsense type in her forties, was approaching at a brisk stride. She wore low heels and a determined smile. A few days earlier, she had sent Pauline her retirement papers, and a notice to vacate.

Pauline, at sixty-five years old, proudly held the position her mother had held before her and couldn't imagine being anywhere else.

"Ignore her, Pauline," said her mother.

"How?"

"She's got no right to force you to move. Speak to your union, like I said."

The too-blonde headmistress had arrived. "Talking to yourself again, Pauline?"

Her mother evaporated.

"I'll pick the tomatoes, madame," said Pauline. "Give you some for the teacher meeting."

"We can't avoid the inevitable. Pauline, try to understand. The union's offered you an apartment. They will relocate you to a new development."

In the suburbs? A place where she'd never stepped foot in her life? Although the young woman who'd been stung to death by the bees had told her the suburbs had gardens, too. She'd said they were pretty nice.

"I was born two streets away," said Pauline. "I've lived here all my life."

"Take it up with your union. They'll find a place closer. Look, Pauline, we need to fix up the *gardien* loge for the new family coming in."

The souls needed her here.

"Read your tea leaves. It's time for you to move on. There's a new generation. I have to enforce the current ministry guidelines."

Move on? She'd seen it all. They wouldn't let her.

Tuesday Evening

"MADAME CACHOU?" AIMÉE peered in the open door of her concierge's loge in her Ile Saint-Louis building's courtyard.

Miles Davis, her bichon frise, ran out and licked her ankles. Sniffed the wig peeking from her bag.

"We took a walk, and he got a burr in his paw, *pauvre petit*," said Madame Cachou, bending down and showing Aimée. "Came out with tweezers."

Her ramrod stiff concierge had mellowed these days; she positively doted on Aimée's fluff ball and her *bébé*. Madame Cachou loved walking Miles Davis.

"Madame Cachou, I just wanted to confirm that when Babette's on vacation—"

"That's what I have to tell you. *Mon Dieu*, I can't watch Chloé anymore—there's been an emergency . . ."

"What?" Aimée had been counting on Madame Cachou covering for Babette so Aimée could make her appointments at École des Beaux-Arts.

"My sister's back in the hospital. No one plans to get sick, do they? I'm leaving for Strasbourg on the night train."

Now Aimée noticed the train tickets sitting on Madame Cachou's desk. A roller bag by the door.

All Aimée's careful planning, and now she was up the creek. She ransacked her brain for options.

"Tell her to get better soon, so you can come back home to us," she said.

"Chloé's papa's here," said the busybody, pointing up the stairs. "Time he pitched in, *non*?"

Melac?

Unannounced and without even telling her?

Two months ago, he and his wife had come to a custody arrangement with Aimée, but then they had just disappeared. Not even a call—fell off the face of the earth. Now he'd just shown up out of the blue? Why hadn't Babette warned her? Why had Babette let him in?

She ran up the stairs, perspiring in the heat, with Miles Davis at her heels. Her key jammed in the door, wouldn't turn. What in the world was going on? Locked out of her own flat?

She knocked, then pounded on the door, panicking.

"*Alors*, such a racket. Hold on, where's the fire?" said an oddly accented voice. *Where's the fire*—that old-fashioned expression Morbier used. She pushed Morbier from her mind. Who the hell was in her house?

Her front door was opened by an older woman with flushed cheeks, tinted glasses, and a sleek grey bob. A lot of makeup.

"Who are you?" Aimée snapped, stepping inside her foyer as the woman made way.

"I'm visiting my granddaughter," the woman said in a taut voice.

A sick feeling hit her as Melac appeared in the hallway with Chloé on his hip. No sign of his do-gooder wife, Donatine, with her organic, homespun everything. He gave her a rueful smile. "*Désolé, Aimée*. I called, but you didn't answer. I know it's not our arrangement, but my mother's passing through . . ."

His mother? That was why the woman looked familiar. Awkward.

"*Excusez-moi*," Aimée said, embarrassed. At a loss for

words, she edged past the woman and took her gurgling baby from Melac. Chloé squealed in delight and burped. Something orange and warm splattered over Aimée's trench coat.

"So *ma puce* has a special treat for *Maman*." Aimée shook her head and glanced at Melac. He and Chloé looked so much alike.

In the kitchen Aimée found Babette cleaning up the floor. Her normal calm manner had evaporated. "I'm sorry, Aimée. Gabrielle's mother picked her up early, Chloé had just woken up, and then my aunt"—she meant Madame Cachou—"was all worked up over my other aunt, who's hospitalized in Strasbourg. Then Melac showed up at the door, and . . . I didn't even have time to say no."

Melac and his mother had steamrollered their way in.

Babette hissed, "She's telling me how to prepare the carrots!" She blew out an exasperated breath.

Miles Davis mewled, his paws covering his face. Even he was upset.

Aimée recognized an emergency—time to prevent her babysitter's meltdown, restore calm, and get Melac and his mother out. As if on cue, Chloé burped up another orange projectile arc.

"*Mon Dieu*, she's so warm." Aimée felt Chloé's forehead. Hot. "A fever."

Could things get worse?

". . . didn't even have the courtesy to introduce herself!" came from the hallway. "I'm waiting downstairs." The front door slammed.

Merde! She'd put her foot in it again. But how was she supposed to have known Melac's mother was going to answer her door?

It was time for all the uninvited to leave.

She took Babette's hand. "Get the baby acetaminophen and start Chloé's bath. I'll take care of everything else."

In the hallway, as she wiped off her trench coat, she cornered Melac. "If you ever barge in here again—"

"*Zut!* Morbier's dying, Aimée." Melac raised a hand in a defensive gesture. "I came to Paris to say goodbye. My mother wanted to see her granddaughter."

He crossed his arms and stared her in the eyes. Defensive.

"So this is all my fault?" she said.

"Considering you had Morbier shot, I'd say yes."

Dumb. Why hadn't she bitten her tongue?

Melac expelled air, ran his hand through his thick hair. "*Alors,* maybe I'd have done the same. Maybe not. But I understand now why it happened, with all the corruption scandals they're blowing smoke over." His shoulders slumped in defeat. "It's gutted me, too. The man mentored me. Like you, I trusted him."

"You think I wanted to believe he killed my father? But when I found the truth . . ." She swallowed.

"Aimée, he's got something to tell you."

Not this again. And from Melac? Just what she needed.

Melac leaned against the hallway wall, as he had so often in the past, his jeans slung low on his hips, those grey-blue eyes searching hers.

"I just can't, so please don't start, Melac. Why are you really here?"

Pause. "I think you know."

"Care to clue me in?"

A warm rush of something drifted between them. He'd gripped her shoulder. Those long fingers drew her close, traced her cheek. That vetiver lime cologne he wore filled her senses.

Chloé's cries reached them in the hallway.

Aimée broke away. He'd left and married someone else. Someone so not like Aimée. What was she thinking? She wished his touch didn't pull her like gravity.

That he didn't still wear that serpent-shaped rose gold wedding ring.

"Look, I've got an evening of work—"

Melac snorted. "Still the same. My daughter's got a fever, and you're—"

"Working? Correct. I run a business," she said, hardening her tone. "By the way, fevers spike in the evening. Did you know that? Chloé didn't have one this afternoon. So don't you dare accuse me of neglecting her. Chloé's my daughter, and if you're here to make trouble about that custody business again, that will ruin any goodwill we established." She caught her breath, so angry she wanted to spit. "Is Donatine going to pop in next?"

Melac met her gaze. "She just got a job offer from the *clinique* in Lille, where she applied last year. It's in her specialty."

Did that translate to the marriage boat hitting rough water? Not her problem. "Sounds like you've got time on your hands."

"You just don't get it, do you, Aimée?"

"Get what?"

"I want to be in Chloé's life. And yours."

He took her hands in his. His eyes bored into hers.

Aimée lifted his left hand in front of his face to show him his wedding ring. To remind him of the woman between them.

She dropped his hand and turned away. Walked toward the kitchen. "See yourself out, Melac."

She wouldn't let this man, the father of her child, disappear and reappear whenever it suited him.

From the open kitchen window, she watched Melac and his mother standing on the bank of the Seine, silhouetted by the silvering surface. Melac's voice drifted. Aimée couldn't catch what he was saying. She couldn't tell if they were arguing or consoling each other. Something struck her as off. Was it the body language?

This was Chloé's grandmother—a woman who would surely be coming back into their lives. Aimée was irritated she'd paid so little attention to the woman when she'd been in her home. But now her curiosity spiked.

Tuesday Evening

"I'VE DONE WHAT you wanted," said Melac. "Now—"

"Keep walking until we round the bend of the quai," said the woman. "She's watching."

Their footsteps crackled in the fallen plane tree twigs. A fat sea gull waddled on the stone wall. Oyster-grey pigeons pecked the pavement. Melac shooed them out of their path.

Past the bend fronting Pont de Sully, Melac stopped. "I need to hear your answer."

He wished he didn't feel like crap, a traitor. He wasn't.

"It's all taken care of, as I promised." The woman opened the back door of the waiting Peugeot, its engine purring. She got in, shut the door. A minute later the window rolled down. She'd taken off her wig, was shaking out her hair. She'd donned sunglasses. "Just see this through the next few days. That's all."

"You mean until Morbier—"

"That's my business," she interrupted, as the window rolled up and the car drove off.

Tuesday Evening

AIMÉE TOOK OVER bath time, letting Babette off for
the night. She cleaned between Chloé's pink-jewel toes
until the baby squealed in delight. "What do you think of
papa, *ma puce?*"

Chloé popped bubbles with her fist.

"My sentiments exactly."

Chloé's brow felt cool to the touch now, thank God.
Aimée cuddled next to her on the linen duvet in her bedroom. Chloé instinctively reached for Aimée's breast, her
little mouth sucking and getting nothing.

"*Désolée, ma puce*, you're on the bottle now. Remember?"

Aimée's milk had dried up on that cold, damp night she'd
watched Morbier go into surgery. Two months ago.

Again, all the sadness and anger washed over her. It was
Morbier's fault she couldn't nurse Chloé. The doctor had
waved her guilt away with, "Sooner or later women stop
nursing. Milk dries up for various reasons—big shock, emotional upheaval. Or it's just time." Guilt still invaded her at
Chloé's anxious tears when nothing came out.

After gentle coaxing, Chloé took the bottle, sucked
hungrily, her little eyelids at half-mast. Aimée grabbed the
pediatrician-psychoanalyst Dr. Dolto's tome, her bedside
bible. She read the section on baby fevers, a worn, book-
marked chapter, and mentally checked off everything Dr.
Dolto recommended.

Chloé's little whistling, sleeping breaths lulled Aimée

into dozing herself. The beeping of her phone woke her. She tucked Chloé into her crib, grabbed a cold sparkling Badoit from the tiny fridge, helped herself to leftover carrots *rapé au citron*, a chunk of Gruyère, and a nub of baguette from the counter. Then, arms loaded with the food, the baby monitor, her bag, her notebook, and Suzanne's envelopes, she sat down on her balcony, Miles Davis beside her.

Below, the quayside lights cast gleaming copper shivers on the Seine's black-gloss surface. The plane trees rustled; the car horns sounded distant.

She checked her muted phone. A missed call. René, ticked off about his nanny cam, no doubt. But there was still a beeping coming from her bag . . . *Mon Dieu*. The burner phone Suzanne had given her.

In all the brouhaha when she'd gotten home that night, she'd forgotten about it.

Damn Melac. And her postpartum anxiety. About to call back on the burner phone, she wondered if she had actually gotten a lead on a ghost.

Tuesday Evening

THE LINE WAS busy. As she chewed the baguette, she added to her to-do list in her red Moleskine:

Banks video footage

But would a fugitive wanted for war crimes buy cigarettes at Suzanne's local *café tabac*? And, if he had, would he let Suzanne get away?

Doubtful.

In the personal column, she drew a calendar and mapped out the days she'd have to bring Chloé to the office. She wrote *babysitter?* on days she was supposed to do IT surveillance on-site at École des Beaux-Arts. Under *TO BUY*, she wrote *lipstick* and *champagne*.

She tried the number again. Still busy.

On the balcony, with her bare feet propped on the filigree grill, she read the investigative file Suzanne had given her. The little she could decipher was the stuff of nightmares. One page was stamped SECRET, and much of it was blacked out, redacted.

No doubt Mirko Vladić was dead. But then death looked too good for him. She wondered what was in the stuff Suzanne didn't have security clearance for—the horrors in black and white. Mirko Vladić was referred to in the same paragraph with Milošević, the butcher of the Balkans.

There were a few more mentions of Mirko in a Red Cross

report, each mention flagged with a cross-reference to an ICTY file. The ICTY file itself was sealed, but Aimée's imagination could fill in the details.

The river slapped rhythmically against the bank in the wake of a passing *bateau-mouche*. From one of the courtyards in Ile Saint-Louis's warren of hidden gardens and old carriage houses drifted piano music, laughter. Her next-door neighbors, who happened to be related to the Rothschilds, were entertaining. The day's dense heat lingered.

Meanwhile, faces flashed in front of her eyes, mental images of mustached men spraying Kalashnikov fire into a pit of human victims, a parrot fluttering its wings, trying to escape a bolted birdcage. Melac's mother's face.

She woke up to Miles Davis's barking.

Disoriented, she tried to grasp what the nightmare had meant, but it slipped away like a greased spoon.

"Psst!" Benoît waved from below the balcony where he was standing on the quai. "Sleepyhead. Your door's locked."

The file spilled from her lap, and papers slid across the balcony. Awake now, she swooped them back into the file, tiptoed inside on her cold, damp feet, and set the file by her laptop.

She combed her spiky hair back with her fingers, ran to check on Chloé, brushed her teeth, and spritzed Chanel No. 5 on the pulse point below her earlobe. Where was her lipstick?

Benoît filled her doorway, lean hipped and grinning, his longish brown hair curling over his collar. Both hands were concealed behind his back.

"What have you got there?" She sniffed.

He pulled one hand from behind his back.

"Night-flowering jasmine," he said, presenting her with a bunch he must have picked himself. Then he pulled out the other hand. "No champagne, *désolé*. Just an amuse-bouche."

Cupped in his palm were several bite-sized buckwheat crepes topped with swirls of smoked salmon peppered with dill.

Delicious. Benoît loved to cook.

"I'll still supply the chaos." She snapped her Agent Provocateur bra strap. "Call me a cheap date."

"I figured." He picked her up, and they made it only as far as her *recamier* by the window.

Wednesday Morning

AT DAWN, BENOÎT crept back home across the courtyard. His scent lingered on the sheets. Once she had a now
fever-free Chloé eating breakfast with Babette, Aimée rummaged in her armoire for something she could wear to beat
the heat. Pulled out a last-season Versace linen miniskirt
from the *soldes*—sales—her blue and white striped Breton
marinière top—for a Left Bank *garçonne* look—and platform
espadrilles. She packed yesterday's disguise in her bag.

She scootered to work. The Seine flowed a murky khaki
below the Pont Marie. Her mind spun with the scads of
things she had to accomplish before Babette left for *vacances*.

Alone in Leduc Detective, she ran ongoing security
scans, savoring the stillness and quiet. René was teaching
at the Hackaviste Academy; Maxence, their intern from
Quebec, was on vacation. The morning light caught a
gossamer cobweb from the high ceiling's carved Empire
moldings.

Time to get their cleaner on task. About to write a note
for the concierge, Aimée stopped and stared at the intricate
spun threads. The web appeared so tenuous and fragile, yet
it would be sticky and cling if she tried to dust. Like her
relationship with Melac.

She'd moved on, hadn't she? Pushed that aside for now.

She wondered what her father would do with Suzanne's
case. She wished he were there so she could ask his advice.

The sadness never went away—she had seen with

her own eyes the explosion that had killed him in Place Vendôme. And now she knew how Morbier had betrayed him and lied to her for years. Tears welled in her eyes. A man her father had trusted. Whom she'd trusted.

She put that aside, too.

She flipped through the surveillance cases in her father's old files. Picked out one she remembered from the late eighties. Read it.

Voilà. She knew what her father would do. Simple is best, he always said.

Call in a favor.

She left a message on the voice mail of Monsieur Guérin, her Paribas bank manager. It wouldn't be the first time he'd helped the Leducs.

Then she changed, packed her Hermès and the information for Dechard, and left a Post-it with the note *Call me* on René's desktop screen.

Was he giving her the silent treatment over some imagined slight? These days anything set him off in a fit of sulking. More and more she noticed it. He'd fumed when she confided her romance with Benoît—told her it wasn't "proper" for Chloé and Gabrielle.

René needed a girlfriend.

PARKED BY THE café near Saint-Sulpice, she pulled the key out of the scooter's ignition and tugged her wig into place. Given the not-so-legal nature of her "surveillance" and this particular fugitive's history, it felt better to don another persona. Keep professional and private life separate. She didn't want anyone to recognize her as the mother who pushed Chloé's stroller to *bébé* swim at the nearby Saint-Germain Pool.

If she didn't see the émigré the young man from the *tabac*
had mentioned, she'd cross him off her to-do list and move
on to her next plan.

The café buzzed. Aimée noted the brisk trade in cigarettes, Loto tickets, PMU horse racing forms. Among the
cluster of regulars at the zinc counter were some already
having a marc liqueur with their coffee.

She ordered a double espresso from the woman she'd
spoken with the night before. As the woman put the espresso
down, Aimée smiled to engage her in conversation.

"Suzanne's friend, right?" the woman said.

"Good memory."

"She's a regular. From the quartier."

A quartier charmingly open yet harboring all manner of
secrets. The woman knew Suzanne—time to press.

"Have you noticed anything about her lately?" Aimée
asked. "Has she changed at all since she's been back?"

The woman raised an eyebrow.

"To be honest, I'm concerned about Suzanne."

The woman looked both ways, leaned over the counter.
"Jittery, tired, *oui*. But that describes a lot of my clients after
work. They come to *déstresser*, chat and have an *apéro* with
friends before going home."

That got her nowhere.

And then she noticed a man setting down a cane at
a table by the window, his dog at his heels. *"Bonjour, ma
belle,"* he said to the woman behind the counter with a
wave. A Slavic accent. "The usual."

The woman hit the red button on the espresso machine.
Arranged a tray with an espresso and packet of Auras. He
must be the one. The *café-clope* émigré with his cigarette
and espresso.

"Let me save you a trip, madame." After sliding a fifty-franc note across the counter, Aimée took the tray.

"*Bonjour.*" She set down his tray, pushed a Ricard ashtray toward him and sat.

He tore the cellophane off the cigarette packet, tapped one out, lit up and exhaled a plume of smoke. "Since when did the waitresses get so pretty? And sit and chat?"

"My treat, Monsieur . . . ?"

"Olgan." He had sharp hazel eyes, a long face, and a grizzled white beard. Stocky and Eastern European looking, with an accent to match. His dog, a grey-whiskered German shepherd, snored below the table.

"Karine Viardot." She pushed a fake card across the table. The phone number on it connected to her answering service. Then she pulled out the photo of Mirko. "I hear you'd know this man if anyone does."

"My reputation precedes me, eh? But why would I know him?"

Two questions and no answer.

"It's a discreet inquiry."

"I read Raymond Chandler, but you don't strike me as that kind of detective."

He'd picked up on her ruse right away. Sharp. "We come in all shapes and sizes these days." She tapped her finger on the photo. "Look, forgive me for bothering you. There's a small chance this man, Mirko Vladić, came into this café the other night. My client wants to contact him."

"Regarding?"

She pretended to hesitate. Glanced over her shoulder. "It's personal," she lied, "but I'm not supposed to say that."

He waved away smoke. "Why are you asking me?"

The truth was she didn't really have a reason. "I'm

reaching out to anyone connected to the Eastern European community here," she said lamely.

"Eastern European community?" He eyed her. "There's an Eastern European bookstore nearby, off Saint-Sulpice. That's what I know."

"This man is a Serb. He was last seen in Bosnia. That help?"

Olgan set down his demitasse so hard it rattled the saucer. His dog sat up.

"We're not all thugs, mademoiselle."

She'd said the wrong thing. Tried to recover. "I don't get your meaning, monsieur."

"Serbs, Bosnians, Croats, we all look alike to you, don't we?"

Stupid. It was true—she didn't know the difference. And she'd hit a nerve.

"Forgive me, that's not what I meant, monsieur."

"I was a university professor. Serb criminals destroyed my family village, massacred everyone in the Vukovar countryside. Ripped Croatia apart." He reached for his cane. "I came here to Paris to teach at the Institut D'études Slavs because I had no family left."

She'd blown it. "I'm sorry. Can you take my card? If there's anything—"

"You think I'd help a Serb?"

"It's more complicated than that," she blurted. "My client thought this man was dead. I need to know if she's seeing phantoms."

She didn't know what else she could say.

His hazel eyes gazed somewhere in the distance. Somewhere far from the café, the bustle of regulars, the grinding of the orange juicer.

"I want to help her move on with her life," said Aimée. "Put the past aside. That's all."

He stared at her, hearing truth in her voice. "Phantoms. That I understand," he said, his voice low. "They roam the countryside, inhabit nightmares."

She'd reached him. Now to play on his loathing for the Serbs. "I'm talking about a rape victim who's afraid the father of her child survived."

She hated that it felt so easy to lie. But she also had only thirty minutes before she needed to be at work.

"A monster," he said.

"Something like that." Alert, she nodded. "Serbs ruined your homeland. Help me. This man might have escaped arrest by the war crimes tribunal."

"What's that to me?"

"If he's in the community here, couldn't you find out?"

"Here? Does he speak French? Why don't you try Croatia or Bosnia? Or little Montenegro, where the Serbs are making all the trouble now? Read the newspapers."

A wanted Serbian war criminal could evaporate better in his own region than here.

"You're right, monsieur. That makes sense. I just need to prove to her he's dead."

He took her card, finished his espresso, and with a whistle to his dog, limped away into the sunshine.

IN THE PARIBAS branch halfway down the block from the café, Aimée stood in the manager's office and flashed her faux police ID.

"*Bonjour*, I'm Karine Viardot with fraud investigations," said Aimée. "A few minutes of your time, please, to facilitate our investigation."

The manager, a middle-aged woman with steel-frame designer eyeglasses, cocked an eyebrow in surprise. "But I met with François from your office this morning."

Merde. If Aimée didn't move fast, this would blow up in her face. She shook her head. "I don't know anything about that, madame. My team works out of Bercy in the counter-terrorism branch. Your bank's video camera looks out onto an area we've put under surveillance. I need to see your Monday night video footage taken between seven-twenty and nine-twenty P.M."

"On whose authority, exactly?" Suspicion clouded the woman's eyes behind her designer frames. She clicked her pen, sizing Aimée up.

"Level three, madame. You do know what that means?" The office smelled like printer toner.

The bank manager reached for a file on her desk. "I'll need to check with—"

"A terrorist sighting," Aimée interrupted. "Please cooperate and furnish the footage. Terrorists funnel money through banks like the rest of us, I don't need to remind you. But we're not looking at accounts right now, only video footage." Aimée opened the file showing the header INTERNATIONAL CRIMINAL TRIBUNAL FOR THE FORMER YUGOSLAVIA. "We're looking for this man. He's a wanted international terrorist who has been spotted in this area. On the street, maybe in your bank. It's time sensitive. I'm sure you'd like to cooperate, *non?*"

"No one has alerted us," the woman said, still suspicious.

A tough nut to crack, this manager.

"I'll need to go through the proper channels," she continued.

But Aimée knew banks furnished *flics* video footage all the time.

"We're working with Monsieur Guérin, the manager at the main Paribas branch at l'Opera," said Aimée, tapping her ballet heel. "It's a routine request, Madame Karon," she said pointedly, looking at the name inscribed on the woman's pen case. "Don't tell me you haven't done this before."

The woman hesitated.

"I can get Monsieur Guérin on my cell phone if—"

In answer, the woman made a call, avoiding Aimée's gaze.

A terse conversation ensued, during which Aimée hoped Monsieur Guérin had listened to the voice mail she'd left and would recognize the fake name she'd warned him she might use.

"*D'accord*," Madame Karon said, "he says to assist and provide you with the footage."

Phew, he'd come through.

The woman hung up, hit a few buttons on her phone to place another call. "Tell David from operations to come to my office and to bring a blank VHS tape."

Join the looming twenty-first century, Aimée almost said. She bit her tongue. She'd convert the footage back at the office.

THE BANK STOP had taken longer than she'd expected. She jumped on her scooter and headed for the École des Beaux-Arts. Her face was a sweaty mess in the heat, her mascara smeared. A total wreck.

Time to get waterproof mascara.

In the model's changing room by the figure-drawing studio, Aimée hurriedly stuffed the wig into her bag, donned her casual IT look. Pastel chalk dust settled in the soles of her espadrilles.

She made a few quick swipes at her face with a cotton pad soaked in Bluet, a blue cornflower astringent she carried; dabbed concealer under her eyes; and popped a *Les Anis de Flavigny* rose-flavored breath mint. The dash upstairs took her to the inner sanctum—the library of the architecture department. According to an early-morning email, this was where she'd be working today. A humdrum database scan.

But the salon adjoining the library was far from quiet. Hot white lights were trained on old masters' paintings that had been propped all over the room: banquet scenes, oil still lifes of plucked pheasants roasting on fires, a medieval scullery.

A photo shoot?

A white-hatted chef prepped intricate plates of hors d'oeuvres, stylish presentations of market vegetables. She watched him primping a red-and-white radish as if it were a model about to head down the runway.

Edible art. Chloé would love it.

Her mouth watering, Aimée edged closer to the long butcher-block table, dying to grab a nibble. Couldn't help herself and reached.

Beside her, a man snorted. "That's not food." It was Jules Dechard.

Startled, she looked where he was pointing. The chef was holding a syringe.

"The chef injects dye and silicon to make it pop for the photo."

"*Merci* for the warning."

"It's all a sham. Not about art or taste. It's business—advertising. They're shooting photos for a big fundraising campaign. Spending money to make money." He sighed. "But it keeps the board happy."

Nonetheless, the photo shoot made her IT tech cover for talking about the case for Dechard easier. There was so much activity in the salon that no one paid her any attention.

"I've got something for you," she said.

He gestured her out of the salon, and she followed him to an office door. Standing in the hallway was a pudgy man holding a sheaf of papers. He was clearly waiting to speak with Dechard. "This is Professor Michel Sarlat, my colleague."

Michel, who appeared to be in his mid-thirties, was a short sausage of a man, with feet so small she wondered how they supported his girth. He wiped his lank red hair from his brow and gave her a perfunctory smile. "*Enchanté.*" He turned to Dechard. "This needs a quick look, Jules, if I can take a moment?"

"Later, Michel."

Dechard led Aimée into his office and closed the door. Michel Sarlat, Aimée thought—his initials would be MS. He could be the staff member with the ms90 email address.

Dechard's vast office was unlike other professors' remodeled offices Aimée had seen in other wings of the school. One faded maroon wall was covered in museum-quality art—centuries-old oil paintings in antique frames. There, too, was the distinctive red ribbon of a Chevalier of the Légion d'honneur, the highest order of merit awarded by the French government. The surrounding three walls were lined floor to ceiling with books: leather-bound antique tomes, tall coffee-table art books, even the kind of cookbooks her grandmother once kept in her Auvergne farm kitchen. Aimée remembered standing on her tiptoes to peer over the counter at those recipes, splotched with béarnaise sauce. How she missed her *grand-mère*—if only Chloé could have known her.

"My weakness," said Dechard, following her gaze. "I'm a bibliophile with a collection running out of control." A practiced smile that didn't reach his eyes. "So you've found all the emails already?"

"*Bien sûr*, that's my expertise." And why he'd paid her a lot of money, but she left that out. She handed him an envelope in which she'd enclosed the printouts of the emails Saj had pulled. "The emails' point of origin was a computer in the Tournon art gallery. There were emails to and from two staff addresses—one of which was yours, Professor." Wondering if he would bring up the blackmail, she watched as he flipped through the pages.

Dechard rubbed his neck. The corners of his mouth turned down. She noted the sallow complexion on his long face. Where had his summer tan gone?

"Now, can I count on you to remain *discret*, mademoiselle?"

He sounded like he wasn't sure. Odd.

She nodded. "A given, Professor Dechard." The blackmail wasn't her business, she reminded herself. She'd finished the job—she was done here. She took a step toward the door. "If that's all?"

"Here's a small token of appreciation, mademoiselle."

He handed her a gift card to a culinary institute. Did everyone know she couldn't cook? Or had he noticed her eye lingering on the cookbooks?

"The bistro is run by student chefs in training," he said. "Make sure you call ahead for a reservation."

"But, Professor Dechard—"

"Food is art, too," Dechard said. He had taken his hat from his desk.

Taking the cue, Aimée turned to leave. Part of her wanted to warn him that accosting a blackmailer never went well. The other part knew he wouldn't listen. And it wasn't her business.

Wednesday, Midafternoon

HER SCOOTER'S MOTOR had died. Again. Aimée checked the oil. Fine. Flicked the ignition again. Nothing. She kicked it.

She stared at the bus stop, where a number of people were checking their watches and stepping into the street, staring down the road. Fanning themselves in the heat. It would probably be faster to walk.

Dropping off a client file at the law school, a last-minute errand for Saj, had taken her out of her way. Set her back. She needed to get to the Métro—then a swift ride would get her to the office in time for her client meeting.

Leaving her scooter parked where it was, Aimée fumed as she cut through the Jardin du Luxembourg to the Métro. Puddles on the gravel paths mirrored the denim blue sky and white puff-pastry clouds above. A moist, vegetal smell emanated from the greenery; the hedge-lined pathway buffered children's laughter. Napoleon had gifted these sixty acres, the lungs of Paris, to its children.

The big pond made her smile. Chloé loved watching the wooden boats, as Aimée had as a child. She emerged through the gold-tipped grill gates, by the Musée du Luxembourg and le Sénat, Marie de Médici's former palace.

Across the street, geraniums lined the windowsills of the hotel at the corner of rue Servandoni. A plaque bore the dates that William Faulkner had lived there.

Her father had told her Juliette Gréco, his not-so-secret crush, hid with *résistants* near here during the war.

A taxi pulled up, blocking Aimée's way. Like she needed another holdup? From the corner of her eye, she caught a couple coming out of the hotel's entrance.

The good-looking man was the Italian boyfriend of Martine, Chloé's godmother and Aimée's best friend since the lycée. She would know Gianni anywhere, with those white teeth bared in a huge smile, that glossy, black, curling hair.

Why was his linen-jacketed arm draped over a woman's shoulder? A woman who wasn't Martine. And coming out of a hotel!

He and Martine were leaving for vacation this week. Martine had urged Aimée to close shop, bring Chloé, and join them in Sicily. She'd been so persuasive that Aimée had browsed tickets. Even René had thought it was a good idea.

Martine had told Aimée she was scheduling a double-date dinner with this cheater and his cousin, whom she was trying to set-up with Aimée.

Aimée had never seen Martine so happy.

Oh God. She didn't want to look. Didn't want to know the other woman's identity.

Some stolen afternoon with his secretary from the Italian Cultural Center? The next moment they disappeared inside the taxi.

Aimée's phone vibrated. She ducked into a doorway. The taxi pulled away.

"*Oui?*"

"So I've got reservations tonight for all four of us," said Martine.

Of all times. Paralyzed, Aimée watched the taxi bump over the cobblestones in the narrow street. Turn left.

"But you said that . . . it would be on the weekend," she said, scrambling. "I've got babysitter issues."

"Okay. Ever heard of takeout? There's an incredible Sicilian restaurant Gianni knows. We'll all play with Chloé."

Merde. How could she pretend she hadn't seen him if he came to dinner? She had to get out of this—and off the phone before Martine sussed out that something was wrong. They'd told each other everything since they were fourteen. Mostly everything.

Could Aimée tell Martine her boyfriend had walked out of a hotel with another woman not a minute ago? She felt a stab to her heart.

"Look, I've got a traumatized *flic* on my hands right now, Martine . . ." she said, going for her sympathy.

"Morbier? Haven't you gotten over that and visited him yet?"

Not her, too. Why couldn't her best friend understand?

"*Mais non,* I haven't told you. It's Suzanne Lesage, the woman who was Melac's undercover partner and helped me when Zazie was kidnapped. Remember? She was seconded to The Hague to investigate Serbian war criminals, and now she's back and shell-shocked—"

"She's not the only one, Aimée. My colleague who reported on that mess still has nightmares—"

"I owe her, Martine," she interrupted. And it was true.

Pause. "And you owe me, too. Remember?"

Put her foot in it again. Could this get worse?

Martine had stepped up and pulled in all her journalist contacts to help Aimée chase down the truth about her father's death—about Morbier. She'd helped Aimée despite the fact that she'd suffered a miscarriage—the straw that broke the back of her go-nowhere relationship. Thank God, Aimée had thought when Martine had finally dumped that boyfriend for Gianni, taken up Tuscan cooking and conversational Italian.

For a cheater.

Aimée didn't know what to say. Her stomach knotted.

"Aimée, you there?" Martine was saying. "Good thing I get repaid in champagne. Let's make that prosecco tonight. It's overdue."

"It's funny, but I think I just saw Gianni," she said, blurting it out.

"You're near Saint-Sulpice?" Martine said without missing a beat. "He's minding the diva from La Scala for an Italian Cultural Center benefit. Poor Gianni. The diva requires hand-holding every minute of the day."

Aimée's shoulders relaxed. Nerves, she was all nerves. Paranoid. Jumping to conclusions. Since when had she gotten so jaded?

So much had happened—Morbier on his deathbed, then Suzanne accosting her, the Dechard blackmailing case, losing her childcare while Babette was on vacation, Melac turning up—Aimée's mind spun. She had to prioritize, stack all these things in mental boxes and shelve away the ones she couldn't get to right now.

"I'll get back to you, Martine. Got to go." Click.

Ten minutes later she reached the Métro. The grill gate bore a sign: CLOSED FOR SERVICE MAINTENANCE.

She wanted to kick someone. How could they? Then the burner rang.

Mon Dieu. When Benoît had come last night, she'd gotten busy with other things and forgotten about it.

"Got anything for me, Aimée?"

"You first. Weren't you meeting your Interpol connection . . . ?"

Aimée stepped under the shade of a plane tree.

"If only the security forces worked together, but it's
always like this," said Suzanne. "Despite our mandate from
the ICTY, prying information out of them is like trying
to open a rusty can. Cooperation takes time with such a
backlog. I'm trying to get Mirko's file to the top of the pile.
New emergencies come in every day."

Aimée had to give her the bad news.

"Suzanne, no one recognized Mirko in the café or any
of the shops nearby. I went three different times. I questioned everyone. Even a woman working the café counter
who knew you couldn't remember seeing him." Silence. She
added, "Things like this happen. I know. I've seen a friend
at a distance and gone up to hug her, and it was a complete
stranger."

"Don't treat me like an infant, Aimée." She heard paper
rustling in the background. Clicking of keyboard keys. "I'm
getting it from everywhere. That's why I came to you."

Suzanne was good. Commander-quality good. Yet . . .

"Suzanne, you're back with your family now. You're not
in the war zone anymore. You have to focus on settling
back in—"

"Settle into administration?" Suzanne snapped. "Because
that's where my boss stuck me, a trained BRI operational
officer . . ."

That was what they did when they were trying to cover
up an officer's mistakes. Aimée wondered if Suzanne's boss
thought she posed a threat to the ministry.

"Why did he put you on administration?" Aimée asked
carefully.

"Why do you think?"

"I think events in the field shook you up," said Aimée. "You're human."

"Our convoy took casualties, so now I'm soft? Only fit for paper work?"

"Calm down, Suzanne. Okay, you wanted proof that Mirko's here," said Aimée. "We'll see what's on the CCTV footage I obtained from the Paribas bank. The video camera covers the front of the café tabac, so it will have caught anyone coming or going."

A sucking in of breath. "Impressive, Aimée. Knew you'd come up spades."

"I'll review it at the office. Compress a file, and email it to you. But unless it shows him, I don't know what more I can do for you."

"There's one more thing I have to tell you," Suzanne said. "Isabelle Ideler is missing."

"Who?"

"Isabelle is the Dutch prosecutor who was leading our team in Bosnia."

Not all this again.

"Past tense, Suzanne. Isn't that over?"

"Isabelle was the one who insisted our team needed to dot every i, cross each t, to nail down Mirko in accordance with regulations." A snort. "More rights than his victims ever had. She's still the expert on this case, the point person coordinating the evidence. Anyway, Isabelle's brother emailed me to say she was supposed to meet him here in Paris—she's in town for meetings, staying with her old roommate. She never turned up when she was supposed to meet her brother, and no one's heard from her for two days. That's unlike her."

"Alert her Dutch counterparts. Standard procedure, *non?*" First it was a dead war criminal; now Suzanne was fixated on a former team member. "For all you know, she got lucky with some *mec* at a wine bar."

"I'm calling her brother." Pause. "You went to the café three times—didn't you find any lead?"

"Look, I'll format the bank's video feed and send it to you. You'll see whatever there is to see for yourself, okay?"

She doubted Mirko would be in it.

"That's not what I asked, Aimée."

Merde. As a *flic*, Suzanne sensed something. Aimée would have to tell her about Olgan, who she doubted knew anything.

"Don't know if an old Croat professor counts," Aimée said. "He hates Serbians."

"Good. Gives him a reason to turn Mirko in. Anything register with him?"

"I gave him my card. I wouldn't count on him making a call. But you never know."

Wednesday, Midafternoon

AIMÉE'S PARTNER, RENÉ Friant, was shuffling something into his leather briefcase when Aimée entered the office and tossed her trench coat over a hook. Startled, he looked up, his green eyes furtive.

"*Bonjour*, stranger," she said.

"You're late, Aimée."

For two days she hadn't seen him. And the first thing he did was jump down her throat.

"*Désolée*, the Métro station was closed. My scooter died . . ."

"Don't go defensive on me, Aimée."

She almost stomped her foot. Childish. "It's true, René."

"I was going to handle your meeting for you, but it's been postponed."

Thank God.

"I thought you'd stopped all that," said René, disapproval in his green eyes.

Aimée controlled her surprise. "Stopped all what, René?"

"Saj left a note on your desk." He was gripping the briefcase handles tightly.

"What's in your case?"

He stiffened. All four feet of him, handsome in his specially tailored café au lait linen suit. A dwarf, René sported an impeccable wardrobe with handmade shirts from Charvet.

"A surprise for me?"

She pretended to reach for the case. She wanted to tease it out of him, not invade his privacy.

Something had fallen on the floor. An admissions handbook for École Alsacienne, the private and exclusive elementary school in the triangle of private schools by Jardin du Luxembourg. Stapled to the front of the handbook was the director's card, an appointment time written on it.

She blinked. "Are you interviewing for another job?"

"I'll explain when you tell me why the brother's at the morgue."

Aimée blinked again. "Whose brother? What do you mean?"

"Read Saj's note."

Isabelle's brother's at the morgue. Suzanne says meet him there.

It took her a moment to make sense of this. Shouldn't Suzanne have called her on the burner phone? She checked. Somehow stuck in the bottom of her bag, the ringer had switched off. Why hadn't Suzanne left a message?

"Suzanne's . . . off kilter, René. She thinks a lawyer from The Hague has gone missing."

"And why's that your business?"

"Like I know? Why is that school your business?"

René's lips pursed. "It's never too early, as I've been saying, for you to get Chloé on a waiting list."

Aimée's jaw dropped. "She's not even walking or talking yet." Good lord. She'd found those Latin flash cards he'd hidden in the toy box. Next it would be Chinese. "Anyhow, I owe Suzanne and will stamp 'paid' on the favor after I go through some CCTV footage."

"Favor? You mean . . . ?" René's brow creased. Then

understanding filled his eyes. "*Mais oui*, that's right. She helped when Zazie went missing." His tone changed. "Saj should have reminded me."

Aimée hit the fan switch. A slow chug of turning metal was followed by a stir of hot air. "So far my legwork's turned up zero. It's a shame, but I think she's suffering PTSD."

René nodded. Thoughtful.

She headed to the old surveillance TV monitor and inserted the bank's VHS tape. Hit PLAY. As she watched, she copied the bank's feed onto a CD she could upload onto her computer. She wanted Suzanne to be able to see the footage for herself.

The feed ran from 7:20 P.M., an hour before Suzanne had remembered seeing Mirko buying cigarettes, until an hour after she thought she saw him. For a mind-numbing hour, Aimée stared at footage of a summer night outside *café tabac*: passing buses, the steady then dwindling stream of people emerging from and descending the stairs of the Métro entrance. She scanned the faces of shop assistants, the office crowd, families—a mother holding a child's hand, the father carrying the child's *trottinette*—a kick scooter—heading home from the Jardin du Luxembourg. As the footage continued, Aimée noticed a shift: now she was watching couples and friends meeting for a drink in the café, locals stopping by for cigarettes—a mixture of young and old, all kinds patronizing their quartier *café tabac*.

No one matching Mirko's photo popped out at her.

She switched the playback to slo-mo and studied the video, hitting PAUSE each time she saw a single man.

No Mirko.

Aimée saw Suzanne's blonde hair as she strode down the pavement. Suzanne paused, looked at her hand. Pedestrians passed by. She'd turned her back. A phone call? Checking a message?

The next moment Suzanne headed into the *tabac*. Aimée watched the time counter. Fifty seconds passed. A minute and a half. A red-haired man entered the *tabac*. A bus passed. Two minutes.

A woman, baguette and leeks peeking from her shopping bag, stopped as her dog sprayed the curb by the Métro stairs. Suzanne exited the café. She looked both ways. Hurried up the street. Paused. Turned back, hesitated, then disappeared from the frame.

Just in case, Aimée wanted René's eyeballs on this. She called him over, showed him Mirko's photo. He hunched forward to stare at her screen, then played and replayed the three-minute clip in slo-mo. He shook his head.

"She can't let go, eh?" René pulled his goatee. "Poor Suzanne."

"Now she's on about Isabelle, her Dutch colleague, being missing, René."

"Say Suzanne gets an email from Isabelle's brother, jumps to conclusions. Suzanne is paranoid about her ghost sighting, and she alarms the brother," said René. "Gets him so worried he's calling the hospitals searching for his sister. No luck."

She knew how that went. She listened to René's scenario sadly, realizing he might be right.

"So now the brother's checking the unidentified female corpses, the *Maries* at the morgue . . ." René shook his head. "Think about it, Aimée. How will Suzanne feel when Isabelle turns up hungover and sheepish?"

She looked at The Hague report. Isabelle seemed like a seasoned professional, with several missions in Sarajevo and Pristina and a commendation for valor.

"On the other hand, what if she *is* in the morgue?" Aimée asked.

"Save yourself the trouble. Forget it. She's not paying you to take this any further."

Aimée picked up her phone and called Serge, her pathologist friend, to see if he was on shift. Got put through to his assistant.

"He's on break."

She hung up.

"Look," René said, "I wanted your opinion on this other school for Chloé. Their scholastic ratings—"

"I know you believe Chloé's gifted."

René nodded. "So bright, and above her percentile in so many areas."

Sometimes René acted as if he'd given birth to Chloé himself.

"You're right, *alors*, but *bébé* geniuses need love first." She grabbed her trench coat. "Back later. We need to arrange a time when you can watch Chloé."

"Where are you going?"

"To tie up loose ends."

SERGE'S BLACK-FRAMED GLASSES slipped down his nose. A thread of carrot was caught in his black beard. Aimée handed him a café napkin from her bag.

"It's freezing in here, Serge."

Serge handed her his cup of coffee. She sipped. Ice cold.

"And quiet," he said. "Nobody finds me in here except you." Around them the stainless-steel handles gleamed on the cadaver drawers. "I thought you didn't like coming to my 'retreat.'"

"Café Cadaver's not my favorite place." She'd claimed

her father's body, what bits remained of it after the explosion, from drawer number five.

She couldn't help but run her fingers over the handle now. Everything came back to her.

She shivered. "I'm supposed to meet Isabelle Ideler's brother. I'm not sure what his name is . . ."

"That the one who's bothering the chief?"

"Dutch?"

Serge nodded. "A big man. They're very tall in the Netherlands. Statistically the tallest in Europe. But he was one of the tallest men I've ever seen."

The door swung open, the plastic panels, hanging like clear fettuccini, flapping as an attendant stuck his face in.

"Open chest cavity in four needs your expertise."

Serge threw the remains of his salad in a bin, finished the coffee, and donned his sterile surgical gloves. She followed him down the chill corridor, their footsteps echoing on the green tiles.

"You're not allowed in here, Aimée," he said.

"Has that stopped you from helping me before? Look, just find out if his sister's on a slab or not. Simple."

Serge paused. "My wife and I haven't gone out in months. My mother-in-law is taking them next month, but she's not here until . . ."

Not babysitting his twins again. Here came the negotiations. Always a price. But that had to mean Isabelle was here. She'd have to find a way to squeeze in time to babysit his kinetic twin boys.

Or.

"How about a culinary treat, Serge? *Très spécial.* Your wife loves not to cook, *n'est-ce pas?*"

She flashed the gift card Jules Dechard had given her.

"At École Ferrandi?" Serge looked impressed. "This books up a month in advance."

"I'll want the autopsy report, too."

He glanced at his watch. "She's in three. A glimpse only." A door pinged open. Serge checked the toe tag on the body on the table inside. "Isabelle Ideler. Identified by her brother."

"Cause of death?"

"Asphyxiation." He pulled down the white sheet from the head. The woman's face was white and her lips blue tinged. Her blonde hair was combed back. So young.

"She was strangled?" Aimée looked for petechiae in the whites of the open eyes.

"Beestings. Closed her air passage." Serge pointed to the swollen neck. "In her case, it only took a minute or two. She was highly allergic. Too bad. With an anaphylactic attack, there are so many things an emergency medical team could have done to save her—CPR, adrenaline, antihistamines." He shrugged. "If they'd gotten there in time."

"Has it been ruled a suspicious death?"

"An accident, Aimée, clear and simple. I've submitted my conclusions. No reason to regard it as suspicious."

"A highly allergic person gets stung by bees . . ."

Serge pulled out a file from the wall. "In Jardin du Luxembourg? Happens all the time. It's summer, remember. She's wearing a sundress. She walked right by the hives."

"Wouldn't she carry an EpiPen?"

"Maybe she did but grabbed it too late."

"How many stings, Serge?"

"Hundreds. She got swarmed." He scanned the report. "Her dress had traces of a sweet, sticky drink on it. I'm guessing Orangina based on the color and content. So she spilled her drink on herself, which attracted the bees. And then, bad luck, she's foreign, doesn't know the garden or that she's walking by the beehive."

"How long before she was found?"

"The storm closed the gardens Monday afternoon."

"Does that coincide with her time of death?"

"Roughly, give or take an hour. The beekeeper found her yesterday morning. Under a hedge."

She'd lain there all night in the storm.

"No one saw her? Aren't the *flics* investigating?"

"An accident?" Serge opened the door to the hallway. "We all concurred. Nothing in the toxicology or marks on her body to indicate anything other than a terrible mishap." He gave her a copy of the prelim autopsy report.

"Where're her things?"

"According to this"—Serge tapped his gloved finger on the report—"her brother, Frans Ideler, signed for her belongings. He's making arrangements for her burial in the Netherlands."

Talk about quick.

Aimée put the gift card in Serge's waiting palm. "And I'll find her brother, Frans, where?"

"Room two eleven. Tell them I sent you."

FRANS HAD ALREADY gone, leaving an address in Utrecht. He'd accepted his sister's death was accidental. Arranged the paper work for her body to be transferred.

Shaken, Aimée didn't know what else to do. For a moment, she'd thought Isabelle had been murdered, that it couldn't have been an accident. But she'd been wrong.

Poor Suzanne. An ache of pity stabbed her. But there was no conspiracy or hit man.

No evidence.

Then she remembered Isabelle's friend whom she was supposed to stay with. Perhaps the brother was staying with her? She checked the report. A mention of a Charlotte Boyer, listed as living on rue Madame.

Maybe Aimée could catch Frans there.

Suzanne might better accept Isabelle's death as accidental if the news came from her brother. Listen to sense, since so far, Aimée's words had fallen on deaf ears.

She rang Charlotte, introduced herself and said she was looking for Isabelle's brother.

"Frans might come. I don't know," said Charlotte. "I'm glad you called. I need to talk with you about Isabelle."

"Why?"

"It's all my fault." Her voice quavered. "Please!"

AIMÉE HURRIED UP rue Madame to Charlotte Boyer's address. A block from the Jardin du Luxembourg, this was a *très* desirable pocket of Paris with nineteenth-century limestone façaded buildings. The neighborhood *had* a playground, a puppet theatre and carousel, tennis courts, boules courts, and an orchard with myriad varieties of ancient apple and pear trees. Crowning it all was Marie de Médici's seventeenth-century palace, her orangery still sheltering orange and lemon trees, palms and oleanders. Statues, fountains, chairs under the hanging chestnuts where people stopped to read or just contemplate. Part of Aimée's childhood and so many Parisians'.

This slice of Paris was central yet tucked away, with a residential air and a tiny hardware store where Nobel Prize winners, politicians, editors, and actors shopped for nuts and bolts. Aimée knew Catherine Deneuve preferred the *café tabac* on rue de Fleurus. Not an area anyone left if they could avoid it. Even three antiquarian bookstores kept their toehold on a single street. If Saint-Germain was the intellectual center—the brain—of the sixth arrondissement, then Saint-Sulpice was the heart and the Jardin du Luxembourg the lungs.

Aimée passed a café whose front tables were almost empty. It was too hot today, too close to the annual August exodus. The city felt listless, lazy. She wished that she were done with this and taking Chloé to the puppet show, that they could cool off in the shade.

"Madame Boyer's expecting you?" said the concierge, holding a squirming little boy's hand. The boy was holding a sand bucket and shovel.

Aimée pulled out the card she had ready. She'd donned her wig and office worker outfit again just in case. "I just spoke to her on the phone."

"You're the detective?" The concierge gave her an appraising look that settled on her ballerina flats. "Third floor, right. I'm taking her boy to the park."

In this quarter, buildings still had dedicated concierges who, in addition to taking the trash out and mopping the common areas and staircases, ferried the local children to and from lessons, camp, and school. In many parts of Paris, concierges had been replaced by Digicodes.

At the apartment door, a puffy-eyed woman about Aimée's age, her light brown hair clipped up, greeted Aimée. "I'm Charlotte." Her hands worried her paisley maternity-blouse sleeve.

"I'm Aimée Leduc."

"I know. The detective." Charlotte Boyer leaned against the doorway, shaking. "Frans went straight to the airport."

There went Aimée's idea to have Frans tell Suzanne about Isabelle's death. Now she needed to think of another way to throw Suzanne off her obsession. "You wanted to talk, Charlotte?"

Charlotte's shoulders shook, wracked with sobs. "I don't know what to do." She sagged against the doorway, overcome by a fit of crying. Concerned, Aimée shepherded Charlotte inside, brewed her a cup of herbal tisane in the eggshell state-of-the-art kitchen.

Ten minutes later she'd settled Charlotte on the designer burlap couch. Light streamed in from the courtyard. Aimée wondered if this woman had anything important to add, apart from grief. How long before Aimée could decently ask for Isabelle's brother's contact info?

"What did you mean about Isabelle's death?" Aimée prompted her. "Why did you think it was your fault?"

"I urged her to come to Paris. Begged her."

Great. Charlotte wanted to vent. Get absolved of her manufactured guilt.

"This will sound terrible," said Charlotte. "I'm ashamed. I was so annoyed with Isabelle." Her lower lip quivered. "I should have been worried."

Aimée gave an inner sigh. Part of her wanted to walk away—she didn't even know the young woman. "What makes you say that?"

"When she didn't come home . . . I should have looked for her." Pause. "At the . . ." Charlotte sniffled. "How did Isabelle look? Did it hurt? Was she in pain?"

The questions people always asked.

Aimée shook her head. Her scalp itched under the wig

in the heat. Too late to take it off now and freak this poor woman out further.

Charlotte covered her eyes. Silence.

"*Alors*, can you give me her brother's contact—?"

"First, I must tell you about her," Charlotte interrupted.

The whole story of their friendship poured from Charlotte. On a law school term abroad, she'd roomed with Isabelle in Utrecht. They'd been friends ever since. Charlotte had just moved here from Bordeaux, because of her husband's new job. She had three-month-old twins as well as the toddler Aimée had met downstairs, and she felt overwhelmed.

"You see all the unpacking left." She indicated the boxes in the hallway. Aimée spotted one labeled ANTIQUES and another labeled CASHMERE. "Isabelle knew we'd just moved in, weren't settled. But she pitched in to help me. She worked morning till night on Sunday putting things away and cleaning. And then the next day she goes out and doesn't come home. She's single, you know—I assumed she'd met someone. I was so annoyed with her for just disappearing when she'd come here to help me, angry when I should have been worried—so selfish . . ." Charlotte dissolved into tears again.

Something niggled at Aimée's brain. "*Alors*, didn't Isabelle have work appointments? Meetings?"

"Did she? Maybe. She didn't mention any. Isabelle seemed so happy. She'd never been to Paris. Since my first baby, we hadn't been in touch as often. Now I'm a full-time *maman* . . ."

With an efficient and obliging concierge and a high-ceilinged, stylishly remodeled nineteenth-century flat. Aimée almost blurted out, *I'm full-time, too, only I also run a business.* How she'd wanted to stay home with Chloé that morning.

Most women Aimée knew worked. But in this part of the Left Bank, work meant something different for a wealthy wife and mother than it did for Aimée. Not all of the women here were stay-at-home moms, though—didn't Suzanne live in her husband's family flat nearby?

Aimée didn't have time to listen to more grief-filled rambling. She was about to ask again for the brother's contact information when Charlotte said, "Wait, I remember now. Two days ago, when she was leaving, she seemed as if she was in a rush. Her colleague—yes, Isabelle mentioned a colleague."

"You mean Suzanne from the ICTY team?"

"A man. Lived nearby."

"What's nearby?"

"The other side of the garden." A vague wave of Charlotte's ringed hand. "I think she went to visit him."

So it was Isabelle's first time in Paris, and she crossed the garden for a meeting, not knowing about the apiary. Made sense, except . . .

"Didn't Isabelle carry an EpiPen—you know, since she was hyperallergic to bees?"

Charlotte gestured to a small roller bag. "The airline lost her luggage. It arrived twenty minutes ago. Can you believe it? I couldn't even get it to her brother. All he could take was her laptop and her rucksack."

New sobs wracked Charlotte's shoulders.

"Postpartum—I'm sorry. Who knows how much longer the twins will be asleep?"

Aimée knew the feeling. Felt guilty she'd been quick to judge this woman whose friend had just died.

A cry came from the back of the apartment. Charlotte blinked and swallowed her tea. Damp spots had appeared on her shirt. "I'm leaking. Got to nurse them."

Nursing twins presented a challenge, Aimée thought, saddened her own milk had dried up. She chided herself for thinking she had it hard with only one baby.

"You've got a lot on your plate," she said. "My daughter's eight months old, and I know how it goes." She moved next to Charlotte and squeezed her hand. "I'm so sorry, Charlotte." Now Aimée had an excuse to be in touch with Isabelle's brother. "Let me take care of sending her suitcase back to Frans, okay?"

AFTER FURNISHING FRANS'S number, Charlotte left to attend the two crying infants.

Aimée unzipped Isabelle's small metallic roller bag. Enough for a weekend: underwear, long-sleeve T-shirt, dress blouse and black pants, toiletries, makeup bag, an epinephrine auto-injector.

A sad, simple explanation for a tragic accident.

About to leave Charlotte and heft the roller bag down the circular stairs, Aimée tried Frans's number and got a short voice mail message in Dutch, English and French. "I'm unable to take your call. You can contact my business line at . . ."

Aimée fumbled in her bag for something to write with. Nothing.

Her phone was almost out of battery, too—at this of all times.

She hunted for a pen in Charlotte's apartment. By the entry, she found a landline and a pad with a blue crayon.

She called back to hear the message again and jotted

down the information. The message cut off before the last digit.

"Charlotte, do you have Frans's other numbers?" Aimée called out.

A yell from the hallway. "On the answering machine."

Aimée hit PLAY, ready with the blue crayon.

A real-estate agent asking for their signatures on copies of the lease agreement, a sales call from a local dry cleaner, a male voice asking for Isabelle.

Aimée's antenna perked up.

". . . She missed our meeting. Can you . . . give Isabelle a message?" Pause. "Sorry, this is Erich Kayser. I've got appointments for the rest of the day, but she can meet me Wednesday at 15 rue Servandoni. Apologies, but she gave me this number. Hope you don't mind." Then he gave his number.

That name sounded familiar. Erich Kayser. Where had Aimée seen it?

Next there was a message from Frans, saying he was going straight to the airport and leaving his contact information. Aimée replayed the messages and wrote down both Erich Kayser's and Frans's work number with a blue crayon in her Moleskine. Punched in Frans's number on Charlotte's land-line to save the little battery she had left.

"*Gooday, dit is het kantoor van* Frans Ideler," said a pert voice.

Great. She couldn't speak Dutch. "Do you speak French?"

"*Bien sûr,*" said the receptionist. "How may I help?"

Aimée explained.

"Meneer Ideler's on a flight to New York. I'll take the message."

"I have his deceased sister's suitcase—"

"Since I can't reach Meneer Ideler until he lands—" Ringing sounded in the background. "Can you hold, please?"

Taped classical music played, and played some more. She fumed.

While she waited, she called Suzanne on the burner phone. Aimée would update her about Isabelle. Let her take it from here. Getting Frans to connect with her had been a last ditch, anyway.

The call cut off before it could go to voice mail. She tried again. Voice mail box full.

Now what?

The pert Dutch receptionist came back on the line. "In the circumstances, it's preferable if you leave it at the Dutch embassy. I've spoken to the ground-affairs liaison. Johan will expect you at their address, 7-9 rue Eblé."

So she was a delivery service? She pulled out her Paris map. It was only a few blocks away.

Now she remembered where she'd seen Erich Kayser's name—in the ICTY file. He'd been part of Suzanne and Isabelle's team. So Isabelle had been on the way to meet with another member of Suzanne's cohort team when she died? What a strange coincidence.

Aimée tried Suzanne's number again. Same result.

Merde.

Looked like it fell on Aimée to reach Erich Kayser. And by default, she'd become the emissary for poor Isabelle and her belongings.

"MY DEEPEST SYMPATHIES," said Johan, the tall young man who met her in the gilt-edged *hôtel particulier* salon. Chandeliers, black and white marble tiles—not too shabby, this Dutch embassy. With a few touch-ups, some cleaning, and quite a few francs, her seventeenth-century apartment could look like this, too.

"Our vice-consul will handle the arrangements. I'll relieve you of this." He reached for that case Aimée had rolled in. "We'll pass it along to Meneer Ideler when he comes in again to pick it up."

Aimée didn't know what else to say. It felt abrupt handing over Isabelle's belongings to a stranger, but then again Aimée hadn't known Isabelle, either. But rendering a service was a way of showing respect for the dead, for the poor young woman she'd seen on the autopsy table.

Serge had nailed it when he'd said these Dutch were tall. Johan's head grazed the doorframe. He grinned, noticing her look. "We drink a lot of milk in Holland."

"Frans Ideler must drink a lot of milk, too," said Aimée.

"Excuse me?"

"Isabelle's brother. He's tall, too. The medical examiner mentioned that. One of the tallest men he'd ever seen."

"Do you mean the man who came to—?" His phone rang. Johan looked at its screen and shook his head. "Sorry, I must take this. Again, thank you."

"Wait." Aimée felt a prickling on her neck. "Frans Ideler stopped by here?" And now she realized Johan had just said, "When he comes in again to pick it up." But the Dutch receptionist had said Frans was on a transatlantic flight, that *she* had made the arrangements with Johan on the phone. Something was off. "Today? A very tall man?"

"*Pas du tout.*" He answered his phone. "Short." He walked off, phone to his ear, rolling the suitcase behind him.

Who had Johan spoken to?

The ghost?

Impossible. *Non,* this was some mix-up, either Serge or

Johan misremembering. None of her business. Isabelle's death was obviously accidental—there was no way someone could have planned circumstances like that.

Was there?

It seemed Suzanne's paranoia was contagious.

On the other hand, a member of Suzanne's team dying in unusual circumstances on the same day Suzanne saw her ghost—it was quite a coincidence. Aimée remembered what her father had always said about coincidences. No coincidences with criminals, only mistakes.

DUSK WAS FALLING. Aimée looked at her watch. All this had taken up precious time. Babette had agreed to bathe Chloé and put her to sleep. Thank God, she thought as she trudged toward Erich Kayser's address.

Her goal—tell him about Isabelle's accident and insist that he speak to Suzanne.

The ground floor of 15 rue Servandoni was a shop front displaying picture frames in the window; above were apartments with white shutters and tall windows. A gallery stood across the narrow, sloped street, a bistro on the corner of rue Canivet, and not far beyond jutted Saint-Sulpice's baroque medieval struts. Lanterns, once gaslit, provided infrequent dots of light on the mostly dark cobbled street. If it weren't for a Renault hugging the fat lip of the pavement, it could have been 1964. Or 1864.

Along the street, several buildings' shutters were flung back, windows open to catch any cool breeze. She heard laughter, voices, a violin sonata playing on Radio Classique, the station René liked. It was so hot and humid. The clinging damp hadn't let up. Dusk had fully fallen, compressing the orange-copper sunset to a thin band over the park's trees.

She had the phone number she'd scribbled in blue crayon, but her phone was out of battery. The cheap burner phone got no reception in this narrow street carved between tall buildings.

No Erich Kayser listed on the building's Digicode by the blue wood door. The lights glowed from within the frame shop.

The framer, a woman in her sixties, peered at Aimée over her glasses. She held a chisel over an intricate Art Nouveau frame that was in pieces on a long table. On the atelier wall were testimonials from clients: a minister, a publisher, a media mogul—all locals, it seemed.

"Never heard of him," the framer said. The woman used the front of her wrist to push her hair from her glistening brow. "But then, I know few of the people upstairs."

Fat lot of good that did Aimée.

"What about the concierge?"

"*Le Sénat* owns most of the flats, I think." The woman nodded toward the wall. "Code's up there."

The local café or shop always had the code for a building's Digicode. A quiet secret in Paris.

The phone on the wall began to ring. Aimée borrowed a pen and wrote the code down on her palm as the woman went to answer it.

Merci, Aimée mouthed, and the woman smiled and waved her off.

She dreaded leaving the bad news for Erich Kayser, a man she didn't know, concerning a woman she'd never met. Yet maybe connecting with him would help Suzanne.

After Aimée let herself into the building, the concierge, a small man, answered the door of the refreshingly cool loge. "But Monsieur Kayser's upstairs, expecting you."

Expecting Isabelle, maybe. She'd use it. Play along.

"What floor?"

"Third floor, left, on the street side. Take another package of lightbulbs with you. His lights burned out. Tell him I checked the fuses, and they were fine. It must be some bad bulbs."

Aimée trudged up. When she reached the dark third-floor landing, she flipped the *minuterie*, but the timed light switch didn't turn the light on. She knocked on the door. No answer. Knocked again, and as she did the door swung open.

"Monsieur Kayser?" she said.

She stepped inside. It took a second for her eyes to adjust to the darkness of the apartment. Only the lamp glow from the street allowed her to make out the silhouette of a chair. She turned and realized she'd walked into a kitchen.

She went back to the hall.

Eerie. She heard what sounded like the bang of a shutter. "Monsieur Kayser?"

A scream came from the street. Shouts. *"Mon Dieu!"*

Good God, what was going on?

Aimée rushed back inside the apartment. "Monsieur Kayser?"

More screams came through the open window. As she hurried toward it, she heard a scraping sound, but before she could look to see what it was, there was another scream.

A hanging light fixture swung by the open window, its old-fashioned plastic cord trailing along the window frame. A stepladder lay on the floor next to it.

Aimée looked out. A body lay on the cobbled street directly below. A man.

Aimée's stomach lurched.

White shirt, black trousers, legs splayed in the way only

the legs of a dead body would. In the streetlight she could see dark red liquid pooling under the blond head and settling in the cracks between the stones.

A couple on the narrow street moved away in horror. Someone had knelt beside the body, feeling for a carotid pulse. A man standing in the third-floor window opposite pointed at her. "There. From that window."

Bystanders looked up.

"Her," the man said.

Idiot! she almost yelled.

Adrenalin kicked in. Had the man fallen by accident while installing a lightbulb, or was someone else here? She felt a chill as she remembered the scraping sound she'd heard a moment ago.

A quick scan of the dark outlines of the furniture revealed no one. She flipped on her penlight, flicked open her Swiss Army knife, and checked the other rooms. No one.

A wallet and a small pocket calculator sat in an open briefcase on a chair. A black suit jacket hung over its back.

She pulled a scarf out of her bag so she wouldn't leave fingerprints and opened the wallet. From his driver's license in the wallet's plastic holder, Erich Kayser stared back at her. It was unmistakably the man lying in the street.

Whether he'd fallen or been pushed didn't matter—she couldn't be here. But she'd been seen. The picture framer, the concierge, the idiot in the window opposite. Footsteps pounded up the stairs. Or were they going down? Away from her? The killer?

Or had Erich fallen while screwing in a lightbulb? Another freak accident like Isabelle's?

Now she was certain—the footsteps were coming up the stairs.

Get out! screamed a voice in her head.

She quickly ran through her memory to see if she could recall touching anything. Only the main light timer in the hall, which would yield tons of unusable smeary prints. She'd get out clean.

She threw the wallet back in the briefcase, and her penlight beam caught on a ring of keys on the table—there was something shiny underneath. The jewel case of a CD-R. Looking closer, she saw the stuck-on label: ICTY 99.

International Criminal Tribunal for the former Yugoslavia.

Knowing she'd regret it later, she grabbed the CD, dumping the keys back on the table, and stuck it in her bag.

She slipped off her ballet flats and stuffed both them and the lightbulb package in her bag. She switched off her penlight, moved into the shadows of the corridor. By the time the footsteps reached the landing, she'd glided up to the next floor. Voices—she recognized the sound of the concierge's and saw the beam of a flashlight.

Someone was calling the *flics* on a mobile phone.

She had to keep going up.

The fifth floor had a narrow corridor with several doors— the traditional *chambre de bonne*—maids' rooms. And a skylight.

Always a skylight and a ladder in the corridor of the fifth floor. Fire regulations.

Slinging her bag over her chest, she positioned the ladder, climbed, unscrewed the bolt, and lifted the skylight. She was out in seconds. She propped the skylight open, pulled up the ladder, then closed it. That should give her valuable minutes.

Breathing hard through her nose, she made her way

toward the tin roof's edge. She crouched at the gutter, keeping low.

Sweat dripped down her neck. Heights—she hated heights. But from here, her pulse jumping, she had an aerial view of the surrounding streets as well as of the people crowding around the body on the street below. Was anyone running, walking fast?

The damn nanny cam was poking her hip. She pulled it out. Here goes nothing, she thought, and pressed record, panning along the street to the opposite building, the neighbor pointing out the window. He was yelling, "It's her! It's her!" at every woman who passed. That kept everyone looking down, and no one was looking up at her. She silently thanked the idiot.

Was that a figure hurrying up rue Servandoni? She panned the camera, but whatever she'd seen disappeared into the shadows. Then came the whine of a siren.

Time to go. Barefoot on the tin-tiled roof, she fought for purchase as heat-slick pigeon poop slimed between her toes. She prayed she wouldn't slip before she could reach the next roof. All the Senate-owned buildings seemed to be connected, from what she could see.

All the buildings except this one and the next one.

A huge, yawning gap to the next building's roof. Below her was a courtyard.

Great.

If this were a movie and she were an action hero, she could try and jump it. But even her long legs couldn't make that leap. She picked her way back to the light aluminum ladder, dragged it to the edge of the roof, and hefted it across to the adjoining roof, hooking its feet into the rusty gutter. She tried not to think of the fallen stepladder in Kayser's apartment. The fact that he had dropped from only the third floor. She was almost twice as high now. If she didn't want to be thrown in a cell for questioning, she had to get to the next roof and escape via the parallel street.

You can do it, she told herself. Just don't look down; that's what they always said. Don't look down.

Wednesday, Twilight

PAULINE LIMPED TO the school yard's grilled gate on rue d'Assas. Her ankles were swollen after a working day on her feet. The evening was the worst.

A young woman stood outside the gate. She'd rung and rung the bell until Pauline responded. Pauline shook her head. "The school's closed."

"Did she suffer?" asked Charlotte Boyer.

She was pushing a double stroller, one of those fancy designer things that looked like space pods to Pauline.

"Who?" One of Pauline's eyebrows arched.

"My friend Isabelle was stung to death by bees, right there by the apiary." She pointed to the Jardin du Luxembourg's closed gate.

"*Alors*, what do you think? Why ask me?"

"Our concierge says you have second sight."

That was what they called it now?

"You see the world beyond, Pauline. Receive visits from the other side. Tania told me. Tania said you'd help me."

Tania and her big mouth. But Pauline had seen this young mother pushing the stroller in the park. She'd registered her older son here for the fall term. A local.

"You're Charlotte?" Pauline said.

She nodded. Then reached for Pauline's hand through the metal bars. "Please, please can you help?"

"Why do you want to know?"

"Isabelle is my . . . I mean, was . . . a good friend. I let her down. It's all my fault."

They all wanted to know the same thing. "Did she blame you? Is that what you want to know? Could you have prevented what happened?"

Charlotte's face crinkled. Tears formed at the edges of her eyes. "I have to know."

"I can't tell you tonight. Meet me Saturday for a walk," said Pauline. "You'll show me the place. But I know already you couldn't have prevented it."

Charlotte took a breath. "How do you know?"

"Because she wasn't alone."

Wednesday Night

AIMÉE SWALLOWED HARD, her mouth dry. She concentrated on crawling across the ladder, focusing on the jagged slate roof line of the next building, not the gaping courtyard below. She prayed her feet wouldn't get caught on the rungs as she braved each yawning gap. The acacia-scented breeze cooled her perspiration-covered skin. Of all the times for there to be a breeze.

Toto, one of her father's informers, specialized in roof work—he was a cat burglar working, *"monte-en-l'air,"* in nineteenth-century argot. Toto always said his *métier* required no trapeze or acrobatic skills—just nerve and sure-footedness. She swallowed again, her mouth like sandpaper.

Her head was full of the image of the streetlight catching the dark red pooling under the man's head. Her legs couldn't stop shaking, making the ladder tremble. Paralyzed with fear, she couldn't make herself move forward. How could she get home if she couldn't get across this ladder?

Get it together. She had to ignore her heart pounding in her rib cage, concentrate on forcing her fingers to release the metal and grasp the next bar. She pulled herself out to the next rung, then the next. Her fingernails scraped the aluminum.

The ladder wobbled, and panic flooded her. She forced herself forward, pushing with her toes. Move faster—less thinking.

Don't think at all about what's below.

One more rung, then one more. Her fingertips reached tile. When her elbows and knees were all safely on the solid, sloping roof of the next building, she caught her breath, her damp collar plastered to her neck.

She'd done it. Her insides quivered with excitement—she'd made it. That old shiver of adrenaline raced through her. What would René say if he found out? She wouldn't have to worry about falling and breaking her neck—he would kill her himself. How irresponsible she'd been—the mother of a baby couldn't go around risking her life scaling roofs. But she'd needed to get away. Still needed to.

She couldn't leave the ladder—a dead giveaway. She pulled it across to her, then dragged it, rattling over the tiles, to a doorway.

She tried the door. Locked.

Sirens echoed in the narrow street below. No time to take a breath, only to keep moving. From where she was standing, the grey slate-tiled rooftop leveled. Reaching the next building, she caught a whiff of cigarette smoke. Someone who'd snuck up on the roof for a smoke? She took off her wig, combed her hair back with her fingers, pulled her scarf out of her bag, and poked her head around a low wall.

An open mansard window emitting murmurs and warm air stuffy with perspiration. Inside, several people worked at desks. On the wall a TV monitor played a live feed from the red-velvet-chaired Senate chambers across the street. Of course, the Senate was on a budget deadline. The senators were working into all hours of the morning with a crew of transcribers and clerks.

"Are you a cat burglar, or do you always meet men like this?" a voice on her right said. A middle-aged man in a white shirt, tie loosened at the collar, sleeves rolled up. He eyed her with a grin from the adjoining building's balcony. So close she could almost touch it. A plume of grey smoke lingered above him, contrasting against the black night sky.

A smartass. Behind him was a half-open door revealing a lighted hallway. Perfect for escape.

She realized her torn blouse and bare feet required a plausible explanation. "Only when my boyfriend's wife comes home early. I escaped out the window."

A knowing grin. Handsome in a clerky *fonctionnaire* way.

"Care to let me out via your building?"

"In return for . . . ?"

She climbed across the short ledge, swung her leg over the railing and slid onto the balcony. "Not telling on you for skipping out to smoke?" She grinned and pretended to slip. Clutched his shirt sleeves.

"What's your name?" he breathed, his hand around her waist. He smelled of cigarettes and musky Dior Homme.

"Thérèse," she said, the first thing that came into her mind. Stars dotted the sky over the dark expanse of Jardin du Luxembourg.

"How about an *apéro* later?" he said.

Like that would happen.

"Why not?" She moved toward the hallway, pulling his hand.

After they'd exchanged numbers, his phone rang. He glanced at it. "I've got to take this."

His wife?

"What's the best way out of here?" she asked.

A door opened on to the hallway. A harried man stuck his head out, ignoring her. "Hurry up. We need the figures, Christian."

He shot her a glance. "Ask the guard for the after-hours exit."

The staircase led down three floors to an inner courtyard—one of three—then down another level. A maze, this place. She figured she was below rue Garancière, near *le Sénat*. She had to get out to the street.

All she could think about was getting out. She wanted to find a taxi and go low profile until she figured out what to do. What this meant.

She wiped off her toes with a baby wipe and slipped on the black heels and large black-framed glasses she had in her bag. She was about to hurry past a session schedule when she spotted the initials ICTY.

"Lost your way?" said a guard.

Her insides curdled. She turned. "*Désolée*, I've never worked this late and need to find the after-hours exit."

Stupid. He'd ask her which office or branch she worked in. *Don't give him time to think.*

"My babysitter's on overtime." True. "And my baby's got a fever." She hoped that was a lie. "I've got to get home."

She acted harried—easy to do—and hefted her bag with her work files sticking out. "Still so much to finish tonight."

The guard gestured her toward a group of suited men and women. "Follow them downstairs. The guard will show you out."

She followed the group but was stopped at the next door by an older guard.

"Not that way, mademoiselle. That's the route for those voting in session." He pointed her toward another narrow door where several people were in line to exit. "You'll take the street exit here." So the senators had an underground passage to the Senate in the Luxembourg. Interesting.

"Everyone gets confused," said the stocky guard. Former military, judging by the silvered *en brosse* crewcut. "It's a warren down here."

She smiled, relieved he wasn't questioning her status. "It's my first time working so late." In a few seconds, she'd be out of there.

As she made for the door, he stepped in her way.

Her stomach fell. He reached for the phone nestled in a control bank with lighted panels and red, green, and yellow buttons.

"That one's reserved. You'll take the next car, mademoiselle."

A car service? Her shoulders stiffened in alarm. She didn't want that—couldn't risk them tracing her to an office where she didn't exist. She just wanted to reach the Métro.

"No need, monsieur . . ."

"Didn't they tell you? Ah, well, it's only in July during the budget sessions. *Le Sénat* provides car service for everyone who works late."

"But I . . . don't think I'm allowed." Think. Play on his sympathy. "No one authorized my overtime, monsieur. Please, that would get me in trouble."

"No worries over that with me, mademoiselle. People come and go all night. I never log names, if that's what you're worried about." He winked. A soft side. "Have a seat."

Nothing for it but to wait. On the bench, she crossed her legs and replayed the scene in Erich Kayser's apartment—the darkness, the scraping noise, the swinging light by the window, the scream . . .

The guard rang for a car, scanned the lit panels, and pressed a yellow button. Then a thought hit her—would she be on video down here? Would she be recognized despite her changed appearance?

"Any security cameras here?" she blurted out. Stupid. What if the question made him suspicious?

If he was surprised, he didn't show it. Shook his head.

"We've got the *gendarmerie* at both ends. Only way out is through a manhole, if you knew where they were."

A talkative type. She smiled again to keep him engaged. "Anyone ever done it? Escaped?" She stole a glance at her Tintin watch. Wished this car would hurry up.

"Hard to do since they sealed the tunnel entrances. Still, the kids at Lycée Montaigne sneak under their school into the old German Luftwaffe bunker. Have parties."

So had she in her student days—those wild raves she'd gone to with Martine. She noticed the framed, yellowed, hand-drawn map hanging on the wall by the control panel. The script was old fashioned—old school. Like this dark, musty, and damp place.

"That map's a bit of history, *non?*" she said.

He shook his head. "More accurate than a Métro map and hasn't changed since the thirteenth century. Except then rue Bonaparte was a canal leading from the Seine."

The guard hit a button on the light panel, illuminating a branch of a tunnel. Several men in suits—senators, she assumed—scurried through, deep in conversation.

Old-fashioned, this network of tunnels. Any *cataphile* worth his salt could breach the system as the *lycée* students did.

Another group of men appeared. What if that Christian was one of them? She put her head down, busied herself with her Moleskine.

"Car's here, mademoiselle," the guard said.

Just in time. Christian's head bobbed in a group coming toward her.

She rushed up the narrow stairs and into a waiting Peugeot with smoked windows. She was the lone passenger, thank god. Her hands shook all the way to the rue de Rivoli. She waited until the car took off before doubling back on the rue Bailleul and turning the corner. After scanning the pavement, she entered her office building.

WITHIN TEN MINUTES she'd charged her phone, powered up her laptop, opened the content from the CD she'd found in Erich Kayser's apartment, and hit PRINT on each document. No time to read whatever it contained—maybe nothing to do with his death—but she'd pore over it later. At least the office printer could handle the job.

She emailed Suzanne the bank's CCTV footage as a compressed file, mentioned that she had information about Isabelle Ideler and Erich Kayser but left it at that. She marked the email urgent and hit SEND.

Only then did she realize René was picking up the pages spilling from the printer tray.

"What's this?" he asked.

"That's what I'm going to find out."

"International Criminal Tribunal for the former Yugoslavia?" René's eyebrows shot up. "Wait a minute. Does this have to do with that supposed missing woman Suzanne insisted you check out in the morgue?"

So much had happened since then.

"You could say that," she said. "That young woman, Isabelle Ideler, is dead."

René's face clouded. "Murdered?"

"No. She died from anaphylactic shock from beestings—
she was highly allergic."

"*Et alors?*"

Her fingers trembled. René hated her investigating anything other than corporate crimes. Since Chloé's birth she'd
promised him—and herself—that it was hands off anything
dangerous.

"I don't know. But there's more." She hooked up the
nanny cam to her computer. "Look at this, René."

"So that's where my nanny cam's gone." He slapped the
pile of papers on her desk.

"Hold on, René. Watch." She loaded up the feed and
played it.

René's green eyes narrowed in worry. "You shot this video
from a roof?"

She took a breath. Explained her visit to the morgue, how
she'd tried to catch up with Isabelle's brother, ended up talking
to the tearful Charlotte and hearing the message Erich Kayser
left on her answering machine. How she'd taken Isabelle's
newly arrived bag with her now-useless EpiPens to the Dutch
embassy. Recounted the strange conversation with Johan.
How she'd then gone to Erich Kayser's apartment in time to
hear the screams from the street where his body had fallen.

René slammed his fist on the desk. "You ran away? Now
you're a suspect in a suspicious death that should have been
ruled an accident. Couldn't you have just told the truth?
Reported it?" René had an innocent trust in the police.
Believed in *liberté, égalité, fraternité.*

"And spend all night in *garde à vue*? Behind bars in a
cell? Deal with *flics*, who bare their teeth at my name, who'd
relish withholding my rights?"

Guilt washed over her. And fear.

"My name's mud," she said.

"What's new, Aimée?"

"It's even worse now."

"And whose stubborn fault?" said René, exasperated. "Show your face at Morbier's hospital bed. That's all you have to do. They're old gossips. Let the police grapevine hear you sucked it up, that Morbier's forgiven you. Have a grand reconciliation."

Like hell she would. "It's the other way around. Morbier should make amends for my papa—not that it would matter, but . . ."

"Haven't you thought he might want to?"

Why couldn't René shut up?

Her phone rang. Martine. Great.

"Martine, I'm still at work. Can't do dinner."

"Party pooper," said Martine.

Thank God Martine didn't insist.

"Gianni's got to work late anyway. We've got to finalize our plans for Sicily. Gianni's family owns a fabulous villa on the beach . . ."

Finalize?

With her phone held between her shoulder and her ear, she scooped up the rest of the papers from the floor. Clipped them together and put them in a folder.

"Did you hear me, Aimée? I'm making reservations . . . Gianni's serious, Aimée. He wants me to meet his mother."

Pause.

"Aren't you happy for me, Aimée? I'd be for you if it was the other way around."

In other words, be a friend.

Aimée's insides churned again. "How many months have you known him, Martine?"

"That's rich coming from you."

"I've never seen you happier, Martine . . ." She had to end this call before she said something she'd regret. "Call you later." Hung up.

René was staring at the folder.

"What do I do, René?"

"You've done what you promised Suzanne. The favor's repaid. But if you don't tell the *flics* what you saw, they'll be looking for you."

"Looking for a brunette woman with a bob." She gestured to the wig and ballet flats in the trash bin. Under them was the box of lightbulbs.

René gave a small sigh of relief.

"What if his fall wasn't an accident, René? I heard a noise."

"Every old building has noises. Didn't you say the concierge had gone up to check the apartment's fuses? The man's lights were out."

True. And the concierge would remember a woman in a mousy outfit, brown hair and her damn Hermès bag. She made a mental note to switch bags when she got home.

"Let Suzanne twist her guts over this, but it sounds plain and simple." René stroked his goatee. "I still don't see connections between this man's changing his lightbulb and Suzanne."

"They connect," she said. "I don't know exactly how. But Isabelle and Erich were Suzanne's colleagues at the ICTY, and now they're both dead."

"*Mais oui*, colleagues in a huge international organization. Big hole number one—the whole thing that got Suzanne all nervous in the first place was she thought she saw Mirko, but there's no CCTV evidence, so nothing to prove he's not dead, right?" said René. He lifted his handmade Lobb shoe and polished a spot with his handkerchief. "He was Balkan. A Bosnian, whatever. Anyway, what would he be doing in France even if he was alive?"

"Suzanne called him a Serbian thug."

"All right, he's Serbian. Do you have any idea how many thousands of Serbians live and work in Paris? Maybe she saw someone who looked like him."

"So there *are* lots of Serbians here?" Aimée said slowly. "Then maybe it wouldn't have been so difficult for him to get here—"

"*Alors*, number two," said René. "How would two accidental deaths benefit a dead Serbian? And even if you think Erich might have been murdered, that there was someone in his apartment when you were there, there's no way Isabelle's death was anything other than an accident, right?"

That was true. She sighed, glanced at the piles of work on her desk. She was done with this, wasn't she?

"It's suspicious, René," she said stubbornly. "Doesn't smell right."

René shook his head. Sighed. "Don't start, Aimée. It's coincidental. Sad and tragic but there's no proof Suzanne's paranoia is anything more than her imagination. You said so yourself—she's suffering PTSD. Forget the whole thing. You don't have time to get more involved." He gestured to the pile of proposals on his desk. "We have Y2K preparations. We have to plan for projected meltdowns in all the networks we service. The new millennium is around the corner, Aimée, and it's getting crazy. And you've got Chloé to think of. Spend your time on what's important, and forget this goose chase."

True. Spending her time on this wasn't fair to him or their business or Chloé.

She nodded, grabbed her scarf. "Point taken, partner."

LATER THAT NIGHT, she transferred the contents of her Hermès into a slouchy Longchamp bag: Moleskine; Chloé's teething biscuits; map; mascara; stub of Chanel red; the old charm bracelet, missing a few charms, from her father; her worn Vuitton wallet; her mini lock-picking set disguised in a makeup kit; her Swiss Army knife; and baby wipes.

Chloé's sleeping breaths came over the baby monitor. In bed, Miles Davis curled on the linen duvet while she sipped a *diabolo-menthe limonade* infused with a splash of *sirop de menthe*. The lemony-mint drink kept her awake and made her mouth tingle. No Benoît that night, or for a while—he had left for Grenoble to teach a summer session.

René was right. She should leave Suzanne's case alone. Still, she pored over the documents from Erich Kayser's CD. Numbers, statistics, charts. Her eyes glazed. Looked like an accounting of finances spent by the French team seconded to the ICTY. So Erich had been the moneyman for the mission, she figured, remembering his calculator.

She sat up, startled by the ringing of the burner phone under her leg.

Suzanne sounded breathless.

"You have information about Erich Kayser? I queried him about NATO corroborating Mirko's DNA, but he hasn't gotten back to me yet."

And he wouldn't.

"Did he mention anything else to you in his most recent email, Suzanne?"

"Said he was busy. Delivering a report at *le Sénat*."

Aimée was staring at the report notes at that moment. Figures and more figures. "I'm so sorry, Suzanne."

Aimée told her what had happened: Isabelle in the morgue and Erich Kayser's fall.

"They got to him," said Suzanne, her voice breaking. "I know."

"Who got to him?"

"First Isabelle and now Erich."

"*Alors,* Isabelle's autopsy revealed a fatal allergic reaction to beestings. Her EpiPen set was in her bag, lost in flight, that turned up today at Charlotte's. I saw it with my own eyes, Suzanne. Visited the morgue, verified the cause of death with the medical examiner. Her death was an accident."

"So it's a coincidence that Erich, who emailed me this afternoon, just falls out a window changing a lightbulb?"

Aimée shuddered, chilled. Pulled the duvet up to her shoulders. "Was there anything else at all in his email?"

"Answer me. You can't think it's a coincidence. He was pushed."

"I got there too late, Suzanne."

"Did you hear anything?"

"Odd noises," she admitted. "But it was probably a mouse, the building creaking, or my imagination on overdrive."

"Trust your instinct, Aimée."

"*Alors,* even putting the events together, it's a stretch. Who would want Isabelle and Erich dead? Why would what they saw and did in Bosnia matter now?"

"I saw it, too."

Aimée didn't want to admit doubt had crept in. What if Suzanne was in danger?

"Erich is reporting . . . was reporting to a commission at *le Sénat* on the Bosnian cases. That's all he said."

Suzanne was in Lyon, over four hours away, meeting with Interpol. Out of trouble. Aimée sipped the *diablo-menthe*, thinking about how to craft her words.

"Suzanne, you of all people know that when you're running an investigation, you have to identify a motive, access, and who benefits. According to those files you gave me, Mirko and his gang were career criminals, paramilitary types. Who'd give him the order to go to Paris? He's not a polished type, sophisticated enough to evade border checks and set up intricate murders in a foreign city where he doesn't speak the language. Never mind making them appear to be accidents—that would take a high-level chain of command. That's what bothers me, Suzanne. You're afraid of Mirko, but the Mirko you showed me couldn't have committed Isabelle's and Erich's murders—if they even were murders."

Aimée paused to let this sink in. "Mirko ran into a tunnel, got blown up. Even if somehow he survived, what resources would he have access to? Didn't you yourself refer to his sloppy technique? Didn't you call him a 'thug'?"

A loud sucking in of breath. "Go see Jean-Marie."

"Who?"

"He was on our team, too. He was in Foča with me and Isabelle and Erich. But he hasn't returned my emails or calls, Aimée."

"*Zut!*" she said, frustrated. Suzanne wasn't even listening to her. "Why would he respond to me?"

"Tell Jean-Marie what's happened. He lost his leg near Foča, but he's out of the hospital, from what I hear."

"Shouldn't you visit him when you're back from Lyon, Suzanne?"

"I don't know where he lives," she said, sounding

desperate. "I've tried to reach him but he's military and they don't share information like that. Find out for me, and I'll visit him tomorrow night."

Or did they refuse to give the information because of her paranoid behavior?

Pause. "Didn't you watch the CCTV? There's no man resembling Mirko going in or out of the *café tabac*, Suzanne."

"Do this last thing for me. Please, Aimée."

Why couldn't Suzanne understand?

"My babysitter's going on vacation," said Aimée. "I'm scrambling right now. This is not a good time."

Pause. A car door and shouts in the background.

"Last thing, Aimée. Please. I promise when you find Jean-Marie, I'll handle everything else. Put it to rest. But I have to talk to him."

Aimée sighed. Took down his full name and the last hospital Suzanne knew he'd been in.

After she clicked off, she remembered she needed René's help with babysitting.

Stupid—in all the panic, she'd forgotten to ask him. And she'd left her damn scooter by Jardin du Luxembourg. Useless, temperamental thing—of course, it was Italian.

Thursday, Midmorning

OF COURSE, THE *flics* were on the lookout after the previous night.

All morning Aimée had felt a tingling down her neck, her nerves on edge. She was worried that the man in the window across from Erich Kayser's could somehow identify her.

She'd worn another brown wig today, with longer hair, had pinned it up in another style. She'd packed several pairs of glasses and an extra pair of heeled sandals in her bag, replenished her scarves.

It was the second day of the fundraising photo shoot at École des Beaux-Arts. The thyme and garlic scents tormented her. How could anyone stay slim in the catering business? But the catering staff all looked like toothpicks. Starving—she hadn't even had time for a brioche that morning—she contemplated popping several silicon-and-dye-injected radishes in her mouth. Her burner phone vibrated. *Merde.* Suzanne pestering her again. She'd been working all morning—hadn't had a moment to look up Jean-Marie.

"I'm at work. Call me back in thirty minutes." Aimée clicked off. Out the window, which overlooked a sun-drenched street, she spied a patisserie.

Clutching a paper bag of macaroons, she walked into a quiet courtyard off the rue Jacob. Stood between beds of purple hollyhocks and bit into a mint-pistachio confection.

Heaven. The phone again. Suzanne. She'd said half an hour! She answered with her mouth full.

"*Oui?*" Green crumbs trickled onto her lap, crème filling on her lip.

"Can you talk now?" Suzanne said. "Any progress on finding Jean-Marie?"

Progress? A pang of guilt hit Aimée. With the million things she had to do, she hadn't felt compelled to carve out the time yet.

"On it," she said.

Suzanne expelled air. "You haven't even looked, have you?"

"Suzanne, first, I do have paying clients I need to service." Time to get firm. "Second, you've seen the CCTV feed I sent you."

"But what about Erich? You got there too late."

Aimée dropped a raspberry macaroon on the gravel. Picked it up and brushed off a pigeon feather.

"And you'd better watch out," said Suzanne. "The police are looking for a woman in connection with Erich's death. There's a message *à toutes les patrouilles.*"

An all-points bulletin. The crumbs stuck in Aimée's throat. Her worst fears realized. She couldn't count on her disguise if they got close. Or if they got to Suzanne.

"How do you know?" Aimée asked.

"Read the paper."

She was involved now.

"Please find Jean-Marie. He's in danger. Just get his address. Warn him."

"Warn a man I've never met . . . ?" *About a hallucination?* But she didn't say that.

"Mirko's a killer, Aimée. If he's in Paris, it's for a reason. He moonlighted as a hit man for his brother."

A hit man? Suzanne had only mentioned what he'd done to little girls. But it was beside the point.

"*Attends une petite seconde, Suzanne.* Did you see any proof of Mirko being in that café on the CCTV footage?"

"I'm back tonight. Please, Aimée, you promised me."

Aimée sighed, angry and afraid. "*D'accord.* After that, *c'est fini.*"

Suzanne hung up. Aimée heard a siren echo on the next street.

IN THE AFTERNOON lull, she'd find Jean-Marie. She wrote out a note for Sybille, letting her know where she was with the computer surveillance and that she'd be monitoring things remotely later. She left the note on the desk in Sybille's whitewashed parquet-floored office.

Aimée wished her place could look like that. With a splash of paint and some floor buffing, it could. More pressing, though, was her need to babyproof the whole flat now that Chloé was crawling.

She looked up the hospital name Suzanne had given her in *Les Pages Jaunes.* Called and, posing as a cousin, discovered Jean-Marie had been discharged a week before and directed to a rehab clinic in his arrondissement.

UPSTAIRS DURING THE library staff's lunchtime, Aimée installed a surveillance program on their vacant terminals. This way, if she'd set it up right, she could monitor activity from home, and René could back up the feed from the office.

Armed with a new spark plug for her Vespa, she sanded the points, got it started. She checked the side-view mirror every block for someone following her. Only the bus.

At a traffic light, she punched in Leduc Detective's number on her phone. "René?" she said without waiting for him to say hello. "Please tell me that program I installed at the École des Beaux-Arts library popped up on—"

"Hold on," said Saj. "I'll check René's computer."

Where was René?

"*Et voilà*, I see it," said Saj. "Glad you alerted me. I'll manage these in my new program. René's teaching today."

Another thing she'd forgotten. Like she'd forgotten to ask him about babysitting Chloé.

SHE PARKED HER scooter at the *clinique* near a treelined square. Blinked at the muscled physique of the smiling physiotherapist, a tawny blond-haired man, even taller than her, who caused her to re-think her aversion to exercise. What wasn't there to like about working out?

But Suzanne's former colleague had a different mind-set.

"Jean-Marie Plove?" said the physiotherapist. "He stopped coming to rehab, dropped out of our program."

Pause.

"You're his cousin, you said?"

A story she'd made up. She nodded. "My aunt's concerned, you know. We want to support him."

He gestured her toward the weight room, empty except for the machines and the tang of recent workouts. "I met him for a drink after he checked out. Nice *mec*, but he's depressed."

And Aimée realized her gaydar had been turned off. So Monsieur Muscle went the other way—Jean-Marie, too. Not her business.

"Did he suffer PTSD?" she asked.

"That's a catchall term. But there's all kinds of emotional

psychosocial displacement caused by an amputation. Physical and mental trauma . . ."

"We had no idea." She hoped her expression showed concern.

"Jean-Marie wants to do this all on his own," the physiotherapist said sadly. "Frankly, amputees need all the support they can get."

A few minutes of conversation revealed that Franck, Monsieur Muscle, had really cared about Jean-Marie, gone beyond his job to try to help. He'd set up a *parcours* so Jean-Marie could train in the square near his place. But after their first meeting, Jean-Marie had failed to show up.

"We keep his file in case he returns. Tell him he's welcome anytime." Franck noticed her hopeful look. "Medical confidentiality precludes me from saying any more. I'm sorry."

A real family member would know Jean-Marie's address. How could she tease it out of Franck?

"Jean-Marie doesn't answer his phone. Our letters have been returned. We think he moved."

"Moved? He said he grew up around there, didn't want to go far away. That's why he agreed to meet me in that square. It's close."

Great.

"We heard he moved after his return from the Balkans," she said. "I came because we're more than concerned. He'd mentioned . . . well . . . he seemed so depressed. We're worried about suicide."

A rap on the glass door. "I've got another patient, *désolé.*"

"Can you just ask the office to let me in so I can check? Please?"

"They've tightened medical record confidentiality.

Again, I'm sorry, but I suggest you try his health liaison at the army. *Bonne chance.*"

Good luck? She'd need more than that with the military. Like they would share medical history or contact info even within their own branches, much less with her.

The waiting room was crowded, and the receptionist was arguing on the phone. Aimée knocked on the counter to get her attention. *"Toilettes, s'il vous plaît?"*

The receptionist pointed to the hall door. Buzzed Aimée into the back corridor. As in her own doctor's office, the patient files lined the walls for easy accessibility for the busy staff.

In the bathroom, she touched up the smudged kohl around her eyes, reapplied Chanel red, and blotted her lips with a café napkin from her bag. Stepped out.

Several of the staff were working with patients in the back room, judging by the sounds of grunts and conversation over a midafternoon radio newscast. The receptionist, back to Aimée, was involved in a heated discussion.

Parfait. Time to grab Jean-Marie's info for Suzanne and get the hell out.

In the rear hallway, out of the line of sight from the rehab rooms, Aimée tiptoed past the shelves, scanning the files. At *P* she looked for PLOVE, JEAN-MARIE. Spotted it.

"That's all I can say, monsieur!" The receptionist was shouting. "If you don't like it . . ."

Aimée tugged. The file stuck.

Footsteps.

She tugged again.

"Mademoiselle? What's your business back there? Weren't you in the toilet?"

In a deft move, she pulled the file free and hid it behind her back as she turned to see the receptionist.

"Warn me next time," said Aimée. "There's only scalding hot water from the tap. You should alert people. I burned myself."

File under the back of her blouse, she hitched her bag on her shoulder to disguise the bulge and hurried through the busy *clinique* lobby, making sure to rub her hands.

Fleeing a scene where a man plunged to his death, stealing medical files to get an address—she could hear René asking what law she would break next.

Thursday, Midafternoon

JULES DECHARD PERSPIRED with nerves as he passed the manicured lawn and entered the *hôtel particulier*'s ground-floor foyer. Upstairs the seventeenth-century mansion had been divided into office suites and apartments with million-franc views overlooking the Seine. This whole area had once been Queen Marie de Médici's personal garden.

The art gallery door was unlocked.

He followed the instructions he'd been left. Told himself he wouldn't let this ruin him.

The salon was boiseried and gilt festooned, the walls lined with paintings. This early in the afternoon there were no clients. Jules made himself walk to the office, go through tall glass-paned back doors leading to a resto kitchen. His hand shook—he needed to take his pills.

The stainless steel kitchen was full of light from the tall windows to the garden but empty of busboys, kitchen crew. Like all staff, they took an after-lunch siesta until preparations for the evening shift.

His contact was nowhere to be found. The envelope dampened under his arm. He needed to get back to École des Beaux-Arts.

"*Allô?*"

No answer—only steam rising from something simmering in the copper pot on the stove. A stock with marrowbones, garlic cloves, a pinch of rosemary, and floating bay leaves.

Jules's hand tremored as he poured himself a cup of water

from a pitcher on the counter. He threw his pills in his mouth and drank.

Where the hell was this mystery contact?

He took out his cell and called the number he'd been given, heard the faint answering ringing from behind the building. He followed the sound through the kitchen and out the back door, his feet crunching over gravel to the delivery bay in the side courtyard. The security guard at the back entrance was turned away from him, talking loudly on his cell phone. Jules felt his apprehension increase.

The hedge-bordered garden was full of blooming peonies. There was his contact, sitting by the remodeled old stables and outhouses. His fear mounted. It must be his contact, *non?* Jules gripped the envelope he'd been about to hand over. The man's back was to Jules. His head rested against a trellis. Bees droned by the honeysuckle.

Something felt wrong. Very wrong. Just then he heard gravel crunch. Felt a blow to his head before the green hedge melted into black.

Thursday, Midafternoon

STANDING ON THE quai, Aimée held Chloé on her hip so Babette could kiss Chloé goodbye. The plane trees rustled in the weak, warm breeze. Lazy clouds hovered and drifted gauzelike over the right bank of the Seine.

"Hate leaving you in a bind. *Désolée, Aimée*," said Babette.

"*Bonne vacances*. See you in a few weeks," Aimée said, wondering what on earth she'd do as Babette piled into the taxi. If only Madame Cachou's sister had not had to go to the hospital.

Selfish. She'd rearrange her schedule, figure it out somehow.

Chloé mewled and bit Aimée's finger. Ouch. She had new teeth. Contingency plan number two: René, who'd volunteered, *non*, insisted on taking Chloé whenever Aimée needed him, hadn't answered his phone. She'd left him another voice mail. The second that day.

Now she knew she needed more backup for the future. Zazie, contingency plan number three, the fourteen-year-old daughter of the couple who owned the café below Leduc Detective, had a summer class and wouldn't be available until the next day.

Benoît had left to teach an Asian studies summer session at the University in Grenoble; his sister—Gabrielle's mother—and her husband had arranged to have their vacation in Ibiza coincide with Babette's.

Weren't people supposed to stagger their holidays in July or August? The boulangeries were mandated to do so by law, so there would always be a place to buy bread. Why was everyone now a *juilletiste* as opposed to an *aoûtien?*

"We'll have baguettes at least, Chloé. That's a good thing," Aimée said. She lifted Chloé's pudgy hand to make her wave bye-bye as Babette took off.

Aimée ran through her other options. Saj had a client meeting this evening. Her go-to dog-sitting standbys, Viard, the police forensic expert, and his partner, Michou, who loved Chloé to death, were in Martinique. Martine was covering a story in Fontainebleau. Even Aimée's cousin Sebastien and his wife and new baby were on vacation at her parents' house in Switzerland.

Toute Paris had disappeared, and it wasn't even August.

Aimée had a lucrative contract to honor, more business than Leduc Detective could handle, and Suzanne on her back.

The police were looking for a female suspect involved in Erich Kayser's death. They were looking for her. The hairs prickled on the back of her neck.

What had she gotten herself into?

Get a grip. She'd work from home. Go low profile. Better stuff down her anxiety and get to work.

Chloé's little eyelashes fluttered, battling sleep. Nap time.

Upstairs, she settled Chloé into her crib under the butterfly mobile, fed Miles Davis the last of the horsemeat from the white-paper package, and made a mental note to stop at the butcher's. One more thing to remember.

She emailed Suzanne Jean-Marie's address, which she found in his medical file. Done, she logged on to her laptop, pulled up the École des Beaux-Arts database, and got back to monitoring.

Her landline rang.

René?

"Aimée, it's me," said Melac.

Of all times.

"I'm at the door, Aimée. Let's talk."

"What? Not with your mother again?"

"Only me. Please."

Panic set in. A former *flic*, Melac still had connections. What if he'd seen the police bulletin about Erich Kayser, somehow put things together?

"We've got nothing to discuss, Melac."

"But we do."

She heard knocking. "Shhh, Chloé's asleep. You'll wake her up."

"Then we'll whisper." More knocking.

Finally, she showed him to the balcony. Clenched her fingers on the wrought-iron railing so she wouldn't hit something.

"I know you're in a bind without a babysitter," he said. "Your concierge told me."

She masked her surprise.

"Can I help?"

Like he'd ever offered before. He'd never even seen his daughter until she was six months old and he decided to pop up at her christening. With his new wife.

But now he'd crouched to examine the baby gate, still in the package, by the balcony door. He took out the instructions.

She wanted to hit him. She couldn't deal with it. Not now. She'd show him the door, get work done while she could.

"There's nothing to discuss, Melac."

Just then, her phone rang from her bag.

"Your whole place needs serious babyproofing," he said. "Not just the kitchen. Look at that exposed outlet. Sharp edges everywhere. Chloé's already crawling and pulling herself up."

"Like I haven't noticed, Melac?" Another thing to do. Chloé's fascination with electrical outlets and the apartment's archaic fuses presented a problem.

Her phone was still ringing. She turned to answer.

Sybille's usually calm voice had gone up a register. "Where are you, Aimée? I checked the library, the terminals, everywhere."

"Didn't you see the note I left, Sybille? I explained—"

"Just grab a taxi. How fast can you get here?"

"Sybille, I'm monitoring your system remotely via—"

"Mademoiselle Leduc, you're under contract." Sybille's voice was coated in frost. "I need you here, not remotely. That's what I'm paying you for."

"*Bien sûr.*" She could hear René saying, *Always humor the client, especially our high-ticket contracts.*

Damn René—where was he when she needed him?

Melac rose. "Go. I'll watch Chloé."

She tried to turn away, but he caught her hand, pointed to his watch.

Her laptop screen showed an error. *Merde.* A system malfunction that hadn't been there twenty minutes ago.

Merde again. How could she trust Melac to watch Chloé? They'd hardly interacted or spent time together. But he'd raised another daughter, Nathalie, who had died after a bus accident. He'd been heartbroken, left the force to be by her bedside while she was in a coma. Aimée knew he was a devoted father.

It would be only a few hours.

Zut! What else could she do?

"Fifteen minutes, Sybille." Hung up.

She grabbed the EMERGENCY list, with numbers for the doctor, poison control, from under the *bébé* swim schedule and tacked it on the wall. Pointed out the blackboard where Babette had chalked Chloé's food likes. There was a new discovery: *compote de cerises au yoghourt.*

Miles Davis, his ears perked up, sniffed Melac's jeans as Aimée slipped into her sandals. "Just in case there's a—"

Melac rolled his eyes. "Think I can handle this. Just point me to the tools." His eyebrows rose. "You do have a tool kit?"

"Bottom kitchen drawer."

"*Bon.* While she naps, I'll properly babyproof this archaic pit."

After a few more hurried instructions, she flew down the worn marble stairs, jumped on her scooter, and revved it onto the quai.

GUNNING HER SCOOTER, helmet on and her phone earbuds in, she wove past a bus on quai de Conti, listening to Saj's take on the system malfunction. He'd discovered malware that had been downloaded through a supposedly legitimate email. They saw this kind of thing all the time. All it took was one careless click. He suggested a system reboot. She prayed that worked.

Ten minutes later at École des Beaux-Arts, she'd donned her IT outfit, flown up the rear building's metal stairs, taken over a terminal, and gotten to work checking the system. It was clear. Saj had installed the antivirus download on his end by then.

"All backed up," Saj said in her earpiece. "Okay, reboot."

She shut down the system. Counted to three and rebooted.

The log-in appeared.

"What's the new password, Saj?"

"4-midable, with a dash and the number 'four.'" She heard him clicking on his keyboard. "Couldn't get so original on short notice."

"Least it's not rata-2-e." She logged in. Breathed a sigh of relief as the normal display appeared on her screen. "Think we're good. No system errors."

"There won't be any more. I found the firewall breach courtesy of that error. The hacker screwed up, Aimée."

"The hacker screwed up? I thought it was that you're such a genius, you discovered the problem."

"Milk this to your employer. Stress the need for employee password privacy education. Someone got stupid. The password hadn't been changed in six months. Lazy. Think of this breach as a good thing. I'm on him now. He's running, but can't hide that sloppy technique."

Sloppy technique—that reminded her of Suzanne's description of Mirko.

Bette, Sybille's assistant, whom Aimée privately thought of as Sybille's lapdog, tapped a pencil on Aimée's screen. She was a fuchsia-haired former art student who thought punk was still a fashion statement.

"*La directrice* needs you, *immédiatement.*" Her voice was self-important and tinged with reverence.

In her office Sybille peered over her terminal. Her normally flawless makeup was smudged. "*Merci*, Bette."

Bette bobbed her head. "À *votre service, Madame la Directrice,*" she said. Aimée could have sworn she almost curtsied.

"All's good," Aimée said. "We've discovered and dealt with the hacker. Sealed the firewall. Your system's back on track."

"*Quoi?*" Sybille was staring at her computer screen. She picked at a loose button on her silk sleeve, distracted. Her composure was ruffled.

"But we've changed the password, so I'll need to educate the staff on—"

"I need you next door," Sybille interrupted. "Follow me."

NEXT DOOR TURNED out to be across the street and down a back passage off narrow rue Visconti. Aimée followed Sybille toward a small townhouse with blue shutters, up a set of steps winding under an arch, past a kitchen garden with trellised bean runners, and along mossy stone walkways. Another world here in the heart of Saint-Germain-des-Prés—what remained of the ancient village and abbey outside Paris's twelfth-century walls.

Sybille knocked at a tall double wooden door, then entered. Aimée found herself in a salon with windows overlooking the garden they'd passed. Jules Dechard sat shirtless on a chair, a doctor with a stethoscope listening to his chest. An intravenous drip was attached to a needle in a vein in his arm. He looked so different from just the day before, his face ashen—the man looked like death. She noticed his concave chest, the visible outlines of his ribs. Shocked, Aimée realized his layered clothing had hidden total emaciation. Bandages were taped to his neck, and she saw dried blood on his temple.

"You've stabilized, Jules," said the doctor, packing his bag. "But I want to admit you to the clinic."

"Like that will happen."

"Stubborn, eh, Jules? *Comme d'habitude*," said the doctor, shaking his head.

"What's the matter?" Aimée asked. "An accident?"

Jules bristled. "Why did you bring her?"

She wondered about this man who blew hot and cold.

"You know why, Jules," said Sybille. She sat down next to him, took his hand. "Now shut up and listen to Dr. Pivot."

A heated argument ensued while Sybille held Jules's shaking hands in her own. Aimée gathered that Jules Dechard suffered a terminal illness, that his condition had deteriorated. And the man was in denial.

She also intuited Jules had kept the appointment with his email blackmailer, confronted him, and gotten beaten up.

But this wasn't her business. She didn't know why Sybille had insisted she come. At least it seemed to confirm Sybille wasn't going to accuse her of a professional indiscretion for taking Jules's cash contract. Was she?

Uncomfortable, Aimée turned to follow the doctor out. Sybille shot out of her chair and ran to stop her.

"*Désolée*, but I must return to work," said Aimée.

"Please, stay. My brother-in-law needs your help."

"I don't understand what this is about," she said, "and I don't think it's my business."

A muscle in Sybille's cheek twitched. "May I remind you you're under contract?"

Doubt it covers this, Aimée thought.

"It seems to me Professor Dechard has a personal problem," Aimée said carefully, remembering her promise to him to be *discret*. "If he is the victim of criminal violence or blackmail, that is a matter for the police, not for the school's IT security advisor."

"*Non*, wait," Sybille said. "It *is* a school matter—they are attacking the École des Beaux-Arts's reputation."

"I don't understand," Aimée said.

"He's being framed."

"Framed? For what? Framed by whom?"

Jules sighed. "I don't know."

Of course he knew. "Please report this to the *flics*. Talk to your lawyer. Not me."

Sybille glanced at her phone. "The lawyer's en route."

"Listen," said Dechard. "This is what happened. I was supposed to meet someone at Galerie Tournon about . . . about a private matter." Dechard's voice quivered. "When I got there, I found my contact slumped over in the garden. He was . . . he looked dead."

A shiver traveled up Aimée's arm.

"Then I got hit from behind."

"You were attacked? By whom?"

He grimaced. "I don't know. Someone knocked me unconscious. When I came to, the security guard had called the police. They were loading the other man in an ambulance—they questioned me, wanted to take me to the hospital. I . . . I didn't . . . I told them I felt fine; I wanted to see my own doctor. I wasn't under arrest, so they had to let me go, but they took down my information. I know the *flics* are going to come for me. Whoever attacked me set me up. Now it looks like I killed that man."

Could she believe him? Or had he confronted his black-mailer, who'd fought back?

"He's being framed," said Sybille, running her red-lac-quered nails through her hair. "That's why he needs your help. We want you to investigate, Aimée."

This was *fou*—crazy. What was there to investigate? Jules

Dechard knew what was going on and should just come clean so he could get the help he needed.

Aimée's eye caught on two blue uniforms in the garden below, a plainclothes *flic* pointing to the window. Her heart jumped. Looking for her?

A dragonfly hovered on sapphire wings between the *flics*, then suddenly took flight. One of the *flics* jumped and swatted.

"You've got guests," she said, ready to bolt. "*Brigade criminelle*. I'll see myself out the back."

Terror filled Dechard's eyes.

Sybille grabbed Aimée's hand. "It's a plot to ruin our reputation, the credibility of the school. Look, Aimée, this would sabotage us. The whole school would implode."

"Sabotage? What are you talking about? Your professor has been attacked—that's criminal assault. You should report it to the police."

Sybille wouldn't release her iron grip.

"They're accusing me of plagiarism," Jules blurted out. "So long ago. Ancient history. They could taint my Légion d'honneur. Endanger my chair endowment."

"The whole department would come under fire," Sybille said. "The whole school—our reputation is on the line."

"Who says you plagiarized, Professor?" Aimée saw him wince at the word, but he didn't respond. "What do they accuse you of plagiarizing?"

"It doesn't matter," he said sharply. "It's all . . . They're framing me. Trying to ruin me to hide their . . . It's . . ." He trailed off.

"To hide what?" Aimée asked.

He flapped a sagging hand, waving her off. "It doesn't matter."

Poor Dechard. She couldn't help but feel sorry for him. But how could she help him if he wouldn't even answer her questions?

"*Mon Dieu, Aimée,*" said Sybille. "Find out who's trying to destroy us."

Footsteps sounded on the landing. A brisk knock. Sybille let go of Aimée and fluffed her hair.

Dechard reached for Aimée's arm with his bony fingers. "I'm being set up." He squeezed so hard it hurt. "We'd worked out a deal. That's what I don't understand. I don't know who hit me. He never even took the . . . what I'd promised to bring him."

The door opened, revealing the *flics* in conversation with a short man who was stuffing his lawyer's robe in his briefcase. Good timing on the part of Dechard's attorney.

She needed to get out of there. But it was too late—a woman stepped into the room, and Aimée was smacked in the face with a familiar wave of old-fashioned bergamot Lanvin fragrance and tobacco. Her stomach dropped a thousand feet.

"Mademoiselle Leduc, we meet again."

That gravel-toned voice, those high heels and that steel gaze—the last person she'd share air with by choice. Edith Mesnard, *la Procureure de la République*.

"Just like you to poke your nose in this. New glasses?"

She'd rather chew tin foil than deal with Madame *la Proc*, the investigating magistrate who was known for her brains and her will of iron. After Morbier's shooting and the closed-door hearing, *la Proc* had had it in for Aimée big-time. The upshot of the hearing was that Morbier would receive retirement, honorable discharge, the full whitewash. Not that he'd benefit for long. Yet unlike his cohorts, he was alive.

The police union rep had attacked and threatened Aimée at the hearing, petitioning for her PI license to be revoked. Even *la Proc*, known for fairness, had admonished Aimée in chambers.

"I'm contracted to École des Beaux-Arts on a corporate security matter, Madame *la Proc*," said Aimée. "Bad timing on my part that I came to deliver a report when Professor Dechard's doctor was here." She shouldered her bag. "If you'll excuse me, Madame *la Proc*."

She made it out the door ignoring the whispered "see you in hell" that one of the *brigade criminelle* inspectors spat at her as she passed. She hurried down the stone walkways, conscious of a coffee grinder in the distance, shutters casting diagonals of light and shadow on the paving stones.

She glanced at her phone. A message from Saj. Another message on the burner phone. Suzanne's muffled voice. "Mistakes were made." An intake of breath. "Jean-Marie . . . in danger . . . Tell him . . ." That was all she could make out. Then an earsplitting crackling as if the phone had been dropped.

Thursday, Early Afternoon

SWEAT STUNG JEAN-MARIE Plove's eye. His aching biceps strained as he struggled for the last chin-up. Go through the pain, ran the training litany in his head. Give 110 percent. And he had, when he'd been in the GIGN anti-terrorist brigade. "Take no prisoners" had been their motto.

Jean-Marie grunted, forcing that last centimeter, willing his muscles taut, going for the aching burn that would turn sweet.

His bristled chin skimmed the tree branch. He'd done it. Euphoria for a brief second until his grip loosened. He landed on his butt, twisting his left leg, which had been fitted with an aluminum prosthesis from the kneecap down. Pain shot up his spine.

"So you work out outdoors now?" said Robert Guedilen, a glint in his heavy-lidded eyes. "No wonder I don't see you at the gym." He held a briefcase and had a wool jacket over his arm.

Robert, a former colleague, had been the fixer on his ICTY team—the man who got the *merde* done. The last person Jean-Marie wanted to see.

Like Jean-Marie would work out in a gym with his prosthesis on display.

"Nature's free," he said, managing a grin.

Here he was, only thirty-two years old, a pathetic fool lying on the dirt in Square Gabriel Pierné. He would have been in his prime if not for the splinter bomb that had taken him down in Foča.

"Your leg is made of metal." Tomas, Robert's precocious four-year-old son, was holding his father's hand.

Jean-Marie straightened his shoulders, fighting the pain in his spine, and winked. "Call me *bionique.*" He ignored Robert's extended hand, grabbed the plane tree trunk, and pulled himself up. His damn kneecap was so chafed and sore from the constant rubbing of his prosthesis.

"Join us for dinner," said Robert. "My wife's preparing her special *salade de crevettes*, your favorite. Perfect for a hot summer evening."

Jean-Marie heard the pity in Robert's voice.

"Got a date. *Désolé,*" Jean-Marie said.

Pause. "A date with Żubrówka?"

The Polish vodka flavored with bison grass that helped him blot out the atrocities. Jean-Marie grimaced. "Don't worry about me, Robert. It's coming together."

Robert smiled down at his little son. "Put our ice cream wrappers in the bin, okay?"

As Tomas walked away, Jean-Marie felt Robert's hand on his shoulder. "You quit therapy, don't answer my calls. Look, my Foča report is due at *le Sénat*. We need to review those details. It's important, Jean-Marie."

Relive that hellhole? He did that every night in his nightmares. The trees were dark green beneath the overcast sky, and drops of rain pattered on Jean-Marie's arm.

"I'll get back to you, Robert."

"It's not the outcome we wanted, I know. But think of it as some form of justice." Robert paused. "Can you call me tomorrow, Jean-Marie?"

"Don't want much, do you?" He brushed the leaves and

gravel from his gym pants, arranged the left cuff to hide the aluminum.

"I know it's hard, but we owe it to those victims."

"I put it all down in my debriefing report already."

"That report from the hospital in Nantes? The one you made while you were still doped up after the amputation? You must be able to add to that."

Why now? Why did it really matter anymore? But he wasn't going to ask and prolong the discussion.

Jean-Marie's depth perception had wavered since the brain injury he'd gotten the same day he'd lost his leg. His vision problems came at random times. He'd made his life routine, took routes he knew from memory, stuck close to this quartier he'd been born in. Every day he forced himself to make a little triangle: the Franprix, his corner *café tabac*, and the square a few blocks from his house. Like clockwork. Next month he'd expand his circuit to the market on rue de Buci, the garden behind Saint-Germain-des-Prés where he'd played as a child by Picasso's sculpture.

"We'll talk tomorrow, okay?" said Robert. "Meet here."

"I'll call you, Robert."

Tomas had returned and was tugging on his father's sleeve.

Robert shook his head and checked his high-tech walkie-talkie. Still on the ministry leash. "Answer your phone. That's all I ask, Jean-Marie."

Like that would happen.

Then the drying sweat on Jean-Marie's neck tingled. He snapped to attention, in that full alert mode he'd known in the field. He was in someone's cross hairs. Being watched.

Thursday, Late Afternoon

THE LEFT BANK café was busy with locals. Two journalists talked over beers about the latest NATO scandal. As they signaled the harried waitress for another round, Aimée's phone rang. Saj. She wedged herself in at the café counter, ordered a Badoit.

"Coming, Saj?"

"Can't. I'm rebooting another program."

Right now her priority was to put together a security protocol for the École des Beaux-Arts staff. Should take an hour, tops. Then she could go home and make sure Melac had coped with Chloé.

"Dechard's been a bad boy," she said. The Badoit arrived with a slice of lime and a frosted glass.

"Tell me later. Listen, I found interesting stuff on the French ICTY team. Mirko, too. René asked me to update you."

Since when had René taken this in his hands? She slapped five francs on the counter and waved off the change. "I'm listening."

"Mirko lived in France as a kid," Saj was saying. "And the team's Bosnia operation is currently under review in Senate hearings."

Her hand paused on the glass. "Mirko lived here?"

"His parents disliked Tito and vice versa. In the sixties the borders were fluid for *travailleur invités*, you know, guest workers. His family lived here two years, then in Belgium."

She cupped a hand over her other ear and concentrated

on what Saj was saying. So difficult over the patron conversation and the *télé*. "So Mirko spoke French."

"At one time, maybe. Then again, he's dead."

And never appeared at the *café tabac*, as the CCTV footage proved. "Go back to the Senate hearings. They're working on the budget now, *non*? How's the Bosnia operation relevant?"

"I know it costs money to subsidize NATO forces, maintain a presence with the ICTY in The Hague and the former Yugoslavia," said Saj. "So the military branch is accountable for their budget."

"Anything on Erich Kayser, the moneyman?"

"I'll keep searching."

Her mind went to Suzanne's garbled message. She fought down nagging guilt again. She hadn't reached Jean-Marie.

But she'd think about that later. Deal with a paying job first.

"Alleged payoffs and bribes by arms dealers," the *télé* newscaster was saying overhead. "Unnamed sources close to NATO's—"

"That's the tip of the iceberg," said one flushed-faced journalist loudly, standing up and throwing francs on his table.

Aimée turned quickly to catch what the newscaster was saying—could it be related?—but the rest was lost in the noise of all the people coming into the café.

SYBILLE HAD ALREADY read her admin staff the riot act before Aimée arrived, but she still felt relieved once she'd delivered her Email Security 101 lecture—never download anything in an email unless you know the sender, and even then, verify; your mistakes open the whole institution to vulnerability; private emails don't belong on the institutional email server; blah blah blah. Sybille seemed to be taking it all seriously, so Aimée thought there shouldn't be any more problems until the next time. There was always a next time— that was how Leduc Detective stayed in business.

Grabbing a piece of chocolate from the bowels of her bag, she scanned her laptop screen. She unwrapped the tinfoil from a Lenôtre raspberry truffle. Took a bite. Heaven, even if it was a little gooey from the heat.

An email popped up from Dechard's lawyer outlining points he wanted her to investigate. Had she actually agreed to do this? Or did her École de Beaux-Arts contract mandate it? A quick check revealed it did not. But what would Sybille say if she refused to help? Would she be kissing any future contracts here goodbye?

She groaned inside. She needed to talk to René. And needed to do a few more things before leaving.

Better check on Chloé, to see how things went so far. But she'd deleted Melac's number. *Merde!* She rang her landline. Heard her own fuzzed voice on the answering machine. *"Laissez un message s'il vous plaît après le beep sonore."* Beep.

"It's Aimée. Pick up, Melac."

Pause.

"Melac, answer."

She hung up. Tried again. Heard ringing.

Why didn't he pick up? Was he out for a walk? But he wouldn't dare leave—he didn't have the keys to get back in.

Still no answer.

Her heart skipped a beat.

She imagined the worst. The drop-in with his mother; this second visit, supposedly to babyproof—was it all a ruse to kidnap Chloé?

Calm down. She needed to breathe and think this through. Tried her landline again.

No answer.

How could she have been so naïve and trusted him again? A man who'd been nowhere to be found when Aimée was expecting his baby, who'd remarried and dropped off the face of the earth, then just burst into their lives again?

Or what if something even worse had happened—a fire? An accident involving Chloé? Good God, had the fever returned? Hadn't Aimée learned from reading baby guru Dr. Dolto that fever is one of the first symptoms of infantile meningitis?

Called again. No answer. If Melac were there, he'd answer.

That settled it. She'd handle the last items later.

Her scooter sputtered. Died. This time she'd forgotten to fill up the tank.

Stupid.

Frantic, she hurried onto quai Malaquais looking for a taxi. None. *Merde*, all these one-way streets going the wrong way. She headed toward rue Mazarine, scrolling through the numbers in her phone. Found her neighbor on the second floor. Her fingers trembled as she pressed CALL.

Ringing.

Idiot, such an idiot to have let Melac in the door. What stupidity to leave her daughter with a man who . . . The neighbor's phone rang and rang, the sound echoing hollowly through her mobile. She bumped into a woman with a shopping bag, spilling her charcuterie and cheeses all over the cobbles.

"Watch where you're going, eh?" the woman said. "You going to pay for my ruined Saint-Nectaire?"

"*Désolée*, it's an emergency. My baby's in trouble . . ." Aimée pressed a wad of francs into the woman's hand and ran to a taxi at the corner. Jumped in.

"In a hurry, eh?" The older taxi driver hit the meter. "Where to?"

"Quai d'Anjou on Ile Saint-Louis." She panted. Hot, storm-charged air blew in the taxi window. "Extra if you get me there in under ten minutes." She choked back the sob rising in her throat. "My baby's missing."

"You're sure?"

"I left her with her biological father. Like an idiot."

"Don't knit your nose hairs, or you'll hang yourself." Another old expression that made her think of Morbier— no. She stuffed that thought aside. The taxi driver shifted into gear and took off, horn blaring, scattering pedestrians in the crosswalk like frightened pigeons.

Her phone to her ear, she tried her neighbor again. No answer. Then her landline again. Please answer, Melac.

Only ringing.

Where had he gone with Chloé? And his mother—was she in on this? What did she even know about the woman?

Everything with him had been a disaster since he'd shown up at the christening. She wanted to kick herself for ignoring the danger signs.

Lying so he could babynap his biological daughter—how low could he go?

As her trembling finger was ready to tap out seventeen for the police, a call came in from an unknown number. A bystander on the quai watching her apartment in flames?

"*Oui?*" Her voice quivered.

"Might want to turn up your landline ringer volume, Aimée," Melac's irritated voice came over the line.

"Is Chloé okay?"

"We're dripping wet on your bedroom floor. Chloé was having a bubble bath until Miles Davis bit my leg, barking like crazy until I finally realized he was hearing the phone."

Good God, last night she'd turned down the ringer to avoid waking up Chloé.

Oops. Relief flooded her.

Miles Davis's acute sense of hearing had won the day. She made a mental note to stop by the horse butcher for an extra treat.

"Melac, sorry . . ." She heard Chloé's soft babbles and Miles Davis whining.

"Quit the panic attacks. We're both sopping wet and getting cold."

"Feel Chloé's head. Any fever?"

"Took her temperature an hour ago. Normal. We're reading her new book after dinner."

"But Melac, if she gets fussy—"

"Fussy over what?" he said.

She heard a crash in the background.

"What's that?" she asked.

Pause. "Miles Davis getting frisky. Knocked over the shampoo or something in the bathroom. *Et alors*, listen, the latest from Morbier's doctor—"

"Don't start, Melac," she interrupted. Her fingers twisted tight on her bag strap. A whoosh of humid air ruffled her hair.

"She's about to eat now."

"Already?" There was a crack of thunder. Any minute it would rain.

"That's the time the schedule on the wall says," he said. "Oh, and she loved my homemade applesauce."

He'd pureed the market apples that she'd been meaning to. "Take your time. No need to rush back."

Hesitant, she glanced at the time. Why not take advan-tage? "I'll be back in an hour."

"Finish what you're doing," he said. "Everything's under control."

"Under control?" But he'd hung up.

Thursday, Early Evening

MELAC HIT THE END CALL button on his phone. Smothered his feelings, the helplessness, and resumed drilling holes for the baby gate. He could at least do one thing right.

"You handled that well." The woman emerged from the tiled bathroom holding Chloé in an oversized fluffy towel. Chloé's sparkling eyes and twisting, damp pink toes peeked out. She'd taken his heart—he'd do anything for this little thing.

"She's got your eyes," the woman said.

Melac stiffened. "Aimée all over."

A sigh. The first time she'd appeared human. "Papa's waiting, my little cream puff."

"We say *mon petit chou*." Melac opened his arms for the damp bundle that was his daughter. Inhaled her sweet, soapy baby smell. Heard a burp and felt the drool.

"You call her your little cabbage?"

"Cabbage, cream puff. Same thing." Melac nuzzled Chloé's champignon nose. He was rewarded with a squeal of delight. He looked up at the woman, who was folding a pile of diapers, bibs, and onesies. There was a mix of longing and happiness on her face.

"I hate lying," he said.

"Come up with a better idea? It's not for long. And it's the only way."

Thursday, Early Evening

UNDER CONTROL? SHE hated to admit that it sounded like it was, apart from her dog.

"Some emergency," said her mustached taxi driver.

"Long story." Aimée pulled out her LeClerc compact. She used her kohl pencil around her eyes, smudged it for a smoky look. Reapplied Chanel red and wished her lips weren't so thin.

The taxi driver's eyebrows shot up in the rearview mirror. "You trust him?"

Did she? Could she believe he wanted to build a relationship with Chloé? Hadn't she always, deep down, wanted them to build some version of their own family?

When she was eight years old, after her mother had left, her father had run himself ragged doing his best to take on the roles of both parents. Her grandfather had stepped in, taking her to piano lessons, for a *pain au chocolat* after playing in the park. Times she'd savored then and still savored now. Morbier had been drafted for ballet duty.

Her heart choked her. How could Morbier have betrayed her papa?

"*Et alors*, my meter's running. Where to now?"

She reined in the memories swirling in her head. Her phone trilled. "*Un moment.*" It was Jules Dechard's attorney. He'd given her his card—good thing she'd entered the number into her phone. She needed to enter Melac's before she forgot. "I got your email, monsieur," she said.

"Mademoiselle Leduc, the victim's gone into a coma and might not come out of it," said the attorney. "Jules Dechard could face manslaughter charges."

Bad to worse.

"I need you to establish his alibi," said the attorney. "Please, talk to the art gallery. Get corroboration."

She hesitated. "This isn't covered by my École des Beaux-Arts contract, monsieur."

"But I'm hiring you, mademoiselle. Faxing a contract to your office. Ten-thousand-franc retainer suit you?"

She covered her phone with her palm and leaned toward the driver. "Change direction." She gave him the cross streets for Galerie Tournon. "That tip's still good if you get me there as soon as possible."

Blaring his horn, he cut over a lane and made a right. Under a threatening sky, the Seine changed from pewter to lead.

The attorney was speaking in her ear. "Jules took a taxi to the gallery earlier today."

"Taxi?" The taxi companies kept records of every fare—that might help establish his alibi. "Which firm, and what time?"

As he told her, she used her kohl eye pencil to scribble the info on the inside of her wrist.

"Get me up to speed in every way you can, d'accord?" the attorney said.

"I'm on it."

Hanging up, she realized she was sitting in a Taxi Bleu, the same service Dechard had used. She eyed the taxi's visor for the driver's name and badge number.

"Monsieur Poncelet, any chance you had a fare to this same address this morning?"

"My shift started an hour ago."

That would have been too easy. "Could you find out who did?"

"Didn't take you for a *flic*."

He had that right. Never in a million years. But going with it could work.

"Because of what happened earlier? *Flics* have babies, too." She pulled out a police ID she'd faked by copying her father's old one and doctoring it with the new logo.

"Never seen one like that."

"I'm with a special branch," she said, improvising, "but Monsieur Poncelet, it's almost like we're friends now after you witnessed my . . . overreaction." Laying it on too thick?

Poncelet grinned. "I've got three sons, six grandchildren. I'm well acquainted with family drama."

He reminded her a bit of her grandfather Claude. She liked how he kept his foot on the pedal, wove down back-streets on the Left Bank. "Do me a favor: check with your dispatch to see who took a fare to Galerie Tournon."

"I'm not supposed to."

"Life's about taking chances, *non?*" she said. "And then, please, after that forget I asked."

"Galerie Tournon?" He was frowning. "But I heard on the radio there was an incident there."

"More than an incident," she said. She'd use this to her advantage. "An attacker's on the loose. It's your civic duty to cooperate."

The taxi swerved as he avoided a tourist bus, throwing her against the seat so that she banged her elbow.

"Don't get me involved," Monsieur Poncelet said.

"Too late, Monsieur Poncelet. I'm calling on you as a citizen to expedite my investigation."

Monsieur Poncelet grumbled, but he radioed his dispatch for Dechard's driver's info. No stranger to drama, as he'd said, she sensed that he liked the excitement of being drafted into a police mission. She listened to a lot of banter—he teased the dispatcher about his wife; the return salvo concerned Monsieur Poncelet's wife, who was a concierge, apparently a busybody like Madame Cachou.

Listening to the back-and-forth, Aimée felt something niggling at her brain, but she couldn't put her finger on what. At least Monsieur Poncelet wasn't an existentialist like the taxi driver she'd had a week ago who'd monologued about Sartre the entire ride to Chloé's pediatrician.

As the taxi maneuvered up narrow rue des Grands-Augustins past Picasso's old atelier, she rooted around in her bag, pushing aside Chloé's rattle and finally palmed her red Moleskine. She thumbed past her to-do lists to a fresh page.

As Poncelet relayed what the dispatcher told him, she wrote down Dechard's taxi driver's badge number and his contact info. Progress.

She gave him double what the meter read in appreciation of his help.

"Need a receipt?" he asked.

She nodded. Business expenses. With the receipt came his card.

"Bonne chance."

Alighting, she saw a FERMÉ sign on the gallery door. Her heart sank. In the back, yellow crime-scene tape fluttered.

Guarding the entrance was a blue uniform who shook his head. "No access, mademoiselle. It's a crime scene."

As a PI, especially one hired by a suspect's attorney, she had no legal rights, no right of entrée. It was late. Fatigue dogged her in this torpid heat. And then the sky opened.

But if she was going to let a little rain stop her, she might as well turn in her license and the fat retainer. She covered her head with the folded *Le Parisien* she'd stashed in her bag and dashed for shelter.

D OWN A SIDE street, she found a café and ordered an espresso at the counter. Rain beaded on her bare arms. The *télé* over the counter blared. The news was dominated by heated parliamentary debates concerning French participation in international military action. Her mind went back to what Saj had told her about the ICTY review at *le Sénat*. She thought of Erich Kayser and the CD holding a report he'd never present now.

On an impulse, she tried calling Suzanne on the burner. Her phone was off. Aimée sighed.

Getting back to work, she confirmed Dechard's fare with his taxi driver and left the lawyer a voice mail with the info and precise time Dechard had been dropped off at the gallery. That might be enough of an alibi. But it also might not, especially if there was a manslaughter charge.

While the rain poured outside, she took a corner table. She needed to draw a timeline as her father would have, write down every detail, and investigate the holes.

She wrote down every question that popped into her head, hearing her father's voice reminding her that for every path that dead-ended, one would open up if she looked hard enough. She had to find something that stood out. But she'd rather be bouncing ideas off René than filling the pages in her red Moleskine in this damp, crowded café.

Her spine prickled. She felt eyes on her.

Uneasy, she turned around. All she saw were beer-swilling soccer fans, their faces redder than before.

She tried René. Left him a message and got cut off midway through. Her unease increased—being unreachable for this long was unusual for a communicator like René. Unless she'd ticked him off again without knowing, and he was giving her the silent treatment.

Seconds later he called her back.

"I know it's crazy, René, but—"

"There's a bulletin on the *télé*. They're looking for you!"

She craned her neck around.

"Police released information that they are following leads in the investigation of the murder of a resident who was pushed from his apartment window by an alleged jealous lover near le Sénat."

She gulped. Turned back around, but not before she'd seen the police sketch flash on the screen.

"That sketch is so generic," she said. "It could be any—"

"Any slender woman with your unusual height?" René interrupted. "Aimée, that facial sketch was not so far off, except the bad hair. And people remember you. The concierge they just interviewed was describing a woman with chipped green nail polish."

A man had noticed her nail polish? Interfering busybody. She hunched down in her chair, dug in her bag, pulled out a packaged nail polish wipe, and started wiping off the remnants.

"I don't get the spurned lover angle," said René. "Why are the *flics* taking the generic route with the investigation?"

"A cover-up, René."

"Aimée, no knee-jerk reactions right now," said René. "Let's think first, act second. Where are you?"

She told him. Explained her work for Dechard's attorney and the retainer.

"Not bad," said René. "So your job is just to help him avoid criminal charges related to the attack at the gallery?"

"So far," she said. "But Sybille was insisting I have to find out who is framing Dechard, because she thinks the school's reputation is in jeopardy. Meanwhile, I'm sure there's more to the story than he's telling us. He said something about plagiarism—is there a way to find out if he's ever plagiarized?"

"I can do some digging," René said. "Let me see what I can find this evening."

"Alors, I can't forget about Suzanne. She might have gotten it wrong, but the two 'accidental' deaths bother me."

"You should be more bothered about being the suspect in a murder investigation," he said. "Concentrate on Dechard's alibi. I'll get Saj on the rest. You stay away from it."

From the window, she watched the closed art gallery through grey sheets of rain. There would be a service entrance behind the gallery. That gave her an idea.

She left some francs on the marble-topped table and headed into the street as the shower stopped. She walked around the block and saw a rear gate and an apartment building next door: 14 bis rue de Condé. As a woman came out, Aimée caught the green door and slipped inside.

She rang the concierge's buzzer. "Madame?"

The door opened to reveal a man wearing an undershirt, an apron tied around his waist. From behind him, a radio talk show played in a language she couldn't understand. Guttural and Slavic.

"Madame's at her other job," he said, his accent thick. A baby boy sat in a booster seat, beside him a little girl spooned soup at the table. "Come back tomorrow."

"Sorry to trouble you, but—"

"Don't you read?" He pointed to the concierge's on-duty hours posted on the door: 9–12, 2–5. What could she say? She was disrupting dinner and now doubting her idea.

But she couldn't give up.

"Please, I need a few minutes of her time," she said.

"Why?"

"Two men were attacked in the gallery's garden—"

He put a finger to his mouth. "Shhh, my daughter doesn't know. You'll have to ask my wife. I was at work."

"Does she have a cell phone? Please, it would help the investigation," she said, showing him her doctored police ID.

"Papa, he's doing it again." The baby had thrown a slice of baguette in his sister's soup.

"All right," he said, harried. "Ready?"

She punched the digits into her phone as he spoke. "*Merci.*"

THE CONCIERGE, GILBERTE, a trim, petite woman with reddish-brown clipped-up hair, was wiping the mirrors of a nineteenth-century marble foyer when Aimée finally tracked her down. "I clean three buildings on my street and the next," she said, her accent Slavic but one Aimée couldn't place more precisely. "If we don't go the extra mile, we'll be replaced with the Digicode."

A hard life. Struggling to survive, to give a better life to her children. In an elite quarter, where residents paid immigrants to clean up their dirt.

"Me, I'm not complaining. It's better than where I come from. Nothing there, no work."

"Where's that?"

"Montenegro." She noticed Aimée's gaze on a turquoise

Gucci bag hanging from her cleaning kit. "My clients like me. One lady gives me her last year's models."

"You're lucky. I get mine at the flea market." Aimée smiled, trying to win the cleaning lady over.

It didn't work.

"*Et alors*, what's so important? I'm in a hurry."

"Gilberte, did you see anything this afternoon in the garden? Did the *flics* question you?"

"*Non*, why?"

"Two men were attacked. One's gone into a coma . . ."

Gilberte shuddered, made the sign of the cross. "I saw the *flics*. Not for the first time either. Last week in our building an old man opened the door to a fake gas-meter reader and got robbed. But I was lucky. I was out taking my daughter to the dentist."

"So no one questioned you about what happened today, even though you live next door? Your building overlooks the garden where the victims were found."

"The garden's big. What time?"

"Between two and four. It's hard to be precise. Two men were attacked, including my client."

"I don't remember. I was busy— mopping and dropping off the mail, packages."

Aimée had to get something. "Did you notice any cars, delivery trucks?"

Gilberte paused.

Hopeful, Aimée watched her thinking.

"Regular ones, you mean?"

Aimée pushed a strand of damp hair behind her ear, nodded.

"Vans from Rungis, yes. I think the usual service vans."

Vegetables, meat and fish came from the giant wholesale

market near Orly Airport. "Wouldn't those deliver earlier, in the morning?"

Further prodding got her more details: sometimes Rungis deliveries came twice a day. Gilberte finally remembered a *camionnette* with a heavyset man in the driver's seat.

"Can you remember the color?"

"Dark colored—blue? That's right, navy blue. Maybe a sign on it, but I can't remember what it said. When I left to pick up my kids, it was gone."

Aimée thought. "That was about four-fifteen?" Gilberte nodded. "*Merci.* One more thing." Aimée had recalled something from her hazy geography—Montenegro was in the Balkans, sandwiched between Serbia and Bosnia. Might as well give it a try. She pulled out the picture of Mirko. "Seen him around?"

"*Non.*" Gilberte's reply came out bullet-like. Her eyes narrowed.

Aimée pressed. "Anything strike you about him?"

"Apart from . . ." She paused. Averted her gaze.

"What? What were you going to say?"

"Look at that mug. Where I come from, no one trusts a face like that."

Gilberte had seen through the photo to the war criminal.

"Seen his type before then, have you? How's that?"

Gilberte threw a dust rag in her cleaning bag. Grabbed her turquoise Gucci.

"Wait, take my card. Call me if you remember anything."

Gilberte stopped in her tracks. Took it.

"You remember something, Gilberte?"

She hesitated. Nodded. "In Kotor, my town, the Serbians put faces like this on T-shirts, like heroes." Her jaw stiffened. "Along with Arnold the terminator."

⌣

A I M É E　W A L K E D　U P　the Métro steps at Pont Marie and stepped into the rain-freshened evening air. Sodden leaves stuck to her heel. As she paused on Pont Marie to pick them off, her gaze caught on the glow from her apartment window. Chloé awake this late?

Voices and laughter rose from below on the quai; waves lapped against the stones as a *bateau-mouche* passed. Ahead she saw a figure in a long raincoat emerge from her building's front door. Passersby jostled her. When she looked again, the figure had gone.

Tired, she climbed the stairs, entered her lit apartment, hung up her trench coat, kicked off her damp heels. Miles Davis's wet nose rubbed her ankles. Thank God she'd remembered to find a butcher.

She followed the familiar sound of Melac's snoring to her sofa. Near the pile of folded diapers and a Babar book sprawled Melac, cradling a sleeping Chloé, who looked like a cherub in his arms. A picture that melted Aimée's heart.

Barefoot she tiptoed through the salon, the dining room, the hallway, noticing the baby-proofing updates. Nice job on Melac's part. Quite the do-it-yourselfer—an aspect of him she'd never known. In the kitchen, she knelt by Miles Davis's chipped Limoges bowl and spooned in the horse-meat she'd wrangled from the butcher just before he'd rolled down his awning.

"*Voilà*, fluff ball. You've earned it."

She picked up Chloé, inhaled her sweet smell, and tucked her into the crib. Pulled up the cotton eyelet blanket, nestled her *doudou* beside her. The *doudou* Morbier had given her and which she couldn't live without. Aimée wanted to burn it.

Childish. And Morbier's face came back to her, reflected in the long-ago memory of a Printemps window. She'd been eight years old when they'd stopped to look at the stuffed Peter Rabbit, le lapin Pierre, in the window.

"Morbier, please, please," she'd pleaded, tugging his arm.

"Your birthday's coming up," he'd said.

She'd squinted at him. Three long months. Forever. "That's so far away."

"Put it on your papa's list," Morbier had said.

She'd wet the bed that night. Ashamed, she'd hidden the sheets, like the time before. When the cleaner came, she'd complained to Aimée's father that she couldn't find any sheets to make the beds. Her father had thrown up his hands in mock despair. "Buy new ones."

And then of course her papa hadn't been there for her birthday at all—he was working surveillance. It was her grandfather and Morbier who bought the raspberry gâteau, sang "Happy Birthday," and clapped as she blew out the nine candles. The big box from Printemps tied with an aqua ribbon had Peter Rabbit and a card from papa inside. Later, when she was older, she'd asked Morbier if he did Papa's shopping for him. "Eh, among other things," he'd said.

Tears wet her cheeks, her eyes stinging with the memory. Guilt stabbed her like a knife. She slid down the wall, hugged her knees, and fought the tears, listening to Chloé's little breaths of sleep.

She didn't know how long she huddled there before she felt hands pulling her up, arms around her, holding her tight. Melac whispered in her ear, "Let it go, Aimée. Things will work out."

But they wouldn't.

"When I was little, Morbier gave me a bunny like Chloé's, and I . . . I . . ." Her voice choked.

"Shhh, let's not wake Chloé." He guided her to bed. "We'll go see him tomorrow. You'll feel better when you've seen him."

"How can I? He betrayed Papa."

"I know. But sometimes people we love do things we don't understand until it's too late. You don't want that to happen, do you?"

"What is there to understand? It won't change that he killed my father."

Melac was rubbing her back, wiping her tear-stained face with his hand. And she hugged him tight. Couldn't help it.

"I found out he'd always kept in contact with my mother, who knows how? Maybe she was in on it, too. Both betrayers."

Melac's arms stiffened. "Playing the judge and jury now? You can't blame your mother for what happened with Morbier, or your father."

"How could you defend her? She left us, disappeared, and never even let us know if she was alive . . ."

Her throat caught. For years after, Aimée had looked, hoping her mother would be waiting to pick her up at the end of the school day with all the other mothers. Dreamed her mother would help with homework like the other mothers, attend her graduation. Damned if she'd ever abandon Chloé like that.

"May lighting strike me dead before I neglect my baby," she said.

Melac lowered his voice. "Not all women are cut out for children."

"Unlike you, I wasn't raised with both parents, a traditional family. Chloé won't be either. But she's loved, will always know and have that. She has René, Martine . . ." Her throat caught again. She had almost said Morbier.

"Put me in the picture, Aimée. I'm her father."

"Speaking of, your wife—"

"And you don't know when to shut up, either," Melac interrupted, frowning. "Nothing changes my feelings for you, Aimée."

Spoken like a true womanizer.

His warm hands still held her, and she couldn't help but remember what it felt like when those slender fingers traced her spine . . .

Her cell phone vibrated. She glanced at it. Nothing. She realized it was the other phone—Suzanne.

"Shut the door on your way out, Melac."

"*Et alors*, we've got to . . ." Those magic fingers cupped her face.

She stood. Knowing otherwise she'd end up under the duvet with him and she'd hate herself in the morning. "You know the way, Melac."

In the hallway, he grabbed his jean jacket, saw the vibrating phone on the secretary. "That phone is just like the burners Suzanne used to use."

Goosebumps broke out on her neck, her arms. Suzanne's husband, Paul, was Melac's good friend—at least, had been. Aimée didn't want this getting back to him—she was sure Suzanne wouldn't like that. Act casual.

"*Vraiment?*" she said. "René keeps a drawerful of these."

"Aren't you going to answer?"

She shrugged. "Later."

His grey-blue eyes, so like Chloé's, narrowed. "Try that

on someone else, Aimée. Are you working with Suzanne on something? Don't you know what she does is dangerous?"

Alarmed, she tried to sound offhand. "Suzanne? Why would I work with her?" Hoped the perspiration on her upper lip didn't show.

"*Alors*, whatever you're up to, there's Chloé to think of. She should be your priority."

She wanted to hit him. "You're one to talk. You're such a shining example."

Melac paused at the door. "Speaking of Suzanne . . ."

Her pulse raced. Melac had worked with Suzanne, knew her well. If only she could ask him what he thought of all this! But she wouldn't betray Suzanne.

"*You* were speaking of her, not me," she said. Yawned. "But how's she doing?"

"She and Paul—*alors*, it's rocky."

Before she could ask more, Melac said, "Need me tomorrow?"

"I'll call you."

Melac's steps trailed down the stairs, and she watched him disappear around the curve of the quai. She checked the phone. One voice mail.

"Call me back if you've got news. I'm worried about Jean-Marie . . ."

But hadn't Suzanne gotten back to Paris tonight? Aimée had emailed her Jean-Marie's address—why hadn't she gone to see him herself?

The voice mail played on, loud voices in the background. "I'm still in Lyon . . . involved in an operation that's going down. They're saying . . ." Two men's voices shouting. A loud sound like a slamming door, or a gunshot. "Can't talk."

The voice mail ended. Aimée's hands shook. She didn't

get it. Suzanne had moaned about being stuck in administration. Yet she was out on an operation.

Saj's call interrupted her thoughts.

"Dechard's attorney faxed me a contract—nice retainer, by the way. But did you see Dechard's latest email that I forwarded you?"

She took her laptop to the kitchen table, switched on the baby monitor, and pulled up her mail. Her jaw dropped. "Dechard's agreeing to meet his blackmailer again after all that? When?"

"Scroll on. Doesn't say, but you'll see his colleague Michel Sarlat has received threats now, too."

"Wait, how did you pull this up?"

"When I was patching the firewall, I got into administrative mode," said Saj. "Never left. I've been keeping an eye out. Dechard's not savvy enough to think that we keep reading his emails."

The blue lights from a gliding *bateau-mouche* rippled indigo on the Seine outside her window. She pressed her toes on the cool, smooth kitchen tiles.

"What were you going to tell me earlier about Dechard—how has he been a bad boy?" asked Saj.

"I know he's got a terminal illness. And he's terrified of being accused of plagiarism, but he won't say what they're accusing him of having plagiarized."

"How can such a famous professor have plagiarized?" Saj said. "The academic community is so critical of its members—scholars all over the world read one another's work. Surely it would have come to light already. He never would have attempted to plagiarize because he never would have gotten away with it."

Aimée thought about this for a moment. "Maybe it

happened before he was famous," she said. "He mentioned something about it all being ancient history. And now he's worried they'll take away his Légion d'honneur and his chair endowment."

Saj whistled. "Must be big. So someone's taking advantage of a terminally ill man?"

"Blackmailers have one Achilles' heel, Saj."

"You mean if they expose Dechard, the 'whatever' dries up?"

"That's in a logical scenario—Dechard should just tell us what they're holding over him. But he's being obstructive; he doesn't want whatever they know exposed, and he's willing to put himself in danger to prevent us from finding out what it is. Illogical or not, he's acting from fear."

"Got a plan, Aimée?"

She'd draft a quick email to René—now she knew how to tell him to refine his search. "I know where to start."

Friday Morning

AIMÉE PUSHED CHLOÉ'S *poussette* over the cobbles, the baby bag strapped around the handle. Chloé cooed, charming the cheese seller on rue Saint-Louis en l'Ile, who pinched her cheeks from the shop's doorway. René updated Aimée over the phone about his Dechard research as she and Chloé crossed the walking bridge onto Ile de la Cité behind Notre-Dame. They skirted the crowds lining up for Sainte-Chapelle and took a quick stroll through the Place Dauphine, quiet apart from locals walking their dogs under the plane trees. Gravel crunched under her heels. Perspiration dotted her forehead by the time they reached rue du Louvre.

At the café window red-haired Zazie put down her broom, waved, and tapped her watch. She was good to watch Chloé later that morning. Aimée breathed a sigh of relief.

She parked the *poussette* under the stairs, strapped Chloé into her designer sling, and shouldered both her bag and Chloé's gear, hoping she hadn't forgotten anything.

The sign on the wire-caged elevator read OUT OF SERVICE. When was it ever *in* service?

Not that she couldn't use the exercise, with that stubborn kilo stuck to her thighs.

Winded by the third floor, yearning for coffee, and wiping Chloé's drool off her linen neckline, she hit the security code. Leduc Detective's frosted glass door buzzed, then clicked open. Light streamed in over her father's mahogany desk, René's high-tech terminal, and the marble fireplace holding their shredder.

"Time for work, *ma puce*," she said, undoing the sling. Chloé's strong legs kicked.

No René. Or Saj. Both out in the field.

She rocked Chloé as she warmed up a bottle and brewed espresso. At her desk she fed Chloé, then set her down in the play area designed by godpapa René. Chloé crawled and scooted backward behind the baby gate. Happy as a *moule* with a *frite*.

Aimée monitored virus scans and checked surveillance logs, then scrolled through email. Chloé babbled and Aimée answered back. Sunlight brightened the wood floor, and happiness filled her—until she read the sidebar in that day's *Le Parisien*.

MURDER AT MINISTRY LOVE NEST.

The sidebar parsed the ongoing investigation of the defenestration of a government employee on rue Servandoni, hinting at a lurid sex life. Mostly a rehash of what she'd heard before. Poor Erich Kayser. The jealous female lover's height was listed as close to six feet.

No wearing high heels for a while.

Her hands shook; her mind spun. She could work incognito, work on Dechard's case, keep her head down, and keep Chloé safe and happy—couldn't she?

But then a thought she'd had the previous day came back to her—the media had been fed a manufactured hush story about a jealous lover. Someone was covering up his death. Could the bees that killed Isabelle Ideler also be a hush story, somehow?

Was someone taking out Suzanne's whole ICTY team, one "accident" at a time?

Aimée had to get to Jean-Marie. She had to warn him just in case.

It would be her last favor to Suzanne—then she'd be done and would focus on her paying clients.

She loaded up Chloé's diapers and her own disguises, checked maintenance systems. All good. Downstairs again, out in the clinging heat on the pavement, Aimée gave Marcel a quick wave and pushed Chloé's stroller into the café.

A family affair, the café was run by Virginie and her husband, and Zazie had grown up behind the counter.

But no Zazie.

"She ran to the market for me." Virginie smiled and opened her arms. Chloé smiled, too. "Until she comes back, *la petite mademoiselle* can charm the customers at the counter." Virginie pointed at the high chair.

Aimée left the pureed *petits pois* and her apartment keys for Zazie, along with a reminder to walk Miles Davis. Gave Chloé a big kiss. Virginie shook her head, eyeing the nail polish Aimée had half-wiped off. "Looks like you're due for a manicure."

The second person to notice her chipped nails. But a manicure fell lowest on the list of her priorities.

SHE WALKED DOWN narrow Left Bank streets, wishing she'd worn a lighter wig. Before she could expire from thirst, she stopped at a small Franprix and downed a chilled Badoit.

The past surrounded her within the medieval city walls. Locals here still differentiated between *dans et hors les murs*—inside and outside the walls—despite the centuries that had passed since the walls set the city limits. The narrow passages within the fortifications—remnants of the first of the city's many configurations—had been walked by kings and cart vendors. They were dark and blessedly cool, even today.

Aimée knocked on the ground-floor apartment door in the dank courtyard of Théâtre de Nesle, part of a seventeenth-century mansion showing the wear and tear of time. A middle-aged woman, eyeliner thick and face stiff with too-pale pancake foundation, set down flyers by the theater's entrance. Her made-up face stared from the poster for *Chichi Andalou*, a production billed as an avant-garde riposte to *Don Quixote*.

"Looking for Jean-Marie?" she asked.

Aimée smiled. "How did you know?"

"Clairvoyant. Another therapist?"

Play along. "And you're an actress?"

"Why don't you people give up?" The hostility in her voice belied her smile. "I'm Bella Delair," the woman said, pointing to the poster. A stage name, Aimée suspected. "Jean-Marie's like my son. Leave him alone."

Wouldn't she want help for him, then?

"I'll tell you the truth," Aimée said. "I'm a friend of his colleague Suzanne Lesage."

"*Et alors?*"

"Suzanne needs to speak with him."

"That woman never stops, does she? Jean-Marie's recovering in his own way. All these calls, reminders of that hellhole, these visits, just set him back."

Aimée noticed the empty bottles of Żubrówka by the pot of geraniums near his door.

The woman caught her gaze.

"I know what you're thinking. That I'm not qualified to say what's best for him." Bella loosened the top loop of her caftan, revealing the crease in her ample chest. "But I know him better than anyone—practically raised him." She pointed first to the door of Jean-Marie's apartment, then to the theater's. "His grandfather, a wine merchant, used to own this place—it was a storefront. We bought it and converted it into two theaters after Jean-Marie's family died in a train accident. Poor kid, contracted the chicken pox and couldn't go *en vacances*—and then lost his entire family. He stayed with us and never left."

A fine mist wafted from overhead as a tenant sprayed geraniums in a window box.

"He's a good boy," Bella was saying. "The army was his life. Ever since he was in short pants, that's all he ever wanted." Then her voice dropped so low Aimée almost didn't catch the words. "Until Bosnia."

Aimée tried for compassion. "Suzanne's worried about him, Bella. She says Jean-Marie's in danger."

That was true.

Bella shook her head. "Quit trying to scare him into therapy. It never ends with you people."

Aimée's antenna went up. "Who do you mean by you people? You mean Suzanne?"

"Suzanne and all your other people who are always calling here, stopping by." She fanned herself angrily. "It doesn't help him. It just brings it all back."

The hairs on Aimée's arms rose. "People come to visit him here? Who, Bella?"

"That's Jean-Marie's business. How the hell would I know?"

Two members of his team had died within days of each other.

Accidents.

"All I know is how it upsets him," Bella said.

"Don't you understand, Bella? His life could be in danger."

"What do you call Bosnia?" Bella's brow creased. "Every hour, every day, a sniper on the roof, death around the corner. I hear his nightmares. Now he needs peace."

So she'd let him drink himself to death?

"Where is Jean-Marie?" Aimée asked.

"Get out. Leave him alone."

Aimée took out her card, scribbled a note on it, then wedged it under his door as far as she could so Bella couldn't reach it.

She checked the Square Gabriel Pierné, which his handsome physical therapist had mentioned, but it lay deserted in the heat.

Two members of the ICTY team had died, but she'd found no proof that Mirko had survived the explosion in Foča.

None of it sat right.

DECHARD'S ATTORNEY'S LATEST email detailed a new turn in the case. Dechard's name had surfaced in allegations of funds mismanagement in his department, and the lawyer wanted to know if this accusation was related. Plagiarism, embezzlement . . . If it wasn't one thing with Dechard, it was another. If only the man would come clean, it would save them all a lot of effort.

Thank God René had been working on the plagiarism accusation. She dialed him now.

"Any luck?" She'd had him researching what he could about Jules's published writing to see if he could find some whiff of plagiarism.

"Hundreds of publications," René said. "He's written for

every art magazine in Europe and has published books besides. But I might have found your needle in the haystack." His voice was excited. "I paid special attention to his earliest publications, as you suggested. There's one very strange coincidence I found. Jules Dechard wrote his doctoral thesis on an incunabulum published in Lyon in 1488, an illustrated text called *L'Ocean des Histoires.* Dechard wrote about the use of illumination in early French printing."

How dry that sounded. Well, Dechard had described himself as a bibliophile. Apparently he'd found a way to bring art history and book obsession together. *"Et alors?"*

"C'est bizarre, but in all the database searches I've run, in all the libraries I've called this morning, there seems to be only one other published academic work on that particular incunabulum. Or at least, only one other work that mentions the incunabulum in its title."

"What's that?"

"A dissertation on the use of illumination in fifteenth-century French storytelling. It was written by Gaston Badot, who was apparently a doctoral candidate in the French literature department at the Sorbonne. That might explain why Jules Dechard was never caught, if this is what he plagiarized. The student who wrote it was in a different department at a different institution—completely different review boards—and Gaston Badot never went on to publish this as a book or to write anything else, so it's never come to light."

Aimée turned this over in her mind. "Could the man he stole from—Gaston?—know about the plagiarism? Could he be the one blackmailing?"

"Unlikely. I've looked him up—the man almost

completed his PhD, down to writing his dissertation, but he never seems to have defended it or taken the degree. He left France very suddenly in April 1983—moved back to Algiers, where he was born. He still lives there now. He's running a family sugar company, it looks like. The manuscript was submitted to the library's collection via the Sorbonne's French department."

"Which library's collection?"

"Bibliothèque Mazarine—they're both there, Jules Dechard's thesis, as well as Gaston Badot's. And while you're at it, you could look at the incunabulum itself—it's in the library's collection, too."

SHE HIKED UP a steep neoclassical staircase surrounded by antique marble and bronze busts niched in the walls. The Bibliothèque Mazarine, part of the Institut de France, was housed in a seventeenth-century palace—an exquisite place to research, all columns, pedestals, and wood paneling. Two gilt rococo chandeliers that had been taken from the Marquise de Pompadour's home hung from near the head librarian's desk. Not too shabby.

The clerk took Aimée's *carte de lecture* and smiled. "We close at five P.M."

Good God, she hoped it wouldn't take her that long.

Dark green baize shelf borders, matching the lampshades on the long study tables, protected the bookshelves from propped ladders. The upper walkway, with its wrought-iron railing, ringed the open-plan galleries. Floor-to-ceiling books, and a world-famous rare books collection. René would have loved this place. Dechard must have been in heaven there.

Armed with René's notes, she felt as ready as one could

when it came to searching for a needle in a centuries-old haystack. She copied down the titles of Jules Dechard's and Gaston Badot's theses. For good measure, she copied down the title of the incunabulum, *L'Ocean des Histoires*.

She set her card and bag down at her assigned seat, 066. Inhaled the lingering scent, the distinctive perfume of old manuscripts and worn leather spines. Her cane-back chair crackled as she sat down. Among the students and researchers at the tables, stillness and a quiet prevailed, punctuated by the turning of pages.

The head librarian, Saget according to his name tag, gestured her over to his imposing reference desk. "Your requested items are going to require time to process."

How long would this take? Hours? Days?

Time for *Système D*, the Parisian way of getting things done by getting around the *rules*.

Flirting, her old standby.

"Don't tell me," she said, smiling. "They're buried in the archives, in the bowels of the building, and haven't been seen since 1979. Or maybe 1799?"

He pulled his glasses down from his forehead.

"Come on, or am I right?"

"Actually, mademoiselle, in one case, the rare book has not been requested since 1984."

She stifled her surprise. That was the year Jules Dechard had submitted his thesis—René had filled her in on the details. Was it a coincidence that no one had even looked at the book since then?

"*Alors*, as it happens, this incunabulum appears unavailable at the moment."

"Unavailable meaning . . . ?"

"We keep these rare documents stored in the

climate-controlled incunable archives," Saget said. "Books such as these, printed prior to 1501, are highly delicate. Fragile."

Mon Dieu. "How long does it take to get them?"

"As long as it takes, mademoiselle." Spoken like a true *fonctionnaire*. Then he winked. "But the other two items you requested have been consulted more recently."

He left to check, and she returned to her assigned seat at the window fronting the Pont des Arts. Off to the right lay the Point Neuf, bright in the warm summer sun. In school she'd learned Marie Curie's husband, Pierre, had been run over by a horse and carriage where the rue Dauphine met the quai de Conti. A widow with two small children, Madame Curie continued her experiments. Compared to Marie Curie, Aimée thought ruefully, she had it easy. Only one child to feel guilty about leaving behind while she tried to get her work done.

She opened her notebook. By the time she'd sketched out her next step, the library page had stopped his cart in front of her carrel and hefted two bound manuscripts onto her table.

She opened Jules Dechard's 1984 thesis. The pages were remarkably crisp and fresh. She read the gist of his work, which seemed to be based on a medieval book written in Latin. *Merde.* Latin had never been her strong suit.

She skimmed through the thesis's third chapter, which was entitled "Fifteenth-Century Religious Art Interpretations in Lyon." At least she understood that. Interesting, too, if you were an egghead.

Clipped to Gaston Badot's thesis, which had been completed in 1983, was a note to the effect that his thesis was simultaneously being submitted for review to the

Sorbonne's French literature department; he'd gifted this then-unreviewed copy to Bibliothèque Mazarine since its subject dealt with an incunabulum in their archives.

She wondered if this was a long shot. René had mentioned hundreds of publications. If only Dechard weren't being so obstinate and secretive when they were trying to help him. Opening Gaston Badot's thesis, she ran her finger down the table of contents. Blinked. Chapter four had the same title as Dechard's third chapter. She flipped to the chapter and started reading. Blinked again. Double-checked, trailing her finger under the words. *Mon Dieu* . . . How could this be? Word for word, the same.

Flipping through other chapters, she realized Dechard had copied Badot's thesis almost verbatim in three sections, even down to the chapter titles. Pages in Gaston's thesis had been folded and showed telltale creases. To her eye, the pages looked as if they'd been copied recently.

She closed both theses, gathered her things. She'd seen enough. Jules Dechard had seemed so honest, but here was proof he'd plagiarized another student's work. Built a reputation and career on work that he'd stolen. Was that what this was all about? How had he never gotten caught?

At the librarian's desk, she turned on the charm again. "Would you be able to help me with one more thing, Monsieur"—she'd forgotten his name, stole a glance at his name tag—"Saget? Would you be able to tell me who last checked these out?"

"Let's see." He flipped through the pages of the request log until he found the entries, one above the other. "It says Jules Dechard." He turned the log for her to see. The date was for

Thursday of the previous week, with a time stamp of 3:15 P.M. The name Jules Dechard was printed in block letters that looked nothing like the meticulous handwriting on the Post-it he'd given her. She peered at the signature. An illegible scribble. Anyone could have scribbled it. Even Chloé.

"*Merci* for your help."

FIFTEEN MINUTES LATER she'd found Dechard's office dark, the door locked. Frustrated, she knocked on Michel Sarlat's open door.

"Professor Dechard's out today, *désolé*," he said, his voice attentive. "May I take a message?"

Had Dechard taken a turn for the worse? "*Alors*, he's ill?"

An evasive look behind the half smile on his round face. "What's this regarding, mademoiselle?"

None of your business, she almost said. Instead she smiled. "As you know, *la directrice* hired me to help with IT issues." True. "My job's to improve routing efficiency and avoid firewall breaches like what happened yesterday."

He'd participated in Email Security 101 and nodded his pink-tinged face.

"I'd appreciate knowing if he kept office hours last week." The sign announcing office hours on Dechard's door read TUESDAY AND THURSDAY, 2-5. If he had kept office hours last week, it would be impossible for him to have been the one to check out the theses at Bibliothèque Mazarine at three-fifteen.

"Did you check with our department secretary?"

Aimée smiled again. "I would, but she's gone for the afternoon."

"*Asseyez-vous*," he said, offering her a seat. "I'll check the department's agenda. I've got it right here."

Aimée's gaze kept getting pulled to his small feet. Today they were encased in soft leather loafers. She caught a wave of the lime scent of Eau de Sauvage as he reached, deftly for a man of such girth, toward an upper shelf.

She gave his desk a quick glance, took in two files, one labeled ANNUAL REPORT.

"*Voilà.*" A moment later he'd opened the leather-bound agenda. "Last week Jules attended an art symposium in Geneva. He returned Friday on the train and kept office hours that afternoon instead."

So he hadn't even been in Paris on Thursday. Someone other than Dechard had requested the theses and used his name. Who but the man across from her?

She debated. Should she probe him with questions, try surveilling him for more information—no, that didn't work with her current babysitting situation—or straight out accuse him?

"And you, monsieur? Where were you last Thursday at three P.M.?"

He smiled meeting her gaze. "Why, mademoiselle?"

"My job's being curious," she said, returning his smile. "I'm charting computer traffic."

"I was here in my office. Where else would I be?"

"Checking out Professor Dechard's thesis at Bibliothèque Mazarine?" She spoke fast to get him off balance.

"Why would I do that?" he said mildly, but something shifted behind his eyes. "I am already very familiar with Professor Dechard's work."

Now the gamble. "Maybe because you're threatening him?"

Sarlat blinked, rolled his swivel chair back. The wood floor creaked. "You know about the threats? *Alors*, I've been threatened, too. I'm scared. There's something going on, and Dechard refuses to tell me. If I'm implicated in it and he goes down, so do I."

That seemed like it might be true, since they worked so closely. And she'd seen the recent threats that had come in to Sarlat's email address. Yet she'd also seen those earlier, cryptic emails between Michel and the blackmailer. This smelled.

"Why blackmail him?" she asked.

"Me? Never."

"I know you've received messages from the same person who's blackmailing Dechard. I think you're involved."

"Involved?" He arranged and rearranged the papers on his desk. His hands shook. "I offered to help, but Dechard refused."

Was he protecting Dechard? Did he know about the plagiarism?

"Help him with what?"

"He's secretive. Look, I don't know. I'm afraid. It's cutthroat here. Academia's a minefield, and things have just gotten worse since I applied for the department chair position Dechard is vacating. I think someone is trying to sabotage my application. Ruin my career."

"Who?"

Michel shrugged uncomfortably, looked at his small leather shoes. "Who knows?"

You know! she wanted to shout. Why wouldn't any of these people tell her what was going on? How could she help them?

She needed to learn more about the other man who was attacked at Galerie Tournon. Did he have a connection to both these professors? She hoped he came out of the coma. Maybe then she'd get a straight answer.

"Look, mademoiselle, I have to finish this article."

Michel Sarlat nodded toward his office door. "Perhaps we can talk more some other time?"

A bad feeling dogged her all the way to Sybille's office.

SYBILLE LOOKED ESPECIALLY petite behind her huge desk in the whitewashed office. She was wearing a soignée cream linen shift and just the slightest kiss of blush.

Aimée took out her laptop. Opened the emails Saj had discovered. Sybille pulled down her polka dot frame reading glasses to scan what Aimée showed her.

"*Quelle horreur,*" Sybille said.

"What's he so afraid of?"

Sybille's lipsticked mouth turned down. She shut her office door. "Depends on whose opinion you listen to."

"Start with the thesis he wrote in 1984."

"I didn't know him then. He hadn't married my sister yet."

Aimée sensed Sybille knew more than she let on.

"Let's make it simple," said Aimée. "Why do you think your brother-in-law's being blackmailed? Plagiarism?"

"Does it matter why?"

"Don't you know the lawyer hired me to find out?"

"All I know is our school's being audited. We can't have a professor's name dragged through the mud right now."

The woman was giving Aimée nothing. Misdirecting.

"Secrets are the gifts that keep giving," said Aimée. "Why doesn't Dechard just expose the truth? Then the blackmailer will have nothing over him."

"It's complicated."

Aimée had had enough. "You're right. Too complicated for me."

She powered off her laptop, stuck it in her bag.

"*Non,* wait." Sybille ran to the door. "There's been

an internal audit here at the school. They discovered a shortfall. In our terms, that means missing pieces in the collection."

Things turned over in Aimée's head. "Do you mean you're afraid your terminally ill brother-in-law appropriated works of art . . . ?"

Sybille didn't reply.

Aimée let the silence hang as long as she could, running through possible scenarios. "Is this somehow related to Professor Dechard's graduate thesis, the one he plagiarized? Or is it some kind of cover-up?"

Sybille wiped her polka dot readers with the edge of her scarf. Nodded.

It still didn't make sense to Aimée. "Why does anyone care fifteen years later? When he's about to leave his job?"

Sybille's phone trilled.

"What's going on, Sybille? What artwork has gone missing?"

She raised her palm to Aimée and answered the phone. "*Oui?* They're what?" Sybille's face crumbled. "Tell them to wait." She scribbled on the back of a juried submission form.

A knock. Outside the glass door, Bette, the lapdog assistant, waved a paper.

"*Merde*, the auditor's here," Sybille said. "I've got to meet him right now."

Bette knocked again.

"Please, Aimée, talk to Jules." In a whiff of Guerlain, Sybille was gone.

What could Aimée do? She called the lawyer to ask for Dechard's mobile number. Voice mail.

Great. Stupid not to have asked Sybille.

She was wasting precious time and had too many things to do. She'd grab his number from Sybille's computer which she'd left on.

Aimée found Jules's contact information in Sybille's digital contact list. As she was tapping Jules's number into her phone, an email popped up with *TIME SENSITIVE: Michel Sarlat Application* in the subject line.

Not her business, but . . . she clicked it open. It was a plea from the board to push forward with prioritizing Michel Sarlat's application for the art history department chair position, which needed to be filled by the end of the year, even without Jules Dechard's recommendation. Aimée scrolled down and read the email from Sybille the board was responding to, in which the directrice had assured them the recommendation was coming but Jules Dechard was unwell and needed more time to complete it, if they could just be patient.

Aimée considered this. What was the relationship between Jules and his colleague? They had both been threatened by a blackmailer. Was Michel covering up his supervisor's plagiarism in hopes of securing the department chair? But if Michel was helping Jules protect his reputation, why hadn't Jules already completed his recommendation of his loyal professor? And why had he hired Aimée to find strange emails that led back to Michel?

And here Sybille was making promises on Jules's behalf. Was the directrice of École des Beaux-Arts going behind her brother-in-law's back?

This all stank to high heaven.

But a signed contract and a retainer meant Aimée would finish the job. She forwarded the email to Saj, then another thread about the audit and school's missing art works, then

looked at the time. Forget calling—Dechard's flat was minutes away off rue Visconti.

SPARROWS TWITTERED IN the lush green foliage
outside Dechard's flat. Footsteps. Aimée saw Michel Sarlat
cross the stone pavers, on his way out. She stepped behind
an overhang of lilac vines, watching Michel consult a card,
his phone to his ear.

Merde. What if he'd told Dechard about her visit? Her
questions and accusations?

When Michel was gone, she mounted the stairs and
knocked on the door. A grey-haired cleaning woman
answered, broom in hand. "Monsieur Dechard's not here."

"When did he leave?"

"The monsieur asked the same thing." She shrugged. "I
haven't seen him."

"But he was going to leave me a message," she lied. "It's
for our appointment."

"You? A message? I gave the envelope to that monsieur."

An envelope? She put it together now. Michel was handling the blackmail for Dechard.

"Where was the monsieur going?" Aimée asked. "Was
there an address on the envelope?"

The cleaning woman shrugged again, pinned a stray hair
up into her bun. Not only did she not care; she smelled like
cheap soap.

"Did he say anything else? Anything at all? Please,
help me."

The cleaner sighed. "I heard him on the phone when he
first arrived. He mentioned the Church of Saint-Germain-
des-Prés. But I told him the rue Jacob's a mess. So much
construction."

Aimée threw a *merci* over her shoulder as she ran down the stairs two at a time. If she could catch him en route, maybe she could figure out what was going on.

Ahead, on rue Bonaparte, she thought she caught sight of Michel's wide figure. Then she lost him in the crowd.

She skirted around the partial blockade on rue Jacob, ignored a catcall from a construction worker in green coveralls, and jogged past a stalled bus.

She looked right, then left. No Michel.

She dodged passersby on rue Bonaparte and caught sight of Michel's back ahead. Then it was gone again.

Reaching the corner at rue de l'Abbaye, she spotted him to the left, standing behind some tourists brandishing a Danish-French dictionary who were blocking the narrow pavement, taking pictures of the Saint-Germain-des-Prés church spires behind them, pointing to the stone arches, struts, and medieval bric-a-brac.

About to cross the street, she saw his brown sleeve flap as he vanished into a building opposite.

Perspiring, she buzzed open the door. Inside she saw one wall of the foyer composed of medieval architraves—an ancient nun's cloister according to the plaque on the wall. A growling Russian wolfhound was crouching in the foyer. The hairs on her arm rose.

"Down, Petrus. *Arrête*," said a highly made-up woman of a certain age, tugging his leash.

Aimée wondered what it cost to feed a dog as big as a pony. His hot drool splattered on her open-toed Valentino sandals. Miles Davis was ten times better mannered than this giant.

Aimée stepped carefully past the dog and the woman and crossed the foyer. The former cloister turned into a suite of apartments lining a cold, high-vaulted passageway. Near the turn, voices echoed—Michel's familiar nasal voice and the voice of a woman that Aimée didn't recognize.

Then a clicking of heels. They were coming toward her.

She ran back into the foyer. Where could she hide? She darted toward a staircase on her left and made herself small on the second step.

All she could see were silhouettes against the bright light streaming through the glass of the door: Michel's rotund frame and a woman in a flared skirt.

Then the door opened. Michel left.

The woman was buckling her bag. After a moment, she followed.

Aimée caught the double doors with her fingertips before they closed. Out on the street, her heart pounding, she waited a beat and followed them.

The woman's long brown hair sparkled in the sun. And then Aimée saw Michel was turning her way.

She ducked through a pair of open pale blue doors. Stepped into, of all places, the courtyard entrance to the *commissariat* of the quartier. Two *flics* were talking. There she was with an APB out for her arrest, walking into the jaws of the police.

Calm down. They were looking for a different one of her personas.

She kept her head down, waiting in the doorway until she thought Michel must have turned again. The old-fashioned *commissariat's* entrance was on a fashionable cobbled courtyard. She remembered coming here once with her father, but that was years ago. No one would remember her, her father's colleagues all long gone.

So far so good. At least she hoped so. From her

unobstructed vantage, she watched the young woman with the flared skirt enter the square directly across the narrow street. She sat down on the green slatted bench near Picasso's famous sculpture of Apollinaire. She took out the latest issue of *ELLE*, with Jane Birkin on the cover—still making magazine covers even at her age.

The woman sat and turned pages for a few minutes. Aimée shifted in her sandals, damp with dog drool. If she hadn't been watching like a hawk, she'd have missed it. The woman's hand slid under the bench by a hedge. Then abruptly she tossed the *ELLE* into her bag, stood, and checked her watch. Aimée heard the metal click as the woman left and closed the gate behind her.

A classic dead drop, like in an old spy movie.

Aimée's eyes swept the square: two disheveled men sharing a bottle of *vin rouge* in the shade, the Danish tourists taking photos of each other, Apollinaire playing ball with his father.

She debated: Should she wait to see who took the envelope? She was dying to retrieve it herself and learn the contents. Jules Dechard and Michel Sarlat had to be engaging with the blackmailer—but over what? Was this related to the audit shortfall, the missing art?

Better hold back, reason told her. The most useful thing she could do would be to identify whoever collected the envelope. Then she'd inform the attorney, let him put the pieces together, and be done with it.

Antsy and hot, she stood perspiring and waiting, wondering if she could just go sit in the square herself. The shade of the plane trees was tempting. She checked her phone.

No messages.

An older man brushed off the bench with a news-paper. Sat down. Laughter came from the toddler. The ball bounced into the hedge.

As the father reached down for the ball, the older man on the bench was speaking to him.

A ruse to disguise a handoff? She craned her neck for-ward, straining to see.

Her phone rang. Chloé's pediatrician's office. Of all times. She had to take it.

"*Oui?*" she whispered.

"We're confirming your daughter's vaccinations next week. Can you verify . . . ?"

Aimée watched as the boy's father sat down on the bench beside the old man, who was leaning toward him.

"Mademoiselle . . . ? Are you there?"

She tuned back into the phone call. "*Oui.*"

"Mademoiselle?"

"*Oui!*" she said more loudly, cringing.

"Spell your last name please."

"Leduc . . . *L-E-D* . . . That's right." She lowered her voice again. "*Oui*, next week then."

Hung up.

"Aimée Leduc? Is that you?"

She felt a tap on her shoulder. Loïc Bellan, the sergeant her father had mentored on the force. Who'd idolized Jean-Claude Leduc and then blamed him for falling from his pedestal. Bellan had investigated a case involving her once, but during the whole process, he'd been suspicious of her, bogged down by the history between him and her father.

Bellan had a few more years on him now, but he was trim in his suit. "You look so . . . different," he said. "Your hair . . . What's brought you out of the woodwork?"

Of all times to be recognized. And she was a wanted person.

"Surveillance, Bellan," she said in a low voice. "And you're in the way."

What else could she say, given her disguise?

She looked over his shoulder. The Danish tourists were consulting guidebooks now, blocking her view.

"Still trying to pay the bills as a PI, eh?"

She didn't need Bellan's attitude. Or a tirade about how she'd gotten a *commissaire* shot.

"Later." She stepped around him and, without another word, hurried across the street. No father and little boy. No old man on the bench.

She'd lost them. Her own fault for answering the phone in panicky-mom mode. Bad luck Bellan had heard her name and held her up.

Across the hot shining pavement, the number 95 bus pulled away on rue Bonaparte. She caught sight of the father in one of the windows. She looked around the square, spotted the old man, who had moved to a shadier bench. His eyes were closed.

Time to change plans.

She pulled out a scarf, tied it babushka style around her hair, and donned Jackie O glasses. She sat on the green slatted bench, pulled out her phone, and pretended to be in a serious conversation. Her other hand reached under the bench. Felt the hedge leaves. Her fingers caught on the rough wood. Then the sharp poke of a sliver—ouch. Had she imagined seeing the woman slip the envelope under here?

"Didn't know you were so old school, Aimée." Loïc Bellan sat down next to her. Grinned.

Annoying. His left hand met hers under the bench.

"*Alors*, Bellan, get lost."

"But I might have to arrest you if you're involved in illegal activities."

"*Moi?*" She tried to calm her nerves. "You've got it wrong. Arrest the blackmailer who will pick up whatever's hidden under this bench."

She felt his arm moving. Heard a rustle of leaves.

"You mean this?" He leaned forward, tucking the envelope into a fold of his jacket. *Merde!*

"Put that back. Quick."

"Only if you listen to me."

What in the world did he have to say to her? It had been years. "Listen to what?"

"Deal or not?"

Great. She was bargaining with a smart aleck who despised her and held a grudge against her father. Aimée nodded.

"The sun's boiling me alive," he said. "Let's sit in the shade over there."

They moved to a bench by Saint-Germain-des-Prés's old stone wall, by a trellis fragrant with roses.

"Tell me about the blackmail," said Bellan.

Stupid. She'd blurted that out in frustration—no way she'd tell him about Dechard's case, especially since *la Proc* already had her teeth in it.

"I thought you wanted me to listen."

Bellan put on Alain Mikli sunglasses. "I lied."

The *salaud*.

"Me, too." She stifled the impulse to get up and leave. "Get your kicks bothering someone else, Bellan." She glanced at her Tintin watch. *Merde.*

"Running late, as usual, *non?*"

When would the jerk leave? How could she get rid of him?

"I'm teaching a surveillance course. Right now you're interrupting my work with a student."

"That's weak." Emotion filled his voice. "I expect better from a girl with Jean-Claude for a father."

"I know I'm not your favorite person, but leave my father out of this."

Bellan's mouth tightened. "He's the whole problem." His loafer ground into the gravel. "*Non*, that's not the right way to say it. It's my problem with your father that's haunted me."

His words and the tone of his voice surprised her.

"There's something I should have told you."

Her gaze never left the empty bench where they'd been sitting. "Go on."

"Especially now . . . with what happened with Morbier . . . I wish I had told you sooner. It's just . . . when it happened, I had my mind on other things. I didn't see clearly back then."

He clammed up all of a sudden.

It came back now—sometime after her father had been framed for corruption and driven out of the force, Loïc Bellan's wife had given birth to a baby with Down syndrome. Exactly when escaped her but she remembered the rumors— that Bellan hadn't been able to deal with it, that his marriage had fallen apart and his wife had left him with the child.

"I remember when your baby boy was born," she said. "You went through a rough time. I understand."

"I lost it. Hit the wall."

"*Et alors?*"

"That's so like your father," said Bellan. "*Et alors, Loïc,* he'd say, *that and five francs buys you a* café crème. *Keep on moving to the better seats.* And that old chestnut, *If it smells . . .* You know."

Follow your nose.

Aimée's lower lip quivered. She fought down the emotion bubbling up. The two men on the far bench were done with the bottle of *vin rouge.*

"A few days before your father left for Berlin, he wanted to meet me," Bellan said.

Aimée's breath caught. Just before the weekend he was killed.

"Did you meet him?"

Bellan took a deep breath. "Stubborn and foolish, I refused. Thought myself on higher ground than my mentor who'd lied to me." He shook his head in sadness. "I was such a fool. He'd called even knowing I'd refuse. It must have been important."

"Any idea why?"

He shook his head again. "I regret how I judged him. Now I'll never hear what he wanted to say."

Pain lanced her. Wasn't that how she'd feel when Morbier passed? Was she throwing away her last chance to spare herself a lifetime of regret?

His phone rang. He answered. "*Oui.* Done."

He hung up.

Things slid into place for her.

"Call me a skeptic, but I haven't seen you for, what, a couple of years?" she said. "Now you pretend to run into me, follow me, and come out with a revelation that amounts to a handful of sand."

Bellan slid his phone back into his pocket. "What do you mean?"

"So it's a coincidence you have this regret about my father to share with me right now?" Her words were coming fast. "*Non,* this has Morbier's tentacles all over it as usual. You're in cahoots to get me to his deathbed. So he can absolve himself of his guilt."

Her words dried up as a woman sat down on the bench she was watching. Sunglasses, large bag—that hair was familiar.

"You're warped, Aimée. Paranoid," Bellan said.

"What?" she said, only half-listening. She wished she could see more of the woman's face.

"Of course this is a coincidence. My branch is DGI," he said. "The only reason I was here was to drop off a case file at the *commissariat* since my little boy's in a learning center nearby. He's writing his own name now. Marie gave me full custody."

The woman closed her bag, stood, and left. Aimée didn't need to see any more. Good God, she'd been so blind.

Bellan stood.

"Wait," she said. "What were you saying?"

"I never trusted Morbier like I trusted your father. So put that in your sick mind, and twist it how you want."

Gravel was sticking to her damp sandals. Despair filled her. Morbier would die with his secrets.

"Go ahead; be stubborn like I was," he said. He checked his phone. "Sounds to me like you're the one who can't face what Morbier will say."

"I got him shot."

"*Merde* happens, Aimée. Old dogs like him have a death wish. All you need to do is own up to your own demons."

Face Morbier's allegations of what her father might have done all those years ago? Someday have to tell Chloé the truth about her grandfather?

"Like you have owned up to yours?" she asked.

Bellan shrugged. "I try." He took off his sunglasses and wiped them with a tissue from his pocket. Pointed to a folder with an École des Beaux-Arts label sticking out of her bag. "I heard *la Proc*'s steamed up about a case involving blackmail at École des Beaux-Arts. If you've stuck your nose in that, consider this a warning."

And with that, he strode out the square's gate. Smart. Dangerous.

Stupid, *non*, careless to let that show. She wanted to kick herself. But had he taken a guess? She wouldn't put it past him to report her to *la Proc*.

Dark thoughts circled in her mind for she didn't know how long. Heat waves rose off the roofs of cars. She sat, perspiration dampening the small of her back. Noises, people, smells, faded in the scorching sun.

Compartmentalize. Worry about Morbier and her father later. Put what she needed to do up front. Her thoughts settled. Dreading it, she pulled out her phone. Raised voices came from the street; she put a finger to her other ear so she could hear and made some calls.

Done, she retraced her steps past the *commissariat* on rue de l'Abbaye. One of the Danish tourists, a thin, straw-blonde woman with a Birkin bag Aimée lusted for, clutched her arm. The Dane pulled her into the *commissariat*'s doorway.

"Please, my camera was stolen, and the idiots don't understand. You were there." The Dane's fair-complected face was mottled pink in the heat, her brow creased with anger.

"Stolen? I'm sorry. I didn't see anything." No way Aimée wanted to get involved.

"But it was those winos—you saw them. Your police, they won't take me seriously."

And then the Danish contingent surrounded her, moving her forward into the chill of the courtyard's entrance to the *commissariat*.

"This wouldn't happen in Copenhagen," the Danish woman said, stumbling over the French. "My camera snatched in front of a police station? Please help me."

She saw a middle-aged *flic* beckoning her into the *commissariat*'s foyer. As if she had anything to do with this. But if she bolted, that would draw unwanted attention.

"This woman insists you witnessed her camera being stolen," said the *flic* by the glassed reception.

"Afraid not," said Aimée.

Aimée felt the Dane's frustration. "But you were in the square. I saw you," she was saying in badly accented French. "It's those two winos who robbed me."

Aimée had been so wrapped up with watching for the blackmailer, she hadn't noticed.

She didn't want to get involved. But she reasoned she'd be less conspicuous to the *flics* if she helped the irate Dane, ingratiated herself.

"You mean those two men drinking wine under the tree?" Aimée asked.

The Danes were directed to a cubicle to make a statement, file a police report. Everyone knew you reported a theft to the *gendarmerie* if you wanted action—never the local *flics*.

"Tourists!" said the *flic* to Aimée. "Always complaining."

"*Alors*, the woman got robbed," she said. Was he even going to do anything about it?

"Very little crime here." His voice was sleepy. "I've

been in this station fifteen years. Quietest post I've ever worked."

Disgusting, his dismissive attitude. She hated these rotten apples. There were always one or two in a *commissariat* in a cushy quartier.

Her eyes caught on the wanted posters behind him. Good God, a fuzzy police sketch of her in a wig, glasses. Those glasses were in her bag right now—she needed to ditch this place ASAP.

She turned to leave.

"Hold on, mademoiselle. The tourist might need you to sign as a witness."

Witness? She itched to get out of there. Yet the *flic* hadn't recognized her. Should she chance it, play innocent, and see if she could learn anything?

"What, no murder or suspicious deaths in your fiefdom?" she asked.

"*Alors*, Pascal!" A sergeant popped his head up from his desk. "Tell her about the spoiled drunk kids partying in Lycée Montaigne's garden." He winked. "Or the couple with the orgy in their rooftop penthouse swimming pool. And all the old people getting themselves duped and robbed every day."

"Old people getting conned, *oui*, but that's everywhere," Pascal said.

She heard the Danes' voices rising in singsong English. The pecking of a typewriter. The *commissariat* didn't even have a computer.

"Then there's the usual punch-up in *quartier de soif*," Pascal said.

Quartier de Soif—the quadrangle of bars and pubs by Marché Saint-Germain.

"I responded to a knifing there last week." A wide grin erupted on Pascal's pudgy face. He liked to talk.

"We had a crime of passion a few weeks ago, if you'd call it that—a concierge was strangled by her son. Serbians. They're all unhinged," he said dismissively.

Something clicked in her mind. Serbian concierges would be a subject to explore.

"That Serb threw himself under the Métro," the sergeant added.

"There was that *mec* pushed from his window near *le Sénat*," said Pascal.

Prickles went up her spine. "I read about that," she said. "Any leads?"

"Around *le Sénat* it's another world. Not our jurisdiction."

That sounded ominous. "What do you mean?"

"The big boys." His voice carried resignation.

Her mind went back to Bellan saying he worked in DGI. Counterterrorism.

State security and foreign relations fell under the jurisdiction of the Ministry of the Interior. Bellan had worn a suit, not a uniform. This smelled.

Friday Afternoon

SHE WAS UP to something, that Aimée Leduc. But when wasn't she? thought Loïc Bellan. He'd followed *l'affair de Champ de Mars* in the papers—she'd ticked off every level of the government. *Bien sûr*, they'd whitewashed it, but everyone knew the truth. He secretly applauded her for having the guts to topple the rotten bunch. Even Morbier. She'd been trained by the best, her own father with his wild style.

Une gamine—the longish pixie haircut, those cheekbones that could cut paper, those huge eyes. So expressive—she spoke with her eyes. When she listened to you, she fixed them on you—it was riveting, felt like the whole world was focused on you. She was the type you felt an urge to take care of, and then the next moment you wanted to chain her high heels to cement.

She'd been a little softened by motherhood, maybe. It had cost her. He saw it, plain as day—more nervous, more worried than she'd seemed before. He'd learned to read people in his job.

"Guilluame had a good day," said the *école maternelle* teacher at the school gate on rue de Jardinet. "He wants to tell you something, right, Guillaume?"

His six-year-old son lifted his backpack. "I spilled my juice. It's sticky all over." His lip trembled. There were tears in his close-set blue eyes. "Teacher said I wasn't careful."

Loïc knelt down, stole a glance at the teacher for a cue. He didn't know whether to scold his Down syndrome son or take him in his arms. He interrogated terrorists, sweet-talked *la Proc*—but right now words evaporated.

He tried remembering the parenting class techniques—parenting a Down syndrome child required patience. You had to remember how intelligent they were, how vivid their memories could be, and try to react to challenges in a forward-looking way. What lesson was Loïc supposed to teach now?

In the end, he came up with only a stock phrase. "Accidents happen, Guillaume."

Couldn't he do better than that?

"But, Guillaume, we talked about how to put your pack under your desk so juice doesn't spill," said the teacher, resting a hand on Guillaume's shoulder. "That's our plan for next time."

Guillaume brushed his eyes. Smiled, his head bobbing. "We always come up with a plan. Figure out how to do better next time."

"That's right, Guilluame." She grinned. "We learn something new every day. You're so good at that."

The next minute Guillaume was hugging his teacher and then Loïc.

"You're not mad, Papa?"

This small ball of love was his boy.

Loïc hugged him back. Tight.

He held Guilluame's hand as they walked into the Cour de Rohan. A private *passage*, but Loïc, like most *flics*, had a master postman's key.

Guillaume loved climbing on the three-legged metal *pas-de-mule*, the medieval mount.

"Remember who used that, Guilluame?" A memory game they always played.

"Nuns and fat priests to get on their ponies." Guillaume, like any six-year-old boy would, gave a whoop and jumped onto the cobbles. He grinned and pointed. "That's the pretty house where the king's girlfriend, Diane, lived."

Diane de Poitiers, Henri II's favorite mistress and rival of Catherine de Medici.

"You remembered. Good job, Guillaume." Amazed that Guillaume retained the factoid, he swelled with pride.

They passed through three small leafy green courtyards to reach Cour du Commerce St-André's uneven cobbled passageway.

Guilluame tugged Loïc's sleeve. "Papa, I remember more."

"*Bien sûr*, you're a smart boy." Loïc squeezed his son's hand.

"I remember we always get a *marroon glacé* right after we pass the place where the doctor made the guillotine."

"That's good, Guillaume. Remember anything else?"

"And Grand-mère gets her pedicure just by the oldest café in the world. There."

His mother had her bunions treated near la Procope. "You've earned a special treat with that good memory of yours."

Headlines on *le Figaro* at the newsagent on rue du Buci proclaimed *New Conflicts in the Balkans—Where Are the Teeth in the Dayton Accord?*

His phone vibrated. His boss. *Merde.* He'd have to get back to work.

Friday Afternoon

IN THE LEDUC Detective office, René rocked Chloé
back and forth in her swing crib as Radio Classique played
Brahms. A steaming cup of green tea sat on René's desk.

Aimée blinked in surprise. "But Zazie was supposed to be
watching Chloé."

"Shh. I just got her to sleep."

She wanted an explanation. She knew she was distracted
these days, but . . .

"What are you doing here, René?" she said, whispering.
"Don't you have the Hackaviste seminar?"

"My friend's covering for me for a few hours," he said.
"You need me here."

He was right about that. Gestured her toward his desk.

"I can't find anything on Mirko Vladić postdating the
explosion in Foča—if he had survived, there would be some
evidence. But he has no family, no traceable acquaintances
. . ." René shrugged. "No DNA confirmation he's dead,
either. Basically no leads in any direction. *Rien.* I've spent
two hours looking. *Alors*, Aimée, you've done what you can.
The *flics* are looking for you."

"A woman who doesn't really look like me," she said.

"Stay away from it. Meanwhile, what is this about? It
looks bad."

She craned her neck over his shoulder. It was the email
she'd forwarded Saj from Sybille's inbox.

"It is bad," Aimée said. "That's our employer at École

des Beaux-Arts. And she's the one blackmailing Jules Dechard."

"You're kidding." He scrolled through the emails. Sucked in his breath. "How does that make sense?"

She shook her head. "It doesn't. But not an hour ago I saw Sybille's assistant, Bette, pick up Dechard's envelope from his colleague's dead drop. Couldn't believe it."

"You're sure? How did this simple IT job go off track like this?"

"Good question. But now we're working for Dechard's lawyer, and we owe him what information we can get to help him get Dechard out of trouble."

"Who's the lawyer really working for, Aimée? And why did Sybille hire you if your investigation would only lead you back to her?"

More good questions. She bit her lip. "Dechard's a victim, René. We have to hurry and figure this out."

René had pulled up Sybille's whole email thread.

"I'd say, based on their ignorance of computers, Sybille doubted we'd delve into her account. But"—his fingers paused on the keyboard—"I don't think this is about blackmail."

"Eh, what do you mean?" she said. Aimée stepped over and straightened Chloé's blanket. Rewound the mobile. "I know he's terrified, René. Now there are allegations of him helping himself to the collection." How did it all fit together? "What if Sybille worked with the blackmailer at the gallery? Did she attack them both? Then why did she involve me, René?"

He pointed to his screen. "Haven't you twigged yet, Aimée?"

"Pray tell, Sherlock."

He pointed to the email thread. "See this 'DAV' alluded to in several emails? This one email mentions a 'da Vinci drawing.' Maybe every 'DAV' reference is the da Vinci drawing—one of the drawings missing from the collection," said René. "The École des Beaux-Arts' collection holds a treasure trove. So much was donated to them in the last century. They could easily have priceless da Vinci drawings."

"Go on."

"Precise thinking overcomes every obstacle, as da Vinci said." René lowered the volume on the radio.

He amazed her. "So you're some kind of da Vinci expert, too?"

He grinned. Shook his head. "*Moi*? Did you forget I grew up in Amboise, where da Vinci died?" He pointed to his screen. "But getting back to Sybille's email thread . . ."

"Sybille's so scared, she's scattered," she said. "She was in a hurry, rushing off to an audit meeting. That's why she forgot to mask this one."

"I'll get to it later, *desolé*, I'm late for the seminar at the Hackaviste." René slid his laptop into his bag and hit the pump to lower his ergonomic chair. He grabbed his tailored Burberry trench coat. Chloé had woken up, and he blew her a kiss. "Blow big bubbles at *bébé* swim, Chloé. You're such a natural in water."

"Spoken like a proud godparent," said Aimée.

René grinned. "Zazie's waiting."

IN BHV, THE rue du Rivoli department store, Aimée paused in the swimwear section. Chloé, in the *poussette*, gummed a teething biscuit.

"You're buying me a *maillot de bain*?" Zazie's mouth was an

O of amazement. Aimée noticed she wore a touch of rose lip gloss, more than a hint of mascara.

"If you're quick about it, Zazie. How else can you get in the pool for *bébé* swim?" At fourteen years old, Zadie had filled out. "No bikini. Your mother would shoot me."

Zazie fell in love with a low-cut turquoise two-piece. They settled on a black Speedo with red racing stripes. Aimée visualized facing this with Chloé someday.

In the dressing room, Aimée checked out her disguises. Chloé squealed at her reflection in the mirror.

"Going on surveillance, again?" Awe filled Zazie's voice. She admired Aimée, insisted she wanted to follow in her footsteps and become a detective.

"You know the drill, Zazie."

Feeling important, Zazie squared her shoulders. "No answering the landline, call you every hour, walk Miles Davis, and keep Chloé hydrated."

THIRTY MINUTES LATER Aimée left Zazie and Chloé at the Saint-Germain-des-Prés pool. The chlorinated aquamarine water made her feel guilty thinking about how she wasn't taking Chloé to swim in the turquoise Mediterranean at Martine's boyfriend's Sicilian villa.

She caught a wink from the male lifeguard—had his Speedo shrunk, or was she imagining it? She didn't have time for that type of fun, sadly. She reached into her bag and pulled out her phone.

Her call to Sybille went to voice mail. Dechard's message box was full. Michel Sarlat's line connected to reception.

Frustrated at whatever game they were playing— why had they had to involve her and get *la Proc* on her heels?—Aimée wasn't paying attention to where she was going. Her foot slid, and her low-heeled Valentino sandal strap tore. Great. She wobbled to the nearest metal bollard, leaned down on the hot, uneven cobbles. Water sluiced in the gutters, swirling with cigarette butts and leaves. She caught the tang of piss and old beer from the corner bar's wall.

She slipped into her spare shoes, metallic ballet flats. Ten minutes' walking brought her to the École des Beaux-Arts locker room. She changed into a jumpsuit, taped a generic construction company logo from her collection on the lapel, donned a navy-blue cap, and tucked her hair under it. Thank God the school was mostly empty that day—only a few bricklayers repairing the far courtyard.

First on her agenda—checking out whether a blue *camionnette* was in the school's vehicle pool. She headed past the courtyard and turned in to another strewn with chunks of Gothic pillars. A graffitied portion of crumbling wall abutted a garage in what appeared to be an old warehouse.

"Mademoiselle?"

A ponytailed young mechanic in grease-stained overalls appeared in front of her. He was holding a small paper cup of espresso, and a cigarette dangled from the side of his mouth. What she wouldn't have given for both those right then.

"*Alors*, the van piston's out of whack," he said. "Tell your boss it's going to take some time."

He had taken her for someone else. Play along.

"And you're right on it, eh?" She grinned, heavy on the flirting. His deep-set brown eyes locked on hers. He filled out the overalls nicely. "*Bon*, he's fine with taking the blue *camionette* instead."

"Which one?"

She wished she didn't want to grab his cigarette.

"That one, you know, the blue one he used yesterday afternoon. He can fit everything in it."

"People sign out vehicles all the time. How am I supposed to remember?"

"Let's check the log."

Ten minutes later, after enjoying a fresh-brewed espresso and a cigarette, she left with a name and a description; in exchange, she'd left him a false phone number.

USING THE NOTES she'd made during her orientation the previous month, she reviewed the school's electrical layout, the locations of the telephone lines and the computer network wires and the cable installations. All the centralized upgrades to the power system made it easy to troubleshoot, according to the building manager.

Time to follow her nose to what stank.

The École des Beaux-Arts had been erected on the site of the seventeenth-century Couvent des Petits-Augustins. The convent's remnants were the small cloister and the church with a supposedly gorgeous hexagonal chapel that exhibited the school's rare art collections and was open by appointment. Which meant twice a year, if that, she'd heard.

The chapel's underground vaults contained the control room for the revamped computer cable network. The building manager had given her the access code, since she'd need it for her job, and had told her where to find the ring of old-fashioned keys in case of a power outage. No one would think it was strange for her to be down there.

The vaulted, pockmarked stone passages were damp and cool. She punched in the code, entered, and bypassed the control room, took the ring of old keys from where they hung. They were as big as her hand and as heavy as lead. Archaic—original.

Further on and to the right, she tried a key in a small wormholed door, which yielded. Behind it, she expected to find the rare art collection within a climate-controlled area like the one at Bibliothèque Mazarine. Instead the door revealed a medieval warren, cold and musty like a crypt. She sneezed.

How could they keep masterpieces down here, protected only by a fire extinguisher, regulation hatchet, and emergency kit at the entrance?

After the Revolution, religious sites were ransacked, and even the Saint-Germain-des-Prés church had been turned into an artillery depot. But more than two hundred years later, wouldn't the school have gotten its act together for the priceless works of art in its collection?

The tunnel she was walking down forked. She followed the passage lit by a string of bare bulbs to a series of moisture-proof metal trailers taking up a huge cavern-like space supported by Gothic arches. Each trailer was marked with a label: PAINTINGS, SCULPTURES, DRAWINGS, MANUSCRIPTS. Locked. But the locks were no problem to pick with the set in her manicure case.

Minimal security, she thought, after you knew the code.

In the portable with the drawings, a temperature-control system hummed. Museum-quality storage racks. Old, yellowed, handwritten tabs divided the folders by century, in a few cases by artists' names. The smell of ancient paper was strong.

The hair rose on the back of her neck in the tepid air as she read the names: Tiepolo, Michelangelo, Leonardo. Name after name she recognized and plenty she didn't.

She'd only seen their work in the Louvre, never this close up. Not touchable.

She donned the white cotton gloves someone had left sitting by some paperwork. Started pulling out the shallow metal racks. Her eyes bulged. Drawing after drawing, arching forms and vibrant colors—it was staggering. Here and there a slip of paper contained a catalog number and said, *On loan to the Louvre* or *On loan to Musée d'Orsay*.

She carefully opened the Leonardo folder, expecting drawings by the master. But it was empty.

"Take your hands off that. Now!"

Aimée spun around to see Jules Dechard advancing with the hatchet.

Friday Afternoon

MELAC SAT ON the stone wall along the quai d'Anjou across from Aimée's apartment, a cup of blood orange Berthillon sorbet in one hand, his phone in the other. Her phone went to voice mail. Again. He'd tried the office, too.

A red-haired girl emerged from Aimée's building, pushing a stroller. He recognized her—Zazie from the café. Those were Chloé's bare feet bobbing from the *poussette*.

He fumed. Aimée had hired a teenager to babysit his daughter, hadn't thought to ask him? He crumpled the paper cup, snapped the plastic spoon, and tossed them in the bin.

His blood roiled for a moment until doubt crept in. Did she suspect something?

He yearned to explain how much he wanted to be a part of their life. How much he wanted to protect Aimée—protect them—from all the dangers the Leducs had brushed up against over the years: the thugs with grudges because Aimée or her father had helped put them away; Aimée's mother's terrorist reputation; the long reach of the Hand. Now that Morbier couldn't protect Aimée anymore, it was Melac's job.

The noise of a shaking rattle came from the *poussette* across the way; Zazie's red hair gleamed in the sun. His phone vibrated in his hand. He answered without looking.

"Aimée?"

Pause. "I thought you were a pro. Why aren't you there?" The woman's voice vibrated with fear. "Find her."

Friday Afternoon

PANICKED, AIMÉE DROPPED the folder. Heard it smack on the table. She moved to the left behind the long table, ducking around the humming wall unit. "Calm down, Dechard. It's me, Aimée."

Fury creased his mouth. The hatchet's blade caught the light. "What in the hell . . . You? Why?"

Had she caught him out? "Put down the hatchet, and I'll tell you."

"You're in collusion with them, Aimée?"

She noticed a chemical smell. A crazed look danced in his dilated pupils—was he doped up? Ready to attack her as he'd attacked the man he'd put in a coma.

"Who?" She wouldn't wait to find out. Keep him talking; get that hatchet out of his hands. "I hate kicking an ill man." She'd pulled her cell phone from her pocket. Prayed there was reception down here. Doubted it. "But I will if I have to."

"I did everything I was asked—"

"Everything Sybille wanted?" she interrupted.

"What?"

"She's playing you. So's Michel. I saw him drop off the envelope you'd left, and it was Sybille's assistant who picked it up."

His shoulders twitched. A convulsive shaking in his arms caused him to drop the hatchet. Aimée winced as it banged to the floor.

"My pills . . ." His trembling hand reached in his jacket. "I need . . . medication . . ." A foil packet tumbled on the table. His breath rasped, ragged and choking.

Mon Dieu. The man struggled to breathe. She grabbed her bottle of Badoit. Empty.

Saliva flecked with blood dribbled down his chin. She punched in 15 for SAMU, the Urgent Medical Aid Service, on her phone, but there was no reception. The man looked like death. Somehow she had to get him upstairs, reach an area with reception. "Take my arm."

Too weak to resist, he swallowed his pills dry.

From the tunnel she grabbed a metal work cart, got the shaking Dechard on it. Ran back for her bag. Then pushed the heavy cart, the wheels spitting stones, over the earthen floor toward the door.

Still no reception.

"Lock up the collection, for God's . . ." His words trailed off.

Later. First she had to get help.

The steep ramp to the door took all her strength. Dechard slumped, groaning. By the time she'd pushed the cart into the main room of the old chapel, she'd gotten reception again. She called emergency and gave them their location.

"There's not much time," she said, looking around.

He gasped, taking shallow breaths.

"Tell me. What does Sybille have to do with the blackmail?"

"Stop. You're lying . . ."

She rolled up his shirt cuff. Took his pulse. Thin but steady. "What should have been in the Leonardo folder in the archives?"

"Not your business."

"The Leonardo drawings are missing. The *flics* will love to make that their business."

"Leave it alone."

"Bit late for that. Hear the siren?"

Panic flooded his face.

"You need my help, Dechard."

He gripped her arm, pulled her toward him. Kept his voice low.

"Last week I discovered there were Leonardo drawings missing," he said, pausing for breath. "Then the emails came."

Then it made sense. "You knew Sybille used her position to hide the theft . . ."

"Sybille's not that stupid."

"Why should you cover it up if neither of you were involved?"

There was real fear in his eyes. "Just leave it alone."

But she couldn't. "The thief raised the stakes, counting on you to swap your past for a missing Leonardo. That it? Anything to keep the chair you wanted to endow intact?"

That was it. She saw it in his face, craggy under the fluorescent lights and caved in with illness and despair.

"So what happened, Dechard?"

He shook his head.

"A man's in the hospital; priceless art is missing. You better talk, or I'll go right to *la Proc*."

"The one who likes you so much?"

He'd noticed. Difficult not to.

"She's hard but fair. That's her job, Dechard."

"I knew the school would suffer . . ."

How blind could the man be? "Your sister-in-law used you. If I can bypass security, so can she as *la directrice*. Where are the drawings now?"

"Gone. Sold. I don't know."

She'd been afraid of that. She forced herself to think about damage control. "All the more reason to talk to the board, explain and give your statement. Scandal gets old after two days. The newspapers will move on, hunting for new fodder. Just get it over and done with."

His gaze wavered.

"Unless you want to keep covering up for Sybille," she said. "Or is it more? Something else?"

Dechard never answered. The *pompiers*, first responders, in their fluorescent green vests had appeared with a defibrillator, oxygen.

"Shortness of breath, pain, any of those symptoms?"

"He takes these pills." Aimée handed over the packet. "Suffers a chronic illness."

A year of premed gave her little expertise, but between the anti-nausea medication and the chemical smell of his sweat, she guessed he was undergoing chemo.

Dechard left on a stretcher. What would she do now? Denouncing an employer for robbery would lose her their contract. René would shoot her.

DECHARD HADN'T TOLD her the whole story. Sybille was keeping secrets, and Michel was playing errand boy. What were they all hiding?

Think.

Her vibrating phone stole her attention. *Merde*, had she missed Zazie's call when she hadn't had reception?

No, it was Saj, mired outside Paris because of a train strike.

She'd figure Dechard's mess out later. Right now she needed to cover Saj's client meeting. Couldn't let her business go down the drain.

"I'm en route," she told him. "Call when you're near."

Jumping in a taxi on the quai, she called Zazie, feeling guilty she'd been out of phone range.

"Tout va bien," said Zazie. Chloé had loved the pool.

Except Zazie had to take her sniffling toddler brother to a pediatric appointment. She'd promised her mother. Chloé would have to come along.

Tant pis. Kids picked up more illnesses in the doctor's waiting room than at home. After that slight fever, Aimée didn't want to risk Chloé coming down with something right now.

She hesitated. Melac had had it under control the day before, hadn't he?

AIMÉE ESCORTED SAJ'S contact, now a Leduc Detective client, out of the office. Sigrid, a thirtyish white-blonde Swedish videographer, had been eager to sign the contract for a ground-up security overhaul of the firm she'd taken over. Ready to sign on the dotted line and pay an up-front retainer. How often did that happen?

Saj rang on the office line thirty minutes later, concerned that the deal had fallen through because he'd missed the meeting. Meanwhile, Aimée had downed an espresso and was running surveillance on the accounts of all Leduc's clients.

"Bravo, Saj. She's in. We'll take her check to the bank." Then she added, since he'd brought in the client, "It's your *bébé*, so you'll set everything up when you make it in." Call waiting clicked. "Later, Saj." She switched calls. It was René, returning the voice mail she'd left him in the taxi.

He sounded breathless. "Damn traffic. A cell phone tower must be down, I've hit so many dead zones. What happened with Dechard?"

She updated him.

"The man needs your help, *non?*" said René. "Time he clued you in."

She agreed. "But I just don't get it," she said. "He's supposed to retire after this year. The man looks like he's on his deathbed."

Creamy afternoon light spangled the chandelier, shooting rainbows onto the white marble fireplace. Aimée rubbed her eyes. Her shoulders ached from pushing Dechard on the steel cart.

"He's almost out to pasture," René said. "Pin a robbery or three on him, blackmail him with plagiarism accusations . . ."

She was tired. She'd gone through all this in her head. "But what does he hold that no one else does?"

"Money, prestige . . ." said René. "He's head of an art history department."

"Wait *une petite seconde.*" She ran over and searched on Saj's terminal, which was still in administrative mode on the school's system network. Scrolled through Sybille's email correspondence with the school's board and trustees. Saw Jules Dechard's resignation.

"He's resigned, René."

"Then I don't get it."

And it stared her in the face.

"He's head of the art history department. That's it. The important thing Jules Dechard provides is the crowning of his successor," she said, printing the email, then hitting FORWARD. She typed in the lawyer's email address and hit SEND. "His recommendation makes his chosen successor a shoo-in for the position, which comes with lifetime tenure."

She scanned Sybille's email for any other clues. There

was a reminder about the board and trustee meeting—it would be starting in twenty minutes. Aimée grabbed her bag, paused at the door. Reminded herself to check: keys, wig, flats, scarf, printouts—all accounted for. With a quick goodbye to René, she flew out the door.

SHE CROSSED BY the statue of Voltaire in the small Square Honoré-Champion, ran into rue Bonaparte, through the school's courtyard, into the old cloisters. She took two steps at a time up to Sybille's office.

"But *la directrice* is meeting with the trustees." The assistant arranged a bowl of hyacinths at the window.

Too late.

"Where's that?" Aimée asked, catching her breath.

"She can't be disturbed."

"It's an emergency."

"Strict procedure. Madame won't allow anyone into the closed session."

Aimée looked past the bowl of hyacinths to the windows across the courtyard. Several grey-haired heads were visible.

The next moment she'd run out into the corridor, rounding the courtyard on her way to the other wing. Another staircase. She felt the pain in her legs as she ran. Her calves seized up.

So out of shape.

Keep breathing. Don't stop.

She pushed one of the tall double doors open. An anteroom.

She kept running. Reached for the handle at the next pair of double doors.

"Mademoiselle, there's a meeting in progress." The

assistant had caught up with her, panting. "You can't go in there."

"Watch me."

At a large, heavy wood table sat six or so men, one holding a gavel, and Sybille, openmouthed in amazement and irritation.

"What's the meaning of this?" Murmurs, the scraping of chairs. "Only board members, trustees, and staff are allowed in the proceedings," said one of the men.

"Then I'm just in time."

Sunlight haloed the grey-haired members of the board in the dark wood-paneled room, reminding Aimée of a Renaissance painting. Her phone trilled. The attorney.

"Good timing, *Maître*," she said. "I'll put you on speakerphone. You've read the emails I've forwarded regarding the candidate put forth for Monsieur Dechard's position."

"Who's listening, Mademoiselle?"

Of course a lawyer would ask that.

"The people who matter." She hit the speakerphone button. "We're in a closed assembly. So can you summarize what you've read in the emails?"

"Where's my client?" The lawyer's voice was tinny, so she upped the volume.

"I rushed Professor Dechard to the hospital." A little stretching of the truth. "He collapsed after discovering— well, I'll let you tell us what I discovered."

Sybille stood up angrily. "I motion we adjourn," she said, turning to the others. "Proceed with voting on the candidate at a later time."

Aimée turned to the candidate. Michel Sarlat, Dechard's colleague and blackmail envoy. He squirmed under her glare, his cheeks flushed. "You've no right bursting in here and—"

"Calling you out on your deception?" said Aimée. "You're blackmailing your colleague Professor Dechard, a cancer patient undergoing chemotherapy treatment, to get him to recommend you for his position." She slapped the printed emails on the table. "Threatening his Légion d'honneur, a sick man's legacy for his life's work." She raised the phone. "But don't take my word for it. It's all printed out, and *le maître* will corroborate, won't you?"

Sybille's hands waved as if she were trying to bat Aimée away like a gnat. "Pwah. Don't listen to her."

"That's ridiculous." Michel's eyes bulged. "She must have faked the documentation."

"And the da Vinci drawings?" said Aimée. "Would you like to explain whom you sold them to with Sybille's assistance? Knocking out your partner at the gallery because he got greedy?"

"I think you're making up stories," Michel said.

Guessing at the truth, more like it.

"I didn't make up how you checked out a blue *camionette* and drove to the Galerie Tournon the day Jules Dechard and the gallery owner were attacked. Your signature's in the vehicle log. A witness identified you."

Again she was stretching the truth, but Michel's jaw dropped. His eyes, with their pale lashes, blinked in fear. He looked like a cornered rat—a well-fed one.

"You counted on Dechard's misplaced loyalty to his sister-in-law and to the school after he discovered the da Vinci's missing," she said. "You had your partner send him threatening emails, holding the ancient plagiarism over him if he revealed the theft. But you underestimated him—he was too upset by the idea of the artworks being stolen to let it go. He hired me to figure out who else had been in contact with his blackmailer, and I led him back to you." She was guessing, guessing—but Michel Sarlat's face was red with silent shock. "Now Jules Dechard would never give you the recommendation you needed to take over the department chair position, which you so desperately wanted. You had lost his trust. He would have ruined your career prospects as his last act before retiring. The poor man, he was trying to prevent you from being promoted, but he didn't want to make things difficult for his sister-in-law, Sybille." Aimée turned her glare on the directrice. "He tried to protect the school's reputation because you'd convinced him the old plagiarism business mattered now. The poor man had no idea you were going behind his back to take advantage of him and help his enemy."

"Who are you, mademoiselle? What right do you have coming in here making allegations, accusing people?" A dignified white-haired man with a South of France tan shoved the printed-out emails to the floor, scattering dust motes. "As chairman of this board—"

"I'm the school's IT system consultant. You, Chairman Bruly, in effect, hired me," she said. "Emails never go away. People think they can delete them. Especially you." She bent down, picked up the papers, and pointed. "Here, Chairman Bruly. Right here, an email from you states that 'the da Vinci drawings are copies. Good ones but nineteenth-century fakes.' Which the board knows, since they all received your email. Only Professor Dechard didn't know."

Bruly shook his head, disheveling his well-coiffed curls. Brushed imaginary lint from his navy blazer. "This is an institution for which you no longer work," he said. "The board handles staff affairs and hiring decisions. None of that is in the public purview or any of your business."

"However, blackmail, coercion, robbery, and criminal assault are crimes," she said, holding her phone aloft, "and prosecutable to the fullest extent of the law. I doubt Professor Dechard's lawyer will fail to bring charges against you."

The door opened, revealing the middle-aged security guard she'd snuck the odd cigarillo with at the rear courtyard.

"Escort this intruder out," Chairman Brûly said.

The guard studied his black shoes.

"Now."

OUT ON THE landing, the guard smiled at her.

"Got them on the warpath. Quite a feat," he said.

She wondered what the guard knew about this tightly closed, crème de la crème world—like a big backstabbing family. He'd know the backstairs version of why Michel Sarlat was the top candidate for Dechard's position, despite everything unsavory and illegal that he'd done.

"More intrigue than at Versailles," she said. "Blackmail, stolen da Vincis—but you'd have heard all that gossip, *non?*"

"Not if I want to keep my job." He went all business, escorting her to the ground floor and insisting on watching her empty her desk and her locker.

She tried again as he was letting her out of the gate. "*Alors*, I'm sure you've heard things."

Nodded. "*C'est ça*, you've stuck your nose where it shouldn't go."

"Professor Dechard's devoted his life to the school," she said. "Now he gets shafted? Disgraced?"

"Dogs bite if you pull their tails."

She shook her head. "They won't get away with it. Not this time." She'd talk to *la Proc* herself. "I still don't get how Sarlat could be considered for department chair. How can that be possible? No one even likes him or wants to work with him."

The guard sucked in his breath. "You didn't hear this from me." He looked around. Lowered his voice. "Sarlat walked in on a three way: *la directrice*; her assistant, Bette; and Bruly, the board chair, in flagrante delicto on the back terrasse."

Aimée visualized the peaceful terrasse, dripping with ivy, as a setting for that threesome. Cringed. Not a pleasant image.

"So promoting Michel is the price of keeping that quiet, eh?" she said.

He'd taken out a cigarillo. Lit it and puffed. Returned the tin to his pocket without offering her one. "Anyone ever told you it's tough being your own worst enemy, mademoiselle?"

SHE KICKED A pebble in the courtyard. Tried to figure out how this could square things for her with Madame *la Proc*. Found a quiet place to make a phone call, then left her a message.

She started walking, feeling a hollowness inside. René would complain that she'd rushed in and alienated the prestigious institution before they'd paid up, as she now remembered they hadn't.

She imagined Martine's reaction—it had been Martine's sister who'd recommended Aimée for the job. She'd face that wrath later.

At the corner of Boulevard Saint-Germain, she noticed

the weekly scandal mag *Voici*—infamous for its dirt on celeb-
rities, royals, and politicians. The huge headline on the cover
read: INVESTIGATION CONTINUES IN LE SÉNAT LOVE-NEST
MURDER—INCONVENIENT MISTRESS?

Her blood boiled for poor dead Erich Kayser and this fake
search for his killer. How could they plant articles like that?
Never mind how—who had this power? Suzanne thought
a Serbian thug was after her, but there had to be someone
much more powerful behind this—whatever this was. If it
even was anything.

She had to settle this once and for all. As long as Melac
held down the fort, she could revisit the scene of Erich Kayser's death, question the frame maker about what she'd seen.

During the humid walk, she reflected on how leads
and evidence guided a police investigation. The *flics* had
accountability guidelines to follow, superiors to answer to,
reports—oh, those reports, her father had moaned; they
tied up your whole day with paper work.

No space for gut feelings, though she knew the best *flics*
followed theirs when they could. Her father had always
talked about that sixth sense, intuition honed by experi-
ence. He'd never ignored it. *Track it down*, he'd say, *before it
tracks you down.*

Powerless at the moment, unable to confront and con-
vict her devils, Suzanne was imagining them on the streets.
How could Aimée blame her? The same thing had happened to her just the previous Saturday. She'd glanced at a
boulangerie window and seen reflected in the glass familiar
tobacco-stained fingers holding a Gauloise. Morbier. There
was his jacket lapel with the ever-present food stain, the
drooping pouches underneath his eyes. The spot by his ear
he always missed shaving. She'd turned to grip his elbow,

overwhelmed by her anger and betrayal. "How could you lie to me?"

"Do we know each other, mademoiselle?" The older man had exhaled a plume of smoke from a newly lit Gauloise, on his face, a puzzled half smile.

She let go. Stepped back, embarrassed. Not Morbier at all. "Forgive me. It's just that I thought you were . . ."

"Someone else," he said, eyeing her. "I'm sorry I wasn't." His eyes were sad. "It's never good to argue and not make up before bed. I know, mademoiselle. There's someone I'd give anything to say I'm sorry to, but it's too late."

Too late.

He'd stood puffing his cigarette, a stone in the river of life flowing around him on the pavement. Then he'd disappeared, leaving her with only the ghost of his sadness.

She was a fine one to talk. She could confront her phantom but wouldn't. Suzanne couldn't.

Yet doubt dogged her steps across the square in front of Saint-Sulpice. The coward in her asked what she could hope to find out. Why not leave it alone?

This plan . . . was it wise? But the disguise she'd changed into was very different from how she looked in the police artist's sketch. Walking down the narrow rue Servandoni, she shuddered remembering how Erich Kayser had sprawled on the street. The pool of blood spreading, veining through the cracks. She thought about what the officer at the *commisariat* had said about the "big boys" who were handling the investigation.

They were still on the lookout for her.

The frame maker's shop doors were open in the late-afternoon heat. She crossed the threshold, stepping on the doormat, which resulted in the tinkle of a doorbell.

The woman, wearing a blue smock and with wood shavings in her hair, turned to look at Aimée. She had been speaking to a man Aimée recognized.

Loïc Bellan.

Aimée froze.

The last person she wanted to see. One who could recognize her despite her disguise.

"*Oui?*" the woman asked.

But Aimée had taken off at a run, keeping to the lengthening shadows of the buildings.

She jumped on the number 63 bus before it closed its doors in front of Café de la Mairie. Head down, she worked her way to the back of the crowded bus, checked her phone. Stole a peek out the window. No Loïc Bellan.

Only Ari, the news peddler who sold to the café patrons *en terrace*. An institution in the quartier; she remembered him from her student days.

If only her heart didn't jump in her chest. If only the waves of nausea would go away. If only all this would go away.

"Look how tense you are, Aimée." Melac was winding up his babyproofing. He set down his screwdriver. "What are you afraid of?"

"Not now, Melac," she said, hot and tired, a thrumming tingle in her spine. She checked her phone. No messages.

"Is it Morbier?"

She was a wanted murder suspect. But she couldn't tell Melac that. Inside she wondered if she was like Suzanne. Damaged.

"You feel so guilty, you're torturing yourself. Why not just go see him?"

Her fingers trembled. "Leave it alone, Melac."

Melac wouldn't let it go. "You still have a chance to make it right with Morbier."

"Quit the crusade." Any minute she'd kick him and his tools down the stairs.

"I'm not thinking of myself." Melac reached for her arm. Held it. "It's you. Morbier can't protect you anymore."

"Since when has he done that? I don't need protection."

"How little you know," said Melac. "He's protected you in his own way for the last ten years, fudged the law for you when you've overstepped and made waves with the *flics*. He's protected you from the Hand, even when you dug too deep and made it dangerous for you both. And he's guarded you from fallout from your mother's terrorist activities. Those champagne socialists would drag you into her wake. Think about it."

She did. More and more these days. She chewed her lip.

"On some level, what happened with Morbier traumatized you. Shootings always do. I went through training, and they still got to me. Plus you're afraid his contacts will retaliate."

"Not will," she said. "They've put me on the poison list already. I expected that."

Melac looked around—Chloé's scattered toys, her blanket on the recamier. "But you're terrified for what you love most, right? Your *bébé*."

Her insides twisted.

If they got to her, what would happen to Chloé?

They wouldn't. Morbier wouldn't let them. Would he?

But he lay dying. Had lied for years, sabotaged her . . . She'd thought his affection for Chloé was real.

"The fear's getting to you," said Melac. "I see it. Go deal

with him, with the phantom in your head. Let him say what he has to say. But then tell him everything—the regret, the guilt, the betrayal of your trust. Give him hell. It might be your only chance to say what you need to say."

Let him know how deeply he'd hurt her?

"You're right. I do feel all that." It bubbled up despite herself. "He ticked me off big-time. The damn *salaud.*"

Melac gave her a wry smile. "Good start. Doubt he'll be too surprised."

Anger flooded her veins. Her temple throbbed. Part of her wanted to confront Morbier, but a big part knew she'd break down. Fall apart. She was helpless to undo what she'd done. What he'd done. The past.

"He's holding on for you, Aimée. To see you, to talk to you."

She'd made him the villain, yet nothing was that simple. Or that black and white. It was all a muddy grey. She pushed it all down—she still couldn't deal with it. Too painful. It would wrench her apart.

Melac had picked up a photo of her and Benoît that Babette had shot the week before when they'd taken the girls to the park. "Who's he?"

Startled at the question, she blinked. "Benoît? He's good for me." It was the first thing that came out of her mouth.

"Sounds like a vitamin."

"He cooks, loves babies, treats Chloé like—"

"His own?" Melac's eyes darkened. Jealous. "She's my daughter. My name's on her birth certificate."

That had been a bitter contest of wills, but in the end, she'd agreed.

"Then act like it, Melac. Don't just stroll in when it suits you."

"I'm trying to." He gripped her hand. "Why don't you try trusting me, Aimée? Tomorrow we'll make a whole day of it."

He stood so close, his vetiver scent surrounding her, and she wanted—stop. Get a grip. She shook loose, and her gaze caught on an expensive tool set.

"Fancy," she said. "Doing some remodeling?"

"Those?" Melac shook his head. "I just borrowed them from Paul to finish babyproofing."

Her ears perked up. "As in Suzanne and Paul?"

"I'm staying at his place. Paul asked me to flat-sit and feed the dog."

"They're both out of town?" she asked warily.

"Paul's in Nantes for the week. And sad news, Suzanne's in the clinker."

She froze. "Jail?"

"Close enough. The police hospital in the Indre."

"In the hospital? *Mon Dieu*, was she hurt in action?" She remembered the voice mail Suzanne had left her.

"Mental stress, battle fatigue. They're calling it sick leave."

She'd heard of this locked rehab facility for police who'd lost it. Rarely did any patients make it back to their positions.

"That's horrific . . ." she said. "I don't understand how they could send Suzanne there."

"Didn't she confide in you?"

Aimée ground her teeth. "Why? We weren't close. Matter of fact, once I thought you two were having an affair, remember?"

Melac nodded. "How could I forget?"

"But this doesn't make sense—she's an elite operative. How can they lock her up?"

Melac shrugged. "Paul called yesterday and asked me to dog-sit. His parents have had the children all week, but Suzanne was supposed to be coming back from a trip yesterday, and their regular dog-sitter was going out of town. He said Suzanne cracked—she was supposed to have another year on her secondment, but she requested reassignment home. PTSD. Seems she hasn't been the same since what happened in Bosnia."

"But PTSD requires therapy," she said, shocked, "not being locked up and deserted by her family." Her heart bled for Suzanne. Harsh institutional treatment didn't make sense. Nothing made sense.

"She saw things on her missions," said Melac. "Terrible things. And it made her a little crazy—she started breaking rules, taking risks that hurt the team. Paul told me she'd raked up sensitive files her boss told her to leave alone. She'd gotten obsessed with this one fugitive."

No wonder Suzanne hadn't revealed anything to Melac. Trying to air out the cupboard, she'd gotten her fingers slammed in the door. Suspected and watched, she didn't trust him or any of them. Now Aimée couldn't either.

Suzanne had trusted only her. Aimée was outside the system of regulations and reports and all the bureaucracy. Suzanne had counted on Aimée to lie, steal. Well, she'd done that, hadn't she? Found no ghost.

Now they'd shut Suzanne up and land-mined Aimée's attempts to investigate.

Isabelle, Erich . . . "They got to him," Suzanne had said. Who were they?

Not my problem, she kept telling herself. Not my problem.

But it was. Suzanne might be obsessed but what had

happened to her was wrong. Like it or not, Aimée'd gotten involved.

Aimée broke away from Melac and went to check on Chloé, who lay asleep, her white eyelet blanket kicked off and her chubby little foot sticking out from under the cotton sheet. Aimée touched her forehead—cool, no fever.

She opened the window a crack. Outside the sliver of a moon hung over the forest of chimneys on the slate roofs. A cat slunk on a nearby balcony.

After a kiss and a quick inhale of Chloé's sweet smell, Aimée went into the bathroom. Closed the door, turned on the faucets so Melac wouldn't hear, and dialed Suzanne's number on the burner phone.

Aimée splashed water on her face as the phone rang ten times, then hung up. No voice mail.

She perched the phone next to her Dior concealer on the shelf under the mirror and scrubbed her face with black soap. Washed off her makeup. Jumped when the phone vibrated, knocking a lipstick tube off the shelf.

Grabbing a towel, she answered. Let the water run.

"*Oui, Suzanne?*"

"Who's this?" said a female voice.

"You first," said Aimée, wary.

"A comedian, eh?" Pause. "I'm Suzanne's friend. She wants to meet."

Aimée's antenna rose. Who the hell was this? Suzanne had been committed to a rehab hospital. "Where?"

"Tomorrow. The statue of Maréchal Ney in front of Closerie des Lilas. Two P.M."

The line went dead. Aimée rang back. Suzanne's phone had been turned off.

Only one way to find out who it was.

Aimée's mind raced, placing the meeting spot—border of the sixth arrondissement, at the far end of the narrow green that continued from the Jardin du Luxembourg, by Port-Royal on the RER B line.

"Aimée, it's Martine." Melac's voice came from the hall.

"Here?" She toweled her face dry, slapped on Clarins moisturizer, rubbing it in with swift oval strokes. Smudged her damp eyes with kohl, swooped down for her fallen lipstick tube, made a quick red slash. She gave herself a glance in the mirror. Dark circles under her eyes. She dabbed Dior concealer but knew only sleep took care of those.

"Going to take her call, or . . . ?"

A call! She stuck the burner in her pocket and opened the door.

He stood with a glass of wine in hand and her landline handset in his other. Definitely at home here.

"Since when do you answer calls on my phone, Melac?"

"Since Martine's name has been flashing for the past five minutes."

Abashed, she took it. *"Merci."*

Only the dial tone.

About to hit the CALL BACK button, she noticed several voice mails. Listened.

A call from her answering service. Olgan, the Croatian professor, fond of *café-clop*, had left a message.

A tingle ran up her arms. She hadn't expected to hear from him.

Before she could jot down his number, Martine rang again.

In the now-babyproofed salon, she answered.

"About time, Aimée."

"Of course. I'm so sorry I forgot your sister's birthday."

"What? No, it's next—"

Her mind had seized upon an idea. "I'll meet you at Closerie des Lilas."

"Wait, I'm at . . . You're up to something, Aimée."

A plan on the fly, but the best she could come up with.

"Give me twenty minutes, Martine. I promise," she said loudly for Melac's benefit.

"Promise what?" Martine was saying, but Aimée hung up.

Melac was standing at the door to the balcony with a glass of wine, which he held out toward her. On the stereo, he'd put on Miles Davis's haunting theme from *Elevator to the Gallows*—the new-wave film with a young Jeanne Moreau, her favorite, roaming Pigalle for her lover who'd killed her husband.

"I can't let Martine down," she said, the lie coming easy. "Mind watching Chloé another hour or—"

"Three?" Melac averted his grey-blue eyes. And for the first time, she sensed there was something wrong—he was worried about something, and all alone. Didn't he have a wife to comfort him?

"I want to talk, Aimée."

"Fine." That sounded abrupt. "You're right. We need to talk. But . . . I need to think." Impatient, she wanted to leave and didn't relish the idea of bundling a sleeping baby in a taxi—but she would if she had to. "*Alors*, it's not the best time. Tomorrow?"

"You're not waking Chloé up," he said, reading her mind. "Go. I'll finish up babyproofing, finish the Merlot."

If he thought he could guilt-trip her, he'd missed the mark.

"Won't be late," she said.

She had a plan.

⁓

HER SCOOTER, RECLAIMED from her mechanic, caught with a purr thanks to yet another tune-up. She took off down the quai, crossed Pont de la Tournelle to the Left Bank. Her hair whipped; her cheeks flushed. She loved riding on hot summer nights, past people filling the café terrasses, spilling from the theaters, piling into bistros—the vibrant life of Paris streets. Rue Saint-Jacques gave her a straight shot to the maternity hospital where she'd had Chloé. A right took her onto Boulevard du Montparnasse. She parked in front of the statue of Maréchal Ney, Napoleon's trusted commander until he turned traitor.

Leafy chestnut trees, backlit by globed streetlights, cast shadows. She keyed off the ignition. Closerie des Lilas, which had once been Hemingway's writing place on cold mornings, appeared as it always had: the polished mahogany, the low light, the red leather, the brass-and-chrome-mirrored bar. And the WC down the stairs with the pay phone. A working pay phone—so rare those days.

She rang Martine.

"You're late, Aimée."

"Order me a—"

"Campari with lime? Done."

"I'm downstairs."

"I know. Gianni saw you."

Aimée sucked in a breath. Gianni? Oh no. What would she say about the trip?

"You're my best friend, Martine." The words caught in her throat. She'd choked up.

Pause. The tinkle of glasses in the background. "I know."

"Up in five," she managed.

She had to act fast. Any moment a staff member or patron would walk by. She'd make it work. In the bathroom she took out the nanny cam, checked the battery, and set the timer. Touched up her lipstick. Back in the hall near the phone, she waited. Listened. No one. She stuck René's nanny cam behind the framed black-and-white photo of the waitstaff in long aprons on the terasse, circa 1900. She secured the camera with the putty she always carried in a thin tray under her blush. She angled the lens, switched the timer on, and hit POWER.

She faked a phone call as a waiter bustled through to the cellar. Prayed to God she'd set the timer right.

Outside on the terrasse, Martine huddled with Gianni. Aimée's drink waited on a paper napkin emblazoned by Dalí's signature S—the napkins all bore signatures of famous patrons. The terasse was full of the usual clientele—journalists, an actor she recognized from the Comédie-Française, bobos and *intellos* sprinkled with a philosopher or two wearing de rigueur corduroy jackets even in this heat, and a few Chardonnay Marxists.

After the customary *bisous*, she sat down and took a long swig. The Campari's sweet, bitter tang hit the spot.

"Going to chew me out, Martine?" she asked.

Martine stretched and winked at Gianni, who held her hand.

"*Alors*, I'm sorry about what happened at École des Beaux-Arts," Aimée said.

"My sister will get over it. Doubt her friend Sybille will."

"You don't know the half of it, Martine."

"And I don't want to know. Keep me in the dark, please. Sybille's a *première*-class bitch. She uses everyone."

Aimée's shoulders lightened.

"Cheers. It's your night out, *si?*" A smiling Gianni summoned the waiter, GQ material with white teeth, a white shirt with undone buttons. He looked good enough to eat.

A wave of relief washed over her. Stress and a baby-addled brain had blunted her focus. Plus the damn humidity.

She downed the Campari.

"*Encore?*" asked Gianni.

Why not?

Martine leaned over the marble-top table. "I can't believe you let Melac babysit."

That reminded her—she checked her phone and saw it was on mute. Stupid. What if Melac called?

She unmuted it.

"Neither can I, but . . . Wait, how do you know?" she asked.

Gianni lit up a triple-filtered Zenit 100's cigarette and sat back. "Don't mind me."

Difficult.

"Melac answered your phone, remember?" Martine said. "Where's his wife, the earth woman?"

"A new job. Maybe trouble in paradise?" Aimée shrugged. "But I don't ask."

She explained how he'd turned up with his mother, his wanting to be in her life, her babysitter issues . . .

"His mother?" Martine said.

"Talk about awkward, Martine." Aimée sipped the fresh Campari the waiter set down.

"Did you know he had a mother? Why wasn't she around before?"

"Never asked. We never got that far. *Alors*, remember my friend Suzanne Lesage, the one who—"

"Not that again." Martine raised her hand. A slim gold-chased bracelet flashed. She nudged Gianni and winked.

"Gorgeous, Martine," Aimée said.

"Let's get to the important things." Martine pulled out a photo. "Here's the house in Favignana."

A sun-kissed gold limestone villa, complete with columns, turquoise shutters, and a garden stretching to the matching sea behind. Breathtaking.

Martine tapped the photo with her lacquered beige nail. "How about a room there for you and Chloé? We'll have dinner in the garden overlooking the sea while Chloé builds sand castles."

More like Chloé would eat the sand, since she put everything in her mouth these days.

If she rearranged the office schedule, got René and Saj to cover a little extra, once Maxence returned, she could, in theory, make it work.

"Of course Gianni's cousin—Federico; you know him—will take us around in his yacht."

Always the matchmaker, Martine.

Before Aimée could reply, her phone rang. Her answering service. "*Désolée*, have to take this."

Under the trees on Boulevard du Montparnasse, she called in. Her service asked if she'd received their last alert, since they hadn't received her usual verification. *Merde.* She'd forgotten in her hurry to get here. Stupid.

Her stomach cramped and it wasn't the Campari. It was imagining Suzanne in a secure facility and thinking of her promise to her.

She took down Olgan's number and reached him after six rings.

"Before you get excited, mademoiselle," said Olgan, his

accented syllables thick, "I put out the word and heard nothing."

And he'd called to tell her that? A welcome breeze gusted the chestnut branches overhead. She pulled a scarf from her bag and wrapped it around her shoulders.

"Until yesterday," said Olgan.

She stiffened.

"Got something to write with?"

Olgan, cautious and scared, had come through with a name—Bartok—and an address and phone number.

"That's it?" Aimée said.

"You want the moon? That's a lead for you. Now you follow up."

"Who is this person?"

"You'll find out. Call during the daytime."

"This person's seen Mirko Vladić?" Chills ran up her arms.

"You didn't get this name from me, *comprenez*? You never met me. Do we have an agreement, mademoiselle?"

"*Bien sûr*," she said, recovering. "A little context would help; that's all."

"If you want context, read the paper."

"*Merci*." She peered past the branches to see Martine and Gianni laughing. Martine's eyes creased from smiling. Happy.

AIMÉE MADE HER excuses to Martine, blaming Melac for getting tired of diaper duty, and pocketed the photo of the Sicilian villa. Promised to check the office schedule and ring Martine the next day.

On her way out, she took aside Edouard, the maître d', a man who had also worked for her father. Edouard, short, trim, with darting black eyes that reminded her of a nervous sparrow's, had been an occasional informer for Leduc Detective—if the price was right. Hiding in plain sight worked best.

"Mademoiselle Aimée, I thought it was you."

"My favorite maître d'," she said, catching his eye meaningfully.

Edouard grasped both her hands, nodding. Message received loud and clear.

He'd clasped the envelope she'd held in her palm. She leaned forward and whispered in his ear. "Tomorrow, two P.M. It's all in the envelope. And a little bonus."

"*D'accord, Mademoiselle Aimée.*" A wide smile. "Always a pleasure to see you."

He'd deliver. The Leducs always greased his palm well.

ON BOULEVARD SAINT-MICHEL traffic slowed; horns blared. Aimée heard a dull thud and ripping metal, squeezed the brakes on her handlebars just in time. A Citroën's and Renault's bumpers were locked as if in mortal combat. Shouts erupted as two drivers piled out, unhurt, fists raised. Why did the heat make drivers crazy?

To avoid the mess, she was about to turn onto the narrow street with the astrological bookstore where she and Martine had browsed as teenagers. Under the yellow lamplight by the irregular steps that were a remnant of the twelfth-century Phillipe Auguste wall, a father was pleading with a little girl: "*Chérie*, it's past your bedtime . . ."

For no reason Aimée could identify, a chill crawled up her back. She looked at the street around her. A man on a bicycle paused at the crosswalk. Blue cap, jeans, dark shirt—nothing special. You wouldn't look twice at him—except he was staring at the little girl. A second later he looked up.

Those dead eyes. Boring into hers.

Her heart skipped a beat. It was the Hague photo come to life.

Mirko.

Her mouth went dry. The next moment she'd revved the scooter, crossing the street and weaving past the father and a disgruntled passerby, gunning toward where the man on the bicycle had been. But he had disappeared.

Maybe Suzanne wasn't crazy.

IN CHLOÉ'S ROOM the mobile fluttered in the soft current of air from the window. A shaft of moonlight kissed Chloé's little arm in the crib. Melac sprawled asleep on cushions piled in the corner, Chloé's half-empty milk bottle in his hand. He looked younger, peaceful with a half smile turning up one corner of his mouth.

Aimée didn't have the heart to wake him.

Saturday Morning

MELAC SMILED AT her from where he stood by the sink
the next morning. "Thanks for letting me sleep."

"You looked tired."

Aimée fed Chloé and sipped coffee in the kitchen as
Miles Davis licked her toes. Another broiling day promising
thundershowers later.

"Let me take Chloé with me to walk Paul's dog and visit
Jardin du Luxembourg," Melac said.

A new tactic to worm his way into their life? But in that
moment there in her kitchen, a perfect family scene, she
found she wanted him to be with them.

"Only if it's okay with you," he said. "We could go to the
market, walk the dog, meet you at the garden after work."

Why did that sound wonderful?

"What about Miles Davis?" she asked.

"He can come, too. Leashed dogs are okay on the east
side. But we'll take him for a big walk this morning."

She needed time to think, work out a plan. What would
she do about the ghost she'd seen who possibly followed
her? She fought back a shiver.

That decided her. "*Merci*. My morning's crazy since
René's teaching."

For a moment, peace reigned: Chloé entranced by a sun-
beam warming her fingers, Melac fiddling with a broken
light fixture, more espresso brewing. Playing at being a
happy family—but when would the illusion break?

Luckily she wouldn't need him to look after Chloé much longer. Madame Cachou had left a message—her sister was fine; *mon Dieu*, such a scare; she was coming back in another day.

But Melac had noticed Martine's picture of the Favignana villa, which Aimée had stuck on the tiny fridge. He whistled.

"What do you think of my new place, Melac?"

He shrugged and made a silly face at Chloé, who was busy smearing his home-pureed applesauce on the high chair tray. "So *Maman* won the Loto and bought you a villa on a Sicilian island, *ma puce.*"

Chloé, now intent on licking her fingers, ignored him.

Aimée gave a mock sigh. "How did you know, Melac? We've been invited on a sun-drenched holiday with Martine and her squeeze, Gianni. *Pas mal*, eh?"

Could she swing it? Decisions. She'd think about that later.

Melac averted his gaze and went back to adjusting the light fixture over the sink. Uttered an expletive as the light-bulb came off in his hand. It made her think.

"How long does it take to unscrew a lightbulb?" she asked.

"That's a joke, right?"

"I'm serious."

"Depends. If it's like this one, no time at all. But you'd need a ladder for the chandeliers."

She thought about Erich Kayser's apartment. She tried to remember the layout, the size, but it came back to her only as dark and small. She'd walked into the kitchen at first, then the salon with a window to the street. There'd been a bedroom off to the right, a small hallway. Mentally she counted: two lightbulbs in the kitchen . . . Came up with a likely total of six.

"Ever heard of a burglar who unscrewed all the bulbs in a house to stage a crime?" she said.

Melac paused. "You're asking because . . . ?"

Should she tell him whom she'd seen last night—at least, who she thought it was? Had it been the Campari? *Non*, she'd recognized those dead eyes . . .

"Hypothetical question," she said.

"I remember a robbery like that in a mansion in the sixteenth. The owners returned and heard the robbers, but it took them ages to find the phone in the dark, and the robbers got away. Why?"

"Wondering. That's all."

"It's kind of brilliant. People get confused in the dark and panic. Gives the robbers all the time they need."

She thought so, too.

After changing Chloé's diaper and putting her in a new peach sunsuit, Aimée made a market list. About to rustle up her spare key for Melac, tell him about the stroller wheels needing oil, she paused. This felt like playing house.

"DON'T HOLD YOUR breath for École des Beaux-Arts' payment," said Saj. He was sitting at René's terminal. Saj handled the bills and accounts in René's absence.

Aimée's hands clenched in anger as she set her bag on her desk.

"So after forcing me to uncover their corruption, they nail us by not honoring the contract?" Aimée slammed an open file drawer shut. "I'll fight it."

Saj sat more upright. "I'm sensing a lot of negativity, Aimée. Try taking a deep breath."

"It ticks you off, too, Saj, doesn't it? Remember how Dechard, debilitated by suffering, with a terminal disease, got used?"

"Listen to this email they sent: *Due to changes in the administration and a transitioning phase, all fiscal commitments will be honored . . .*"—he paused, looking up at Aimée—"*in the near future.*"

She wanted to spit. Disgusted. "The next blue moon, eh?"

"Wait! Get this." Saj grinned. "A follow-up email from the clerk René had dealt with: *looks like la directrice cut the check yesterday before her forced administrative leave, so I'll just ignore that last email. Let's have that promised drink, René.*"

Aimée whistled. "The Friant charm at work."

Sybille was out. Aimée felt a thrill of glee—until she thought of Dechard. "What a mess at the school." She sighed. "And so much for future business there."

"The river of life flows and ebbs. And it's especially deep with our new Swedish videographer contract."

"Win some, lose some, Saj." Her father would have added, *Keep showing up and never let go.*

Time for an espresso and work. She brewed a demitasse, savored the jolt it provided, and itched for a cigarette. Fondled the packet of Auras in her pocket. She popped a stick of cassis-flavored gum into her mouth and took out the number Olgan had furnished.

She got a recorded message for a construction company saying the business wasn't currently open. Tempted to leave it at that, she hesitated. The old émigré had gone to bat— although for what, she had no idea.

She suppressed a shiver.

Lost in a swarm of thoughts, she did what her father would have told her to do: she took out a blue dry-erase marker and went to the whiteboard behind René's desk. She taped the photo of Mirko to the whiteboard and then listed all Suzanne's team members whom she knew about in one column: *Suzanne Lesage, Isabelle Ideler, Erich Kayser, Jean-Marie Plove.* Next to that she made another column of things she didn't understand: *ICTY funding? Suzanne's message, "mistakes were made"? Mirko family in France? Accidental deaths?*

How could Isabelle Ideler's death be murder? A killer would have had to know she was hyperallergic to bees, and then would have to have somehow forced the bees to sting her. It sounded more and more unlikely the more Aimée thought about it. How could a person force bees to attack? On the other hand, honeybees were not aggressive creatures; they shouldn't sting unless they felt threatened. How strange was it that they had stung Isabelle Ideler at all?

Had Mirko known Isabelle was allergic? Also somehow engineered the loss of her luggage? She thought about the strange feeling she'd had at the Dutch embassy—how the liaison had described Isabelle's brother as short, which was contrary to Serge's description.

She sat back down at her laptop. Searched the Dutch embassy staff list, found the liaison and the vice-consul. Shot them an email.

An auto-generated reply from both came back immediately. *Out of the office until next week. Please contact the ambassador's secretary if this is urgent.*

Hopeless.

"Anything strike you, Saj?"

"Besides an aura of intense concentration? I thought you'd washed your hands of this case."

"I had. Until I learned Suzanne had been shoved into

a hospital. Then I spotted him last night. *Alors*, at least someone who looked like Mirko."

She filled him in on Suzanne's hospitalization, the man on the bike, and the contact from Olgan.

Saj sipped a tepid rose-hued infusion of petals and stems.

"What do you think, Saj? What am I missing?"

"If I broke it down . . ." He unfolded his long muslin-draped legs and stood. Took a marker. "May I?"

"*Bien sûr.*"

He put a big X through Isabelle Ideler and Erich Kayser. "Passed on." Then through Suzanne Lesage. "Locked up." He met Aimée's gaze. "Who's left from the team?"

Jean-Marie.

"You said Suzanne hadn't spoken with him. Shouldn't you try again?"

She nodded. "And I'm concerned about this woman who called on Suzanne's phone and wants to meet." She caught him up on the call from Suzanne's number the night before. "I think it's a setup." She flicked the camera control button installed on René's laptop.

"You hooked up René's nanny cam again?"

She checked her Tintin watch. "I set the timer for two P.M. at the Closerie des Lilas pay phone. Record it, okay?"

"Watch yourself, Aimée. Let's do some asanas and breathing work."

Before Saj could pull her onto the mat to meditate, she grabbed her bag.

"Later, Saj."

Olgan had thought it important enough to ask around and deliver her a name. She'd check in with this Bartok at 24 Impasse des Deux Anges. A place to start.

Ten minutes later, she parked her scooter off Boulevard

Saint-Germain at Cathédrale Saint-Volodymyr le Grand, the Ukrainian Catholic church. She knew it well. A decade earlier she'd taken premed classes close by at the Faculté de Médecine.

The gate was locked. In the evenings, the small garden often held gatherings of Eastern Europeans—men's and women's groups, people coming to look for job postings on the church's bulletin board. Why hadn't she thought to ask here before?

The humidity was a damp blanket over the Impasse des Deux Anges. And it was only 9 A.M.

Bartok's construction company nestled in a small court-yard surrounded by a ragged hodgepodge of roof lines. Aimée caught a whiff of garlic.

FERMÉ, said a sign hanging on the door.

Next door, a bright-eyed young woman answered Aimée's knock. Her cheeks were flushed and her hair piled in a knot on her head. She responded to Aimée's query about Mirko's photo with a shake of her head.

"I don't know him," the woman said.

"He's a carpenter," Aimée said, faking assurance.

"Ah, one of them? I don't know who my uncle hires."

"But Serbs work here, non?"

"Some."

"There's a problem. I need to reach Bartok—he's your uncle, right?"

"What kind of problem?"

She needed this woman helpful. Time to take control, or she'd have wasted a trip.

"It's not for me to say, but . . . it's a family emergency. Serious." Through the window of the closed dispatch office, Aimée spotted a chalkboard with names, but she couldn't make them out from where she stood. "May I see the workers' schedules?"

"Serious how?"

So full of questions.

"I'm sure you want to cooperate," Aimée said. "Can I speak with your uncle? Please."

The girl hesitated. "My uncle does apartment remodels when work's slow."

"Got an address?"

"Hold on." A few minutes later she returned. "He has a renovation at thirteen rue du Dragon. But he moves around to different job sites."

"*Merci.*"

As Aimée left, out of the corner of her eye, she saw the young woman making a sign warding off the evil eye.

RUE DU DRAGON ran from Boulevard Saint-Germain to the junction of Croix-Rouge, below which lay an abandoned Métro station she'd partied in during premed. A block later the street blended into rue du Cherche-Midi— now with designer consignment shops, local bistros that had become chic—and joined rue de Vaugirard, the old Roman road. She remembered the *café tabac* on rue du Dragon, the regulars—many elderly people protected by *la loi de 1948*. When they passed on, so did their old controlled rents.

Number thirteen had an art gallery on the first floor— the open door emitted the whining of a drill. She heard shouting in a language she didn't recognize but which she was sure came from the vicinity of the Danube.

"Monsieur Bartok?" she called out.

A plaster-dusted head poked out from a ground floor window.

"Back tomorrow," came the accented voice. "Not here."

As if she'd leave it at that. "Sorry to bother you, but could you help?"

She'd walked through the open door. A fine white powder covered the plastic sheeting on the floor. Hammering and drilling hurt her ears. Three workers had looked up at her entrance. One was in his forties, the other two in their twenties. None resembled Mirko.

Now that she had their attention, she'd play the helpless card. "Bartok's niece over at Impasse des Anges told me he'd be here. I think I wrote down his phone number wrong."

"What number do you have?" one of the men said.

Great.

"Oh no," she said. "It's here somewhere, I think, but, it's his business number . . ."

"Give me your number. I'll give Bartok the message," the man said.

She couldn't read a thing in any of their expressions. Sweat dripped down their dust-covered faces. They were like mute white phantoms. They'd sooner drill a hole than reveal anything.

Brazen it out. "Look, I've got a dispute with his cabinet supplier. Not him," she said.

After a back-and-forth that escalated to a threat to inform the better business bureau at the *mairie*, she obtained Bartok's cell number.

The drill started again before she was even out the door.

That went well.

Out on rue du Dragon, disgusted, she shook her head to get the dust out of her wig.

Tried Bartok's phone number.

"*Allô?*" a voice answered.

"Monsieur Bartok, I need your help."

"I heard. Later."

Click.

SHE'D FEEL GUILTY if she didn't try to find Jean-Marie one more time. He hadn't called her, and when she tried his phone number in his file now, he didn't answer . . . What if whoever "got to" Erich Kayser had gotten to Jean-Marie?

So she hopped back on her scooter. She'd try the square again. With all the roadwork, she ended up taking a circuitous route. Her elbow scraped the wall threadlike rue de Nevers. On the quai, she wobbled, almost hitting a man who darted out toward a taxi.

Idiot. Running in the damn heat.

Off quai de Conti, she turned left at the Institut de France. Academicians in robes spilled out the back doors. Sneaking a smoke? Pretty grand for a rear exit.

She parked by the dark blue storefront of Roger-Viollet, a photo archive with windows displaying black-and-white photos of the quartier's former inhabitants—gems of Picasso looking out from his studio on quai des Grands Augustins, Albert Camus smoking on Boulevard Saint-Germain.

Opposite, she unlatched the metal gate of the small square. A couple read in the shade. A man did push-ups on the trampled grass near the base of a chestnut tree. Only the army instilled the discipline to train in a heat wave like this.

She counted an impressive series of fifty, then sat down on a bench. "Jean-Marie, I'm Aimée, Suzanne's friend. You're not an easy man to reach."

"I like it that way."

A sliver of aluminum glinted from below his sweat pants where his ankle would be.

"Understood, Jean-Marie. I respect that."

"Then why hunt me down here? *Non*, I don't care why. In case you haven't figured it out, I want to be left alone."

"It's not about you, *désolée*. Just hear me out, and I'll go. Promise." She fanned herself with her scarf and continued talking before he could interrupt. "Suzanne saw Mirko Vladić last Monday night in her *café tabac*. The same Mirko Vladić who your team saw blown up near Foča. I'm a detective; Suzanne asked me to investigate."

"That's got nothing to do with me."

"True." She pulled out a bottle of Evian, glad she'd bought an extra, and set it in the grass. He ignored it. "While I was investigating, two other members of your team, Isabelle Ideler and Erich Kayser, both died in freak accidents," she said. "Meanwhile, Suzanne's been taken off her job and hospitalized for stress or trauma, or whatever they're calling it."

Pause. She wished she could read his expression. "Again, nothing to do with me."

"Suzanne thinks you're next."

She tried to read his body language. Stiff as a rod.

"Suzanne intimated that mistakes were made during the operation in Foča." Aimée paused, stretching the truth. "Is that what this is about?"

There was a metal click as Jean-Marie adjusted the prosthesis. "Who are you?"

He hadn't thrown her out of the park yet, even if he wanted to. Maybe he couldn't.

"Someone who'd prefer to handle paid investigations," she said. "I'm only here because I respect Suzanne too much not to follow up when she begs me to help."

"Suzanne? Beg?"

Aimée half-smiled. "I owe her a favor." She sat down

on the grass cross-legged. "Look, we both know how smart Suzanne is. If she's concerned for your safety, you should be, too."

"Mirko's alive and in Paris," he said. "And he's going to come for me. That's what I'm supposed to get out of this?"

Her phone vibrated. René. But she couldn't interrupt the conversation or stop Jean-Marie now.

"You'd know better than I would," she said.

For the first time, he looked up and held her gaze. His azure eyes were full of pain and anger. "Tell me what Suzanne told you. In exact detail."

She took out her Moleskine, consulted her notes. Told him all the details. He nodded as he listened, giving her his full, quiet concentration. She figured he'd be a good operative in the field. Suzanne's team must have been a crack commando unit.

When she got to the part about the bank's CCTV footage, he said, "So that café's in front of the Métro, right?"

"*Exactement*. It's at the corner of rue de Rennes and rue du Vieux Colombier."

He nodded, his short hair glinting in the sun. "Been a while, but I know it. Isn't there another door for the *tabac*?"

"Not that I saw."

"Like I said, been a while."

"But you believe Suzanne?"

"I think she's too good to make a big mistake like that," he said.

"What could she mean about mistakes being made?"

"It's complicated."

Translation: forget it. She had to walk on eggshells, make sure he didn't shut back down.

"Not something you want to talk about, I understand,"

she said. "Or remember. But she's been locked up. Taken out of commission."

He uncapped the Evian she'd offered him. Took a long sip. Then another.

Progress.

"So unlike Suzanne," he said. "Where is she?"

"The police rehab hospital in Indre."

Jean-Marie shuddered. "They wanted to shuffle me in there."

"But you're army, *non?*"

"The crazies of every stripe and medal get complimentary care there, if you know what I mean."

She could just imagine. Nodded.

He leaned forward, retying his perfectly tied shoelace. "Two days ago I felt like I was being followed. Then again yesterday."

She shivered. "Did you tell anyone?"

"I avoid everyone."

"Why?"

"My old advisor, a military attaché, Robert, is trying to get me to . . . give a report." He paused, struggling with something. "I don't want him asking me any more questions."

She shouldn't ask him any more questions, either. Best thing she could do was to wait, listen—maybe he would talk on his own if she was patient. Some things took time.

Jean-Marie swigged the rest of the Evian. The couple had left. The square lay deserted. Lilac leaves drooped. Not another soul there.

He scooted back into the retreating shade of the chestnut, and she followed. He was talking in a low voice, almost to himself—he'd waited until the park was empty.

"Bosnia made you feel dirty," he said, crushing the plastic bottle in his hands. "Stained you. You tried to do good— never enough. If you turned over one dunghill, you found another. It never ended. One thing you learned to help you survive was those people never forget. Memories like elephants. Some twelfth-century dispute over land, a daughter who got pregnant in 1917, a boundary wall of a farm that hasn't been planted since before the war—it's like it happened yesterday."

He paused. Had his words run out? Or did he expect a comment?

She pinched herself to keep herself quiet. Prayed he'd continue.

"At our orientation, the Hague liaison stressed how the people held on to old loyalties, seethed with pent-up emotions about decades of conflict. Ready to explode without rhyme or reason, at least none we could understand." Jean-Marie's low voice continued. "After the Second World War, Tito deep-froze the ethnic divisions. He thought he could strong-arm Catholic Croats, Bosnian Muslims, and Serbian Orthodox all into one country. Then Tito died, the decaying communism eroded, and the Croats, Bosnians, Serbians, all wanted their old piece of that country."

He sounded as if he knew a lot about what he spoke about. He wasn't just some army beefcake.

"Some orientation to a mop-up zone," he said self-consciously. "That's what they call ethnic cleansing, a mop-up. You want to make sense of senseless violence? You don't. Just understand where it comes from."

She slid off her sandals. The grass felt good, cool under her feet.

Once he'd started, he couldn't stop talking. "Now Mirko

. . . He was only small-fry. A monster, a thug, but no mastermind. It was Arkan who was the big fish—Arkan and his Tigers."

Her phone vibrated again. René.

"Arkan, who's he?" she asked.

"Arkan's the Serbian godfather crime lord. A mastermind. He speaks several languages. He first came to Interpol's attention in the seventies and eighties for robberies and murder all over Europe—he's on the most wanted list."

Her mother, an American, had also earned that distinction. Aimée batted that thought away.

"Arkan vacuumed up jobless soccer fans in the Belgrade streets," Jean-Marie was saying. "That's how you build a paramilitary organization, you know. The hungry young without a future who are about to explode. Guys like Mirko Vladić. Arkan channeled their hate into a perverted nationalism, creating an army of thugs that made him rich and powerful. He used them, his Tigers, he called them. He gave them a cause, a heavenly mission. They went from fans to hoodlums to wealthy, well-armed gangs."

For the first time, she noticed the tremor in Jean-Marie's good leg.

"Arkan, always a trendsetter, paved the way for Croats and Bosnians to organize quasi-legitimate paramilitary outfits. Criminals let out of jail signed up for this 'legitimate' army. Opportunistic politicians used them to cut down inconvenient opposition."

Jean-Marie's face flushed. "People had lived in mixed ethnic families for generations. Sarajevo had more Muslims than any other group. It didn't matter. The paramilitary groups took out anyone they didn't like. The UN sanctions did nothing. NATO was a joke."

"Mirko was one of Arkan's Tigers?" she said.

"I don't know how, but after they caught Arkan, he managed to break out of a Dutch prison in the 80s. He must have been helped. Someone was protecting him. Always protecting him." Pause. "But yes, Mirko was one of Arkan's Tigers and stepped into a power vacuum in Sarajevo after the war. He'd done heinous things, and now he'd emerged as a head thug."

"Could he have reconnected with Arkan?"

"Anything's possible."

"Do you think Mirko could have survived, tailed Suzanne, and engineered accidents for . . . for Isabelle and Erich?" It sounded hard to believe to her as she was saying it. Suzanne and now Jean-Marie had both described Mirko as a thug. Could he have pulled off something so complex?

"What does your investigation tell you?"

He sounded like Morbier. *Just the facts, Leduc,* he'd say, *backed up with evidence.*

She took a breath. "I think if he's here, he had to have had help." She told Jean-Marie about Erich's dark apartment, the sound in the darkness, the horrific scream, escaping on the roof.

Her phone vibrated. Melac. Chloé—was there a problem?

"I have to take this. And if I don't hurry, I'll be late to see who shows up at Closerie des Lilas."

"You're seriously keeping the appointment?"

"I know the maître d'. I have a plan and a nanny cam."

He grinned. The first time she'd seen him smile. "Now I understand why Suzanne enlisted your help."

She stood, brushed grass bits from her skirt, surveyed the square. No one except long-robed academicians.

"I've got a new phone," said Jean-Marie.

For all his bluster, he'd taken precautions.

"Call me after Closerie des Lilas," he said. "I'll give you my number."

"Only if you'll answer," she said.

"Tell me who shows up."

"You mean you'll help?"

The look in his eyes had changed. "Mirko was considered a small-fry criminal. Nothing special except that we'd gotten a sealed indictment from the ICTY that nailed him directly to the Foča massacres. However, we were after big fish, too. Hervé Gourmelon, a French agent, had met clandestinely with Karadžić, the fugitive former Bosnian Serb president. Gourmelon was suspected of passing him information about NATO plans to capture him."

"A French agent helping the fugitive Serb leader?"

Jean-Marie gave a little nod. "A diplomatic disaster trying to cover it up. Someone leaked the details of the secret arrest plan and jeopardized the operation and NATO troops."

"But what does that have to do with Mirko?"

"As the *merde* hit the fan, we discovered Mirko was Gourmelon's Serb contact. There was a rumor of an arms deal. Gourmelon, probably his cover name, vanished, and no one's seen hide nor hair of him."

She tried to piece all this together. Recalled Suzanne's words: "Mistakes were made."

"Mirko's death in an explosion would have been convenient." Aimée rubbed the back of her neck. "Especially if it was staged. He could move around Europe without a trace, carry out the aborted arms deal. Is that what you're saying?"

Jean-Marie took her phone and entered his new number.

"I'll take that as a yes."

⌐

AIMÉE WATCHED THE awning of the Closerie des
Lilas through her palm-sized mother-of-pearl opera glasses,
a nineteenth-century pair her grandfather had found at auc-
tion. From her vantage point across the street and behind a
plane tree, she made out bicyclists, a family walking toward
the Jardin du Luxembourg, tourists in sun hats consulting
maps.

No Suzanne.

At 1:59 a man in a nondescript light fabric suit
approached Maréchal Ney's statue. Lingered reading the
plaque. At 2 P.M. he consulted his watch. Just then a waiter
in a long white apron, one of the maître d's crew, appeared
and handed the man Aimée's note. All according to plan.

Her digital camera's zoom lens caught his face as he
looked up. She snapped a photo. He followed the waiter
into the Closerie des Lilas.

She hit Saj's number on her cell phone.

"Saj, please tell me the nanny cam's running and you see
something."

"Hmm . . . black and white floor tiles, a pay phone."

Thank God. The camera was working. A small relief
filled her.

"Record it, and if anyone comes in, get a freeze-frame of
their face and print, okay?" she said.

"Oops, a lady's stepped up to the phone."

Suzanne.

Aimée pulled out the burner phone Suzanne had given
her. It rang in her hand.

Aimée counted to three and answered. "Suzanne?"

"I have a message from Suzanne."

Fear danced up her spine. "Who is this?"

"Suzanne said to deliver it in person."

"Where's Suzanne?"

"Hospital, but you know that. This happens face-to-face. No phone, no email."

"Write your message and leave it with the maître d'." Aimée hung up.

Saturday Afternoon

SAJ MET AIMÉE on the bench in the rose-brick courtyard of the Institut Catholique de Paris on rue d'Assas.
She'd picked this spot for its proximity to Saj's upcoming
meeting. His blond dreadlocks were tied back under a bandanna. His laptop whirred as he downloaded her digital
camera's photos of the man.

"It was a double-team," she said. "He handed off to a
woman waiting inside."

She'd checked the photos of the woman that Saj had
printed out from the nanny cam. No one Aimée knew.
Or who matched the staff photos Saj had pulled up from
the ICTY website. Then again, an agent operating in the
shadows wouldn't merit their salt if their image got out.

"René's got a new software program for facial recognition," said Saj. "The trick's finding the correct database
to compare the images to. I'll work on that back at the
office."

Edouard's call came at the arranged time.

"Mademoiselle Aimée, I'm afraid no reservations were
made."

Disappointed, she thanked him and hung up.

"The double-team didn't play," she said. "No message
from Suzanne."

Saj looked up. "A setup?"

"Looks that way. Ministry intelligence in some form."

Aimée glanced around. Students. A priest.

She had the feeling she was being followed. And not for the first time since Suzanne had sought her out. Lax security on her part? She'd changed in the school's religious-studies wing restroom, removed her wig, donned her Jackie O sunglasses.

She moved closer to Saj on the bench. "Jean-Marie, the wounded one with a prosthetic, might recognize either the man or woman."

"How's that?"

She explained Mirko's links to Hervé Gourmelon, a French agent. Rumors of arms deals. How meetings with the fugitive Karadžić caused a scandal.

"Why don't Jean-Marie or Suzanne go public on this?"

"Maybe Suzanne tried. It's not that simple, Saj. It stinks."

"You're telling me." He lifted his arms and stretched, his eyes scanning the courtyard. He'd caught her wariness.

Laughter came from a group of students clustered by a poster about summer seminars. Everything felt normal apart from the shiver up her neck.

Saj fingered his rosewood prayer bead bracelet, then reached in his messenger bag. Slipped a printout into her bag. "A little more on Mirko."

"Brilliant. Now can you see what you can dig up on a military attaché named Robert something. Jean-Marie's old advisor. Lives near him."

Saj nodded. "What am I looking for?"

"More about their mission. Any connections to arms dealers. There's someone involved who is powerful enough to plant lies in the media."

"Don't ask for much, do you?"

"I don't need any more surprises," she said.

"You're stressed. Those knots in your neck, your tight shoulders—how about a massage?"

Why not?

"Beats a cigarette," she said.

His large hands kneaded her shoulders. "Breathe, Aimée. From your diaphragm, like this. Now. You're all knotted up." He leaned forward and whispered in her ear. "What's with the eyes on us? I feel it, too. You picked this site at random, *non?*"

Her mind clicked over the possibilities—Mirko? The *flics?* She'd been so careful, hadn't she?

"Not sure." The knobs of tension she carried in her shoulders melted under Saj's fingers. Her gaze flicked up to the mounted cameras at each end of the courtyard. "Think you can worm your way into the good graces of the receptionist?" She gestured to the laughing, long-haired blonde receptionist standing in the doorway across the courtyard. Aimée recognized the woman from when she'd taken a web security seminar here two years ago. "Ooze some of your charm, and inspire her to play back the last fifteen minutes of their video surveillance system footage. If anyone looks out of place or suspicious, get her to print out a few frames. Think you can do that and still make your client meeting?"

Saj winked. "Old school. I like that." He stood, shouldering his Indian cloth bag. "I'll call."

Saturday Afternoon

PAULINE CROSSED HER ankles on the bench beside Charlotte.

"A red crayon?" Some of the wax caught under Pauline's thumbnail. She sniffed. "Don't you have anything else?"

Charlotte crinkled her brow. "Isabelle's clothes, her bag, everything's been returned to her brother. My little boy told me Isabelle drew him a picture with this crayon."

Charlotte's right hand shook holding a half-torn drawing.

Pauline took the drawing, held it to her chest, and closed her eyes. Sometimes the visitations took time. Sometimes they never happened.

"Pauline, did you really mean I couldn't have prevented Isabelle's accident?"

Pauline waved her silent. She needed stillness for the energy to settle. Charlotte's bounced around in electric sparks.

An image flickered—fat drops of rain were pelting. Isabelle in her lime sundress running for shelter. The man running after her. The man catching her.

"The man . . ." Pauline trailed off.

"What man? Who?"

"The man spilled Orangina on her dress. He's holding her arms . . ."

"What else?"

"If you want more, you must still your emotions, harness

the energy," said Pauline, standing. "Please stay here. I must feel this alone."

The minute Pauline walked away toward the apiary, Charlotte rooted through her bag. That young woman— where was her card? What was her name? Charlotte found it, grabbed her cell phone, and dialed Aimée's number.

Saturday Afternoon

"SHE'S A CLAIRVOYANT caretaker at the school across the street?" Aimée strolled with Charlotte under the allée of arching chestnut trees.

"Pauline calls it having visitations."

The clank of boules rose from the sandy pit as they passed, and resounding shouts came from the players. Several men in short-sleeve shirts wiped their foreheads with bandannas.

"You mean she sees dead people," Aimée said. "Does she charge?"

Charlotte bristled. "It's not what you think."

"What do I think, Charlotte?" Aimée tried to control her crankiness. Almost breaking her neck to rush here in the traffic, Charlotte insisting it was an emergency, and all for this? A psychic old-lady con artist?

"She refuses even a centime," Charlotte insisted. "It's what the spirits ask her to do, she says. I begged her, Aimée. She didn't want to. And she says Isabelle wasn't alone when she died."

Aimée stopped on the gravel path. "Who was with her?"

"Pauline saw a man spill Orangina on her."

She thought of Serge's autopsy report, and goosebumps rose on her arms.

BY THE NINETEENTH-CENTURY apiary, a sixtyish woman with short, brushed-back, greying hair stood with her hands in her smock coat pockets. A woman you wouldn't look twice at, Aimée thought, noticing the pouches under her eyes, how tired she looked.

"It happened here," Pauline said. "Isabelle knew him."

Charlotte took Pauline's arm. "Who was he?"

"My legs swell in the heat," said Pauline. "Doing this takes it out of me. I need to sit down."

Aimée followed them to the concrete steps of the Art Nouveau building where the beekeeping classes were held. Children ran up and down the path, their parents calling after them.

"Can you describe him, Pauline?" Aimée asked.

Pauline fanned away a fly. "A cap, with a brim."

Aimée pulled out Mirko's photo. "Does he look familiar?"

Pauline lifted the readers hanging from a chain around her neck. Bees droned. "Not the mustache."

But the man she'd seen the other night sported a mustache. A fake one?

Now the important question. "Did he spill something on Isabelle's dress?" Aimée asked.

"Orangina."

Aimée controlled her shiver. "Is that a guess, Pauline? How could you tell?"

"*Mais* I recycle glass at school."

"*Désolée*, I don't understand."

"I know an Orangina bottle when I see one," she said. "Monday, just before the storm, I was reading my union's rehousing notice on that bench. There." She pointed. "I saw the man in the cap. He had an Orangina bottle. He must have been waiting for her. The sky opened; it started to pour. Thunder cracked. Whistles blew. The garden was closing. I was leaving, and I passed the girl hurrying through the gate."

Anything the woman was saying she could be making

up on the spot, or she could have rewritten her memories to feel important—that happened with witnesses all the time. It was only her knowledge of the Orangina that made Aimée wonder if she could get more.

"I've seen this man." Charlotte's finger tapped the photo so hard it fell from Aimée's hand to the gravel.

She picked it up. "Where, Charlotte? Why do you remember him?"

Charlotte's brow furrowed. "I'm trying to think."

Had Mirko cased and surveilled the street, their apartment, watching to come up with a plan to take out Isabelle? Aimée turned to Pauline, whose face was flushed. Forget all the woo-woo. The woman might have actually seen something.

"So you saw this man and Isabelle together?" Aimée asked. "It's important, Pauline."

Pauline's eyes fluttered. She got to her feet. "I don't see anymore. I'm tired."

Aimée looked around, noticed a trash bin under the sign pointing to the *pépinière*, the nursery with espaliered pear and apple trees. She calculated the distance from the hedge where Isabelle's body was discovered to the bin—only a few meters. Close.

"*Alors*, do you remember if he threw the Orangina in the trash bin?" Aimée asked.

Pauline rubbed her forehead. "The guards' whistle sounded; they were closing the park because of the rainstorm . . . So I came back on Tuesday after the park reopened."

"You came back? For what?"

"To recycle. I collect glass, and Pilou picks it up from me every week."

The frugal *gardienne* made extra by taking recyclables out of the bins in the park.

"You took the Orangina bottle?" Aimée asked.

The crime-scene technicians had assumed Isabelle's death was an accident, so there'd have been no collecting of evidence. The discarded Orangina bottle would have still been there.

Aimée grabbed Pauline's arm. "Can you show me your recycling? If it's still there, we'd have fingerprints."

"Pilou comes Saturdays. Maybe he's already gone . . ."

"Then let's hurry."

They rushed out the gate and up rue d'Assas to the school's courtyard. The bin was empty.

"Too late. He's gone," Pauline said.

"Where does he go?" Aimée asked.

"His truck's just up the street. There."

A faded yellow postal truck, bags bungee-corded on the roof, paused at the stop sign at rue Vavin.

Merde. "Call him," Aimée said.

"Like he has a phone," Pauline said.

Aimée took off running. Her sandals pounded the hot pavement. The light turned green.

She burst across the zebra crossing, just avoiding a screeching Peugeot. The driver leaned out the window and swore. "*Idiote!* I almost killed you."

Aimée had been an *idiote* all right. Why hadn't she remembered the Orangina Serge mentioned in the autopsy report? If—and a big "if"—Mirko existed and if he had—another "if"—held the Orangina bottle long enough to leave fingerprints . . .

Her legs pumped.

If so, she'd have the one solid piece of evidence in this shaky story of visitations, a ghost.

A lot of ifs.

She sprinted with her last bit of energy up rue Vavin, crossing rue Notre Dame des Champs. She spied the old postal truck double-parked by the tiny triangular *place*, a wedge of trees and benches.

A hunched-over man with grey hair rummaged through the trash bin by the green metal Wallace fountain.

"Pilou?" she gasped.

He looked up. Smiled a toothless grin.

"How much for Pauline's glass recycling bag?"

Without a moment's hesitation, he shot back, "Two hundred francs. I'll throw in her metal bag, too."

"Okay, two hundred but only the Orangina bottles." She panted, catching her breath. "Keep the rest."

SHE CALLED CHARLOTTE, asked her to stop at the *pharmacie*. Twenty minutes later the three of them, all wearing latex gloves, had separated out the bottles.

Seventeen Orangina bottles were in the scruffy old Monoprix bag Pilou had thrown in "on the house." Aimée dialed Jean-Marie's new number and arranged to meet him.

ON RUE DE Nesle, she pulled up on her scooter, the bottle bag bungeed in her straw basket. "Let's go, Jean-Marie."

"You drive a pink scooter." Jean-Marie shook his head.

"No time to worry about your image, Jean-Marie."

"Forget it. Not even if I could get my prosthesis over the seat."

What, pink wasn't his color? The tall, muscle-bound ex-soldier filled out his jogging suit; she didn't think she could force him to get on.

"I've carried shopping, laptops, wiretapping equipment, and my eight-month-old daughter, who didn't complain. Now get on."

"I'm not your daughter, so don't talk to me like that."

She wanted to explode. But she read the fear in his eyes and remembered what the physical therapist had said. Jean-Marie preferred to stay close to home.

She grinned at Jean-Marie. "My office is right there." Pointed. "Just over the Pont Neuf. We'll make it in two minutes. I have photos from the Closerie des Lilas to show you. I'll be able to explain everything in privacy. There's an espresso machine."

"Espresso makes me jumpy."

As if he wasn't already? "Tisane, green tea, whatever you'd like. I'll send you back in a taxi."

"No way. Not a good idea."

He turned. She saw his shopping bag, a Żubrówka bottle peeking out.

"Bring that with you," she said. "Listen, Suzanne's in trouble—both of you are. And I might have Mirko's fingerprint."

"He's alive?"

"I'll know if you help me. And we can't do it here. Please."

Jean-Marie blinked. His voice changed. "You need a database to compare prints to."

The next minute he'd gripped her shoulder wedged himself on her cracked leather seat. "I'll ride sidesaddle. We shift our weight and lean into the turns, or we'll go heads up."

Aimée revved the handlebars, took the corner, and roared down rue de Nevers.

—

IN THE OFFICE, Aimée handed Jean-Marie the Hague documents Suzanne had given her. Together they skimmed the contents of Erich Kayser's report. Saj was printing out what he'd found on DGSE in Bosnia, NATO's movements in Foča, and their ICTY team.

Not much. And no luck, Saj reported, with the Institut Catholique courtyard. The CCTV was down.

"There are two options," said Saj. "We can try ICTY—I have a contact in their IT department and can see if he can dig deep and rustle up Mirko's file. It may or may not contain his fingerprints. The other option is hacking into Interpol, but that's only relevant if he's wanted internationally, not just in Bosnia."

"There's a third option," said Jean-Marie. "The Belgrade office. I spent six months there in tactical support, and Robert's got connections there, too."

"Robert?" said René, who was working at his terminal, his shirt collar loosened.

"Robert Guedilen, my old colleague, the fixer on our team. He's been after me to beef up his report anyway. I'll call him."

"Let's not forget France and Belgium," said René. "Mirko lived there from . . . Hold on." He scanned a document on his screen. "Born in Zagreb in 1963, family entry into France, 1973, as émigrés—he was ten, so unlikely to have fingerprints on file from then. Then, 1975, the family moved to Brussels. Belgian customs exit records show 1977. He'd have been twelve to fourteen there—possible someone printed him, although unlikely." René opened another window on his screen. "We could look for juvenile delinquency reports if there were any. But would they contain fingerprints?"

"Only one way to find out," Aimée said.

They divided up the work.

Her contact in the forensics unit at the *préfecture* was on a break. She left him a message. She couldn't bring him the Orangina bottles until she had Mirko's fingerprints to compare them to anyway.

Her old *lycée* classmate at the Paris school rectorate, Nina, answered on the second ring. "What now, Aimée? I'm going *en vacances* and wasn't even going to answer."

"Then good thing I caught you. Here's what I need."

Nina clucked her tongue and took down Mirko's particulars. Aimée was trying to find his family's old address in Paris.

"Don't ever make it simple, do you?" said Nina. "Those archives are in the cellar." A sigh. "Same as before?"

"Exactement," said Aimée. "And for you?"

Nina told her. That gave her two hours.

She didn't know how the address would help, but anything to flesh out the little she knew. She was still waiting on Bartok's return call.

"Instead of spinning our wheels," said Saj, "can't Jean-Marie speak up, say he's seen this Mirko? With a second sighting, they've got to take action, right? Demand a file with fingerprints."

René nodded. "You would think—"

"That's missing the point." Aimée stood. "Suzanne reported, and look what happened to her. There's no actual proof that Isabelle's death wasn't an accident unless we connect Mirko's fingerprints to those on the Orangina bottle. If that's even possible." She fanned herself with a sushi takeout menu. Hit the switch on the ceiling fan. "But it would be proof Mirko's alive," she said. "That's what

Suzanne needs. That's our goal. And under the war crimes statute, his ICTY case would be reactivated, and he'd be arrested here in France."

"She's right. We do this on our own," said Jean-Marie. She'd supplied him with water to hydrate him before he could hydrate himself with the Polish vodka. His leg was propped on the recamier by the ICTY reports. "We need solid evidence. After the scandal of Karadžić getting away, the French military prefers to stay hands off."

Saj pulled out a second laptop from his bag. "Say we get Mirko's fingerprints, and there's no match. Then what?"

"We'll go from there, Saj. Step-by-step," Aimée said. "Jean-Marie felt someone watching him. The whole thing smells, down to the setup at Closerie des Lilas. Whatever's going on . . . it's real. In the meantime, Jean-Marie, do you recognize either of these people?"

She'd pulled out the printed-out photos of the man by the Maréchal Ney statue and the woman at the pay phone. Now she taped them to the whiteboard.

"Spooks." Jean-Marie nodded. "These two came around at my debriefing. Types like these get involved when they want to cover up."

Aimée's stomach churned. She saw alarm cross René's face. "Alors, politics? Not our field," said René.

"Think of Suzanne," she said. "I need to figure out if this Mirko's alive. She'll be the one to turn him over."

Jean-Marie nodded again. "I'm with you. They're not. And better face it that you're in the equation now."

She chewed her lip.

They all returned to work. Jean-Marie used the extra laptop. René rewatched the bank's CCTV feed of the café. "I feel like I'm stuck in a Georges Perec novel," he said.

"You read too much, René," she said. "Another thriller?" René loved detective novels.

"You're kidding, right?" said René. "Perec wrote this whole book sitting in Saint Sulpice cafés, on the bench by the church, a stone's throw from that *café tabac*. It's nothing but three days of chronicling everything passing by."

"Sounds like a page-turner," said Jean-Marie.

"Fascinating," said René, ignoring Jean-Marie's sarcasm. "Perec took note of everything—old ladies, children holding their mothers' hands, the numbers of buses passing, the trucks making deliveries."

"What about the dogs?" Jean-Marie said.

"*Mais oui*, even the dogs."

"So a stakeout novel?" said Aimée.

"A novella," René said.

"I don't get the point," she said.

"There is no point," he said. "It's literary."

She thought for a moment. "How's what you're seeing now different from what Perec chronicled?"

"That was twenty years ago," said René. "Now people talk on cell phones; clothing styles are different. Buses still go the same routes, but the Métro runs quicker."

Aimée paused at the whiteboard. "Say that again."

"The Métro runs quicker." René looked up. "Now trains arrive every minute or so, but back then—"

"*Non*, not that. Cell phones." Of course. She put down the marker and joined René by his terminal. "Play the feed again."

He ran the short clip they'd edited it down to.

"Watch Suzanne," she said. "She's holding something, I assume her phone. Then she stops; people pass; she's turned. Like she's gotten a call or message."

René went back, sped the tape up. "Here?" René had eyes like a hawk.

"*Exactemente*. Now rewind . . ."

"It's digital, Aimée," he said.

"Right. Go back. Check for any passersby on a phone." She stared. "*Alors*, there's a heating and cooling service truck that wasn't there earlier."

René played it further. "A serviceman goes in. Comes right out. Then he lugs a ladder around the corner. Gone."

Aimée paused to think. To recall details. Overhead the fan stirred the warm air from the window open on to rue du Louvre.

"That's right," she said. "I remember when I went in there on Tuesday night someone was working on the fan unit above the *tabac* shelves. On a ladder."

"Look, Aimée," René said. "The serviceman's coming out the front door without the ladder. How?"

"Show me again."

René did, slowing the clip to view it frame-by-frame.

"So here he leaves the truck with his ladder." René's finger pointed at the screen. "Doesn't go in the café door. Three and a half minutes later, he emerges out the front without the ladder. Where'd it go?"

Aimée and René looked at each other.

"There must be a side door to the *café tabac*," she said. "The ladder must have blocked it when I was there."

"That's what I remembered," said Jean-Marie. "I thought you could enter the *tabac* via rue du Vieux Colombier."

So Mirko could have come and gone via the other street.

"I got a hit." Saj hunched in front of his screen. "Lojane, Macedonia, 1993, a drunk driving charge. Mirko was arrested, and they took his prints."

Aimée's jaw dropped. "Don't tell me you just hacked into Interpol? Europol?"

Saj winked at René.

"*Pas du tout.*" René shrugged. "Don't we always tell you, Aimée, simple is best?"

She sat cross-legged on Saj's tatami mat. "What's this? Greek? I can't read this."

"Serbia's in official control of the Serb-Macedonian border," said Saj. "Lojane's the border town."

Jean-Marie nodded. "Infamous for a people-smuggling network for people trying to get into the EU. A network stretching from Thessaloníki to Scandinavia."

Saj had pulled up an arrest record. "Lojane's records came through our band of brothers."

Hacker speak for white hats—the good hackers.

"Brilliant, Saj," said Aimée. Now to butter up her connection at the *préfecture*. "I need Metallica tickets, René. Front row."

René tugged his goatee. Clicked his keyboard.

"We're in luck. They're touring in September."

That would have to do.

SHE COULDN'T ENTER the *préfecture* with a police bulletin out on her. Couldn't beg for Morbier's help as she'd done in the past. So with Mirko's Macedonian arrest file burned on a CD and a bag full of Orangina bottles, she made her first stop: the morgue.

Serge met her in the off-white-and-green lounge on the morgue's lower floor. A place where family members waited to view their loved ones. It reeked of despair and pine air freshener. The second time she'd been here this week.

He looked around furtively to see if anyone was listening. "You want me to plant evidence, Aimée?"

"Not yet."

A pained expression crept over Serge's face.

"Maybe not at all," she said, with a reassuring smile. "I need to know if any fingerprints on these Orangina bottles match the ones on the arrest record on this CD."

"Seventeen bottles? Do you know how much work that takes?"

"An hour tops for my contact in the fingerprint lab at the *préfecture*. It's direct comparison, like slicing butter. Either a fingerprint matches or it doesn't."

Serge looked behind him. "That's assuming clear prints show on the bottles."

True. So many ifs. "It's what we've got to work with, Serge. *Alors*, we both know things get in the wrong file. Evidence mislabeled. It happens. Maybe the right Orangina bottle has been in the wrong file."

"I won't break the law."

The prints on the bottle had to go through the police system to show chain of custody. Authenticity. There was nothing official connecting the bottles with Isabelle Ideler's death right then, and if their true chain of custody were known, they would be inadmissible as evidence. She needed Serge to bend the rules for her if she was going to get the law on Mirko.

"We'll figure it out, Serge."

"If the prints match, is my ruling on Isabelle's death as accidental going to be challenged?" he asked.

Aimée twirled a strand of hair from her wig. "Anaphylactic shock killed Isabelle. No challenge there." She took a deep breath. "But if his prints show on the bottle, that's all

I need to force an investigation into a supposedly dead man who might be alive and engineering murders."

Serge hesitated. "*Alors*, I'm jammed. You know how it goes."

She'd give him a script. "You say the Orangina bottles arrived late and are now thought to contain evidence pertaining to another case. You insist they be checked against the prints on the CD. Put Loïc Bellan's name on it, and then bingo, you are top of the class. If Bellan questions you, just say, 'The report lists you in the chain of command.' Simple." She tugged Serge's sleeve. "The man's a Serbian criminal wanted by The Hague for crimes against humanity. A sealed indictment gets reactivated if there's proof he's alive." She leaned closer. "Serge, if he's the same man, he raped eight-year-old girls. Murdered them and threw them in a pit."

Serge's eyes bulged behind his thick lenses.

"We need proof. That's all."

Serge took off his glasses. Wiped the lenses with the edge of his lab coat. "You trust your contact in fingerprinting to keep his mouth shut, Aimée?"

"With these I do." She flashed the receipt for the tickets for the Metallica concert. "He adores heavy metal. He's helped me before."

"I'm not sure, Aimée."

"Did I forget to mention babysitting the twins on your upcoming anniversary?"

"You mean for a long weekend? It's a special anniversary."

She groaned inside. Envisioned making the twins run laps in Bois de Vincennes to exhaust them. As if anything could.

"Done," she said.

Serge took the disc and the bag of bottles, taking another furtive look around the lounge.

On her way out, Aimée dialed her fingerprint contact's number. "We're on. He's ready."

She hoped to God this brought answers. She couldn't pinpoint why, but she believed Pauline. Her habits fit a frugal school *guardienne* on a fixed income. Just forget the seeing-dead-people thing—just as long as the collected Orangina bottle came through.

On her scooter, she climbed the heights of Belleville, passed Saint-Fargeau Métro, and parked on rue du Groupe Manouchian. If they pertained to any school in Paris, from *école maternelle* to university, even going back a century or more, the records existed here at the rectorate.

The homeless man who'd made the back doorway of the rectorate his abode sat reading. Everyone in the quarter knew him as Flaubert since he read *Madame Bovary* front to back every six months. Had done so for at least the last ten years. He frequented the soup kitchen line; locals left him blankets; staff at the rectorate gave him odd jobs. Once a professor of literature? An academic? He had a story, like all those without a home.

"*Bonjour, Flaubert,*" said Aimée.

He looked up from his mattress in the doorway. A groomed beard, sandals, and the overcoat he always wore. She imagined he kept most of his life in the bulging pockets.

Even in this heat.

"You're here for a pickup, mademoiselle?"

"*Oui, Flaubert.*"

Flaubert handed her the manila envelope.

"Any message?" he said.

"Tell Nina it's taken care of," said Aimée, slipping him a fifty-franc note. "She'll understand."

Nina had a restraining order against her ex, but it didn't stop him from sending harassing emails, trolling her online. Aimée had blocked the ex's email account for good. Slashed his credit score as an added thank-you.

IN THE SHADE of the kiosk by the Métro, she opened the envelope. Inside were smudged photocopied pages.

Mirko Vladić had attended the *école élémentaire* at 42 rue Madame. The street Charlotte lived on. A beige-and-salmon-brick school a stone's throw from Jardin du Luxembourg.

Shaken, Aimée read further.

His father had been a construction worker; his mother a concierge; domiciled at the building that employed her, 3 rue Palatine. The short block crossing rue Servandoni, Erich Kayser's street.

Was Mirko back "home"?

Her phone trilled. A number she didn't know.

"It's Bartok. I meet you. Now."

BARTOK MET HER at Odéon under Danton's statue, a popular meeting place. Dove-grey pigeons fanned their tails, their white V markings creating a random beauty on the street. In summer, even the rats with wings looked *beaux*.

"Monsieur Bartok, if you can help me—"

"I know what you want," he interrupted. Checked his phone. "Let's walk and talk. I've got a work site to check."

He didn't look back. He expected her to follow.

She caught up as he crossed the crowd in line for the cinema.

"My name is good," said Bartok. He was short, stocky, and muscular. "My people are good. My work is good, and clients trust me." He paused, and she almost ran into him. "You know how hard such a thing is?"

She figured that was a rhetorical question.

"Hard for anyone. But for an émigré like me, even harder." He was walking fast. "It takes time to build trust. Fifteen years I'm here. When I first come, I sleep in a friend's bar in the storeroom. I learn my French at the counter, do any job I could. Thank God I'm good with my hands. Now I employ good people, do good work. So good I've remodeled six of the bars in Saint-Germain and am contracted for three more. I work like dog, have different teams who I train and inspect every day. I work, but . . ."

A truck passed, clattering on the street.

Bartok continued. "In Croatia, there's no work, no buildings left, and no money to rebuild. Here, this country give me a new life." He paused at a red light. "I have choice when I arrive, you know. Steal and live the old way or a chance for a different life. That's what I tell my team. I take you on. You must prove to me you're serious."

She realized he was talking about Mirko.

"In other words, Mirko wasn't serious," she said.

"Listen," he said, his thick, calloused fingers motioning her forward. "Not a good one to know. Mirko brings *bura*, we say, a bad wind."

"'A bad wind'? How's that?"

"A lot of young guys are like that. Like me, once. I give him a job, show him. A chance, you know, like I had."

Aimée's pulse picked up. "Recently?"

He shrugged. Took out a bandanna and wiped his

forehead. "Three, no, maybe four years ago. I haven't seen him since."

That would have been 1996 or '95. A dead end.

"Have you heard if he's back in Paris?" she asked.

"If he was, I don't want to know," said Bartok, checking his phone again. "But Professor Olgan, he say I should talk with you. That's it. I talk to you."

She felt desperate, sensing there were things he hadn't told her. A silver cross hung from a chain amid Bartok's dark chest hair. "Did you find Mirko at Cathédrale Saint-Volodymyr, that place where men search for work?"

"*Mais non*, he is a friend of a cousin . . . like that kind of connection."

"I don't understand. If he's a Serb and you're Croat . . ."

"It's complicated."

Everything was complicated lately.

"Simplify it for me, Bartok."

"Simple? You want simple? Where I come from, nothing's simple. My father's Croat from Hungary, okay? My mother's a Serbian born in Croatia. My brother married a Bosniak. You understand?"

"Bosniak?"

"Muslim background, born in Bosnia. My family, you know, it's like so many mixed families in my village. We never care. But then Tito dies. The politicians come." Bartok gave a long sigh. "Neighbors turn on neighbors, Bosnians and Serbs who grow up together. How can they stir such hate when the mosques and churches are right next to each other?" He shook his head. "We marry each other; no cultural divides until Milošević, his greed, his myth of Greater Serbia. But then all the stockades; the UN food workers black-market, you know; they put the profit in their pockets."

Jean-Marie had said as much.

"Most people, like us, we never want this senseless fighting."

"So you're saying, you give Balkan men a chance for a job . . ."

He nodded. "And it works or doesn't. Mirko didn't."

"How?"

He paused. Diesel exhaust from a bus filled her throat. The light turned green, and he took off. She ran to keep up with him.

"Like how you say . . . place-holding?"

"Holding a place in what way, Bartok?"

They'd reached the half circle in front of the Odéon-Théâtre. A cat stretched on the tiles of the resto La Méditerranée under Cocteau's logo.

"I mean, it's cover, you know. Right away I understand he's connected."

Bartok's phone rang. And then he was speaking in a language she didn't understand and hurrying back the way they came.

She scurried after him, checking her own phone. Melac had left a message saying to meet in the park in half an hour. She heard Chloé's cooing in the background, and her heart warmed.

So glad she was only ten minutes away.

Bartok turned down rue Monsieur-le-Prince. She found him in the first café on the left at the counter, still on his phone, beckoning her inside. Nicotine-stained walls, a browned mirror with business cards stuck to it behind the counter, and a sleeping corgi sprawled sausage-like on the chipped tile. The place looked like those cafés she remembered accompanying her father to as a little girl. A place where he knew the owners, followed up a clue as she drank *chocolat chaud.*

Bartok had ordered an espresso, its steam coiling above the zinc counter. The older woman behind the bar had a helmet of tight grey curls, the type of cat-eye glasses that were popular in the sixties, a cigarette hanging from her mouth, and a questioning look in her eyes.

"I'll have the same," said Aimée. *"Merci."*

Bartok slipped his phone into his pocket. *"Désolé,* supplies didn't arrive; burst water pipe; the joists full of rot . . ." He sipped. "There's always something."

"Who's Mirko connected to?"

An old fan blew hot air. The corgi snorted awake, opening his big brown eyes. A second later closed them again.

"He's protected," Bartok said. "Everywhere it's the same. You're connected, and *then you're protected.*"

His words resonated with what she'd heard from Jean-Marie.

"It's all about who you know, who you can help, who can help *you* down the *rue.*"

"Getting favors owed to you, you mean?"

He lifted his shoulders. He'd gotten the Gallic shrug down perfectly. "Or it's what you know that someone needs, or what you hold over them. Mademoiselle, I don't read you as naïve."

"Maybe I'm confused as to why a Serbian war criminal's protected," she said. Downed the espresso.

Bartok threw down a five-franc coin. Leaned forward to kiss the woman behind the bar on both cheeks. "Louise, if I weren't married . . ."

She grinned. "You'd wine and dine my daughter, if I had one. Go with God, Bartok, and my disposal valve's clogged when you have time."

They stood outside in the shade of la Maison d'Auguste Comte, a museum and former home of the positivist philosopher, Aimée remembered from a school trip.

Bartok took her hand. His calluses rubbed her thumb. "No one accuses me of being intellectual—me, I never finish school. But I read people, mademoiselle. Have to. Developed that thing in my gut and go by what it tells me. Sometimes, I just know."

There was more; she knew it.

"After Mirko was with me two days, I knew. Bad news."

"Did you ever hear where he went?"

Bartok let go of her hand. Looked both ways. "You never heard this from me. In fact, you never heard this, okay?"

"I promise."

He leaned closer as if the walls had ears.

"He was in arms, munitions from Dravić. A man whose father was Ustaše." He said it close to a whisper.

"Ustaše?"

"Ustaše were the fascist, nationalist Nazi Croats during the war. They run their own concentration camps. Their Jasenovac complex was a hell."

"But what does that have to do with Mirko?"

"The father's dead. Last year Dravić, the son, an arms dealer, dies in a shootout in Kotor. Those are the kind of people Mirko is connected to, *comprends?*"

"You're saying that Mirko had connections with a big-deal Croatian arms dealer. Maybe took over his business?"

He sucked in air. "More or less."

Could this relate to Mirko's ties to the elusive Gourmelon? The mistake? Protected, but by whom?

"Bartok, one more question, please. Do you remember him as a thinker, a planner, or more of a thug, unsophisticated?"

A siren wailed in the distance.

"Eh, that's a long time ago," Bartok said.

"But Mirko made an impression on you. Didn't you say you can read people?"

Bartok shrugged. "Street-smart, that's what I remember. Nondescript yet savvy. I'd say he is all of these. I think he use working with me as a cover, then move on. When I hear who he is connected to, it make sense. Make me glad he moves on."

SHE WALKED AND thought. Walking cleared her head and helped the pieces settle. Sometimes even fit them together.

From Bartok, she'd gleaned . . . what? That Mirko had had connections to arms dealers—that he'd been protected. Things she'd already known.

Right now she needed to check in with the office before she met Melac and Chloé at the park.

René answered. "Nothing new so far. What about you?"

"Can you put me on speakerphone?"

She updated them on her visit to the rectorate and her talk with Bartok.

"So Mirko knew the area," said René, his voice tinny, "spoke passable French."

"I'm looking up the arms dealer, Dravić." Saj's voice came over the line.

Jean-Marie piped in. "When Robert returns my call, I'll ask him if he knows of Dravić."

"Ask him why your team would be targeted here in Paris. Why now? We don't know if someone else is behind Mirko. All we have are questions."

No answers.

"*Attends,*" said René. "He had the opportunity and the means. He knows the quartier. That's if he's alive. Maybe it's a simple case of revenge. Wipe your team off the earth because you hunted him down and saw proof of his crimes?"

"But he was reported dead," said Saj. "Why risk being discovered to come back here?"

There was more to it, and she didn't know what.

"Gourmelon, Mirko's contact, who engineered Karadžić's escape and facilitated murky arms deals . . . According to Robert, he's gone to ground," said Jean-Marie. "*Alors,* as Saj says, why would Mirko chance it if he were alive?"

And how long would the fingerprints take?

They were no further than before.

A click indicating another call. Serge with good news? Or Serge apologetic that he'd reconsidered, gotten cold feet, gotten called to another case? She could imagine a hundred scenarios.

"I'll call you back," she said.

But it was an unknown number. She glimpsed Chloé across the gravel path at the Jardin de la Roseraie sandboxes. Her heart melted, as it always did. She waved. Melac, in the sandbox with Chloé, looked up, took Chloé's chubby fist, and together they waved back.

She wanted to ignore her phone. Wanted to join them and play in the sand. Share ice cream with Chloé and her father. They formed a slice of heaven in her line of vision.

The phone stopped ringing.

It rang again immediately. She couldn't ignore it. Maybe she should have.

"*Oui?*" she said.

"Okay, mystery woman, I asked myself why you wore a

disguise and wig in the hottest part of the day," said Loïc Bellan, "and why *la Proc* has it in for you."

Of all people. Of all times.

"I can't talk now, Bellan," she said.

"Then a professor at the Beaux-Arts is hospitalized, the directrice steps down, and *la Proc* takes an interest in my investigation."

"What investigation?"

"A Hague war crimes investigator's defenestration on rue Servandoni."

Erich Kayser. Her blood ran cold. She remembered Bellan talking to the woman in the framing shop.

Now it made sense. The fact that he worked in DGI now meant he was part of counterterrorism and the "big boy" investigation near *le Sénat*. And who knew what else? He was looking for her. *Join the crowd*, she almost said.

Perspiration collected behind her shaking knees.

"Lo and behold, I get some good news," said Bellan. "Some fingerprints arrive in my email, and zip, it's an auto-generated match to someone I don't even know."

So Serge and her contact had made good on what she'd asked them to do. A brief second of relief. Had the finger-prints on one of the Orangina bottles matched Mirko's?

"*Et alors?*" she said.

"Why do I think it's got you all over it?" he said. "I think you should tell me the story, and I need to listen."

"You give me too much credit, Bellan."

But now she'd need him for this plan to work.

Chloé sent sand flying with her shovel. Melac wiped his eyes, brushed the sand off Chloé.

"Aimée, Aimée," Loïc Bellan was saying. "Talk to me, please."

Chloé's little cries erupted as Melac lifted her up.

"Is that . . . Jean-Claude's grandchild I hear?" Bellan asked.

If only Jean-Claude could have seen her. Aimée pushed that thought aside. "Bellan, tell me whom the fingerprints belonged to."

"You'll make it worth my while?"

She tapped her sandaled toe. "I'm waiting."

"Tedsolovic Nowak."

Her shoulders sagged with disappointment. "Who?"

"You might know him by one of his other names, Mirko Vladić."

Alive. Mirko was alive. She made her legs move. "I'll call you later."

"*Non, non*, meet me at your office in ten minutes."

"Make it forty if you want to land a big fish."

FIFTEEN MINUTES LATER she'd given Chloé a bottle, hummed a lullaby, and pushed the stroller until her little coos turned into snores.

"Why don't we walk through the garden?" Melac suggested. His sunglasses hid his eyes.

"I've got to rush back to work."

"What? I planned this afternoon since you said—"

"Complications came up, Melac. *Désolée.*"

She parked the stroller by the sandbox. Set the brake with her toe. Her gaze caught on a drawing in the sand—the outline of a mouse wearing a crown drawn in deft strokes. Familiar. Oh so familiar.

The story she'd loved as a child—Emil, the mouse who lived in the Louvre.

But Emil wasn't from a children's book.

Now the realization came crashing down on her. Why Melac's mother had seemed so familiar to her—the woman hadn't resembled Melac. Aimée's mouth dried; her stomach was queasy. If she'd paid attention, she should have recognized her despite the makeup, disguise, wig. The odd accent. Put it together.

The bile rose in her stomach and she almost threw up.

Emil, the story her mother had made up and illustrated with drawings. Just for her. The mother who'd abandoned her.

And it stunned her like a punch in the chest.

She spun around. Saw the woman sitting on the bench in the shade of the roses. She looked thin, unwell under the makeup.

"I thought you'd . . ." Aimée's breath caught.

Her mother.

"Why now?" Aimée took a breath, sat down.

"I wanted to see Chloé, touch her. Like you, I wish Jean-Claude could have seen his granddaughter."

All Aimée's childhood pain welled up—nights looking out the window hoping her mother would walk across the bridge. Aimée wanted to hurt her, make her pay.

But she'd never been this close to her mother since she was eight years old. Caught that whiff of muguet, lily of the valley, the same fragrance she remembered her mother wearing. Something shifted inside of Aimée.

"Selfish of me, I know," said her mother.

She felt sorry for this woman—imagined her life as lonely on the run. How sad to think of all she'd missed.

"I'll never leave Chloé, ever," Aimée said. "Not like you left me."

A downward flick of the eyes, and then her mother's gaze met hers straight on.

"Your father taught you the important things in life. Me, I discovered them too late." Sydney reached over to touch Aimée's arm lightly. "Or have I?"

"You want in on our life?" Aimée wanted to pull back. Couldn't. "What right do you have? Why lie? Make him lie for you?"

Melac, the liar, was pushing the stroller toward the fountain. Giving them time alone?

"Don't blame him," Sydney said. "It's safer this way, incognito. I explained the situation. He agreed."

"What are you talking about?" Aimée asked.

"Morbier's dying. No one can protect you anymore except Melac."

"Protect me from what?"

"Think of Chloé, Aimée."

She pulled away. Anger battled with tears. "You're still wanted. Up to your old tricks. Don't pull me into this. I won't play the victim."

"For years, I've kept you out of this." That accented voice stirred a strange sense of familiarity inside Aimée. "But I know things about the Hand, those in power who murdered your father."

Hadn't Aimée taken care of them? Caught and exposed them? "But it was Morbier."

"You really should pay attention, *Amy*." The American way she said "Amy" made Aimée feel eight years old. "It's bigger than that. So much bigger."

Her skin crawled. "So that's whose been watching me?"

Alert, Sydney sat forward, pulled out her cell phone. "Who do you mean?"

"Don't play with me."

Sydney murmured something into her phone as she

scanned the garden. Stood. "You've been followed. But not by anyone interested in me."

Mirko.

Aimée looked over her shoulder.

Green, dappled leaves; couples strolling; children.

Sydney slipped something into Aimée's hand. "Read it, and destroy."

"Like I should believe anything you say?"

A click came from Sydney's bag. The unmistakable snick of a pistol's safety sliding off.

"A gun in your handbag?"

"We need to work together on this, Amy," she said. "Call Melac, and tell him to take Chloé to that address. Find a taxi in front of *le Sénat* and lose your tail."

"And you?" Her voice choked. She couldn't help it.

"We pretend this never happened."

Aimée felt a warm hand on hers. A squeeze.

Sydney disappeared behind the trees. Leaving, as she always did. Aimée's hand trembled as she punched in Melac's number.

"Listen, I've been followed," she said.

She told Melac what to do.

For once, he didn't argue.

"I don't know who's following me, but there's a chance he knows Suzanne's place."

"What?"

"Explanations later. I'll meet you as soon as I get things for Chloé." She gave him the address on the paper, the door code, memorizing them as she recited them. "This is safest."

"For now," said Melac and hung up.

SHE TOOK THE path along the back of the Musée du Luxembourg, her heart almost thudding out of her chest. She forced herself to keep a steady pace, tagging along close behind a couple and then mingling among the people at the narrow exit on the side of the museum.

No taxis.

She pulled out the card she'd gotten from Monsieur Poncelet, her taxi driver from the other day, and called him. She joined a group assembling for a guided tour, tried to blend in, and kept her eye on rue de Vaugirard.

A Taxi Bleu.

"Good thing I had a fare nearby," Poncelet said. "Life treating you better today?"

A murderous Serbian war criminal on the loose and out for her blood, her daughter's safety to worry about? Not to mention her deadbeat spy mother turning up out of the blue?

"It's complicated." She slipped two hundred-franc notes by the gearbox. "You're going to lose whoever's trailing me. He might be in a car, or on a bicycle—maybe on foot."

"You mean a tag team, like when the *flics* trade off to avoid suspicion?"

He watched too much *télé*.

"Close enough," she said. "No chase scenes, though."

She outlined her plan. The hot air whipped in through the rolled-down window. "So keep your meter off. I'm engaging you for a couple of hours. *D'accord?*"

"*À votre service.*" He fiddled with the meter. "I'll tell my boss it jammed."

THE ARTISTS' SQUAT, a graffitied, pitted stone *hôtel particulier*, had avoided the wrecking ball. Not for much longer, Aimée figured, in this desired chunk of real estate. Hôtel de Choiseul-Praslin, built by an aristocrat on the old road to Versailles, had become the National Savings Bank, then a postal museum that was later taken over by artist squatters. Great parties, Aimée remembered.

She jumped out of the cab on rue de Sèvres. The overgrown front garden hid the fact that the building had access to the next street. She picked her way over discarded metal and found herself under a soaring ceiling flaking plaster, chipped-nosed cherubs forever caught in flight in the boiserie. A collective artists' squat. She waved at Artaud, the metal sculptor, who put down his welding torch to wave back. No one else paid her attention. In the old kitchen, she pulled on a silk jacket, another wig, new glasses. Slipped on her Louboutin sandals and left through the art gallery, which doubled as an underground cinema at night.

The taxi pulled up on rue Saint-Romain exactly per the plan.

"Anyone follow you?" she asked.

"I lost the motorcycle three minutes ago." Poncelet described the rider as he wove through traffic: black helmet, visor, and black leathers on a matching bike—could be anyone. "My son will pick up your scooter, then park it at that garage on Ile Saint-Louis."

"Brilliant, Poncelet. The spark plug's temperamental. It's Italian."

"What do you expect?"

She struggled to wedge her scooter key off the chain, nicking her cuticle. *Merde*. She sucked the welling blood, and her mind went to the warm hand that had enclosed hers not twenty minutes earlier. She heard that wobble in her mother's voice: *Selfish . . . I wanted to see Chloé, touch her*

. . . We need to work together . . . Aimée's heart thudded. It jarred her, how thin Sydney had appeared under her blazer. All that effort she'd gone to, enlisting Melac . . .

Aimée's phone rang. René.

"Why don't you update me? We're worried," said René, petulant.

"We're going to plan B, René."

"Remind me again—what's Plan B?"

She lowered her voice. "The prints came back a match."

There was a sound on René's end that sounded a lot like his tea cup smashing on the floor. René cursed. "*Mon Dieu,* Mirko's alive?"

She sucked in her breath. "On the loose and on a mission. I've been followed all day. I've just lost him—for now. Make sure the building back door's open, okay?"

She glanced behind her. A bus.

"Go to the *flics,* Aimée."

"Matter of fact, one should arrive in a few minutes. Don't let him in until I get there. I'll pack my things and Chloé's."

"You two should stay with me," he said.

And fit where in René's studio lined with computer terminals?

"We're camping at Martine's, more room," she lied. "You and Saj take the laptops, and work at home."

"What about Jean-Marie? He's hit the vodka big-time. The guy's a mess."

"Has he talked to this Robert?"

"Not yet."

She had to come up with a plan.

"Get Robert's number," she said. "Find an excuse to look in Jean-Marie's phone. Then drive him to a hotel; put it on our card. Can you do that?"

"If Mirko's loose, Aimée, you're in danger."

"Tell me about it. We don't want Jean-Marie taken out next. So see that he gets settled somewhere safe. Then get in touch with Bella at Théâter de Nesle—a real battle-ax. Get her to keep watch over him."

"Got it."

AIMÉE LEFT THE taxi on rue Saint-Honoré, nodded to a woman working in a boulangerie as she passed through, and left a twenty-franc note by the crusty browned baguettes cooling on the racks. In the boulangerie's rear courtyard, she opened the back cellar door of her office building. She crossed the stone-walled cellar and passed the garbage bins, reached her building's staircase and mounted three floors. She hit the Digicode and stepped into Leduc Detective.

Loïc Bellan chewed on an apple, gazing at the dry-erase board. *Merde!* Why had René let him in?

"Your partner, Monsieur Friant, was having trouble with a big *mec*—quite drunk," said Bellan. "So I helped them downstairs. He said I could stay."

Bellan's eyes hadn't left the dry-erase board, where Aimée had taped up Mirko's photo.

"You do have a story to tell me, Aimée," he said. "And your hair's different again. Fascinating. I'm listening."

She threw her bag on her desk, unclipped her wig, and kicked off her sandals. Hit the ceiling fan switch and headed to the espresso machine. Her mind raced.

"Café?" she asked.

"Guess I'll need it."

The dark brown stream dripped into the two demitasse cups. Simple, keep it simple, her father always said.

"Sugar?" she asked.

"I'm sweet enough. *Merci.*"

She'd forgotten his corny sense of humor.

Only after she handed Bellan the espresso did his gaze swivel around and take in the office. Chloé's crib by the old sepia sewer maps on the walls; Aimée's father's mahogany desk, where she worked; her grandfather's photo in his old *Sûreté* uniform. The original Leduc Detective license.

"This place breathes Jean-Claude and *le vieux*—that's what we called your *grand-père*," Bellan said.

"I know what you called him," she said, thinking fondly of her grandfather. She packed Chloé's stuffed owl and a few bottles into a leather holdall. "But you're here for a big fish. If you want to land him, I'd like something in return."

She needed Bellan on her side.

"Everything I say stays here," she said. "Between us."

"How can I agree if I don't know what 'everything' means?"

"Look, someone's been following me. I lost the tail for now. But I won't put my baby at risk, *comprends?*"

"Who's asking you to? *Alors*, tell me from the beginning."

"Let's start with the fingerprints. You got a match to Mirko Vladić?"

"Via the National Central Bureau in Nantes. And a confirmation from Interpol. It's all automated now." He snorted. "How can I use the prints in an investigation if I don't know which one? But that's why you need me, *non?*"

Smart. "This works both ways. Get me off the hook, and you land a big fish wanted by the ICTY, the International Criminal Tribunal for the former Yugoslavia."

He liked part of this; she could tell. Would be stupid not to. And her father had once said Bellan ranked at the top of all recruits he'd known.

"I'm listening." He handed her a fingerprint match verification so fresh her palm smudged the printer ink.

"These match a Serbian war criminal who was under indictment from the Hague," said Aimée, "until an ICTY team saw him blown up near Foča about a year ago. Or thought they did."

Bellan tossed the core of his apple in the trash. "According to this evidence you brought to my attention, Mirko Vladić's here in Paris, alive. And you'll make a statement to this effect?"

This part got tricky. No way in hell did she want to make a statement.

"*Alors*, two members of the ICTY team from Foča died in engineered 'accidents,' and a third—the drunk you met—could be next."

Bellan's phone rang. He glanced. "Nantes' calling."

"Please let it wait."

"That was you in Erich Kayser's flat," said Bellan, his tone matter of fact. "A witness claims you pushed him. Can identify you."

"Me? He saw me for one second in a window across the street—a brunette in a dark room—and he's going to pretend he saw me commit murder? I didn't push Erich Kayser. I never even met him."

"You ran away. Looks pretty guilty."

"Put yourself in my place, Bellan. Would you stick around? Get pushed next?"

"You could have told the truth," said Bellan, sipping his espresso.

"And be questioned, spend all night in a cell?" She pushed up her sleeves. Damn heat. "Like I can pay a babysitter that kind of overtime. Get real, Bellan. Erich Kayser was killed by Mirko Vladić. You know it. I'd gone to see him after Isabelle's death and was too late to save him. You'll never prove I was there—the concierge thought I was Isabelle."

"We'll get back to that," said Bellan. "Let's see your theory of how the fingerprints on the Orangina bottle connect him to the murder."

"Theory? We've done the work for you."

She pulled another dry-erase board down so she could sketch a map of the quartier as she spoke.

"We'll start here at the *café tabac* on the corner of rue de Rennes and Vieux Colombier, with the Métro in front. On Monday night, the CCTV camera shows Suzanne Lesage, formerly of—"

"I know her. Go on."

"Who recognized Mirko inside buying cigarettes. We figure Mirko left out the side door, which the camera doesn't cover."

She continued through the pieces of her puzzle: Isabelle Ideler's death; her visits to Charlotte, the morgue, and the Dutch embassy; how she'd wound up attempting to inform Erich Kayser—arriving too late.

Bellan, demitasse and saucer in hand, had moved to sit on the edge of René's desk.

"Get practical," he said. "How could a Serbian paramilitary thug engineer all this?"

Aimée sipped. Nodded. Bellan's remark was a good sign. "I wonder, too. It's an elaborate plot, sophisticated, involving access to airline luggage, medical records, surveillance." She paused. "If there's a mastermind behind this, using him . . . *Alors*, I'll just keep to what I know. Mirko speaks French—how much, I don't know, but Mirko's family lived here when he was ten to twelve. He attended school on rue Madame and lived on rue Palatine—close to where the deaths of both Isabelle Ideler and Erich Kayser happened. He's back in his old hood, knows the quartier."

Bellan pointed. "Tell me more about this."

She drew a line from the *café tabac* to Charlotte's apartment on rue Madame, showing him where Isabelle had stayed. Another line up rue de Fleurus to the gates of Jardin du Luxembourg. Aimée described Isabelle's path through the park. Made an X for the apiary, where Isabelle's body had been discovered and where Pauline had picked up Mirko's Orangina bottle.

"He's a murderer making it look like accidents," Aimée said.

Bellan twisted his watchband of worn brown leather, flicked the buckle. Thinking.

"A dead Serbian war criminal surfaces in Paris," he said, his words measured, "to knock off members of an ICTY team who could identify him. That's what you're saying?"

"I think it's more than that. Why resurface now?"

"You mean why chance it? That's easy. *Le Sénat*'s hearings on the Balkans will determine the military budget there."

"How does that threaten him?"

"It threatens the military."

Tingles ran down her arms.

"That's too broad. Vague." She tried a hunch. "What about an arms dealer who had too much to lose?"

"I'm a *flic*, good at my work, love what I do. Now my job's liaising with a branch that's carrying on a long rivalry with the military. You know how that goes."

Like she cared. But if Bellan was mentioning this, it meant something important.

She decided to throw out the names, see if they stuck on Bellan's brain. "Anything to do with Gourmelon, the snitch, or Dravić, a dead arms dealer?"

Bellan's demitasse rattled on the saucer as he set it down.

She'd hit a chord. Suzanne's words "mistakes were made" again came back to her.

But he was too good a *flic* to let anything slip and brought things back to Aimée. "If I'm to proceed, you need to make a statement, Aimée."

"Bellan, if mistakes were made—maybe supplying arms via Mirko or supporting the ethnic cleansing—someone wants it quiet. The ICTY operated under a sealed indictment."

"*Et alors?*"

"Mirko survived, and whoever got him out of Serbia and to France wants things quiet. He's protected."

"Conjecture."

But he was thinking; she could tell.

"Come to the *commissariat*, and I'll take your statement," he said.

With an APB on her? She wasn't spending the night in a cell. "You're kidding, right? Make my part go away."

"I'm a *flic*, like your father was. We do this the right way."

"The right way's open to interpretation," she said. "You'll get the credit, engineer the coup of arresting him for crimes committed here and abroad."

His phone rang again. He glanced at it. "That's my Interpol contact. Mirko's fingerprint identification has hit all the agencies. The Hague, local forces in Serbia. Do we do this or not?"

If only there were a way to do it without her name on it. She had to nail Mirko. She nodded, sat down, and began typing at her computer. "Right here. Right now."

"That's the deal?"

"Along with protection for Jean-Marie and vindication for Suzanne."

He sighed. "Then I need Mad Max." He noticed her look. "Not the movie. A general. He's a legend. The mastermind leading to Carlos the Jackal's capture."

"In return you get the CD I found in Erich Kayser's apartment with his report. Maybe you'll find an answer in *le Sénat*'s hearings."

"You stole it from his apartment?"

"Better me than Mirko." She slid it over her desk. "It's yours now."

Admiration and irritation fought each other in Bellan's expression. "You're wasted here, Aimée. I could keep you busy in a legal way."

Like that was going to happen. "What's Mad Max's claim to fame besides the Jackal? That's ancient history."

"*Pas du tout*. The legend operates out of Hôtel de Brienne with carte blanche to consolidate all Balkan intelligence. Agents and officers report directly to him, even over their superiors."

Mad Max had the chain-of-command thing down. Sounded like the one to get things done.

"Who's following you, Aimée?"

"The spooks who committed Suzanne, maybe? Or your people?"

"My people?" Bellan shook his head. "I've removed the APB."

"*Vraiment?* Where do you get the authority?"

"I convinced *la Proc*. Took doing. So you owe me."

"Not as much as you owe me for this feather in your cap."

"Mirko's a gangster, hit man, right?"

"And a war criminal who raped and murdered little girls."

Bellan looked startled at this. Paused. "And you know this how?"

"Look at the reports on Foča's mass graves. Sickening."

"If you know about Mirko, no doubt he knows about you, Aimée."

She pushed that aside. All she could imagine, if they caught Mirko, was the long road to trial. Her required testimony. Then a knock on the door one night, in a year, three years—a gun in her face.

How far did Bellan's influence stretch? Could she trust him? But she had to cut the doubt, the luxury of worry—no other option existed.

He took her printed-out statement. His phone trilled again.

He answered this time. Turned away. A few *ouis* before he hung up, pocketed the CD. "Mad Max thanks you for your cooperation. Your name will be kept out of the investigation, at least for now. And he says to please leave this to the investigators."

"He said please?"

Bellan gave a half shrug as he stood to leave. "I added that for *politesse*." His eyes turned serious. "Sounds better than an order, *non*?"

His footsteps echoed down the stairs.

Loud and clear—she was supposed to stay hands off. She'd fulfilled her promise to Suzanne. So why the creeping unease as she packed extra diapers into the carryall?

She tossed in several burner phones, extra SIM cards, from the collection René kept in his drawer. Left her laptop.

On René's desktop screen, a message had popped up.

Robert Guedilen, 56 rue Jacques Callot. A number at his office on Boulevard Saint-Michel at l'École des Mines.

No time like the present. She punched in his number.

"Monsieur Guedilen's in a meeting," said the receptionist over the phone. "He'll be back within the hour. May I take a message?"

"I'll call back," Aimée said. "*Merci.*"

She worried over Jean-Marie and wanted his colleague's information, if he had any. She wanted to assure Suzanne but had no way to reach her now. Her call to Melac got a busy signal.

Frustrated, she left the way she'd come. Poncelet was waiting in the taxi and shifted into first as she closed the door.

"Where to now?" His eyes gleamed.

As she pulled out the address given to her by her mother—how odd that sounded—Aimée's cell phone rang.

"You gave me your card," said a breathy, guttural voice she recognized as that of Gilberte, the Montenegrin concierge of the building by Galerie Tournon. "Showed me a photo. Remember?"

Aimée stiffened. "I remember. What about the photo?"

"Fourteen bis rue de Condé." The phone clicked off.

Saturday, Late Afternoon

"So you're on her speed dial? Good job, Montenegrin whore. Glad I followed her here." He held a knife to Gilberte's baby's throat in the booster seat. The baby whimpered. "Do I take care of him now, tomorrow, or—?"

"*Non, non,* I say nothing," Gilberte pleaded. "I disappear. We go."

The *zanata,* filthy Montenegrin whore, shook, still on her knees. Clutched his leg. He shook her off, stamped her cheap phone to pieces.

"I beg you . . ."

He kicked her. Again and again until she crumpled, moaning, on the tiny kitchen's floor littered with children's toys. That desperate, pathetic look in her eyes. Not enough.

"Maybe I wait until your little girl comes home," he said.

"I do more. You like again?"

He rifled through her turquoise handbag. Found her fat ring of building keys.

"You listen to what I tell you, and the baby lives," he said. "Maybe your daughter, too."

Saturday, Late Afternoon

AIMÉE RANG GILBERTE back, her heart in her throat. The call went dead.

Was Mirko at that address?

A setup?

"Where to?" Poncelet had pulled over on rue Saint-Placide.

"Drive past 14 bis rue de Condé."

She called Bellan. Needed backup. Got his voice mail and left the address. Then she rang René and explained.

"Call the cavalry, Aimée."

"The cavalry doesn't answer."

"Don't you dare, Aimée. What if it's a setup? What if he's waiting for you?"

"That's what worries me," said Aimée. Her mind raced. "But if Gilberte recognized him from the photo I showed her, saw him at the address . . ."

"Or Mirko followed you there. Coerces this Gilberte to call you . . . wait."

Quiet except for clicking.

"René?"

"Hold on." In the background, she heard René in conversation. A minute passed. Two.

The soles of her Louboutin sandals stuck to the taxi mat. Her neck dripped perspiration. The radio channel playing in the car stuttered with static.

"René?"

"Cavalry's en route," said René. "Keep out of the area. I've called the bomb squad, robots and sniffer dogs."

She gulped. "That's overkill, René. You're overreacting."

"Someone has to. Stay the hell away, Aimée."

She rolled down the taxi window. Sirens wailed. A blue-and-white police car raced by the taxi. Fire engines pulled up at the other end of the block.

"Talk about quick response time!" she said.

"With le Sénat, the ministries right there?" said René. "They're in-house, prepared for a moment's notice. Use a burner phone from now on. The military alert means they'll be tracking all GPS and calls via the signal towers."

"Wait, what if Mirko slips away? Did you give a description?"

"Done."

René hung up.

Poncelet turned in the driver's seat, his eyes wide. "Did your friend just do what I think he did?"

"If I told you, Poncelet, I'd have to . . ."

Pause. "Kill me?"

"Not until your son brings my scooter." She tried for a grin. "Mais non, let's keep this quiet, eh?"

"A little hard to with those." The sky filled with the sounds of helicopters. "My shift's almost up. I'm an hour over our agreement."

Translation: he wanted out. She didn't blame him. If she were smart, she'd be out already.

Her phone rang. "Didn't you get the message, Aimée?" Bellan's voice, hoarse and panting, came over the line. "Back off."

"Mirko's been seen at fourteen bis rue de Conde," she said, glad he couldn't read her face and see the lie. "Check on my source, Bellan." She gave him Gilberte's address, phone number. "I've got a bad feeling."

"You and me both. But me not the way you think."

AIMÉE COULDN'T CALL Melac and check on Chloé, not with the military monitoring all cell-phone transmissions. Not a good idea since her mother had provided the "safe house." Aimée didn't want to jeopardize Sydney, despite everything.

Stuck. Her fingers worried her bag strap. She wished the taxi could go faster. That they could escape the cordon the *flics* were erecting at street corners.

A net to catch Mirko.

Would it work?

Staff and workers, evacuated for safety from *le Sénat*, grouped on the hot pavement. One read a newspaper; another filed her nails.

To them, it was just another bomb threat. *C'est la vie.* So many these days.

Aimée scanned the faces as the taxi passed. Despite the rapid response, the combined police and military, how simple it would be for Mirko to merge into a crowd, get lost in the passersby. Or maybe the *flics* already had him in cuffs in back of the police van screeching away ahead of them.

Stuck in the traffic bedlam, she shouldered her bag, about to get out and walk to the safe house, when a black Peugeot with blackened windows pulled up, blocking the taxi. Her passenger door opened, and a steel grip closed around her arm.

Before she could fight back, she felt herself lifted in the air by a large cocoa-skinned man in a black suit and

sunglasses. A wire trailed over his collar. He smelled military. "This way, Mademoiselle Leduc."

"Get your hands off me—"

Too late. His companion flashed a security badge at Poncelet and tossed a wad of francs on the seat. "You've never
seen us or your passenger. *Comprenez, Monsieur?*"

With an expert move, the black suit had her in the back
seat of the Peugeot and buckled in all within ten seconds.

"You must practice that," she said, fuming inside. He
needed a lesson in manners.

He nodded. "Quite a bit."

"You pinpointed my location because I used my phone?"

"Comes in handy," he said.

The Peugeot took off and wove expertly through traffic.
Trapped. Stupid. Her reaction time had been too slow.

"So what's the occasion?" she asked.

"You'll find out," the black suit said.

A FEW BLOCKS later, on Boulevard Saint-Michel, the
car turned into the limestone-façaded entrance of l'École
des Mines, the *grande école* of engineering and geology,
founded by Louis XVI, bordering Jardin du Luxembourg.
With a shudder, she remembered it as Guedilen's office
address. Men in suits and military uniformed men and
women clustered in the dank, cool courtyard.

She clutched her bag as the seat belt was unbuckled
and the door opened. Both men escorted her up a
sweeping marble staircase, through a wide hallway, and
past double doors. Another corridor, more tall double
doors.

"Why am I here?" she asked.

No answer.

She was thrust in a room, the doors pulled closed behind her. Metallic clinking as they were locked.

Great. No hinges to pry off, no way to escape. No option but to wait.

She found herself in the school's mineralogy museum, surrounded by rocks and minerals in dusty blond wood display cabinets. The whole place smelled old; musty. The herringboned floorboards creaked with her every step.

How many years had it been since she had come here with her grandfather? She remembered the dollhouse-sized theater maquette; the realistic mock-up of a coal mine, a working pulley, the coal lumps, slate and shale layers descending to the mine's core. How her hands had come back smudged and gritty with shale. It was still there, worn by time and layered with dust.

Chloé would wonder at the amethyst crystals, purple blooms of desert rocks. Aimée would bring her here—that is, if she ever got out.

If she climbed out the window, managed to land without breaking an ankle, got through the police cordon . . . *Non*, she wanted answers from Guedilen, who she figured must have been the one who'd had her brought there.

A glass cabinet circa 1800 displayed maps of the old quarries and catacombs under Paris. One yellowed map showed what lay under the sixth arrondissement, riddled like Swiss cheese with traces of quarries dating back to the thirteenth century. Right below where she stood.

Her breath caught as she recognized parts of this map she'd seen under *le Sénat* buildings—those nearby tunnels below rue Bonaparte, which had once been the Abbey of Saint-Germain-des-Prés's moat.

With her index finger, she traced the quarry map's blue

lines—at different points jagged, straight, or spidery, stone walled routes leading to vaulted caverns, staircases to the surface. A subterranean world connected by an intersecting system of tunnels and hollow pockets under the garden and buildings above. A *gruyère*, all right.

She was looking at a location on the map—there was an entrance to the tunnels right below the apiary. Mirko Vladić had lured Isabelle Ideler into the apiary, then disappeared—down this tunnel? The same tunnel adjoined an old German bunker under the Pharmacy School, and another offshoot led to rue Garanière by *le Sénat*. By Erich Kayser's apartment. Could Mirko be using his own version of this map?

Metal scraped. The lock turned, the sound echoing in the mineralogy gallery. Two men entered, accompanied by a chorus of creaking footsteps. The younger was in his thirties, had heavy-lidded eyes and a darting gaze. He wore a blue shirt, red tie—the ministerial look under a black wool suit.

In this heat?

The other sported a full army uniform with stripes on his shoulder. He had a hawk nose, slit ice-blue eyes, and short-cropped silver hair. The kind of *mec* you wanted on your side and not the opposite in battle.

"Lost?" she said. "Or has the army gone into taking over museums?"

"Requisitioned, Mademoiselle Leduc," said hawk nose.

She didn't like him. Or the military. "The Germans requisitioned this place, too."

"You must be thinking of the Luftwaffe at Lycée Montaigne." The name Rondot was embroidered on his lapel.

"And who are you?" Aimée asked the man in the black wool suit.

"I'm Robert Guedilen, mademoiselle." He flicked a switch on a walkie-talkie hooked to his belt. Gave a thin smile.

"You're a hard man to reach," she said.

"Excuse the secrecy," he said. "But we feel it's better this way."

Secrecy.

"Abducting me from a taxi? No need to go to the trouble. *Alors*, I've been trying to reach you, as has Jean-Marie. Mirko's alive, but you must know that by now."

"Tell us your source, mademoiselle," Rondot demanded.

She blinked. "What difference does that make?"

"I think the colonel means how you contacted Mirko," said Guedilen. "Where did you obtain sensitive information?"

The military, suspicious and wrong, as usual.

"Doubting my credibility? Mirko's prints have been identified in an investigation run by DGI. Interpol, the ICTY, and other relevant organizations have been alerted," she said. "Why waste time?"

She looked for an answer in their faces. Expressionless.

Had she gotten it wrong?

She pulled out Mirko's photo. "We're talking about the same *mec, non?* This Serbian war criminal who was under a sealed ICTY indictment."

"How does this case involve you?" said Rondot.

"Loïc Bellan of DGI is investigating Mirko's connection to two murders here of people from the same ICTY unit. Jean-Marie Plove was on the same team." She stared at Guedilen. "Your team, *non?* He referred to you as the military attaché, his advisor. He's been trying to reach you, as I have."

Guedilen shrugged.

"Don't you understand? He's next."

Guedilen took the photo. He didn't do a good job of hiding his recognition. He pulled out his high-tech walkie-talkie, the kind in René's geek tech magazines. Barked an order.

The two men conferred in low tones.

She caught their attention and pointed to the map. "Mirko escaped down here in the tunnel after pushing Erich Kayser out the window on rue Servandoni."

"You're a pest," said Guedilen. Shook his head. "A real nuisance in heels. Obstructing an investigation."

"Shutting down *le Sénat* at the army's expense," said hawk nose. "Wasting resources like that will earn you military accommodation."

Put her in a military prison?

He was bluffing. "Get real. I didn't report a bomb scare. Even if I had, it's a citizen's duty." She paused, frustrated. "But I get it now. The tunnels. That's how Mirko escaped in Foča, too. He's some kind of underground rat."

The door opened and the two men who'd lifted her from the taxi appeared. They approached her, and each took one of her arms.

She'd read this all wrong. They had no interest in learning what she knew or had discovered. They wanted to shut her up.

Guedilen and Rondot silently watched her be escorted out of the room.

FIVE MINUTES LATER she'd been locked in an old classroom on the ground floor with barred windows overlooking a garden.

Frantic, she looked around. No way out.

She pulled out a burner phone from her bag, as well as the encryption card she kept in her wallet—her and René's private code. Dialed his emergency burner phone number.

"Where the hell are you, Aimée?" he said.

She hoped René could control his emotions and do what she needed him to. "Remember our drill. Quick. Write this down."

She gave the message in their code as quickly as she could: *Call LB. M escaped. EcdeMines. C bottle.*

Hoped to God he kept the code key handy.

She hung up. Under sixty seconds and the call would still be traced. René needed to act fast.

She caught sight of a figure outside the window, heard fragments of a phone conversation. " . . . The woman? Confiscate her cell phone, *d'accord*."

Merde! The signal had been detected. She stuck the thinnest burner phone and two SIM cards in her bra. Her wallet into the elastic of her lace thong, trapping it tight against the base of her spine.

A young female army officer appeared. She wore a starched uniform of a pale grey skirt and double-breasted jacket with black shoulder boards and shiny gold stripes. Her brow was creased in irritation. Just out of officer training school by the look of her.

"No calls," the officer said. "Give me your phone."

"I'm not under arrest, am I? I've got to pee."

A sigh. "Hand over your phone. I'll escort you."

Aimée did.

The officer's nose was running. She dabbed it with a clumped-up tissue.

"Allergies?" asked Aimée.

"Summer cold." She looked miserable, red-rimmed eyes and chapped skin around her nose.

"The worst." Commiserating might get her somewhere.

"First take off your shoes," she said. "Leave your bag."

No woman would escape without her bag. Or Louboutin sandals.

The officer escorted her, clutching Aimée's elbow in a tight grip.

"*Désolée*, but the last thing I want is my baby getting your germs," Aimée said.

The officer let go. Showed her into a locker room marked FEMALE ONLY. A few uniforms hung on hangers. Sinks lined the wall. Aimée noticed the upper windows weren't barred. There was a tang of mildew.

It gave her an idea.

"Look, I'm sweating, smell rank," Aimée said. "Can I sponge off?"

"No time. We're short staffed. I'm on the desk alone."

The phone rang from the office across the hall.

Aimée sighed noisily. "*Alors*, I'm ripe as Saint-Nectaire . . . Can't you just lock me in for a few minutes?"

The officer's irritation deepened. "That's against regulations."

She had to soften her up. But how? "I just want to clean up before I'm questioned."

The phone's insistent trill echoed. The officer looked at her watch. Hesitated.

"Who's going to know? Please!"

The phone kept ringing.

"Make it quick," the officer said. The key turned in the door.

Aimée turned on the faucet in the cracked porcelain

sink. She stripped, pulled on the first uniform about her size, balled up her clothes, stuffed them in a bin, and grabbed a black hat with a gold insignia. Found low black heels only one size too big and stuffed the toes with tissue.

She had just finished rooting through the lockers when she heard the lock turn. She would either make it out the window or ambush the officer if she had to.

Saturday, Early Evening

THE PHONE TRILLED again. Aimée heard a muttered
"merde." Receding footsteps.

She climbed onto the sink, praying it would hold her,
and stood in the splashing water to pull a top window
all the way open. She hoisted herself up to the ledge,
which was narrow and covered in cobwebs. The window
opening was just wide enough for a petite-sized woman.

Being a medium, she needed to squeeze through like a
sardine. If she got stuck, the officer would laugh and leave
her there.

Her elbows scraped the wood as she pulled herself
through. Splinters pierced her arm. She felt her hips scraped
even through the thick material of the uniform. She caught
hold of a rusted pipe outside the window and tugged. Her
hips squeezed through.

She tumbled out of the window sideways. Somehow she
managed to keep her hold on the pipe and swung, slapping
into the limestone façade. Her whole body stung. The too-
big shoes slipped off.

Footsteps echoed off the tile inside. The officer had
returned. Aimée had to move.

She ground her teeth and dropped, feeling the gravel cut
into her bare feet on impact. She stuffed the tissue back in
the shoes and took off into a vaulted arcade. Her mental
compass pointed her right—east to the exit, she hoped. But
the corridor ended with a locked door.

Shouts. They would find her in no time. Her getaway depended on speed. On finding the entrance to those stairs that led to the tunnels. Then she'd get away underground. Like Mirko.

The handle finally turned on the third door she tried. She burst into a back corridor. Pipes ringed the walls above cable junction boxes. She ran along the corridor, searching for a service exit. From a window, she saw a few soldiers and jeeps in the adjoining courtyard. Recognized the far wall that ran along the Jardin du Luxembourg. Beyond that a gate to the *caserne*, lodging for the gendarmes who policed the garden, and the gardener's tool sheds. All parallel to the underground tunnels.

She heard footsteps. More shouts. "A woman's escaped! A civilian."

She fought her impulse to run. That would be stupid.

She adjusted the hat. Play the part, and get out of here.

Didn't this corridor lead to the cellar with the staircase? What if it didn't? She turned the corner, and her ugly black shoes skidded on the worn pavers.

She'd run into a soldier. "*Merde*" was the first thing that popped out of her startled mouth.

"*Excusez-moi*," said the soldier, snapping to attention and saluting, a Kalashnikov strapped across his chest. A tang of rifle oil came from his freshly oiled machine gun.

She executed a poor imitation of a salute she remembered from a movie.

"The counterterrorism team's in there," he said.

Who the hell did he think she was? She brushed down the jacket, feeling the multiple stripes and gold braid of a high-ranking officer. She straightened her spine, copying his rod-stiff posture, and her thong tightened over her wallet. She followed the young soldier. Out of the frying pan, as that old saying went, and into the flames.

Maybe she could at least learn something. "Get me up to speed . . ." She didn't want to misstep, say something that revealed she was an imposter. "No one's updated me on progress with the bombing suspect. Who do I talk to first?"

"Colonel Rondot in the command center."

Great.

With soldiers massing in the courtyard to protect le Sénat, René's bogus bomb scare had done more harm than good. They'd never catch Mirko; he'd gone underground.

She spied a small door by an exit sign with the symbols for staircase and evacuation route.

"Dismissed," she said to the soldier.

With a salute he was gone. If only they were all that easy.

A loud voice boomed from a room packed with men in uniform. She saw a wall-sized map of Paris's twenty arrondissements. She looked at the men—a rainbow of hard-set faces. Mercenary types who'd entered the Foreign Legion, exiting with a new name, a French passport.

Guedilen stood less than a meter away, his phone cupped to his ear, lips pursed. No use trying to persuade him to shift the search, to believe her that Mirko would go into the tunnels. No time to uncover the snake's real agenda. She wanted to shake him, but that would only land her behind bars.

Head down, she kept a measured pace. She looked both ways and slipped inside the stairway exit. Closed the door.

Right then she needed her penlight, Converse high-tops, and a crowbar. All, except for the crowbar, sat in her bag back in the room where she'd been held. So did Chloé's baby pictures. Aimée's heart ached at the thought. At least a lock of Chloé's hair was wrapped in a sugar cube paper and tucked among coins in Aimée's wallet.

She made herself focus. Right now getting out unnoticed was all that mattered.

She pulled the jacket sleeve over her fist, punched and broke the glass cabinet protecting a fire extinguisher. Holding her breath, she waited, counting to five. No alarm. No shouts.

Five kilos heavy, she thought, clutching the fire extinguisher's handle in her left hand. With her right she felt her way down the steep stairs, following a smoky, faint blue glow from the war-era lanterns. Her fingers came back chalky and damp from the dirty residue on the sweating stones. Down, down. The steps kept going. Her ears popped. The air smelled dead and old, reminding her of a mausoleum.

In the dimness she came face-to-face with a grey metal door, rivets beading it in what seemed a happy face design. Had she come down all this way to be locked in? To her surprise, the well-oiled door yielded to her yank. It opened with a sighing whoosh of metal. Well used.

She flicked on the rounded porcelain light switch. Now she saw a dim row of bare lightbulbs, strung on a cord hanging from hooks along the stone-walled tunnel. The temperature felt even, not too cold or humid, almost pleasant. The air here had a musty, earthy fragrance she could almost taste. Nothing too intimidating apart from the old German signs painted on the walls: RAUCHEN VERBOTEN—smoking forbidden. She'd never wanted a cigarette so much in her life.

She closed her eyes. Listened. Silent as a tomb.

She visualized the quarry and catacomb map, the tunnels and exits she'd seen. Remembered an all-night party she'd been to as a student, in the bowels of Lycée Montaigne. With her direction in mind, she moved fast.

She needed to get out and use Bellan's influence on Mad Max to refocus the troops. Mirko would wait it out. In his shoes, she'd hide out down here.

Except she wasn't in his shoes; she was in someone else's. The disgusting pumps were too big, slowing her down. She was constantly afraid she would walk out of them. Armed with the heavy fire extinguisher, she headed west. At least, she hoped it was west.

Parts of the tunnel were so low she had to bend down. She hunched her way through an *abri*, a bomb shelter for the Luftwaffe, past rotting benches where they'd placed their derrieres, a metal toilet, rusted and leprous. Wartime graffiti was scratched into the soft limestone: "*Hansi liebt Muti*, April 1942," "*Fritz und Inga*" scratched by a heart dated 1941. She imagined young men crouched here in wartime, far away from home and occupying a country that hated them. She wondered if any of them who'd sheltered here ever made it home.

Ghosts hovered, their lives unremembered except here. A sad feeling, a miasma of loss that she couldn't explain, propelled her to cover the distance here below faster than she'd cover it above. No stranger here in her partying days, she still remembered how the bunker linked to rue Guynemar and the northern side of Jardin du Luxembourg. There it was, the ancient, dried-out Chartreux fountain of the Carthusian monks. Just beyond that, the old stairs up to the street.

She almost made it.

Saturday, Early Evening

THE SKIPPING OF her heart didn't mask a faint rhythmic thumping on the earth. The sound of tires coming toward her . . . ? She could swear it sounded like a bicycle with a flat. Closer and closer.

The stairs were just a few steps ahead. She gulped the musty air and ran.

The man came into view on a *trottinette*. Attached to his cap was a head lamp, and he wore a jumpsuit with a roll of rope sticking out of the pocket.

A city worker or one of the *cataphiles* who roamed the underground exploring the quarries?

But when he looked up, she saw those eyes. Her heart beat so hard she thought it would jump out of her chest. No mistaking that face.

Mirko.

The tunnel rat. A nondescript man with a sallow face, this killer of little girls. No one you'd notice in a crowd. Only the dead eyes gave him away.

The head lamp illuminated the limestone-powdered earth and her shoes. As he directed the beam, he took in her uniform. She moved the fire extinguisher behind her back, her mind racing. No service down here—she couldn't call for help.

"Where's my contact?" No fear in his accented French.

Contact? Think quick. Her uniform was army—he must have been expecting an army officer.

"I'm ordered to guide you to safety," she said, keeping the tremble out of her voice with effort.

"You? Some bitch called in a bomb scare," he said, his tone amused. "How the hell will you help me?"

Play on appearances; don't give him time to think. "Plans changed. We're moving you."

"Don't I deserve respect?" he said. "The big man should come himself. Not send a minion."

He struck a match, lit up what she figured was an Aura, and checked a walkie-talkie hooked to his utility belt. The same high-tech one Robert Guedilen had carried.

Robert Guedilen, whom Jean-Marie, she now remembered, also had called his team's fixer.

Who would have known about Isabelle's bee allergy, Erich Kayser's report.

"I'm just following orders," she said, thinking fast. "I'm to escort you to the safe house."

"What safe house? He said nothing—"

"No time to debate. This bomb scare complicated things. The van's arriving"—she pretended to consult her watch, edging toward the stairs—"in one minute up on rue d'Assas. You need to be on it."

A flicker of distrust crossed his eyes. "I'm supposed to meet him at the—"

"It's a contingency. Plan B. Guedilen sent me to meet you."

"Bet he gives you a nice cut, too." Mirko hadn't blinked an eye at Guedilen's name. Good God, Guedilen had had his own team members assassinated . . . and for what? To silence rumors about some arms dealings?

Mirko set the scooter against the wall. Unzipped his jumpsuit, stepped out of it. Underneath he wore jeans, a dark sweatshirt. Then she noticed the crowbar in his fist.

"Why do you need that?" Panic flooded her as she edged backward.

"For real, you don't know?" He snorted. "To open the sewer manhole up there."

Crowbars were used for opening manhole covers from the street, not below.

Liar. He took two steps toward her and raised the crowbar. "Why don't you show me what's behind your back?" He sneered. His cigarette dangled from his mouth.

Her mouth went dry. When she didn't answer quickly enough, he said, "Those shoes don't fit. See, I knew Guedilen wouldn't send me a low-ranking officer."

"You're so important?" she said, stepping back. She had to get the hell out.

A big grin. "Matter of fact, yes, I'm that valuable." Cocky. He exhaled a puff of smoke at her. "What do you know? I'm his, how you say, ace in the hole. I feed his bank account."

"But what about Gourmelon?" she blurted.

A snicker. "That's a code name. Seems you're not in the know." He stood back. "Maybe you're the one he called a pest," he said, "the one who took that cripple for a ride on a pink scooter. Yes, I recognize you now. That busybody brunette in Kayser's apartment." He advanced with the crowbar in one hand, unzipping his pants with the other. "That's okay. I know what to do with a busybody."

"I don't think so." She pulled out the fire extinguisher pin, squeezed the lever, and aimed the hose at his face. Dry white powder exploded in a cloud, covering everything. He roared, blinded momentarily, raised his hands to wipe his face. The crowbar fell, clanking against stone. But he was coughing, shouting, coming at her, fighting his way through the cloud.

She swung the heavy tank. Heard a thwack as it hit the wall. Then swung it again. A cry of pain, more coughing.

She couldn't see. More cries of pain. A ruse?

She held the fire extinguisher aloft, her eyes tearing, feeling her way along the wall.

Then he grabbed her ankle in a viselike grip.

Thrown off balance, she squeezed the lever again, spraying wildly until he let go. In the hazy cloud, she swung until she hit something. Hard. She heard a crack. An ouf . . . then quiet.

In the dissipating haze, she saw him sprawled on the dirt. Then she whacked him again.

"You really should have put out your cigarette," she said. "Didn't you see the no smoking sign?"

While he was unconscious, she took off his belt and looped his ankles together. Pulled off his sweatshirt and used it to tie and knot his wrists behind his back. Strapped his head lamp onto her military hat.

As she was finishing up, he moaned. Struggled in the dirt, his shoulders twitching.

A kick in the head shut him up. Then another for the little girls. And for Isabelle and Erich, Suzanne in lockup . . . Caught herself before she kicked him to a pulp.

Death was too good for him. So she removed his walkie-talkie and stuck it in the belt of her uniform, lugged and dragged him toward the Chartreux fountain. Leaving him there, she climbed two, three flights, up to the fourth level running under the street. Sweat dripped between her shoulder blades, behind her knees. Her breath came in gasps. She needed to get back before he woke up or someone came for him.

She pulled herself up the rusted metal rungs to the

overhead manhole. Awkwardly she reached up and ran her hands over the worn greasy manhole cover illuminated by the head lamp. Pushed. It didn't budge.

Nothing for it but to climb higher on the rungs, put her shoulders below the manhole cover and push up from her bent legs, using them like a piston. She shoved and pushed the cover, using all her strength, sweating and gasping for breath. Again and again until finally, little by little, the heavy metal cover budged. She kept at it until she could wedge herself through and pull herself out. She'd never been so happy to breathe humid air and feel the beating sun. Staggering to her feet, she pulled the burner phone and a SIM card from her sweat-soaked bra and called René.

"Mirko's tied up," she said.

"*Quoi?*" René said, incredulous.

"I mean literally. But I don't know for how long. Tell Bellan to put on his flashing blue light and get here. Rue d'Assas."

"Are you all right, Aimée?"

"Fine." Took a deep breath and looked around. Noticed a jeep at a hastily set-up army checkpoint by the law school. "*Alors*, René, Colonel Rondot and Guedilen are protecting Mirko. Guedilen is the one using him for arms deals. Who's that contact you've got at *Le Parisien?*"

"You want to call the press?"

"Paparazzi will do."

"You need to get the hell away, Aimée."

All of a sudden she was going to lose it, break down. She choked back a lump in her throat.

"Listen to me, René," she said. "They're going to hide the murders, the guns, everything. They don't care about crimes against humanity, what he did to those little girls.

They've been hiding him, and they'll keep doing it—he's important to the military."

"How?"

"I'll tell you when you get here. Hurry."

She punched in the number René gave her to *Le Parisien*'s tip line.

"WHERE'S THE ESCAPED Balkan war criminal?" said the perspiring press photographer, cameras slung around his neck. Almost a caricature. "I brought my climbing shoes like I was told."

"Five floors down to the left," Aimée said.

He was snapping pictures already as she leaned against the grilled gate in the torn army jacket.

"*Non*, no photos of me," she said.

"That's the deal, *chérie*. Make or break. You decide."

He wanted a coup—a female army officer capturing a fugitive war criminal, who'd murdered members of an ICTY team and was wanted by the ICTY and Interpol.

She thought. Maybe a good idea. "Give me your sunglasses." She couldn't be identified; impersonating an officer was a crime.

Too bad she didn't have lipstick. She put on his Ray-Bans, opened two buttons of her army jacket, stuffed her hair under her hat. Pinched her cheeks for color.

He clicked away. "Sexy. I like it."

Bellan had pulled up with a squeal of brakes, flashing lights, and a flotilla of police vans.

"Better hurry up or the *flics* will beat your scoop," she said.

AIMÉE PACED IN the anteroom of Hôtel de Brienne, the Ministry of Defense's plush heart of operations.

A double door opened, and Bellan rushed out. He tossed her bag onto the gilt chair, dropped her sandals on the floor.

"Thank God," she said, rummaging inside for a baby wipe and lipstick.

"We're keeping this quiet for now."

"What?"

"Just listen, Aimée—"

"Guedilen, aka Gourmelon, is the one who furnished Mirko all the info he needed to assassinate the ICTY team. It's a big damn cover-up. Deliberately distracting from the investigation of Guedilen's shady business."

"Which is?"

"Suzanne knows details. All I know is that Mirko helped Guedilen supply French arms to paramilitary groups in the Balkans. Geudelin needed Mirko's connections to a network he'd inherited from a dead Croatian arms dealer named Dravić. They both must have gotten rich off of it. And meanwhile, French weapons were used to carry out ethnic cleansing."

"And Mirko's here why?"

Aimée pulled out her phone, checked for messages. One from Melac.

"The ICTY operations were at odds with Guedilen's shady dealings, so Guedilen had Mirko removed from the Balkans to France—the whole explosion in Foča was a sham," she said. "Guedilen's a fixer. Got Mirko to do his dirty work here in Paris."

"How are we going to prove that?"

"Look at Guedilen's financials; that will tell you. Mirko boasted about how important he was. He's a murdering rapist who gets away with everything." She wanted to hit something. "I could have taken care of him down there myself."

"Oh, that," said Bellan with a little smile. "Mad Max has taken care of him."

"You mean . . . killed him and destroyed the evidence?"

"Not quite. If it makes you feel better, Guedilen and Rondot get a one-way ticket to prison."

"So you already knew this?"

And let her spout off anyway?

"I just found out. But they're handling it their way."

"Meaning?"

"A sexy sergeant's solo capture of a fugitive war criminal. Nice touch, eh? Backslapping the army."

He pulled out page proofs of *Le Parisien*'s special evening edition. Her photo, air-brushed to make it look as if several more buttons were undone. "Quite an accomplishment, Aimée. They're secretly pleased you gave them the capture and sabotaged Guedilen's operation."

And did all the work. She got it.

Bellan paused. "Aimée, consider going on a vacation."

"Think I've earned it?"

"It's a good time to be out of sight."

"I'm not afraid of the military, or the *flics*," she said with more bravado than she felt.

"That paparazzo's quite taken with you. He wanted an exclusive. I'm afraid . . . You know how they are. He's discovered your identity."

Her stomach skidded. No peace.

"Vacation sounds like a good idea, Bellan," she said. "My daughter's never seen the Mediterranean. Time she did."

Loïc grinned. "Never too young for sun and sand." After a moment, he added, "My son loves apples. We're going to Normandy."

"Got a picture?"

Aimée stared at the smiling, almond-eyed little boy wearing a backpack, his hand gripping Bellan's.

"Looks like a boy who's easy to love," she said.

"You got that right. It took me a while, but he's made me realize what's important."

Realize what's important.

Monday Morning

MARTINE HAD ORDERED a taxi *monospace*—a min-ivan—to take them to Orly Airport for their flight to Sicily. She claimed that with Chloé's car seat, stroller, and accou-trements they needed a cab that big. She'd neglected to mention her Louis Vuitton luggage set.

Martine worried about missing the plane, about meeting up with Gianni at the airport in Sicily, a million little things. She insisted they arrive early.

On quai d'Anjou, René kissed Chloé, then strapped her into the car seat in the waiting taxi. "I'll hold down the fort."

Thank God. The business would be taken care of in her absence. Melac would dog-sit Miles Davis. Suzanne had been released from the police hospital and reunited with her children.

All bases covered.

They crossed the Pont de la Tournelle, the khaki-grey Seine flowing below.

Aimée had handled everything, hadn't she? So why did she have this niggling scratch in her heart?

Chloé gurgled and tightened her fist on her *doudou*, her scruffy stuffed bunny.

"Martine, I've got a stop to make," Aimée said.

"*Quoi?*" Martine looked up in alarm. "We'll miss the plane."

Aimée glanced at the time. Shot her best friend a pleading look. "We're three hours early, Martine."

WITH CHLOÉ IN her arms, Aimée walked into la Maison de Santé du Gardien de la Paix.

Her damp collar stuck to her neck, her fingers trembled, but this time she didn't turn around.

She saddled Chloé on her hip, passing through the dark-walled lobby. When she came to the hospital room door, she rapped with her knuckles, then opened it.

Crocus-and-jasmine-filled vases standing by rows of get-well cards. Photos of his grandson and Chloé were propped by his bed.

Morbier's short-sleeved hospital gown revealed tubes running from his arms, just-visible chest patches connected to an EKG machine that beeped. His eyes were the same. He looked like the Morbier she'd always known. Except that his hair had gone stone white.

"About time, Leduc," he said, as if they'd spoken the day before.

"I like your hair," she said. *"Très distingué."*

She'd never seen his lip tremble before. But then he'd always had a mustache before.

She put Chloé into Morbier's open arms. Then leaned down and kissed his brow.

"So what do you have to tell me?"

Acknowledgments

I HAVE SO many people to thank for their time, extraordinary help and generosity: Jean Satzer, cat *maman* and reader extraordinaire; Libby Fischer Hellmann, accomplice in all things crime and writing; Kevin Curtis, Chief of Investigations with UNICEF, former ICTY Investigations Team Leader; Nicolas Sébire, Investigation Specialist, Investigations Unit, UNICEF, former ICTY investigator; Catherine Driguet, former Brigade Criminelle and ICTY investigator who lived parts of this story; *merci mille fois*.

In Paris: huge *mercis* to Françoise Deygout; Gilles Fouquet; Jean-Claude Mules, former Brigade Criminelle; above and beyond to Arnaud Baleste, former Brigade Criminelle; Patrick Bourbotte, Brigade Criminelle who shared his first case; Marie-Pierre in le Tribunal; indefatigable Ingrid au Clair; dear Naftali Skrobek, *ancien Résistant* who never lets me forget, and Lidia; Dr. Alan and Marie-Paul Marty; much appreciation to Doctor Christian de Brier and Blandine de Brier Manoncourt and family, who shared their *quartier* and much more; Jean-Luc Boyer, Chirine Ghiafiar and family, who helped in so many ways and introduced me to the *real* Bartok.

Deep gratitude to generous Karen Fawcett (and her concierge) for all those afternoons on rue Joseph Bara. *Toujours merci* to Anne Françoise Delbègue and Cathy Etile and to Benoît Pastisson. Gilles Thomas for all things underground and Carla Chemouni Bach, *l'entrée* to École des Beaux-Arts and more.

Nothing would happen without James N. Frey, or Katherine Fausset, or my patient, brilliant editor, Juliet Grames, or *chére* Bronwen Hruska and the entire, incredible SOHO family. And forever thanks to my son, Tate, and Jun.